PRAISE FOR

Blood Wyne

"The Otherworld novels are a tapestry of excellent writing and interesting character development . . . always fun, sexy, and magical, and *Blood Wyne* is no different." —*Fresh Fiction*

"*Blood Wyne* has action, sizzling romance, and some majorly startling discoveries that will cost dearly . . . This series just gets better and better!" —*The Bibliophilic Book Blog*

"I am excited to read what happens next in this series."
—*Night Owl Reviews*

Harvest Hunting

"Readers are in for an action-packed ride that is sexy to the max!"
—*RT Book Reviews*

"Heartbreaking and enlightening with twists and turns that will surprise all of us who are fans of the series—and leave us eager for the next book. A five-star read." —*Fresh Fiction*

"It's not too many authors who can write a series as long-lived as this one and make every book come out just as interesting and intriguing as the last, but Yasmine Galenorn is certainly one of them . . . *Harvest Hunting* is a must buy. Don't miss it!"
—*Romance Reviews Today*

continued . . .

Bone Magic

"Erotic and darkly bewitching, *Bone Magic* turns up the heat on the D'Artigo sisters. Galenorn writes another winner in the Otherworld series, a mix of magic and passion sure to captivate readers."   —Jeaniene Frost, *New York Times* bestselling author

"Quite simply A-M-A-Z-I-N-G!"   —*Sidhe Vicious Reviews*

Demon Mistress

"As always, [Galenorn] delivers intriguing characters, intricate plot layers, and kick-butt action."   —*RT Book Reviews* (four stars)

"Just as exciting as the last episode in the Otherworld series."
     —*The Romance Readers Connection*

"The tense fights, frights, and demon-bashing take front and center in this book, and I love that . . . All in all, *Demon Mistress* certainly makes for enjoyable summertime reading!"
     —*Errant Dreams Reviews*

Night Huntress

"Yasmine Galenorn is a hot new star in the world of urban fantasy. The Otherworld series is wonderfully entertaining."
     —Jayne Ann Krentz, *New York Times* bestselling author

"Yasmine Galenorn is a powerhouse author; a master of the craft who is taking the industry by storm, and for good reason!"
     —Maggie Shayne, *New York Times* bestselling author

"Yasmine Galenorn hits the stars with *Night Huntress*. Urban fantasy at its best!"
     —Stella Cameron, *New York Times* bestselling author

"Love and betrayal play large roles in *Night Huntress*, and as the story unfolds, the action will sweep fans along for this fast-moving ride."   —*Darque Reviews*

Dragon Wytch

"Action and sexy sensuality make this book hot to the touch."
—*RT Book Reviews* (four stars)

"Ms. Galenorn has a great gift for spinning a compelling story. The supernatural action is a great blend of both fresh and familiar, the characters are each charming in their own way, the heroine's love life is scorching, and the worlds they all live in are well-defined."
—*Darque Reviews*

"If you're looking for an out-of-this-world enchanting tale of magic and passion, *Dragon Wytch* is the story for you. I will be recommending this wickedly bewitching tale to everyone I know!"
—*Dark Angel Reviews*

Darkling

"The most fulfilling journey of self-discovery to date in the Otherworld series . . . An eclectic blend that works well." —*Booklist*

"Galenorn does a remarkable job of delving into the psyches and fears of her characters. As this series matures, so do her heroines. The sex sizzles and the danger fascinates." —*RT Book Reviews*

"The story is nonstop action and has deep, dark plots that kept me up reading long past my bedtime. Here be dark fantasy with a unique twist. YES!" —*Huntress Book Reviews*

Changeling

"The second in Galenorn's D'Artigo Sisters series ratchets up the danger and romantic entanglements. Along with the quirky humor and characters readers have come to expect is a moving tale of a woman more comfortable in her cat skin than in her human form, looking to find her place in the world." —*Booklist*

continued . . .

"Galenorn's thrilling supernatural series is gritty and dangerous, but it's the tumultuous relationships between all the various characters that give it depth and heart. Vivid, sexy, and mesmerizing, Galenorn's novel hits the paranormal sweet spot."

—*RT Book Reviews*

"Yasmine Galenorn has created another winner . . . *Changeling* is a can't-miss read destined to hold a special place on your keeper shelf."

—*Romance Reviews Today*

Witchling

"Reminiscent of Laurell K. Hamilton with a lighter touch . . . a delightful new series that simmers with fun and magic."

—Mary Jo Putney, *New York Times* bestselling author

"The first in an engrossing new series . . . a whimsical reminder of fantasy's importance in everyday life."   —*Publishers Weekly*

"Pure delight . . . a great heroine, designer gear, dead guys, and Seattle precipitation!"

—MaryJanice Davidson, *New York Times* bestselling author

"*Witchling* is one sexy, fantastic paranormal-mystery-romantic read."   —Terese Ramin, author of *Shotgun Honeymoon*

"Galenorn's kick-butt Fae ramp up the action in a wyrd world gone awry . . . I loved it!"

—Patricia Rice, *New York Times* bestselling author

"A fun read, filled with surprise and enchantment."

—Linda Winstead Jones, author of *Come to Me*

Shaded Vision

An Otherworld Novel

YASMINE GALENORN

JOVE BOOKS, NEW YORK

THE BERKLEY PUBLISHING GROUP
Published by the Penguin Group
Penguin Group (USA) Inc.
375 Hudson Street, New York, New York 10014, USA
Penguin Group (Canada), 90 Eglinton Avenue East, Suite 700, Toronto, Ontario M4P 2Y3, Canada
(a division of Pearson Penguin Canada Inc.)
Penguin Books Ltd., 80 Strand, London WC2R 0RL, England
Penguin Group Ireland, 25 St. Stephen's Green, Dublin 2, Ireland (a division of Penguin Books Ltd.)
Penguin Group (Australia), 250 Camberwell Road, Camberwell, Victoria 3124, Australia
(a division of Pearson Australia Group Pty. Ltd.)
Penguin Books India Pvt. Ltd., 11 Community Centre, Panchsheel Park, New Delhi—110 017, India
Penguin Group (NZ), 67 Apollo Drive, Rosedale, Auckland 0632, New Zealand
(a division of Pearson New Zealand Ltd.)
Penguin Books (South Africa) (Pty.) Ltd., 24 Sturdee Avenue, Rosebank, Johannesburg 2196,
South Africa

Penguin Books Ltd., Registered Offices: 80 Strand, London WC2R 0RL, England

SHADED VISION

A Jove Book / published by arrangement with the author

PUBLISHING HISTORY
Jove mass-market edition / February 2012

ISBN: 978-0-515-15035-3

JOVE®
Jove Books are published by The Berkley Publishing Group,
a division of Penguin Group (USA) Inc.,
375 Hudson Street, New York, New York 10014.
JOVE® is a registered trademark of Penguin Group (USA) Inc.
The "J" design is a trademark of Penguin Group (USA) Inc.

PRINTED IN THE UNITED STATES OF AMERICA

10 9 8 7 6 5 4 3 2 1

Dedicated to
Meerclar, my own little black "panther"

ACKNOWLEDGMENTS

Thank you to my beloved Samwise—my biggest, strongest, and most handsome fan. And my gratitude to my agent, Meredith Bernstein, and to my editor, Kate Seaver—thank you both for helping me stretch my wings and fly. A salute to Tony Mauro, cover artist extraordinaire. To my assistant, Andria, who helps me in so many ways. To my furry little "Galenorn Gurlz," LOL-cats in their own right. Most reverent devotion to Ukko, Rauni, Mielikki, and Tapio, my spiritual guardians.

And the biggest thank-you of all—to my readers, both old and new. Your support helps keep the series going. You can find me on the net at Galenorn En/Visions: www.galenorn.com. For links to social networking sites where you can find me, see my website.

If you write to me snail mail (see my website for the address or write via my publisher), please enclose a self-addressed stamped envelope with your letter if you would like a reply. Promo goodies are available—see my site for info.

The Painted Panther
Yasmine Galenorn
July 2011

A doubtful friend is worse than a certain enemy. Let a man be one thing or the other, and we then know how to meet him.

—AESOP

The battlefield is a scene of constant chaos. The winner will be the one who controls that chaos, both his own and the enemies'.

—NAPOLEON BONAPARTE

Chapter 1

"I'm going to be sick! Move!" Iris shoved past me and ran to the bathroom. I could hear her retching and then, after a moment, the toilet flushed and the sound of water ran in the sink.

Grimacing, I decided she could manage on her own and busied myself by putting the finishing touches on my outfit. I wasn't a fashion maven, and all I could think was, *Please, oh please, let me be dressed up enough for tonight.*

My jeans were new, for a change, with no rips, and dark black, and I was wearing a bright fuchsia tank top with a rhinestone kitty on the front. I'd traded my utilitarian brown leather belt for a white leather one with a silver buckle, and I'd grudgingly changed my shit-kicker boots for a pair of suede ankle boots with three-inch heels, which put me at an even six four.

My spiky hairdo was back to the golden shade it normally ran from the horrible calico mess that it had ended up, although I'd waffled and finally asked Iris to add in some chunky platinum highlights and a few thin black ones, and now I had tiger-striped spikes. The vining leaf tattoos on my arms had darkened some—with each passing week, they seemed to fill in a little more. Camille had helped me with my makeup, and I looked reasonably ready for clubbing, even though my typical evening was spent hanging around in front of the TV with Shade, curled up eating junk food and trading kisses. That is, when we weren't out kicking demon ass.

I slipped into my black leather jacket and patiently sat on the edge of the bed, playing with one of my kitty toys. The squeaky mouse had become a favorite of mine and—even in human form—it made me grin. I shook it until it let out a string of loud squeaks.

Iris poked her head out of the bathroom.

"Will you *stop* that damn noise? You've been obsessed with that toy night and day for the past two weeks. If you don't put it down, I'm going to toss it in the garbage."

"Not my squeaky mouse!" I quickly dropped it on the floor. I *loved* my squeaky mouse, and nobody was going to take it away from me.

Iris had fixed her makeup, and, with a look that told me she wasn't at all sure about our plans for the evening, she edged out of the tiled room and shouldered a smile. "Do I look okay?"

Grumpy notwithstanding, I could tell she was anxious. About six weeks' pregnant, even though she wasn't showing yet; her hormones were playing her fast and furious—like Jimi Hendrix played his guitar. Add to that, tomorrow she was getting married, and our Talon-haltija sprite was as jumpy as a cat in a thunderstorm.

"You look beautiful," I said.

Iris was radiant, for all she was going through. Her ankle-length hair shone like spun gold, and her skin was smooth and flawless—pregnancy agreed with her in that regard, at least. Her eyes were luminous, round, and blue as the early morning. And she still had her figure—she was curvy and buxom and, standing at three ten, she put me to shame in the girly department. But the feminine demeanor was deceptive—Iris could pack one hell of a punch, both magically and physically.

She stared at me for a moment. As she cautiously dashed at her tears, trying to keep from messing up her mascara, she gave me a blissful smile. "You're so sweet. Can you braid my hair for me? I sure wish I had Smoky's ability to order it to fix itself."

"I think a lot of people want a taste of Smoky's talents. Among other attributes of his." I sat her down and divided her hair into three sections. "I know *I'd* love to come out looking peachy clean every time we fight a battle."

After I wove one section over the other and finished it off with an elastic-coated rubber band, Iris coiled it around her head in an intricate pattern, leaving the tail end of it hanging down to her midback like a tidy ponytail. We added a brilliant yellow bow. It reminded me a lot of Barbara Eden's hairdo in *I Dream of Jeannie.*

"I wish you could, too. Then I wouldn't have so much laundry to do."

She laughed and smoothed her skirt—a gorgeous cobalt blue number she'd paired with a pale gray button-down shirt and a pair of pumps that matched the color of her hair bow. The Finnish house sprite looked like a pretty secretary rather than the high priestess she was. Talon-haltijas were good at blending in. Even when they could whip your butt in a battle.

"You don't think Menolly is upset about putting off her promise ceremony to Nerissa? They had decided on February second and now . . . they changed their plans because of me."

"Are you kidding? Both of them are fine about it. And it gives them more time to get ready." I knew that Iris felt she had upstaged them, but neither my sister nor her lover were upset in the least.

"As long as you're certain I didn't tread on their toes."

"I'm sure. Now, are you ready?" I stood, reaching for my purse.

She closed her eyes and pressed one hand against her stomach. "My stomach feels like it won't ever be ready for anything again, but let's get a move on." As we left my room, she glanced up at me. "By this time tomorrow, I'll be Iris O'Shea. Bruce's wife. What the *hell* am I doing?"

I laughed at her panicked expression. "You're marrying the leprechaun you love, Iris. And you're going to have his baby, so you might as well get used to it. Life's changing." Cocking my head, I added, "So, you're taking his last name?"

She nodded. "If Kuusi were my family name, I'd hyphenate. But . . . as much as I loved the Kuusis, they weren't exactly family. I worked for them, I cared about them, but when it comes down to it, they were my employers. So I figure, since I'm starting over yet another time, so I might as well start with another new name. Only this time, someone I love is attached to it. You're right. Life is changing. And I'm embracing it."

As we headed downstairs, I realized that was so true for all of us. Life was changing all around us. Some things for the better, some things not. And there was no way to stop the ride now that we'd all gotten on board.

The guys were sitting around the living room looking guilty. Not sure what they were up to, I gave them a sideways glance as we passed into the foyer and then the kitchen, where my two sisters—Camille and Menolly—were waiting with Menolly's lover, Nerissa. A trail of wolf whistles followed, and Iris gave me a look and shook her head.

"They'll be out like a light by the time we get home, want to make a bet?"

"I kind of hope so." I really didn't want to think about what kind of trouble they could get up to without us here to supervise.

Menolly's coppery cornrows shimmered under the lights, and she was dressed in blue—tight jeans and a denim jacket over a rust-colored turtleneck. Her boots were even made of denim, and they sported thin stiletto spikes, almost as high as Camille's.

Camille, on the other hand, was fully decked out in her usual fetish noir. Chiffon skirt, with a green underbust long-line waist cincher with black boning and silver hooks and eyes, beneath which she wore a shiny black spaghetti-strap top that left nothing to the imagination with regard to her DD breasts. She balanced on a pair of sky-high stilettos that I couldn't even imagine wearing and was carrying a sparkly black wrap.

Nerissa, who was munching on a bread stick she'd found in the cupboard, wore a flirty tiered powder pink skirt that barely covered her butt, and a glitzy tank top. Strong, lean, and muscled, she was an Amazon of a woman, a werepuma who wasn't afraid to tackle life with my sister the vampire— and she was always ready to party.

Camille lit up as we entered the room. "You both look great. Sharah's meeting us at the club. Come on, let's get this show on the road and leave the house to the guys. Trillian told me they've got a fully stocked bar, but he didn't say anything about a stripper . . . I'd be surprised if they don't just end up playing games on that damned Xbox all evening."

Supes or not, some of our lovers and cohorts had developed an addiction to video games. It seemed odd to watch two grown demons battling it out over Super Mario or whatever was the latest Xbox rage, but they took it seriously.

"What about Maggie? Who's looking after her?"

"Don't you worry about our baby gargoyle. Hanna's watching her. Maggie has really taken to her." Iris picked up her purse. "I'm ready."

"Then we're ready." Camille arranged her shawl. "Bruce gave us the use of his limo and driver. Ladies, our chariot awaits."

"At least we aren't headed out to get our butts kicked."

I peeked back in the living room at the guys. They looked innocent enough, but the amount of trouble an incubus, a demon, a leprechaun, a dragon, an FBH (full-blooded human), one of the dark Fae, and a half dragon, half shadow walker could get into boggled my mind. Without us to keep an eye on things, I fully expected to come home and find the house trashed.

Iris must have been reading my mind because as we

clattered down the porch steps, she muttered, "Here's praying Hanna can keep those men in line."

"Hanna's a tough woman, but I don't know if she's that tough." Camille nodded to the limo. "Bruce's driver is named Tony; tip him big tonight. Okay, let's go, ladies. Iris, this is your last night as a free woman; we're going to live it up."

"Just so long as my supper stays where it's supposed to," Iris countered.

As we maneuvered through the melting snow—spring was finally on the way and though it was still cold, most of the harsh winter snows were standing puddles of slush and mud now—Tony got out of the car to open the doors for us.

The limo was lush; roomy enough for six in the backseat. I pushed my worries away for the evening. Nothing would go wrong. It was the night before Valentine's Day—and the night before Iris's wedding. The gods had to be kind to us at least once, didn't they?

The Demented Zombie lived up to all the hype except for its name. Though not a high-class club, the disco seriously rocked. Run by a Fae couple from Otherworld; the club was named it after a cocktail they served. I was determined to find out if the drink was as good as the rumors had it.

We slid through the crowd. "Do you think we'll be able to find a table?" I looked at the crowd on the dance floor. Most of them were women, and I had a sudden suspicion Menolly and Nerissa had brought us to a lesbian bar. "Hey, this a gay bar? Not that it matters, but . . ."

"Not so much. And we've got reservations for the big table in back they keep for parties, so chill." Menolly shouldered her way ahead, and after a moment, we caught sight of the bar. She winked at the bartender, who looked like your average hunky guy, except I could tell he was Were. He motioned us over to the big table that had balloons surrounding it. *Dangling* ribbons. I stared at them for a moment. My

Tabby self stirred, wanting to come out and play, but I forced the instincts back long enough to turn to Camille.

"Balloons—ribbons? You think such a good idea around me?"

She snorted. "Can't you control yourself for one night? Sometimes I think you use the fact that you're a werecat as an excuse for bad behavior. Now, be a good Kitten, Delilah, and don't tear up the joint."

As we slid into the booth around the table, a familiar voice echoed through the crowd and Sharah hustled up, carrying a large pale silver box wrapped in a pink ribbon. Her blond hair caught back in a sleek ponytail, the elf looked very sixties. Waiflike in her go-go dress and white knee-high boots, she made retro work.

Sharah was Chase's girlfriend, and Chase used to be *my* boyfriend, but we knew we couldn't make it work so we broke up. Now we were good buddies. Sharah had slipped in to fill the void, and they seemed to be grooving together. Whatever the case, I knew enough to keep my nose out of it.

She handed me her present for Iris, and I put it with the others on a side table as the waitress came up to take our orders. We quickly went around the table. Iris couldn't drink, of course, so she ordered a glass of orange juice. Camille ordered a rum and Coke, Nerissa asked for a mai tai, Sharah and I ordered Demented Zombies, and Menolly ordered a Bloody Vamp—which was actually just blood, but it sounded better with a cool name.

"Here—you have to wear this tonight." Camille pulled out a rhinestone tiara with a miniature veil attached and plunked it on top of Iris's head.

"Only if you guys are wearing party hats, too." Iris shook her finger at us, at which Nerissa pulled out a pack of sparkling princess crowns. We all slid the cardboard hats on as Iris grinned and adjusted her tiara.

The music started—Lady Gaga's "Born This Way"—and Menolly and Nerissa excused themselves to the dance floor. A stunning pair, their dancing got dirtier and they began to pull in looks from both sides of the fence. I stifled a snort—some of the women looked jealous, while others looked at them like they were the best thing since sliced bread. Not a gay bar, my ass. Most of the men around didn't seem interested in anybody but each other.

A rather tall biker chick tapped Camille on the arm. "Dance?"

Camille blinked but then grinned and excused herself to work the floor as the music turned to "Weapon of Choice." After a few seconds, Biker Chick was looking mighty impressed; Camille had lost herself to the music and they went spinning around the floor, Biker Chick's arm hooked around Camille's waist.

"I'm glad to see her smile," Iris whispered to me.

"Yeah, after Hyto's attack, I wasn't sure how she'd come through." I leaned down so Iris could hear me. The noise in the place was deafening.

"It will take her awhile to fully move on, but I think she'll be okay, eventually. Her men help a lot, especially Smoky, though it can't be easy for them since he looks so much like his father."

Sharah leaned across the table. "Nerissa's counseling is helping. At least Hyto didn't infect her with any disease."

"My sister's a rock, though Hyto almost smashed her to bits. But she always pulls through."

I couldn't forgive our father, though, for not standing up for her after he knew what had happened. That he'd sat in our living room, listening as she told him what horrors the crazed dragon had put her through, and then chosen to leave, had hardened my heart to him. His own daughter, kidnapped and raped, and he walked away. Our cousin Shamas had threatened to go home and confront him about it. We persuaded him to hold off, but I had the feeling he was so pissed that he might do so without our consent.

Iris tapped her fingers on the table in time to the music as the others returned from the dance floor.

"Did you want to dance?" Menolly asked.

She shook her head. "Not the best idea. Stomach's queasy."

Sharah handed her a packet of saltines. "Here, these will help."

Iris munched on them. "I see presents—and they're unopened." Her eyes glittered as she motioned to the stack of boxes on the side table. We'd brought gifts from the guys, too.

"Not just yet," I said, glancing at Camille and Menolly. I'd been in charge of the party, much to their dismay, and one of the first things I'd decided was we were going to entertain Iris to the max. "Up, you two."

Camille grimaced. "Oh please, do we *have* to?"

"Yes, as excruciating as Delilah's yowls can be. We have to." Menolly's eyes were pale as frost, but she smiled a toothy grin. "Come on."

A path opened in front of our table to reveal the stage and a karaoke machine. I snickered.

"You just wait. I'll get you for this." Camille shook her head, leaping lightly up on the stage.

"Hey, Menolly's not complaining."

"*She* can *sing*! You and I are pathetic . . . well . . . mostly."

We clambered up on the stage and Menolly swung around in front of us, striking a pose with legs spread and both hands around the microphone. Camille and I took up our stations as her backup singers. The music swept in, and, with a deep breath, we dove into our rendition of "We Are Family."

We turned on the glamour, dropping our masks so our charm shone through, and the crowd went wild, laughing with us and clapping along. We spun and twisted to the music, throwing our hearts into it. Even though Camille and I weren't that great in the vocal department, we warbled away while Menolly carried the song. We'd been practicing in secret for over a week now, and though we weren't polished, we were doing a pretty good job keeping a beat to the music.

Menolly leaped off the stage, carrying the microphone

with her, and danced her way over to Iris. Gently lifting the sprite onto her shoulder, with another leap she made her way back onto the stage, where she set Iris down and we surrounded her, singing as she clapped and swayed to the music.

People started throwing dollars on the stage, "for the bride," and by the time we finished, jazz hands and all, we'd collected seventy-five bucks and a couple rounds of free drinks, which put an end to Camille's and my being able to sing anything.

"You guys are great," Iris said as we headed back to the table. "And thank you. Presents now?"

I laughed, a little too loud, and burped. How many drinks had I managed to put away? I counted—there were only four glasses in front of me, but the Demented Zombie was one hell of a drink and packed a punch. I wasn't sure what was in it, but it was better than catnip.

I glanced around. I'd arranged for some special entertainment for the evening and—and . . . *there he was*. The guy was fine, gorgeous, with dark hair to his shoulders. Even beneath his policeman's outfit, it was obvious that he was ripped. I motioned to him and he sidled over to the table. The music dimmed and everyone around us turned to watch.

"Are you Iris Kuusi?" His voice was smooth—so smooth it made me want to slide up against him.

She blushed bright red and her eyes glistened. "Yes . . . ?"

"Iris Kuusi, you have the right to *scream as loud as you want*. You have the right to *let me arouse you*—" And with that, he motioned to someone at the counter, and Amanda Blank blared out from the speakers as his hips began to move.

He was a great dancer, keeping up to the beat in perfect rhythm with the rapper even as he—*woo-hoo*! There went the jacket, tossed on the ground near him. As he slid his hands to the cuffs of his shirt, he jerked and the shirt landed in Iris's lap. Gleaming muscles flexed as he clasped his hands behind his head and swiveled his hips in a move that put Elvis the Pelvis to shame.

"Wow," Sharah said, breathing softly. "Just . . . Wow . . ."

"Wow is right." I felt a little glassy-eyed myself. He looked far better than I thought he would and his dance was just . . . well . . . the way he moved his hips had me thinking about a different kind of bump and grind. Oh yeah.

Camille was looking at him suspiciously, and Menolly looked bored, staring at the crowd, but Nerissa, Sharah, and Iris were all fixated on the dancer. He slid his hips from side to side and caught my attention once again, as he grabbed hold of the waistband and—just like that—the pants flew off and over to the side.

Now in a tight G-string leaving nothing to the imagination, with fringe shimmering down the sides and in front, he began to gyrate toward Iris, whose eyes had gone immensely wide as she stared at what was coming toward her.

I was staring, too, but suddenly realized that my attention was no longer on the stripper, but on his fringe. Boy, that fringe looked like it would be fun to play with—to bat around, to yank on, to chew on . . . to . . .

Before I could stop myself, I was shifting right at the table. A few screams echoed around me, but mostly, I heard a lot of laughter. None of it mattered as I pounced on the object of my lust. Those strings—those glorious strings, all dangling and fluttering, calling my name—and all I wanted to do was reach out and grab one and have my way with it.

"Delilah! No!" Camille's voice echoed from across the table, but the fringe was too pretty and too dangly. The next thing I knew, I'd sideswiped Stripper Boy's thigh and was hanging from his G-string, several of the pieces of fringe in my mouth, tugging on it.

"What the fuck? Where'd the cat come from?" The guy suddenly didn't sound quite as thrilled as I felt. As he tried to pull away, I yanked harder.

Menolly put her arms around my tummy and tried to pry me away. Determined that the fringe was going to come with me—it was *my toy*, damn it—I held on for dear life.

Riiiipppppp . . . and the G-string gave way. Triumphant, I gripped the fringed banana hammock in my mouth and shook it, purring. I glanced up at Menolly, waiting for my praise. The least she could do was tell me what a good girl I was.

The stripper, trying to get away from my claws, fell toward Iris in the process but managed to catch himself on the edge of the table. Iris stared at the dangling penis that now hung free as a bird, hovering inches away from her face. She looked fascinated at first—or so I thought from my cat's fuzzy brain—but then as she opened her mouth to speak, she started to cough and, the next moment, vomited all over the stripper's goodies.

From there, it was all downhill. There was no way to salvage the evening after that. As the stripper disgustedly wiped down with a towel the barkeep gave him, I managed to gain enough control to shift back. Still tipsy, and with the taste of sweat-soaked G-string in my mouth, I cleared my throat, trying to stay steady on my feet.

Iris was wiping her mouth, totally embarrassed. Sharah and Menolly were taking care of the stripper—I saw a few extra twenties pass hands. Camille had moved over to their side.

"Dude, you've got some sort of glamour going on. Don't deny it—I can sense it a mile away. You're an FBH—full-blooded human. So what gives?" Her voice was low, but loud enough for me to catch.

He jerked his head up and stared at her. "Babe, I dunno what you're talking about."

"Don't even try blowing smoke with me, dude. You have no clue who you're dealing with. I just want to know where you got the potion. There'll be an extra fifty in it if you tell me the truth. And I'll know if you lie." She pulled out her purse and waved a fifty-dollar bill under his nose.

He paused, then cleared his throat. I tried to focus on what he was saying, but it was hard because the drinks and shifting and the promise of those dangling fringe pieces had all clouded my mind.

After a moment, the stripper shrugged. "What the hell.

Why not? I got it from a little shop in south Seattle. Name's Alchemy for Lovers, and they said that if I put three drops on my dick before a performance, it would increase my profits. Boy, were they right." He gave a sideways glance to Iris, then me. "Well, until tonight, that is. Damn stuff burns a bit, but hey, it makes sex better, too."

He sounded vaguely hopeful, but Camille motioned for him to leave.

The bartender was giving us dirty looks, so Menolly gathered up the presents. With Nerissa carrying the cake and Camille helping to guide me, we stumbled out to the limo. Tony was waiting for us right where he'd parked. He opened the doors and we crawled in.

Nerissa sat up front with him, holding the cake; Camille and Iris sat on one side, while Menolly, Sharah, and I sat on the other side of the backseat, and we set off for home to finish partying where we wouldn't chance ruining anybody else's evening.

We pulled in the driveway and slid out of the limo just in time to see Vanzir and Roz tossing each other around the yard. They were both stripped to their waists, oiled down, and involved in what looked like some sort of Greco-Roman wrestling match.

"What the hell . . . ?" Camille stared at them, then shook her head.

"I'm not *even* going to ask." My head was pounding. Apparently the Demented Zombies weren't agreeing with me. As I squinted, I saw Bruce stumbling around, chasing a dog that looked suspiciously like Speedo, the neighbor's basset hound. He was carrying a pair of bunny ears. Bruce, that is. Not Speedo.

"Holy crap, how much have they had to drink?"

"I dunno, but we've got a pair of dragons on the roof." She pointed to where Smoky and Shade were sitting on top of the roof, dangling their legs over the side. Neither looked too cozy, but they were talking and not arguing for once. A pile of rocks near the cars told us they'd been taking potshots. At least they hadn't broken any windshields.

As we stumbled our way into the house, we found cousin Shamas, Morio, and Chase in the living room, playing poker. The table was covered with change and dollar bills, and it looked like Chase was wiping the floor with both of them. Empty bottles of Nebelvuourian brandy and Elqaneve wine were strewn about, along with a couple empties of Irish whiskey. The smell of cigars made me want to hurl, and I glanced at Camille, who was also wrinkling her nose. She opened the window to air out the place.

"Honey, you're home!" Morio glanced up at Camille. As he stood up, he tripped and went sprawling at her feet, where he stayed down, reaching out to play with her strappy shoes.

"You're drunk." She moved her feet just out of reach.

"Ya think?" Morio burped and promptly dragged himself to his feet, where he threw one arm around her shoulders and one arm around Menolly's. Camille glanced at Menolly, who quickly sidestepped out of Morio's embrace. He still wasn't over the bond that had developed when some of her blood was injected into his veins, but Menolly seemed to have shaken it off . . . or at least she acted like it.

"You're *all* drunk." I glanced around as Shade and Smoky followed us in, clutching Bruce between them. "Well, maybe not those two, but geez . . ."

The pair seemed relatively sober, but then again, they were dragons and it probably took a whole keg of hard liquor to even *begin* to get a dragon bombed.

Smoky took the cake from Sharah and carried it to the kitchen, returning with Trillian, who had his nose in a book. One look at Iris's pained face and Trillian set down the book and slipped back into the kitchen, returning a moment later with a package of saltines and some ginger ale. She smiled and sipped the soft drink.

As the guys sprawled out in the living room and we joined them, Iris made the mistake of telling them about the stripper.

Smoky leaned forward, his eyes whirling. "You watched

another man remove his clothing for entertainment?" He glared at Camille.

"Chill out, Iris threw up on him and that killed the mood."

Trillian snorted. "You're lucky we live Earthside and not back in Otherworld. You'd be punching out guys right and left for the way they look at Camille there. Get used to it. Your wife's hot and people notice."

"Smoky, give it a rest. Trillian's right. Just accept it and move on," Iris grumbled. "And it's not my fault that I have morning sickness all the damned day!" She looked hurt and Camille slipped over to give her a hug, then settled onto Smoky's lap. His hair reached up to stroke her shoulders and entwine around her waist.

"I'll bet the gentleman wasn't expecting *that* response." Shade laughed.

"I'm not so sure he was that much of a gentleman." Camille repeated what the dancer had told her about the potion and the shop. "Sounds like sorcery to me. I don't like it."

I was about to say something when the phone rang. Yugi's voice echoed through the line.

"Delilah?" Yugi was Chase's second in command at the FH-CSI—the Faerie-Human Crime Scene Investigation unit. And he sounded so frantic I could barely understand him. "Please, we need you over here *now*. Sharah and Chase especially. It's an emergency."

"What's up?" A tingling in my gut told me that whatever it was, we were in no shape to deal with it.

"There's been a bombing at the Supe Community Council. Four confirmed deaths so far, and two people are in intensive care. We don't know how many others were in the building. Rescue teams are heading in as soon as the bomb squad confirms no more danger. Get over here. *Now*."

As I hung up, staring helplessly at the phone and wondering if any of my friends were among the dead, I realized that despite the celebrations going on in our private lives, we were always on call. There would never be another moment when we could fully relax—not until we'd pushed back the demons and stopped Shadow Wing and his cronies. And even then . . . there were other horrors in the world waiting for us to stop them.

"Sober up any way you can," I said, setting the receiver back in the cradle. "We've got work to do. And it can't wait till tomorrow."

Chapter 2

The room fell silent. I took a deep breath and barked out orders. "Smoky, Shade—you guys are sober, but I'll be damned if Smoky's touching a car."

"I can drive," he protested, but I shook my head.

"Right, and I can blow smoke and fire out of my mouth. Nice try." I tossed my keys to Shade. "You drive my Jeep and take Vanzir, Roz, and me. Menolly, you're sober. You can drive Camille's car and take her and her men."

Iris piped up. "Bruce's driver can take Chase and Sharah. But somebody has to stay here. Someone not drunk out of their minds."

"Right . . . okay. Smoky, you stay with Iris and the others. You can handle trouble if there is any."

"Check." He blinked, the smile wiping off of his face. Ever since his father had captured Camille, the dragon had taken security around the place to a whole new level. We practically lived in a compound now.

"Crap, is there *any* way we can get some of this booze out of our systems?" I didn't want to go in drunk. And I had the feeling that—from now on—we wouldn't be partying with booze. At least not all of us at the same time.

Iris blinked. "I can help—I've got an herb that works wonders, but the effects won't be pleasant in the morning."

"We have no choice. Can we all use it?" I didn't care if we all had the dry heaves in the morning. Tonight, we needed to be on our game.

"Not everybody. But you, Camille, Shamas, Trillian, Sharah . . . it might also help Rozurial since he was Fae before he was turned into an incubus. I'd be hesitant to try it on Morio or Vanzir, though. I'm not sure about Nerissa."

"Then bring it on. Shade's fine. Nerissa's staying here, so go ahead and try to sober her up after we're gone. That just leaves Vanzir and Chase."

"I don't need it." Trillian held out his hand. It was steady. "I had two brandies a few hours ago. I'm sober."

Iris nodded. "Fine. While I might consider giving it to Chase . . . hell . . . just a minute!" She turned and raced for the bathroom.

Meanwhile, Smoky picked up Camille, tossed her over his shoulder, and headed up the stairs. "I'll get her dressed for action," he called over his shoulder. Trillian and Morio followed.

I pulled off my boots and asked Shade to bring me down a pair of mud stompers and a heavy denim jacket. The rest of my outfit would be fine. He nodded and dashed up the stairs.

Meanwhile, Iris reappeared and motioned for Menolly to help her. I followed them into the kitchen, where Iris pulled out a packet of a foul-smelling herbs, but instead of steeping them into tea, like I thought she was going to, she began packing them into gelatin capsules. Then she whispered some sort of enchantment over the capsules and handed me one of the giant horse pills along with a bottle of water.

I stared at it, finally slipping it into my mouth. I struggled to swallow it with a big swig of water. It began to open on the way down and I burped, an earthy, tangy taste filling my mouth. As I winced, Iris slapped a piece of bread spread with butter in my hands.

"Eat. It will help cushion the impact of the *damishanya* root."

"Damishanya? Oh crap. We're fucked. But yeah, it will help."

Damishanya was an Otherworld herb that was as harsh as it was effective. I'd forgotten about it until Iris mentioned the name, but now memories of the root flooded back. The first time Camille, Menolly, and I had gotten pie-faced drunk—before our father gave us permission to drink—we'd sneaked some of the herb to keep our father from finding out. But he could smell the booze and herb a mile away, and we'd all suffered his wrath. We'd all been on cleaning duty for a week straight. He'd blamed Camille most, since she was the oldest and he held her responsible. She'd been on house arrest for two weeks.

As Camille and the others entered the kitchen, Iris doled out the capsules and food, and then we headed out for the cars. Roz had declined the drug; come to find out he was barely tipsy and just blowing off steam. He did, however, wash off the oil and dress. Vanzir stayed home—he was too wasted to be of any help in the field.

So Shade and I took Chase and Sharah with us in the Jeep, while Menolly drove Camille's Lexus, ferrying Camille, Morio, Trillian, and Shamas.

As we headed down the driveway my thoughts began to clear. The root was working fast. With a poignant regret, I realized how much I'd welcomed shutting down my mind for a while. For just a moment we'd been able to let ourselves go wild, forget about all we'd been facing. But now, I realized just how much steam was left behind the barrier.

As we pulled into the parking lot at the Supe Community Council, I realized I was stone-cold sober. The hall—a small building that sat on a weed-infested lot with a parking lot full of cracks in the pavement—was smoldering. The smell of smoke saturated the air and it was hard to breathe. I opened the door and slowly stepped out of the car.

At first glance, I thought maybe we'd lucked out and the building hadn't been hit too hard. But as the others joined us—with everybody but Morio looking relatively intact—we moved forward, and I realized that the place had been gutted by the fire and explosion.

I stared at the fractured hall, my heart skipping a beat. I was an integral part of the Supe Community Council. I could have easily been here. The planning committee for an upcoming dance was supposed to have met tonight. And what if this had happened during one of our monthly meetings, when we'd have up to a hundred members joining us?

The thoughts of *what might have been* began to run through my head, an unending stream of bloody images, until I realized a lump the size of a golf ball had formed in the back of my throat. Camille took my hand as we surveyed the damage. The firemen were still pouring water on parts of the building, but by now, most of the flames had burned themselves out. There wasn't much left for them to feed on.

"It's bad." Yugi saw us and hurried over. Second in command to Chase, the Swedish hulk of a detective had grown into a friend—he'd always been helpful to us. He was an FBH, but he was also an empath, and now he looked into my eyes and I saw him shiver. He turned to Chase, who stepped up.

"I'm sorry I wasn't here—" Chase started to say, remorse filling his voice.

"You can't be on duty twenty-four-seven, boss. Nobody knew this was going to happen. We didn't have any warning. Sure, hate crimes have been up, but nobody expected anything like this." Yugi handed him a file. "Here are the details we have so far."

"Run it down for us, please." Chase flipped through the file, but it was too dark to read, even under the streetlamp.

Yugi nodded. "Sure thing. We got a call at ten forty-five p.m. that there had been an explosion, but we weren't sure how big or bad. Fire trucks were on the way. Team assembled and headed out. We got here to find the building engulfed by flames, and the firemen weren't able to put a dent in the fire. I noticed an odd smell, and I still can't place it—it might be gone, but I can't say for sure. By now my nose is filled with the smell of smoke."

Camille and I stepped forward and began to sniff around. Shamas did the same. After a moment Shamas let out a shout, and we looked at him.

He turned to Chase. "Explosive all right, but not from Earthside. This is *canya*, a volatile magical mixture. Liquid—but it's usually mixed in small amounts into a bigger bomb. While it's sold in the back alleys of Otherworld, it's illegal in most of the cities there."

"Canya? Are you sure?"

"Trust me. I know that scent."

Camille let out a long sigh. "The one place in Otherworld you could find it in any great measure would be the Southern Wastes." She frowned. "And the Southern Wastes are controlled by sorcerers, goblins, and the Goldunsan Fae—who work their way into some of the northern mountains. The Goldunsan aren't like us. They're alien, a little like the seers of Aladril."

"That's the second time the mention of sorcerers has come up tonight. You think Van or Jaycee had something to do with this?" I stared at her.

Two sorcerers had escaped our net a few months back after seriously putting the bite on a bunch of local werewolves, and they'd done some heavy damage to Camille in the process. We'd done our best to capture them, but they managed to vanish. We couldn't win them all, and we'd taken down their illegal drug operation and saved several werewolves from a horrible death. So, we'd counted ourselves lucky.

Sucking in a deep breath, she caught my gaze. "I don't want to go there. I really don't, but we'd better put that down as a possibility. Revenge, perhaps, for shutting down their Wolf Briar business?"

Wolf Briar was a skanky drug used to subdue werewolves. And the production of it required the torture and dissection *of* werewolves. We'd put a stop to an underground production line, but the main players had managed to escape and were still out there.

"Good possibility. They're Tregarts, so they'd have access to the explosive." I rubbed my head. Tregarts—humanoid demons who could pass easily in society—were becoming a constant issue. We weren't sure how they were getting in from the Subterranean Realms, but since Shadow Wing had one of the spirit seals, chances were he'd figured out a way to make it work for him.

"There's one other possibility that we can't overlook: Telazhar." She pressed her lips together.

We'd gotten word that Telazhar, the necromancer who'd trained Stacia Bonecrusher—a rogue demon general whom we'd barely managed to put an end to—had escaped from the Sub-Realms. He'd been deported there when he was kicked out of Otherworld. We had reason to believe he might be Earthside now.

"What if somehow he hooked up with Van and Jaycee?" I didn't even want to entertain the thought, but we had to.

Camille shook her head. "If he does, we're fucked. Sorcerers and necromancers together? They'd be such powerful allies, they'd rival a demon general. But since Van and Jaycee were connected to Stacia, that's not a wild-card bet. We'd better check it out."

Chase cleared his throat. "Keep it in mind, but let's not start on that assumption. One thing I've learned: Never assume. Go by the facts, and conjecture all you like, but remember it's just speculation until proven." He let out a long sigh. "You say four died?"

Yugi's jaw tightened. "Five. We found another body after I called you. Two are on the cusp—Mallen's taking care of them back at headquarters. Sharah, you need to get over there. Mallen needs your help."

As he moved to call an officer to drive her, I stopped him. "Can we go poke around the building?"

Yugi shook his head. "Not till morning. Still too dangerous to go in. The rest of the roof could easily cave, and then where would you be? The flames aren't even doused yet.

And we have to go through it with a fine-tooth comb for evidence, and also to look for . . ."

"For more bodies." I clenched my teeth. I had too many friends from the Supe Community. Chances were, I knew at least one of the victims. "We'll take Sharah to HQ. I need to see the victims, to see if any of them are . . ." I couldn't finish the sentence. Instead, I asked, "Has anybody called yet wondering if the victims are okay? I imagine word about the explosion has made the news already."

He nodded. "Yeah, a bunch of family members are waiting at the station. I was hoping you'd volunteer to come help. The news might come better from . . ." Pausing, Yugi ducked his head.

"From one of their own?" My voice was soft; I knew what he meant and there was no disrespect there. As I spoke, I felt an arm snake around my waist and Shade pressed against me, his lips brushing against the side of my head.

I leaned into his embrace. Even without words, I could read his intent. He had my back, during the good times and the difficult. My heart swelled as the slightly exotic musk that marked him as part dragon swept around me, shoring me up, giving me strength.

Camille caught my eye and smiled. She understood. She knew what I was feeling because she had that reassurance, too. Having a dragon lover—even a half-dragon lover— brought with it a special sense of security. That security could be broken, but it took a lot to shatter the safety.

As if reading my mind, Trillian placed his hands on Camille's shoulders. Ever since Hyto's attack, my sister had pulled her men close to help strengthen her boundaries, and they'd been more than willing to help, in whatever way they could. Morio and she had started headlong back into their death magic rituals as soon as he was out of the wheelchair, Trillian had been teaching her how to fight street-dirty, and Smoky had been securing our land with his own crazed vigilance.

I looked up at Shade, intensely grateful for his support. "Thank you. Let's go," I said to the others. "We can't do any more here tonight." And with that, we turned and walked away—even though it was torture to think there might be more of my friends under the rubble—and headed for our cars.

So who am I? Taking a moment here to introduce myself, let me first say that some days I'm not exactly sure *who* I am. Oh, I know I'm Delilah D'Artigo, a two-faced Were, meaning one shape I shift into is a long-haired golden tabby who loves to get into trouble, and the other is my black panther self—ruled over by the Autumn Lord. There's no memory problem . . . but I've been changing so rapidly over the past year, it's hard to catch my breath, and sometimes I stare at myself in the mirror, wondering who's looking back at me.

One of those changes includes the fact that I've also become a Death Maiden—the only living Death Maiden at this time. Most of the Autumn Lord's servants are dead, their souls gathered in Haseofon to work for him, but I'm alive. And someday, he has promised I will bear his child via my lover Shade. How and when that's to be, I have no clue, but it's destined to happen, and I believe in Fate.

At first, the transformation into the Autumn Lord's service was hard for me. When my sisters and I came Earthside a few years back, I was still fairly naïve. I believed in the goodness of people. Now—well, I'm still an optimist, but I lost my rose-colored glasses along the way. And I no longer automatically assume the best of everyone I meet. Now, I'm embracing my duties, and I feel honored to hold the title.

Along with my sisters—Camille, a wicked good witch, who is also a priestess of the Moon Mother, and Menolly—a *jian-tu* acrobat and spy-turned-vampire, we were sent over from Otherworld. We were members of the OIA—the Otherworld Intelligence Agency—and after the portals dividing the worlds opened, we were assigned Earthside.

At first, the people here opened up their arms to their magical brethren. At one time the two worlds were united and the reunion caught the heart of most of Earthside. But now hate crimes were on the rise as interaction between the Supes—supernaturals—and the FBHs increased and the novelty wore off.

Our mother was human—she's long dead—and our father is Fae. Near the end of World War 2, when Sephreh was over Earthside on some secret mission, they met and fell in love. In the true nature of whirlwind romances, he swept her off her feet and took her back to Otherworld. Losing Mother was hard on our family. Losing our father's support was even harder. But he turned his back on Camille, and in doing so, we turned our backs on him.

We resigned from the OIA and told our father that we'd return to duty when he came around to accepting Camille's pledge to the Earthside Fae Queen's court. Now we're on our own, still facing the demon lord Shadow Wing, who intends to raze Earth and Otherworld for his own private amusement.

He's after the spirit seals, and so are we. Originally one seal, the artifact was formed after the Great Divide, the time when the great Fae Lords ripped apart the worlds. They created the seal to keep Otherworld, Earthside, and the Subterranean Realms separate, then broke it into nine pieces, scattering them to the Elemental Lords to keep them hidden. Separate, the nine seals have kept the realms safe. If brought back together, they can rip open all the portals.

But sometimes things work as they will and not as we wish. The seals began to surface. They came to the attention of Shadow Wing. And that's where we come in. We were plunged into a race to find them as they made themselves known—hopefully before the Demon Lord gets hold of them. He managed to steal one of them from us before we could secure it. We've found five. So far the odds are in our favor, but the fact that he possesses even one of them puts everyone in danger.

Technically, we now work for Queen Asteria, the Elfin Queen back in Otherworld, who's hiding the spirit seals as we take them to her. But in reality we work on our own, trying to ensure that the future makes it here in one piece without too much damage or demonic interference. Some days are easier than others . . .

"What are you thinking about?" Shade glanced over at me as I leaned back in the passenger seat, wincing. I had the beginnings of a headache and wondered how long before the side effects of the damishanya were going to hit.

"I'm wondering who I know among the dead. Which families I'm going to have to shatter with the news." I rubbed my temples, glancing into the backseat at Chase and Sharah. "You guys have it worse . . . I know. I'm not complaining. It's just never . . ."

"Never easy," Chase said, finishing my thought. "Trust me, I understand and if I didn't think you'd be a helpful influence, I'd never ask you to join me for this. I wish we'd brought Nerissa, too. This is part of her job. She's a wonderful grief counselor."

I pulled out my cell phone. "Let me give her a call and see how she's doing." The phone rang three times before Iris picked up. I ran down what we'd learned and where we were going. "Is Nerissa in any shape to drag herself out of the house and down to HQ?"

"Hold on." Iris set the phone down, and as I waited, I thought about how entangled we'd all become in each others' lives. After a moment, Iris returned. "She's sober. I'll have Bruce's driver take her down to headquarters in the limo. If you could see that she gets home when necessary . . ."

"No problem. Bless you and bless Bruce. Tell her we'll see her when she gets there." I punched the End Call button. "Nerissa's coming down."

Chase grunted a thank-you. "Odd . . . how this has all worked out." He didn't say anything more, but I knew he'd picked up on my mood—I'd been around him long enough to tell.

We'd been involved, after he struck out with Camille, and we'd made a good stab at a relationship, but the rocks on that ocean were just too sharp to navigate. Now he was involved with Sharah, the elfin medic, and they seemed to be a more compatible couple. He'd hired Nerissa as a crisis counselor, and she and Menolly were promised to each other. One by one, our extended family kept growing involved in ways we'd never have been able to predict. It kind of made up for the isolation we'd first felt when we came over Earthside.

By the time we arrived at the FH-CSI headquarters, Morio was fully sober. Apparently alcohol sped through his system quickly. Camille looked vaguely ill, as did Shamas, and I was starting to feel as rough as they looked. But we were all clearheaded as we followed Chase and Sharah into the building.

The Faerie-Human Crime Scene Investigation building took up at least four floors, though there was a rumor of a hidden level. The top floor housed the police headquarters and medical unit. First floor down was a highly secure arsenal. Second floor down—the OW offender jails. And on the bottom floor were the laboratory, morgue, and archives. Tonight, we were headed for the morgue—a place we had been all too often.

As the elevator descended with a silent rush, a somber mood settled over the group and I stared at my feet, Shade's hand on my shoulder. I didn't want to go in—didn't want to look at the faces of my fallen friends. The Supe Community was tight-knit; everybody knew everybody else.

The doors opened with a swish and we stepped out onto the hard tiled floor, our boots leaving a series of staccato tattoos echoing in our wake. The walls here had been recently painted sterile white. Whether they thought the color made the atmosphere brighter than the pale blue had, I didn't know, but now the complex felt cold and hollow. As Chase pushed through the doors, Sharah right behind him, I watched them go in.

They fit together . . . they really fit. Both of them had to deal with the leavings of society—the aftermath of battle. Whereas I was on the front lines, Chase was better suited to picking up the pieces and making sense of it all, of organizing the back lines. We'd never found our niche together. And yet we both had our place in the battles we were facing. And we'd become blood brother and sister. No matter what, we had each other's back.

Chase glanced back at me, his eyes shimmering, and he blinked, then slowly smiled and inclined his head, as if he'd heard me speaking. He was changing, evolving, and none of us knew what he was becoming. Not even him.

He stood back, holding the morgue doors open for us. Sharah headed over to examine the bodies and talk to Mallen, her right-hand man, who was also an elf. He handed her a series of charts and she flipped through them.

I slowly approached the tables—five of them, each covered with a snow white sheet. Or what had started as snow white. Blossoms of blood spread across them, petals staining the undersides of the sheets, and as I watched, the patterns seemed to form the silhouettes of flowers. Or perhaps it was my imagination—like some gruesome Rorschach test.

The bodies were still, no breath, no movement. No fear they'd turn into vampires, like when Menolly had come here to identify victims. Just . . . dead. Cold, forever gone. I took a deep breath and looked up at Mallen.

"How bad are they?" Swallowing my fear, I tried to remind myself that I was a Death Maiden. I escorted—or would soon escort—souls over through the veil as part of my duties. I would be leaving the empty bodies of not just my enemies, but anybody whom the Autumn Lord ordered me to take.

He sucked in a deep breath and let it out slowly. "They aren't good. It's not . . . it's bloody. But the faces are fairly intact. I think they're recognizable enough. The bodies were pretty mangled and burned. Four of them were right near the blast. The fifth . . . he never made it through the ride to the hospital."

Menolly and Camille joined me. I reached for Camille's hand as Mallen pulled back the first sheet. I flinched. I knew the face. "Tom. Thomas Creia. He's a member of the Verde

Canis Clan. They were a group of Weres working for environmental causes. He's married. Two children."

Sharah jotted down the information as we moved to the second table. Again, the sheet came down. Again, a familiar face.

"Crap. Trixie Jones. One of Marion's sisters. Coyote shifter. Single. I think she might have been engaged, but I'm not sure." The fire in my belly began to burn brighter. Whoever did this, I wanted to find them. *Now.*

The third sheet. Another man. This one, I knew by name but not to call *friend.* But his death had not been pleasant, and the grimace on his face told me he'd died in pain.

"Salvatore Tienes. Werewolf. He recently moved up from Arizona. I don't know what pack he was with, but he's been staying with a werewolf family up in Shoreline." I bit my lip, wanting to stop. I couldn't shake the feeling that I didn't want to see who was left—an irrational fear took hold, that it would be someone even closer. Mallen drew back the fourth sheet.

I stared. Menolly and Camille squeezed my hands, and Camille let out a little gasp. Even Chase moved closer, hanging his head.

"Exo Reed," he said quietly.

Everybody in the Supe community knew Exo. He ran the Halcyon Hotel, catering to Supes. He'd called us in on several jobs and was an upstanding member of the NRA and a member of the chamber of commerce for the greater Seattle area. And now, he was so much fodder for worms. Bloody . . . gone to whatever afterlife awaited werewolves when they died.

Tears threatened, but I sucked them back, holding myself rigid. Camille was doing the same, and Menolly had one of those horrific looks on her face that told me she wanted to do nothing less than hunt down the scum who did this and rip them to shreds.

"Show us the last, Mallen. Then we should talk to the survivors." Chase glanced over at the elf but paused when Mallen held up his hand.

Mallen barely looked old enough to be in high school, but he was far older than most of us. "They aren't in any condition to talk. They may not be for a long time. But I'll do my best to have them conscious by tomorrow."

"Crap. We need to know everything we can about this blast." Chase looked flummoxed but then shrugged. "Whatever . . . we'll play it as we go. So, who's our last victim?"

We were all afraid that it was going to be someone else we knew, but this time it wasn't a Were, but an elf, unfamiliar to any of us. Neither Mallen nor Sharah recognized him, either.

"We'll have to go through the records of who came over from Otherworld recently . . . track down anybody who might have seen him come through the portals." I was shaken, and I hated to admit it, but I'd been relieved that our last casualty wore a stranger's face. Somewhere, he had to have family or friends who would miss him. But for us, he was easier to handle—a cold statistic in what had become a terribly personal crime.

"Did the fire or explosion kill them? I know it's an obvious question, but is there anything we overlooked? That we don't know?" Camille spoke up, looking to Mallen for answers.

"Good question," Chase said.

Mallen consulted his charts. "Toxicology is still out, but the most obvious cause is massive trauma due to whatever explosive device this was, and third-degree burns over most of their bodies. Although . . ." He paused.

"Although what?" I pulled out my notebook and began making my own notes.

"The odd thing . . . when a bomb detonates—a homemade bomb like those commonly used by hate crime groups—they usually make sure it's loaded with shrapnel. Now, there are injuries due to shrapnel here, but it wasn't from the bomb. The fragments obviously came from the surroundings. Wood from the beams, metal from the tables that exploded. Whatever blew up doesn't seem to have left much of a residue."

"That's because the explosive factor was canya." I watched as Mallen's expression turned from perplexed to horrified. "Yeah, we're thinking sorcerers. The question is: Who did it, and how did they get hold of this crap?"

"Then toxicity results aren't going to show anything." He closed the folder and set it down on the table. "The fact is, the amount of canya needed to blow up a building the size of the Supe Community Hall points to some very powerful enemies. If they have enough canya for that, I wouldn't put it past them to have other tricks like this up their sleeve. You have to find them, or I predict a body count like we haven't seen in a long while."

Chase let out a long sigh. "We so didn't need that information. Okay, let's go have a talk with the families. I know some of them are waiting upstairs." He shook his head, looking resigned. "I'm used to breaking bad news to people, but the sting never goes away."

Chapter 3

Chase told everybody but Shade and me to go home. There were family members out there, and it was better to avoid overwhelming them with too many faces, too many questions.

After Camille and the others left, we followed Chase, filing through the cubicles, waving to the night crew, until we reached Chase's office. Nerissa hurried in behind us, looking a little worse for wear, but she was dressed in jeans and a pretty blouse, sober, and ready to work.

As soon as he closed the door, Chase turned to me. "I hate this part of the job. I know you do, too. But we have to word this carefully. We know this was no accident. So we have outright murder and arson."

"What do we tell them?" It was better to defer to Chase on this one—he was the one who had to deal with the fallout, especially if it took us a while to find the murderers.

He stared at a piece of paper on his desk, tapping his fingers on the wood. After a moment, he looked up. "Let's go. Just follow my lead." With a decisive nod, he motioned for us to follow him.

We headed out into the waiting room, where a group of anxious Weres sat around the room. I caught sight of Marion Vespa—owner of the Supe-Urban Café—and quickly looked away before she could catch my eye. I dreaded being witness to when we told her that her sister was dead.

Exo Reed's wife, Claudia, was there. She'd left the kids home. And others . . . most likely family of the dead and injured. Surveying the anxious faces made me want to weep. So much needless death and destruction went on in my world. The dead were usually okay—off doing other things—but here was the real aftermath of tragedy.

As we approached, Claudia glanced anxiously at us, scanning our faces. She must have read our energy, or perhaps it was simply body language, but whatever the case, her expression crumpled and she began to weep. Marion glanced at her, then hung her head, silent tears streaming down her face.

Chase glanced at them. "Will the families of Trixie Jones, Thomas Creia, Exo Reed, and Salvatore Tienes please come with us." He turned to Sharah. "Will you talk to the others?"

She nodded, silently leading three people aside. They must have been family of the injured. I glanced at her as we led the others into a quiet conference room. Nerissa gently steered Claudia, who looked like she might collapse.

As I closed the door, Chase motioned for people to sit down. "I'm afraid I have bad news." He let out a long sigh, pausing.

"They're dead, aren't they? My Exo is dead." Claudia struggled to speak, her voice barely audible.

He nodded. "I'm sorry to have to tell you this . . . and in this manner. There was an explosion at the Supe Community Council tonight and seven people were caught in the blast—seven that we know of so far. Two are in intensive care fighting for their lives. The others . . . I'm sorry but they didn't make it."

I watched as he skirted the delicate line between caring too much and sounding too callous. He didn't dare let himself get caught up in their pain, but neither could he remain totally detached.

Marion sucked in a deep breath and raised her head, letting out a long cry—a howl almost. The others, one by one joined in. Coyote, canine, wolf . . . they were all part of the tableau and they were all shifters under their superficial differences.

Chase waited till they finished, respecting the tradition, and then he gently passed around pictures of the elf. "I'm sorry to ask this, but first, do any of you have any idea of who this man was? He was caught in the blast, too, but we haven't been able to put an ID to him yet."

One by one they studied the picture, tears streaming, and shook their heads. Marion held it last, staring long and hard.

"I think he might have come into the café the other day, but I'm not sure. It was a slow day and I seem to remember . . . yes, Trixie was there, she was talking to him. But I don't know his name." She handed it back. "Who did this?"

"We don't know yet." Chase let out a long breath. "I'm sorry, but the sooner we ask you some questions, the sooner we'll be able to catch whoever it is that did this." He glanced around at the silent, tear-stained faces.

After a moment, Claudia Reed spoke up. "Ask your questions, Detective. We'll do all we can to help." She looked at the others, and they nodded their assent. Apparently, Exo's wife was tougher than I had first thought.

"Thank you. I know this is a rotten time to ask, but it might help." Chase shuffled a few papers and flipped open his notebook, pen poised over the paper.

"Have any of your loved ones mentioned anything out of the ordinary—any enemies? Anybody who might have been making threats? Anybody unhappy with them?"

He settled back in his chair while Nerissa unobtrusively passed out tissues, patted shoulders, and brought a blanket for Marion, who was shivering. I wanted to go over, put my arms around her shoulders, whisper that it was all okay, that it was a mistake and her sister was still alive and well.

Claudia shrugged. "Exo has . . . had . . . he's made a number of enemies, definitely. Anybody turned away from the hotel could be out to get him. And there are a few members in the werewolf packs who don't like the fact that he's made such a public name for himself."

I glanced at Chase, who gave me an imperceptible nod. "Do you know if any sorcerers have been hanging around the hotel?" If Van and Jaycee were part of this, chances were they had brought more of their kind over from the Sub-Realms.

The werewolf flinched, her eyes gleaming in the dim room. "Sorcerers? Crap—I didn't know sorcery was involved." Most werewolves didn't care for outright magic.

Marion cleared her throat. "Delilah, can I speak to you in private?"

I led her out of the room, to an empty one next door. "Yes?"

"Could this have anything to do with the Koyanni? You cleared out a lot of them, but some got away. You know I'd have told you if I knew where they were, but it's well known among the coyote shifters that you are connected with the Supe Community Council. And a strike at the organization you help run would be a strike at you."

I cleared my throat. "You might be right. We've talked about this already. Which means I'm going to have to talk openly about the Koyanni. I know your people have kept them a secret all these years, but let's face it, that barn door was left standing wide open and the horses are long gone."

She closed her eyes and leaned against the wall. "I suppose it is."

"When they attacked Luke's sister, they forfeited their secrecy. Eventually, everything is going to come out in the open. We can't keep a lid on old legends when they prove to be true and still deadly. And if the Koyanni are involved in this, we've got a huge problem on our hands. Would you like me to tell the others, or do you want to? You know their history better."

Mario bit her lip. "I broke my vow of secrecy when I first mentioned them to you and your sisters. I guess . . . now it's moot. And if the Elders can't understand why I'm speaking up, then that's their problem. We can't keep them a secret when they may be terrorizing the entire Supe Community. Especially if they had anything to do with my sister's death. And if they did, then I will hunt every last one of them down and slit their throats."

"You don't think they targeted Trixie because they knew you were the one who originally told us about them, do you?"

"I don't know." She shrugged, then covered her eyes with her hand as tears slowly rolled down her face. Her voice throaty with tears, she added, "Whoever did it, I just want them *dead*."

I swept the gaunt, lean woman into my arms and hugged her. She was so creative and nurturing in her restaurant; it was a shock to hear her talk so harshly. Grief was like that, though. It could make killers out of ordinary men and women. Heading back into the other room, I gave Marion a moment to compose herself. I motioned for everyone's attention and glanced at Chase, who nodded for me to go ahead. He trusted us. We did our best not to abuse that trust.

"We have a situation that started back in October. Whether or not it relates to the bombing tonight, we're not sure yet. But I think it best if we tell you about it in case the events spark off any connections . . . anything that might help us locate who killed your family members. Again, as Chief Johnson said, we're sorry to have to put you through this tonight—we understand how hard it is. But the sooner we can gather clues, the sooner we can begin looking for the perpetrators."

The word *perpetrator* felt odd on my tongue. To my mind, they were murderers, but the inflammatory tone of the word might further sidetrack the family members, who were reeling as it was.

Marion quietly joined us again. She slipped into her seat. I glanced at her, and she gave me a resigned look. I smiled at her and continued.

"Last October, some of you may remember hearing of several killings that happened among the werewolf community. We were investigating the case of several werewolves who were murdered—"

"I remember that," the weredog said. "I'm Shane Creia. Thomas was my little brother. He was only a couple of years out of high school. He's got a wife and twin boys." He pinched his nose, the tears glistening in his eyes. "What kind of people do this?"

The other man—a werewolf—cleared his throat. I could tell his nerves were raw. Weres were readable; we were like open books at times thanks to our heightened body language. "Geraldo Tienes . . . Salvatore's uncle. Word about the murders filtered down into Arizona, though there wasn't much information released. Do you think those killings were connected with the explosion tonight?" He straightened, his nose twitching.

I nodded. "Right, we didn't release a lot of information, and with good reason. We're walking on treacherous ground here. There are things going on that we just can't talk about right now. When those murders happened, we caught a number of the perps . . . but some got away. We think they may be back—not necessarily for their original reason, but to wreak revenge on the Supe Community. Maybe on Marion, or me or . . . who knows. The murders were connected with Wolf Briar—"

"Wolf Briar! Wolf Briar is loose in the community?" Geraldo's eyes glittered with fear.

"Yeah, it is. We think we destroyed most of it, but we can't be sure, so be cautious. And we know for a fact it was being made by a couple of sorcerers and a group of Koyanni."

Doing my best to skirt the whole spirit seal–demonic invasion theme, I kept it to "sorcerers" and left out the *Tregart* part, then hashed the rest of the information together in a way that made sense.

"Koyanni?" Salvatore glanced up. "Who are they?"

I was about to defer to Marion, but Geraldo spoke up.

"Coyote scum, that's who." He pressed his lips together, the bridge of his nose turning unnaturally white.

"Oh, hell." Claudia shifted in her seat. "Exo mentioned

that he thought the Koyanni were in the area. He had trouble
with them when he was on a special ops assignment for his
unit, years ago, down in South America. He told me that
they were a vicious breed of coyote shifters . . ." She turned
to study Marion for a moment. "Does *she* know anything
about this?" Shaking an accusing finger at the café owner,
the werewolf slammed her chair back.

Marion slowly stood, meeting Claudia's angry gaze. "Do
not confuse me with the Lost Ones. They walk to their own
vision, and any coyote shifter who follows the true path of the
Great Trickster will have nothing to do with them. The Koyanni are dangerous and a tribe unto themselves. They left the
old ways behind eons ago and are considered outcasts."

Before fists—or fur—could fly, I stepped in. "Stop and sit
down, both of you. Marion has *nothing* to do with the Koyanni. I see that you're familiar with them, so for now we'll
forgo discussion of their past. Marion's just as much a victim
as the rest of you. Her sister was caught in the explosion."

Claudia mumbled an apology and returned to her seat.
Marion shrugged and slouched in her chair again.

Trying to ignore the scent of pheromones in the air—the
energy was thick and volatile—I quickly laid out a highly
edited version of what had happened last fall.

"What you need to know is this: Several Koyanni joined
in with a couple of sorcerers to produce Wolf Briar. They
were capturing werewolves from the area, beta males, and
hyping them up on steroids in order to kill them, to harvest
their pituitary glands and adrenals. We managed to put a
stop to the operation and captured several of the main players, but the sorcerers—Van and Jaycee by name—got away.
As did some of the Koyanni."

"And you think they're the ones who blew up the community hall?" Claudia bit her lip.

"The explosion was caused by a sorcerer with ingredients
from Otherworld, as far as we can tell." Chase cleared his
throat. "Which means it's going to be hard to trace. What
we need from you—and I know this is asking a lot—is that
you comb through every memory you have. We need any

clues . . . anything that might be of help. Any strangers who your loved ones mentioned, anything that seemed off—I don't care if it seems minute, it might be an important clue."

Claudia frowned. "It's so hard to think . . ."

I could feel the weariness flowing from her. She—and the others—were all close to breaking down. And when Weres broke down, it was never pretty. I motioned Chase to follow me. Meanwhile, Nerissa passed out coffee and cookies, speaking in soothing low tones while we slipped out of the room.

I leaned against the wall.

"Chase, we can't push them. *Trust me*, unless you want a couple wolves, a coyote, and a dog in there—probably at each others' throats since emotions are so heightened—then I advise you to let them think it over for the night. We're not going to learn anything right now."

He crossed his arms. "I'd like to fight you on this one, but I know you're right. All right, we'll give them the night, though I really want to get on top of this. But the fire marshal probably won't be done until tomorrow anyway, and since we know it was a magical signature, we're not going to be finding much in the way of typical evidence. Even if we do, I doubt if it will be useful."

I nodded. "Give them the night and by tomorrow, they'll be able to focus more. Right now the shock is playing havoc with their emotions."

"I know, I know." He shook his head, scuffing his foot on the floor. "I just don't want to deal with the aftermath if the investigation takes us a while. The pressure's going to be coming from all sides in the Supe Community to find out who did this. And what if we're wrong and we find out some wacko hate group executed this whole rotten plan? We're going to be looking at another whole can of worms."

I bit my lip. Tensions had been growing between a vocal minority of society and the Supe Community. "You really think a hate group would go to these lengths?"

Chase flashed me a sad smile. "They'd go a lot further. Look at my history—at the history of mortals. Look what we've done to each other in the name of religion, in the name of moral superiority, in the pursuit of money. I fully believe some crackpot group like Freedom's Angels or the Church of the Earthborn Brethren would toss a bomb into the mix."

"You've changed a lot since we first met you." I studied him. "You've gone from being . . . well . . . an arrogant and totally by-the-book detective with a stick up his ass to someone who digs in deep. Who isn't afraid to get his hands muddy."

"I've changed." He lowered his gaze away from mine. "I've changed a lot. Especially since Karvanak got hold of me. I've never told anybody what happened. Chances are, I never will. But it made me realize what we're facing—how you and your sisters are right. Sometimes you have to skirt the rules." He paused, then added, "Everything shifted again when you gave me the Nectar of Life. Sometimes I feel like there's so much going on inside me that I'm caught in a whirlpool. Or like I'm in the center of a tornado, spinning out of control, and I have no clue where I'm going to land."

He gave me a long look and I could see the flurry of emotions battling within him. I reached out, put my hand on his shoulder, and kissed him lightly on the cheek.

"I'm sorry. We really haven't had much of a chance to sit and talk about your transformation, but we need to. Chase, Camille and Menolly and I really want to discuss the changes you're going through. Sharah can help you learn to cope with the changes you're undergoing, but . . ."

"Yeah, I know. You don't have to say it. Now that she and I are dating, she might not be unbiased enough to pick up on potential problems. Trust me, I've been mulling this over for a long time and the incident with the Elder Fae—the spider freak—sealed the deal. I know things are happening to me that I can't figure out. Hell, I can barely explain them. That's why I asked Camille to make me an appointment with the Triple Threat. I took their tests and am waiting for them to contact me with some answers."

"She mentioned you'd come to her." Some odd magical connection had sprung up between Chase and Camille. She'd noticed the bond developing and mentioned it to the rest of us. Whether it was just the magical energy or something deeper, we weren't sure.

"So you really think you might be able to help me? Once I know more?"

"We'll do everything we can to try." I paused, not knowing whether to say something that had been lurking in my thoughts. Chase and I hadn't really spoken about our breakup, either. It was almost as though—once it happened—we'd pretended like it was over and done with, a blip on the map. And though I was happy now, and we'd made the right decision, I wanted to be able to talk about our time together, without recriminations, without regrets.

"Chase . . ."

He gave me a look that said he knew where I was going and wasn't ready to go there himself. "Yes?"

I paused again, then shook my head. "Nothing. Let's get back inside."

We headed back in, and I slid into my chair again while Chase made a show of straightening his papers. He folded his hands on the table and leaned forward.

"We know this is a rough time for all of you, so we'll be in touch. Please, think about what we asked. Delilah and I will be dropping over to your homes tomorrow to see if you've remembered anything that might help us. Meanwhile, if you'd like, we'll have an officer escort you home."

Marion and Claudia stayed, but Geraldo and Shane were up and out the door before Chase could say another word.

Claudia stared at her hands, spread out on the table. "Before I go . . . I just remembered Exo said that he had a meeting with a new client who was interested in booking the hotel for a convention, but that he'd declined. He said something felt off about the man."

"When did this happen?" I leaned forward as Chase jotted down the information.

"A week . . . five days ago? Sometime the past week. I know because when Exo told me he turned away a convention, we got in an argument. I said it was foolish to turn down that kind of money. He told me they weren't good people. I . . . I . . ."

She swallowed, hard, and stared at us like a deer caught in headlights far too bright and blinding. "I told him he didn't love his family, that he was always putting his ethics ahead of our welfare. Exo tried to talk things out, but I pushed him away and made him sleep on the sofa. Yesterday he brought me roses before he went to work and told me he loved me. I wasn't over being mad yet—I didn't say it back! And now . . . and now I'll never have the chance. He died thinking I stopped loving him."

As Claudia crumbled before our eyes, Nerissa was beside her, arms around the woman's shoulders, whispering something in her ear.

I glanced at Chase. This was too intimate—we were witnessing a private breakdown, a moment of grief and regret to which no one should be privy. As Nerissa cradled the fragile woman, we quietly walked out of the room with Marion, who was shouldering her own trauma.

"At least Trixie and I parted on good terms. The last time I saw her, we were discussing plans for her upcoming trip to Europe. She'll never make it now." Marion shrugged in that resigned sort of way that tells you someone's given up hope. "When I heard about the explosion on the radio . . . I knew. She was going to help plan out the spring dance and had gone down to the hall to meet some of the organizers."

The spring dance—Viva la Primavera—was scheduled to take place on the weekend right after the equinox, but those plans had been blown sky high. I draped my arm around Marion's shoulders.

"How about you? You need a ride home?" I stopped her, brushing her hair out of her eyes. Coyote shifters were gaunt; they were lean and always had a hungry look in their eyes, even when well fed. But now, Marion just looked tired.

She shook her head. "My husband's on the way. I'll go through Trixie's stuff tonight, to see if I can find anything that might indicate the Koyanni or Van and Jaycee are around. Somehow, I don't think I'll be able to sleep very well. Tomorrow, I'll call you if you don't reach me first."

And with that, she pushed her way through the cubicles. As

we watched her hurry out of headquarters, toward the main doors, I had an uneasy feeling that she might vanish into the night—a victim of whatever phantom we were facing.

Exhausted, I followed Chase into the visitor's room, where Shade was waiting. I'd given the keys to my Jeep to Camille so they could drive home in comfort, rather than everybody squeezing into her car. Now I dropped into a chair, wondering how the hell we were going to get back home, but then I saw Bruce's driver standing by the door. He gave us a little bow.

"Thank you, Tony," I said. "You didn't have to wait for us. You must be exhausted, too."

"Mistress Nerissa asked that I do so. She said she'll catch a ride with Mistress Menolly." He was oh-so-formal and looked so young, but I had a feeling he wasn't as young as he appeared.

I flashed him a weary smile. "Oh, Tony, skip the titles. It's just Delilah, Nerissa, and Menolly. We'll be out in a minute."

"Yes, Mistress." He tapped his hat and exited the building. I turned to Chase.

"So, can you meet me here tomorrow morning? I'd really like you to come along when I question them." He tapped my head with the file folder, smiling faintly. "Please?"

"I can't go with you *tomorrow*. It's Iris's wedding. I need to help with preparations." I knew talking to the families was important, but sometimes you just had to say no. "And you'd better show up at the wedding. Iris has done a lot for you."

He closed his eyes and let out a long, loud sigh. "I'll be there, no problem. It's in the evening, anyway. But can't you come in for a few hours in the morning? I need your help, Delilah. I wouldn't ask, but . . ."

"But you can trust me." It was my turn to sigh, and as I did so, I blew my bangs off my forehead. He knew I'd say yes; I could tell by his hopeful stance.

Shade wrapped his arms around my waist. "You could come in for the morning. Iris won't mind."

"All right. I'll be here around ten but I have to leave by one. Maybe Iris will be too excited to notice." Were we ever going to be able to cut loose again without some trauma spoiling our fun? Were we ever going to catch another break?

Chase hugged me, then shook hands with Shade, and we headed out to Bruce's limo. It boggled the mind that only a couple hours before we'd been on stage, singing and drinking, and now we were facing another ride on the demon-go-round. I slid into the car and stretched out, and without a word, we headed off into the darkness.

Chapter 4

The alarm blared through my dreams, and I blinked, glaring at the light that was filtering through the curtains. My head was plagued with a case of thunderbolts from hell, and I realized this was the side effect of the damishanya. The pounding was worse than any hangover I could imagine.

There was something else . . . something about today that I needed to remember . . .

"Get a move on, woman!" Shade's voice penetrated my foggy mind as he yanked the covers off me, exposing my all-too-naked body to the chilly air. "In the shower with you. You can't go help Chase, or attend Iris's wedding, smelling like a wet cat."

Iris's wedding! That's right, tonight she was getting married and we had to set up all the decorations and get everything ready. I tried to force my eyes open as Shade grabbed my arm, yanked me none too gently to my feet, and gently trundled me over to the bathroom, where I heard the water running.

Grimacing, I squinted, trying to see through my eyelids,

which were stuck together by gunk. I hadn't taken off my
makeup the night before. A glance in the mirror told me I
looked like a fright.

The shock of the warm water on my skin hit me like a
thunderbolt. I hated getting wet but couldn't stand the
thought of being dirty for long. Sometimes I wished I could
just give myself a bath in cat form and turn back nice and
spiffy clean, never needing a shower. I even refused bubble
baths—the thought of soaking in a tub gave me the willies.
No, showers were definitely the lesser of two evils. Sputter-
ing, I ducked my head under and lathered up, quickly wash-
ing away any lingering grime, sweat, and mascara. As soon
as I felt clean, I hopped out of the shower and pressed a soft
towel to my face, wiping the water out of my eyes.

"Feel better?"

I peered over the top of the towel. Shade was leaning
against the door, looking all too sexy and tidy. At six two, he
was an inch taller than me, and his long, honey-colored hair
shimmered with amber highlights and danced down his
back in a tangle of curls, caught back in a neat ponytail till it
hit his waist. His skin was a warm bronzish-brown, and he
looked like an Asian-black mix, but it wasn't human ethnic-
ity that gave him the exotic look. He was part shadow dragon,
part Stradolan—shadow walker. I wasn't clear exactly what
that side of his heritage meant, but I was slowly learning
about him as the days and weeks passed.

He was wearing a pair of brown cargo pants, holding an
olive green ribbed turtleneck. His abs—rippled, muscled,
with scars here and there from the past—led up to a chest
that looked strong enough to bend bars. He probably could,
being part dragon.

I glanced over at the bed where his boots—hiking
boots—sat on the floor. I licked my lips, staring at his feet.
They were handsome feet . . . and many a times I'd grappled
those ankles in cat form. He'd just laugh and scoop me up
and rub my belly while I purred, and then he'd throw my fur
mice for me.

The sight of him standing there, a soft, slightly sly smile

on his face, made my heart stand still. Maybe it was the fact that Iris was getting married. Maybe it was the realization that we'd lost five members of the Supe Community to some mad bomber. But right now, right here, all I could think of was how happy I was that Shade was with me. He was here, alive, and I loved him.

I slipped over to him, dropped my towel, and reached out. He took my hands in his, leading me back to the bed, where he sat down and I straddled his lap, staring into his eyes.

"Thank you," I whispered.

"For what?" His gaze was heavy, lidded, sultry. I ran one finger down his nose, then hooked it into the corner of his mouth gently.

"For being here. For being with me. For becoming my anchor. My rock." And then, leaning forward, I pressed my lips against his, feeling the creamy velvet of his hands catch me around the waist and pull me to him. His fingers sizzled against my skin, lazily tripping up and down my spine.

As he stood, I wrapped my legs around his waist and he turned around to lay me on the bed. I let go of his neck and fumbled with his belt, unbuckling it and unzipping his pants. He slid them down and off, standing between my legs still, staring down at me with a gentle smile as his erection grew.

I sucked in a deep breath, staring at him, feeling the pulse in my stomach grow as my nipples stiffened. I bit my lower lip, waiting, as he ran his gaze over my body, his eyes lighting up as he knelt between my legs, his arms on either side of my waist.

"You up to this today?" Shade always waited, always let me take the lead. I hadn't been used to it at first, but now I welcomed the question. I was growing stronger, and he seemed to recognize that I needed to learn how to be in charge.

I nodded. "Oh yes. The damishanya twisted my stomach, but the shower made me feel better. I need you."

And I did. The loss of my friends, the attack on the hall, the realization that Iris was growing away from us—that she was not just here to make our lives complete but that she had a life of her own—had all conspired to bring the tears to the forefront. I tried to blink them away, but they were stubborn and before I could help it, they spilled out, trailing down my cheeks.

"What's wrong, baby? What's wrong?" Shade stared at me for a moment, and then, quick as a cat, he was by my side instead of looming over me, taking me in his arms and holding me.

"I . . . so much has happened. The explosion . . . Iris is pregnant . . . Camille's assault—and our father didn't even give a damn." The pressure in my chest was hitting me hard and I ducked my head as I cried, leaning into his arms, shaking.

Shade scooted so he was up against the headboard of the bed, pulling me with him till we were leaning back against it. He brought the covers up over us and tucked me against his shoulder.

"Camille will be okay. Your father will—or will not—come around."

"You don't understand. All our lives, Camille was the strong one. If she can be hurt so badly, then anything can happen. You know how you always rely on someone to be there? To be the backbone? That's gone. She'll be okay, but there was a time when . . . I really thought she was dead. And everything changed."

"But don't you see, my love, that means that you have to step up and be the strong one. For yourself—not for anybody else, but just for you. And you've done that without realizing it. Do you know how strong you are? How incredibly proud I am of you?"

I looked into his face. His eyes were ancient—and I could smell the soft hints of bonfire smoke in his aura, a comforting scent that had become, for me, a cologne.

"Thank you." I let out a sigh. "I do know that I'm stronger. I do know I'm growing up and I'm actually happy about it. But . . . it's just . . . "

"Just what?"

Sucking in a deep breath, I finally shook my head. "Nothing. I just don't deal with change well." I shrugged, coughing off the phlegm that had gathered thanks to my waterworks. "I'm a cat. You know that we have trouble when our routines are interrupted." As I tried to dash away the tears, he caught my hand and brought it to his lips, kissing it gently.

"Shhh . . . no—no, don't blow this off so quickly. Don't shortchange your emotions. Tell me everything."

I closed my eyes for a moment. There was no getting out of it—that much I'd discovered about Shade. Once he wanted to know something, he made sure to find it out. He gave persistence a new meaning.

Searching inside for the right words—for the right meaning—I finally let out a long sigh. "Okay. Last night, at the bar, we were up on stage singing to Iris. It was a lot of fun, but the song—'We Are Family'—set me off. I realize now I was starting to slide into a depression, but then Iris threw up and the stripper got pissed and the bar wanted us out. So I pushed it away. By the time we got home and Chase called, I was primed to spiral down."

"Why did the song depress you? You aren't that bad a singer." Even as he said it, I knew he was joking, trying to goad me into a smile.

I shrugged again, not wanting to admit the truth, even to myself. But the words took on a life of their own and burst out of my mouth.

"Are we *really* still family? Oh, we love each other and we're here for each other, and I'm not unhappy that we're each finding our niche, but damn it, we used to be so close. So tight. And now, now we're lucky to eat meals together. We hardly ever have time to sit around and talk. We plan movie and shopping dates when we used to just take off whenever we wanted. I hate that things are changing so fast."

Even as I spoke aloud, I blushed. "I don't mean to sound like a little girl hanging on the coattails of her sisters. I'm not that anymore, but damn it, I miss the days when we were first in the Y'Elestrial Intelligence Agency, when Father still loved all of us, before Menolly was turned into a vampire. Before . . . before . . ."

"Before you came Earthside?" Shade didn't flinch, didn't pull away.

Feeling embarrassed, feeling selfish, I nodded. "Yeah. Before we came Earthside. It's like, we got sent over here and everything changed. The spirit seals started showing up. The demons are pounding at the gate. Camille got married— three times. Menolly found a girlfriend—and apparently, a steady source of party-hearty vampire invitations. We met Iris and now *she's* getting married. I know it sounds petty, but who the hell is going to remind me to clean out my cat box? I need those things. I need . . . a mother. And until now, Camille filled that spot and Menolly was the one who pushed me into trying new things."

Shade laughed then, a deep, honey-rich laugh that echoed through my body. "Honey, you don't need a mother to remind you of those things. You need a personal assistant. I'll do it. I'll remind you to clean your cat box and pick up your clothes. For one thing, if I don't I'll be doomed to sit around smelling—and looking at—cat poop. As for your sisters, be happy for them. And before you say it, yes, I know you are. But, I also know that you want the impossible. You want life to be as uncomplicated as it was before you came over Earthside. Yet you also want the good you've encountered here. It can't happen, love. It just can't."

I dashed away the tears. "Do I sound horribly selfish?"

He shook his head. "No, no, sweetie. Just confused and set in your ways, and looking for a hidey-hole in which to crawl. But, Delilah, my love, life moves on. It has to evolve. Look at you. Look how far you've come."

Biting my lip, I couldn't help but agree. "I guess I want my own changes, but not for them to have theirs. I want them to be there for me when I'm ready, not the other way around. And you're right, it can't be that way. We *all* grow or we all don't. But it's hard to face . . ."

"And it will be harder to face over the coming months. But I'll be here, to help you. *I'm not going anywhere.* I'm not afraid of the challenge you present. In fact, I rather enjoy it," he whispered, nibbling on my neck.

"You really like me?" My voice came out smaller than I'd expected, and I realized that I needed to hear him say it. I needed the reinforcement.

"Really *like* you? No, my sweet. I really *love* you. Now kiss me, fuck me, and then get your ass dressed so we can go help one of your best friends on the happiest day of her life."

He rolled on top of me, hard again, and I opened my legs. As he stroked my body, he lowered his lips to my nipples and I gasped, purring as he licked and tugged them. We fit together, like the pieces of a puzzle, and he slid inside me, jostling from side to side to find the right rhythm. We settled in, gently rocking, and then he picked up the pace, thrusting deep into me, liquefying my center, his cock pulsing inside me. I gasped as his hips ground against me, Shade's fire igniting my own.

I ran my hands down his back, my nails digging in, and he flipped me, rolling with me till he was beneath me and I was straddling him. Smiling now, I slid my hands up to cup my breasts as he held my waist, his eyes glistening with delight. I rubbed my nipples, my head dropping back, feeling freer than I ever had with Chase or Zach.

"Oh yeah, that's it," he whispered. "Come on, baby, give it to me." His hands slid around to hold my butt, and I moaned, suddenly out of my funk and fully in the moment. I leaned down and pressed my breasts to his chest, reveling in the feeling of his skin against mine. The scars on the side of his face and forehead gave him a rakish look. He moved his arms up to coil around my waist, holding me tight on top of him, then wrapped his legs around mine and once again, we rolled over.

Unfortunately, we had apparently been on the edge of the bed and rolled right over onto the floor with an unceremonious thump.

"Ouch!" I hit my elbow on the corner of the nightstand as we tumbled apart. As I rubbed the offended body part, Shade started to laugh.

"You're not getting away that easy. Unless you broke your funny bone, get your ass over here." He started crawling toward me, on hands and knees, and delighted, I flipped over so he could enter me from behind. Rear entry was my favorite position—though I wasn't much into butt sex. I knew Camille liked it, but for me, it was a once-in-a-while treat . . . like rich food. Good now and then, but too much just ruined the effect for me.

As he rubbed against me, his cock sliding back inside, I peeked over my shoulder. "Oh gods, that feels so good. You can get so much deeper this way." With Shade, talking during sex seemed natural.

He let out a chuckle. "Deep is good, baby. Definitely good. And I'm going as deep as I can, love. Up to the hilt." As he began to thrust harder, I forgot about talking and, bracing myself on the floor with my hands, I closed my eyes as the fire grew and his hips swiveled against mine, spooning my butt as he slid in and out of my pussy.

Catching my breath, I let out a low moan. "Oh yeah, that's it, sugar. Deeper . . . deeper . . . I can't believe how delicious you feel inside me. Never leave me . . . never stop."

"I'm here for the long haul, baby. I'm yours . . . and I'm not going anywhere." And then he picked up the pace, and everything fell away in the raw heat of our passion as I came, and came again.

By the time we were dressed and headed downstairs, it was nearing eight. Iris and the others were up and in full swing. Camille looked like she had the headache from hell, and she was shoveling in the waffles and bacon like she hadn't eaten in a week. Menolly was, of course, in bed for the day, but looking out the window, I could see Smoky, Roz, and Vanzir erecting poles for the long tents we'd be putting up for the ceremony.

Once the tents were up—pale blue awnings and walls—we'd cover them with wreaths and silver ornaments.

Iris hadn't wanted to hold her wedding in a fancy hall. She wanted it here, at her home, with all of her friends and family attending. Bruce's mother and father were coming in via the barrows from Ireland and she was nervous. Time to meet the in-laws. Right now, though, she was holding Maggie, rocking back and forth with a cup of tea.

Hanna and Trillian were preparing breakfast. In the past couple of months, Hanna had adapted quickly, learning to use most of the household gadgets without fear. Trillian was teaching her how to read, and she'd learned enough English that her broken speech was passable in stores. She'd thrown herself into the task, grateful to be away from Hyto's madness, away from the unending cold and gloom that had accompanied her indentured servitude.

I sat down at the table, Shade sitting beside me, and grabbed a clean plate off the stack. I stabbed two waffles and eight slices of bacon. Shade loaded up, too, and I blinked, suddenly thinking about our monthly food bills.

Even with the gardens Iris had put in, and the occasional cow Smoky brought home to fill the freezer, we were going through quite a bit of money. I also knew that Smoky supplemented the budget from his treasure trove. No one knew just how much he had stashed away, but he was a dragon, and over the centuries he'd accumulated quite a nice haul.

Shamas also pitched in, helping out from his salary, and Menolly from the Wayfarer. I wasn't sure where they got the funds, but Trillian and Morio also contributed. Since everybody lived on our land except Nerissa, there wasn't extra rent for them to think about. But still, we had to be spending a good fifteen hundred to two thousand a month on food.

Shade touched my hand, lightly brushing his fingers over my knuckles. "What are you thinking about?"

Startled, I glanced up, shaking away the thoughts. "The food bill, actually."

Camille let out a strangled sound. "Yeah, it's time for shopping again. Iris will be away on her honeymoon, so someone will have to go with Hanna to help out. I'm volunteering myself, you—Delilah, Morio, and Shade. This coming weekend."

"Oh, on that matter, I have something for you." Shade reached in his pocket and pulled out an envelope, handing it to her.

She set down her fork and opened it, her eyes widening, the violet hue glimmering in the sudden wash of sunlight that came streaming through the kitchen window.

"Oh! Are you sure? This is . . . very generous." Camille pulled out a stack of bills, and I saw they were fifties.

"I'm staying here now, so I'm adding to the household expenses. Never worry—I come by my money in an honest way." Shade grinned at her, then down at me. "I want to help."

"There's five thousand dollars here!" She glanced up at him again. "This is . . ."

"Enough for about two and a half months of food. Take it. I eat like a horse." Shade pointed to his plate, stacked high with waffles and bacon.

Smiling gently, Camille nodded and tucked the money away in the kitchen safe, namely the Spongebob cookie jar. "Thank you. We manage, but this will help a lot."

Trillian arched an eyebrow, then pulled out his wallet. "If you're going grocery shopping again, that means it's cough-it-up time, people. Let's see the coin on the table. Give what you can." He handed her five twenties.

Smoky produced another stack of bills, Morio handed over what looked like about eighty dollars, Shamas—who was dawdling over breakfast for once—handed her a check for three hundred, and Vanzir, who'd just come into the room, surprised everyone by producing a couple of fifties out of his pocket.

"I got lucky last night at poker. Here, take it." He looked so proud I wanted to hug him. Vanzir was the least likely among us to ever have money to spare.

"We can stock the pantry and pay the utilities for a while with all this. We have no mortgage. Henry's bequest allowed me to pay off the Indigo Crescent Café. The OIA pretty much bought the building the bookstore and the Wayfarer are in . . . so we're doing good. We still need to come up with the cash to build Iris and Bruce's house with, though." She worried her lip between her teeth.

"No worries there," Iris said from the rocking chair where she was playing with Maggie, who seemed to enjoy the bustle of the morning breakfast routine. "Bruce will pay for that. He's a leprechaun, you know—they have a special way with turning thin air into gold. And stocks into a pile of cash that defies even the market fluctuations."

Laughing, Camille nodded. "Good, then. As soon as the weather clears up a little more, the guys can get busy building, so come up with plans and get the permits we need. Now, let's finish eating and get the place decked out for your wedding."

I pushed back my chair, finishing breakfast post haste. "I hate to be a party pooper, but I promised Chase I'd give him three hours this morning. We need to go talk to the families of the Supes who were killed last night in the bombing. I also want to look through the remains of the hall while the energy is fairly untainted. I don't suppose you could go with me?" I turned to Camille.

She frowned, but Iris spoke up. "Take her. Just be back this afternoon to help me get ready."

Trillian nodded. "Go, both of you. We men may not have quite the same sensibilities you womenfolk have, but Iris will tell us what to do and we'll carry through. Shamas, are you working today?"

He shook his head. "Yeah, I'm going in a little late."

Smoky, Trillian, Morio, and Shamas started chattering with Iris about plans as she handed Maggie to Vanzir, who began playing a rousing game of tickle-belly with her. Shade headed over to join them. Camille and I glanced at one another.

"Get the feeling we aren't needed around here?" She was joking, but I sensed a little bit of hurt beneath the surface. Camille had always been the one everyone turned to, and while I knew it dragged on her, after the trauma with Hyto, we'd all quietly pulled back a little, become a little more independent so she'd have the time to recuperate.

I shrugged and grinned. "Eh, they'll need us soon enough.

But right now, Chase *does* need us, so let's get a move on. I'll drive."

She nodded, and, gathering our coats and purses, we headed out the door for my Jeep. First stop: the Supe Community Hall, to find out everything we could about the freaks who'd destroyed five lives.

Chapter 5

In the harsh light of morning, under the dismal rain that was
pouring down, the charred ruins of the Supe Community
Hall looked like a burned-out shell. Part of the building was
still standing, but it looked dangerous, and the fire marshal
had cordoned it off with bright yellow caution tape. The
smell of smoke hung heavy in the air, scorched wood and
flesh—acrid and pungent on the lungs. The rain formed riv-
ulets of black water, thick with the ash and soot from the fire,
the channels streaming along the street toward the grates
covering the drains. I watched as little flakes of what had
once been a beautiful building silently glided into the sewer
system.

Frostling, a full-blooded Earthside Fae officer, stood
guard. She'd recently joined the FH-CSI and was proving to
be a fantastic addition. I waved to her and she waved back.
"Delilah, Camille, hello. Chase said you might show up this
morning."

"Anybody try to get in here?" I glanced around. "Anybody skulking around?" The bushes near the main hall had

been scorched in the fire along with the building, but there were enough trees on the lot that somebody could conceivably hide and keep watch.

She shook her head. "Not so far. I've made the rounds several times. Oh, there have been plenty of gawkers wandering by, but nothing out of the ordinary. Most of them were human, though a few Supes came by this morning who hadn't heard of the fire. They were here to prep for the dance. I had to give them the bad news." Her face fell, and I could tell it hadn't gone over well.

Supes—especially Weres—weren't the most gracious when startled or hit with upsetting news. They could turn surly really fast, and a surly Were was five seconds away from a dangerous Were. Even those of the avian variety—they were just as wild as the four-footed and finned ones.

"You okay?" I glanced her over, looking for possible damage, but she just smiled and waved her hand.

"Nobody threatened me. Don't worry about that. But, Delilah, if you want my opinion, you need to hold a community meeting as soon as possible to discuss this and to calm everybody down. I smelled a lot of fear rising off the group." She opened the tape to let us through. "You can go in, but be cautious. The building's not safe, and you really shouldn't stay long."

"Thanks. We need to examine the area, but we'll be careful. I promise." Leading the way, I motioned for Camille to follow me as we gingerly skirted a pile of charred rubble. "Camille, why don't you look around out here—you're not exactly dressed for climbing over broken lumber."

"Okay, but be careful in there," she said, starting to edge around the outside of the building, opening an umbrella she'd brought with her. Her spidersilk jacket would keep the chill away, but not the rain.

I cinched my denim jacket tighter and blew on my hands. It was cold, still bitterly cold even though the snow had, for the most part, vanished with the torrential downpour. As I picked my way toward the building, the scope of the destruction began to hit home. It looked like some giant fiery mouth had come down and taken a huge bite out of the hall, leveling it to the ground. Shattered pieces of wood and glass lay everywhere, most of it scorched. Where the doors had been, a gaping wound yawned, painful to look at.

To the right of the gap, the building was a pile of ashes and timbers, and most of the roof had crumbled. To the left, walls still stood—leaning precariously, but still upright. The timbers had been blasted, though, and at any moment, the rest of the building could come tumbling down. I caught my breath as a sharp twinge stabbed me in the ribs. They'd healed up fine from Stacia Bonecrusher's attack back in October, but now, when it was too cold and I was too tense, I'd catch a stitch in my side every so often, deep in the bones. I wasn't sure if it was stress or something physical. I'd been meaning to ask Sharah but kept forgetting.

As I cautiously placed one hand against a still-standing beam and breathed through the spasm, I glanced around. Rubble was scattered everywhere. The fire had been bad enough, but the explosion was worse. The hall had been demolished. Everything would have to bulldozed. No amount of shoring up or renovation could make the hall safe again.

The spasm eased and I moved forward, setting my foot in a clear space between the scattered piles of broken wood and shattered glass. A shard of window pane I hadn't noticed crunched under my boot, and I shook my head. So much destruction.

"Looking for something?" A familiar, unwelcome voice echoed from behind me, and I whirled around.

Andy Gambit stood there, leaning against the perilous beam I'd just passed, a smirk on his weasel-like face. Star reporter for the Seattle Tattler—a rag as yellow as a daffodil—Andy had made it his mission to harass every Supe in town and to stir up antipathy toward the Fae and vampires. He was xenophobic to the extreme, and yet we knew he had a fetish for Supe women and would probably cream his pants if he had the chance to actually fuck one. If he hadn't already forced his way . . . surely no sane woman would touch him.

"What the crap are you doing here?" I glared at him, setting my hand to the hilt of my dagger. My blade was strapped to my leg. I didn't trust the little perv, especially since I'd decked him for harassing Nerissa at our house, uninvited and unwelcome. "Gambit, why don't you just slither back out that door and leave me alone?"

"Are you kidding? This is the story of the month—and a welcome event, if you want to know what I think." He curled the corner of one lip in a heckling smile and winked at me.

"I don't give a damn what you think." I stopped, then gave him another long, measured look. "So tell me, where were *you* last night?"

"First, you aren't a cop so I don't need to answer you. But to put your mind to rest, Blondie, I was at a meeting of the Fellowship of the Earthborn Brethren. We were discussing the evils of allowing demons like you loose in our society." His lips might have said "demons," but I could see the lust in his eyes. My fist still hadn't put out his fires.

I took a step toward him. "You sneaked in here, you little pervert. You managed to get past the guard because if she'd seen you, she would have whipped your butt all the way home. If you don't get out of here, I'm going to haul your ass outside and hand you over to her for trespassing. Yet another charge on your rap sheet."

He straightened his shoulders, looking at me warily. "I warn you—you touch me again and I'm getting a restraining order. My nose still hurts from the beating you gave me."

"Get out of here or I'll knee you so hard you'll wish you were dead. And I guarantee, if I go after that part of your body, your right hand will have one less job to do." I'd had enough. I didn't care if I got in trouble for assault. Andy Gambit had outworn his welcome, and the only thing I could think of to do was to smash his face repeatedly against the trunk of a tree or break his balls. Or both.

Tripping over the debris, he began to back up. "You're a menace and a freak! I swear, one of these days I'm going to take you down a peg. You and your sisters have played queens of Seattle for long enough, and I'll make you sorry—don't doubt it! I'm going to make you so unwelcome here you'll beg to leave."

Letting out a low growl, I began to transform into Panther, and the minute he saw the air shimmer around me, he turned tail and ran. Luckily I was in midtransition, because if I'd managed to shift into full panther form before he left, his running away would have just triggered my instincts to follow and destroy. As it was, in the time it took me to shift, he vanished out of my sight.

Once I was Panther, I decided I might as well sniff around. Sometimes things were clearer to me in this form, and my sense of smell was heightened. I began scouting around, hunting for anything that might give me a clue that we could use. My rhinestone collar—both a sign of my bond with the Autumn Lord and also my clothes for when I transformed back—tingled, and suddenly I sensed a presence. It was *him*. Hi'ran, the Autumn Lord. I transformed back into my two-legged form.

I hadn't seen him since Shade and I had gotten together, and now a tingle raced through my body as he came in on the north wind, a whirl of flame and fire and burning leaves and chill autumn nights. His long black cape fluttered, and his hair—as jet as his cape and past his shoulders—glimmered with sparkles of frost that had landed and stayed frozen to the strands.

A wreath of burning maple encircled his head, and around his neck, he wore a golden cord from which hung a skull, small and human-looking. His boots—dark leather with stacked heels—left a trail of frost in their wake with every step he took. Hi'ran was seven feet tall, and the Elemental Lord's eyes glimmered, a whirl of stars against the blackness.

I caught my breath at his beauty and stepped into his embrace. He pulled me close, and I rested my head against his chest. As I stood there, safe in the shelter of his arms, he murmured low whispers I couldn't quite catch. I searched his face, and he lowered his lips to mine and then, my breath was whistling out of my body and into his as he leaned me back, sucking the life out of me, and then with a soft hiss, breathed me back into my body again. He held me tight, the energy of his aura crackling like a pulse through me, vibrating every cord, every muscle, and I began to soar as he brushed my breast with one hand.

"My Delilah." A low growl ripped out of his throat and he pressed his lips firmly against my own again, his tongue meeting mine, forcing me to acknowledge his power. I moaned low as the flames erupted through my body and I ached to have him, to feel him in me, to know what it was like to embrace the power of the Harvest. As if reading my thoughts, he swept a hand down, brushing my thighs, and I came hard and swift, crying out as a swirl of sparks echoed through me, struck by the heat of his touch.

"My lord," I whispered, when I could think again. "What do you ask of me?" Whenever I was around him, all I could think about was making him proud of me, making myself worthy in his eyes. He was my dark lord who had reached out and yanked me forever into his world. He brought out my panther side, and for that I would forever be grateful.

"You will be facing a trial with Greta soon. It will test your heart, but follow through, knowing that it is what must be."

Greta was another one of the Death Maidens, and she was my trainer—teaching me to harness the powers that the Autumn Lord had given me. She, along with the rest of his harem, lived in Haseofon, the temple that existed in his realm. And I had fallen in love with the Harvestman as surely as I loved his emissary—Shade. Though separate, distinct beings, they were connected. And my love encompassed both of them.

I nodded. "I won't disappoint you, Hi'ran."

"You think you won't, but when the time comes, I guarantee you will question whether it's the right thing to do. When that happens, search your heart, search your soul, and you will know."

And then, with another quick kiss, he vanished from my side and I was once again standing in the rubble. As I shook my head, blinking, I looked down and saw something sparkling among the ashes.

As I leaned over and picked up the item, shaking the ash and soot away, I heard a shout from outside and hurried back through the door to find Camille and Andy Gambit. The fiery imprint of her hand marked his face.

I started to run forward but then stopped, waiting. Camille needed to ask for my help. She had to face her battles on her own; she'd made that quite clear over the past month. Hyto had damaged her self-esteem, her confidence in her ability to fight back. Even though she put on a good show, I knew she worried constantly about being weaker than Menolly or me.

She leaned toward Andy, hands on her hips, her voice low. "If you ever dare to touch me again in any way I'll run my stiletto through your dick and claim it was an accident. And *then*, I'll let my husbands come after you. All *three* of them. Got it?"

He rubbed his face, eyes glistening. "Bitch. Whore. You fuck three men and you dare to call yourself married? You're a slut! Marriage is a contract between one man and one woman—"

Before he could continue, she backhanded him again—launching him backward into the rubble-strewn grass. I heard the crisp, clear sound of lightning overhead as her hand connected with his cheek. Maybe her self-esteem was coming back faster than I thought.

"Don't speak to me. Don't look at me. And *never, ever* touch me again. If you do, I'll kill you."

Leaning over him, she grabbed him by the collar and dragged him up. We were all strong, but Camille wasn't as athletic as Menolly or me. I was surprised to see that she'd been working out. As he protested, she yelled for Frostling, who came running around the corner. When the officer saw Andy Gambit, her eyes lit up and she strode over and dragged him away from Camille.

"I told you last night if you didn't get the fuck away from this place, I was going to run you in for trespassing. Thank you for making my day, Gambit!" As she spoke into her radio that was clipped to her collar, requesting a car, Andy let out a sigh and gave up struggling. Frostling was a lot stronger than even me, and she must have put the squeeze on him.

"You have the right to remain silent. You have the right to an attorney . . ."

As she read him his rights, Camille and I slipped out, giving her a wave. By the time we were back at the Jeep, another patrol car from the FH-CSI had driven up. We watched silently as they hauled Gambit away in cuffs.

"I hate him." Camille opened the door and crawled back in. "I hate him and I wish he'd fall off the face of the Earth."

"You left quite the imprint on his face." I glanced at her. "What happened?"

"His hand decided it needed to squeeze my boob. I should just tell Smoky and then we'd be done with it." She cleared her throat. "So you find anything?"

"I didn't have much time to look around, to be honest. We have to get over to Chase's office. But look—I picked this up near the door." I handed her what I'd found. It was a pendant, with strange markings on both sides, made of gold, or a gold alloy, and it gave me the creeps.

She took it. "This clenches matters. It has the stench of Demonkin on it. But more than that—this writing—it's Runetongue."

"Runetongue? What the hell is that?" That alone sounded suspect, but even more worrisome was the fact that it smelled of Demonkin.

"Sorcerer's tongue." She stared at it for a moment, then let out a little gasp. "I know what this is! A trigger talisman. It's a magical detonator. This is proof that sorcerers are behind this—or someone trafficking with sorcerers."

Flipping it over, she paused. "So, we have the stench of Demonkin, Runetongue . . . and . . ." She held it to her nose and inhaled deeply, grimacing as she did so. "I can smell the canya on here. I know Chase doesn't want to jump to conclusions, but we're right. This was crafted in Otherworld. The alarms are ringing a mile wide."

I stared at the pendant in her hand. "Do you think we

really could be facing Telazhar?" The thought of facing a necromancer as powerful as he had become over the eons down in the Sub-Realms left me shaky. Facing demons was bad enough, but their powers were usually incidental. A necromancer that ancient and that strong would be like magic incarnate. "The idea of going up against him . . . He *trained* Stacia Bonecrusher."

"I know. There's no chance Morio and I can take out someone that powerful, even with our death magic. Even the magic Telazhar taught Stacia was stronger than what we know. But we lucked out with her. When she was in her natural form, she couldn't use it." Camille wrapped her hand around the circle of metal and stuffed it in her purse.

"We'd better go meet Chase. I certainly hope this day gets better."

She smiled then, wide and beaming to make me feel like a ray of sunshine had broken through. "It has to. Tonight's Iris's wedding, remember?"

"Right." I let out a long sigh. Iris's wedding, and then she and Bruce would be off to Ireland on a their honeymoon via the barrow mounds. Hanna would take over for her until they returned. And as much as I liked Hanna, she just wasn't Iris.

When we entered headquarters, Yugi motioned for us to wait. "The Chief asked me to let him know when you got here. He'll be right out." The detective looked worried as he punched the intercom.

"Something wrong, Yugi?" I dreaded getting yet more bad news.

He frowned, then handed us a newspaper. The *Seattle Tattler*. We hadn't had a chance to see it this morning, and as Camille and I opened it up, the front page had a huge spread on the bombing. The slant of the article was congratulatory to whoever had instigated it.

"We've had three calls already this morning since this piece of trash hit the streets. A Were got beat up over in the

alley back of Pike Street by a couple of thugs. They kicked
him around pretty bad. And an Otherworld visitor—Fae—
was accosted downtown. She's okay because she knew how
to fight back, but the guy was out to rape her. I just sent out
two of the men to talk to another Were. His house was tagged
with graffiti last night. Pervs wrote *Back to the doghouse,
you filthy Werefuck* on it."

I bit my lip, thinking how much hatred there was in the
world—in both our worlds. People sucked, and I was all too
quickly finding out just how much. A glance at Camille told
me she was thinking the same thing.

Just then, Chase came hurrying up, shrugging into a
trench coat over his jacket. "Glad you're here on time. Let's
head out."

We climbed into the patrol car with him as Camille ran
down what she'd figured out from the pendant we found.

"Crap." He paused to buckle his seat belt and motioned
for us to do the same. "I guess it was foolish for me to hope
this might be a simple hate crime—if there is such a thing as
that. So what we're really looking for here is info that will
lead you guys to the sorcerers behind this? Because while I
can give you backup, you're the ones who know the ins and
outs of these creeps."

"*Creep* is a good word for them . . . but not nearly powerful enough. Speaking of . . . I guess you heard about Andy
Gambit?" I stared at my hands. We'd already had a number
of run-ins with him, and Chase had tried to get us to ignore
him, but when the little freak got in our faces, none of us
were capable of holding our tempers.

"Yeah, he's already out on bail and no doubt writing up a
lawsuit protesting police brutality. Camille, did you want to
press harassment charges against him?"

She leaned forward from the backseat, snickering. "What
do you think? Should I? Especially since Smoky will find
out what happened? Because frankly, I'm tempted to just
tell my husbands and then Gambit would never bother us
again."

"Don't say things like that in front of me! I'm supposed to

keep people from getting murdered, not encourage it!" Chase gulped. "*No*. Definitely not. Although it might solve the problem in the short run, in the long run somebody worse would take his place. No, give Gambit enough rope and he's going to hang himself. You wait and see. His kind always do."

As we eased out of the parking lot, he motioned for me to flip open his notebook. "Where are we headed first? Your call."

I glanced over the names. "Let's go talk to Claudia. She mentioned Exo recently turned down the conference with somebody he felt was 'off' . . . plus, her guilt is eating her up. I think she could use a visit."

Privately, I was worried about the werewolf. When Weres lost their mates, it was like any other couple except the animal side came out too easily under the stress of the grief. And then the loss became dangerous to others. If Claudia lost control of herself, she could end up roaming the city in wolf form, attacking from the frenzy of her grief.

Claudia and Exo's house was in the Queen Anne neighborhood. Quiet, classy, understated. We parked in the driveway next to the chain-link fence that prevented her children from running out in the road. The kids were out in the yard, home from school, and their older brother was watching over them. I did a double take. He could have been a carbon copy of Exo, only years younger.

As we swung out of the cruiser and headed up the walk, I jammed my hands into my pockets and shook my head. At least the hardest part was over—notifying her of the loss. But now we were intruding into her sorrow and pain. I hated what we were about to do.

As we entered the gated yard, the kids gave us a brief glance, then went back to their games. The teenager watching them nodded but kept quiet. His eyes were ringed and red, and I could tell he'd been crying.

Chase knocked on the door and Claudia opened it, standing back silently as we filed into the house. She motioned to the living room, and we gingerly sat on the sofa as she quietly lowered herself into a wooden rocking chair and pulled an afghan over her legs. An older man came out—he also looked a lot like Exo—and gave us the once-over.

"Orick, this is Chief Johnson from the Faerie-Human Crime Scene Investigation team. And Delilah and Camille D'Artigo. Orick is . . . was . . . he's Exo's brother." She said the last in a flurry of words infused with pain. As she said Exo's name, she cringed, then hung her head. "Please, some tea?"

"Of course, Claudia." Orick gave us a two-fingered salute and retreated into what was probably the kitchen.

"Excuse us for intruding, but last night you said that Exo had refused to book a convention?" Chase quietly slid out his pencil and notebook and flipped it open. He kept a gentle eye contact with Claudia, but a nonthreatening one, letting her know through body language that the lead was hers. Wise move. Very wise move. Chase had learned a lot since we first met him.

Claudia paused, then motioned to an appointment book on the coffee table. "I don't know who it was. Like I said last night, we had a fight over the fact that he turned them down, but I was mostly concerned with the money he said no to." She coughed, wiping her nose with a tissue.

"That sounds horrible, doesn't it? I was worried about money . . . I didn't trust his judgment and now look what happened."

"It's not your fault, Claudia. You didn't do anything to cause this." Chase started to pat her hand, then stopped, merely flashing her a gentle smile.

"Yeah, right." She let out a shudder, then said, "You might find something in his appointment book. This happened about a week ago. It was on a Wednesday, I remember. Thursday is garbage day and I was fretting that Exo had forgotten to put the cans out. He took off for the hotel after the fight, and so I remember asking my son to do it instead." She lingered over the words, as if simple memories of daily life could erase the pain.

"I suppose we want to look for something that seems out of the ordinary around that time." I picked up the book as

Chase continued to gently question Claudia. As I flipped through, her voice echoed softly through the room. Camille scooted close to me, peering over my shoulder.

I flipped back to a week and a half ago, starting on Monday. Nothing seemed odd there. Nor on Tuesday. But Wednesday there was a meeting penciled in between two and three p.m. The notation read *V & J/The Energy Exchange*.

"V & J? Van and Jaycee?" The words burst out of my mouth before I could stop them as I jerked my head up, looking at Camille.

Camille blanched, slowly shaking her head. "The Energy Exchange. *Fuck*. We should have checked that place out before. I knew it was trouble from the first time we saw the sign. And I'll bet . . . we suspected they had something to do with it." She looked up as Claudia leaned forward.

Claudia started. "Yes, that was the place he mentioned. I remember now, he said it was a convention for a group of . . . vampires? No . . . not vampires, but . . . I don't know. I can't remember."

As we gathered our things to leave, taking the appointment book with us, I wondered just what we were facing. We'd suspected Van and Jaycee were involved with the club—but we'd gotten sidetracked after we shut down the Koyanni the first time. We suspected the Energy Exchange of being a hangout for the magical set—namely sorcerers. It wouldn't surprise me if it also attracted necromancers as well. The two groups weren't all that different. Which might just point to a connection between the pair and Telazhar.

Thanking Claudia, we exited back to the prowl car. All I could think of was I wanted this over and soon. But a creeping feeling in the back of my neck left me thinking we had a bumpy ride ahead of us.

Chapter 6
❧❧❧

Back in the fresh air, which hung heavy with the scents of rain dripping from cedars, we paused by the children, who were playing on the swing set.

"They have no father now," Camille said, biting her lip. "But at least they knew he loved them."

I knew she was thinking about our own father. "True . . . but not all fathers can show their feelings in the right way. They'll be okay." I touched her arm lightly. "They have a strong mother. Claudia will continue to run the hotel. She won't let Exo's dream die."

My cell jangled as I slid into the passenger seat. It was a text message from Tim Winthrop. Tim—aka Cleo Blanco, female impersonator turned computer whiz—ran the website for the Supe Community Council. I scanned his text and sighed.

"People have been overwhelming the site with e-mails—wondering what to do now. And a few of the more shallow have been whining about the dance and asking where it's going to be held now."

"Callous idiots, worried about a dance after what hap-

pened." Camille leaned forward between the front seats, as
far as the bulletproof glass would allow. "Frostling was
right. We need to call an emergency meeting—but we'd better not advertise it. Go through the phone trees. We don't
want these freaks setting off a bomb in the main area when
there's a big gathering."

"I don't know why they didn't wait till the actual dance." I
pondered the thought and the more I poked at it, the more it
bothered me. "Why not?"

"Why not what?" Chase asked, pulling into the right-turn
lane. We were headed to Marion's café next.

"Why *not* wait until the dance? Why set off the bomb
with only a handful of victims inside? Wait a few weeks and
they could have had a lot more casualties. It doesn't make
sense."

"Maybe, maybe not. If they were going after volume,
you're right. But maybe they were looking to instill fear
instead?" Chase pulled into the parking lot to the side of the
Supe-Urban Café. "Let's run with the thought that they
weren't just looking to kill Supes . . . what else could they
want?"

"To stir up unrest?" Camille said.

"Maybe." I thought about it for a moment. "What about to
throw suspicion on somebody else? To start a hate war between the FBHs and the Supes?"

"But there was clear evidence of who created it—
wouldn't they take the trouble to hide the canya if they were
trying to bring it on between the FBHs and us?" Camille
shook her head. "There has to be more to it than that."

"Not if they didn't think we'd recognize the smell. After
all, we aren't sorcerers. It was Shamas who recognized the
scent. And that talisman, it was just luck that we found it. By
rights, that metal should have melted in the fire."

"You have a point there. Then maybe they were trying to
drive a schism even deeper between the FBHs and the Supes.
But why?" Camille chewed on her lip. "Whatever the answer,
we've got to find them and soon. We can't let this happen
again."

Chase cleared his throat. "Yeah. Tell me about it." He fell silent, then let out a long sigh. "I have something to tell you. I got the results of my tests from the Triple Threat. Aeval summoned me to come out to her barrow at five this morning."

"And?" We were all ears. Ever since Chase had been given the Nectar of Life, he'd been changing. Powers that had been lying latent within him were coming to the surface, and we'd seen some interesting flashes of what he might become, but nobody was quite sure what the potion had done to him. So Camille had talked to Titania and Aeval, and they had grudgingly agreed to test him in order to ascertain just what was going on below the surface.

As he parked the car, then turned off the ignition, his hand seemed to shake for a moment. "They said they've never seen anything quite like it. Most humans, when they drink the Nectar of Life, pretty much just stay the way they are only . . . a little stretched out as the years go by. They looked into my past—I don't know how, so don't ask—and Aeval said that I don't have Fae in my background, but I do appear to have had some great-great-great-great-and-so-on grand-mother or grandfather who was part elf. It's not much—just a drop in the bucket—but enough to set off my powers."

Camille snapped her fingers. "I knew it had to be some-thing. You always had a glimmer that was beyond the nor-mal human energy signature, but I knew it wasn't Fae. But that means . . ."

He grimaced. "What it means, apparently, according to Aeval, is that I'm related to my girlfriend. And to Queen Asteria. They were able to trace it."

As Camille sputtered, I stifled a laugh. It seemed so ridic-ulous . . . our detective, who was so very human, was related to the Elfin Queen.

"That's why you have been having these bursts of power come through. It's coming from the buried elfin heritage." Camille nodded as if she'd just made a discovery. "Of course . . . but it's going to be severely fucked with due to the fact that you are mostly human. You're going to be in the same position, relatively, to my sisters and me—powers amok because of the mixed blood."

"That's pretty much what Aeval said. As I said, my elfin heritage is terribly diluted—so much that I wouldn't ever think to call myself an elf. But it's apparently enough that the Nectar of Life set things off. She couldn't tell me exactly what those powers are, except that I'll have my best attempts if I learn magic dealing with the astral plane or with the voice. Language, commands, communications, and astral travel are apparently my strong areas."

He stared up at the sky. The clouds were thick, promising fat raindrops, and while the chill of winter snow was gone, now we were in the throes of the days of icy rain. Everything felt waterlogged: the ground spongy, the very air laden with moisture.

"I have no idea what to do or where to go from here," he said softly.

"Take it one day at a time." I put my hand on his shoulder. "And about being related to Sharah—you're such distant relations, that isn't a problem."

"No," he whispered. "I suppose not."

Then, turning, he headed for the door and we followed, just as silently.

Marion was in her office. The smells of hefty biscuits and pie and old-fashioned meat loaf smothered in gravy filled the diner, which was packed as usual. The Supe-Urban Café served Supes from all over the city, but also a fair number of FBHs came here to eat, totally stoked by the quality of the food.

My mouth began to salivate as we entered the room, and I decided that I wouldn't be leaving without one of her cinnamon buns. But for now, we followed the waitress through the maze of tables to the back, where we found Marion hunched over her desk, patiently adding up a column of numbers.

Her face was placid, calm—and I wondered just how the coyote shifters dealt with death. They followed the Great Trickster, and where he walked, danger always followed.

•

As soon as we entered the room, she popped her head up and gave us a half smile, rising to greet us. She motioned for us to sit down and we did so, Camille and I in the chairs in front of her desk, Chase taking a side seat as he once again pulled out his notebook.

"I dug through everything I could think of, but I'm afraid I don't have very much for you. Except . . . perhaps one thing and I don't know whether it's going to help or not." Marion wasn't one to stand on ceremony.

"What's that?" Chase asked, taking his cue from her.

"Trixie has a new boyfriend. He's a vampire. Trixie's always had a thing for the bloodsucker set. I disapproved, and our parents disapproved, but she was a grown woman and we couldn't do anything about it."

"That's hard," Camille said, and I knew she was thinking about Trillian and our reaction to him when she first started dating him.

"Yes, it causes a lot of stress and we knew that if we said anything, she'd just hide the relationship. So we . . . tolerated him. Anyway, they went out clubbing not long ago and Trixie came in the next day, upset. She told me the whole evening, a group of Bryan's friends—Bryan is her boyfriend's name—kept badgering her for information on the coyote shifters in the area. So much so that she got uncomfortable and left."

I sucked in a deep breath. "Let me guess, the name of the club was the Energy Exchange?"

Marion shifted in her seat, a worried line creasing her brow. "Yeah, how did you know?"

"Exo Reed was contacted by a group from there. They were trying to schedule a convention or conference or something at the Halcyon. And we think that the group was headed by Van and Jaycee, the sorcerers who were working with the Koyanni to produce the Wolf Briar."

One beat. Two . . . and then Marion said, "Okay, but why the fuck are the Koyanni getting mixed up with the vampires, then?"

"We think the Koyanni have gotten themselves involved with a very powerful necromancer, who is also connected with the sorcerers—at least with Van and Jaycee. Now, some vampires hang around necromancers, at least back in Otherworld they do. It could be that Bryan was trying to cadge information out of Trixie to give to them. They're probably paying him something. My bet is he's one of their toadies—a rogue, not connected with the local vamp groups. They probably singled him out and formed some connection, whether paid or through blackmail. How long did you say Trixie has been seeing him?"

"A few weeks. She was so excited. As I said, she's got a real thing for the vamp set." Marion began to rifle through her desk.

"How many people knew she liked vampires?" It occurred to me that if it was common knowledge that Trixie liked vamps, it would be easy to orchestrate a meeting between her and Bryan.

"Too many. She frequented several chat rooms, but mainly the one called Fang Girl Wannabes." Marion shook her head. "Trixie was always too open. She never learned that it was dangerous to give too much away. She even used her own name online. But why would they kill her? Was she targeted?"

"We don't know that yet. But there has to be some connection there, if they were badgering her for information." I glanced over at Camille. "We're going to have to dig deep into that damned club."

Marion found what she was looking for in her desk and tossed it across the desk. "Trixie left this in the break room last week."

I picked up the matchbook. The cover had a logo of a green flaming wheel with an X in the center of it, against a black background. Across it, in white lettering, it read, The Energy Exchange. I flipped it over and read the address, but I already knew where it was. We'd seen it before.

"Okay. So we've got an ancient necromancer, sorcerers, the Koyanni, and this club. And somehow they're all linked together. I don't think the vampires as a whole are involved, Bryan not withstanding." I tossed the matchbook to Camille, who held it in her hands and closed her eyes.

After a moment she opened her eyes and hastily put it down on the table. "Yeah . . . we'll have a talk about this in a while. I don't like the places it's taking me." She glanced at me and mouthed *Demonkin*. Marion was too preoccupied to notice.

"Did she talk about Bryan much?" I figured Menolly could track him down and—if Roman backed her up—they might be able to question him.

"She didn't say much. As I said, our parents had a fit when they found out. And I knew he was trouble. It's not that I don't like vampires . . . but this guy . . . he felt predatory— all vampires are, but he felt on the verge, constantly. I worried about her safety."

Marion pushed back a stray strand of her hair that had escaped the ponytail and let out a deep sigh. "Truth is, Trixie was the rebel of the family. She didn't fit in. For one thing, she didn't want children and that was a big issue. The folks wanted her to get married and have a passel of kids. And they wanted her to settle down, to build a life like I have. But she hopped from job to job. She hitchhiked to California a couple years ago to live with the drummer from Dead End Boys—she was a fang hag all the way. But that didn't work out, so she came back and went to work for me."

She looked at me, her eyes glittering with unshed tears. "Find out who killed her, please. Trixie wasn't the brightest bulb in the socket, but that made her special. And . . . she was my sister."

As she suddenly busied herself straightening up her desk, we took that as our clue. I scooped up the matchbook and put it in my pocket, and we filed out. By the time we hit the front door, I'd forgotten all about buying myself one of her cinnamon rolls. The pain on Marion's face had killed my appetite.

Back in the car, Camille held out her hand for the matchbook again. She shuddered as I dropped it into her palm. "This is nasty. Demonkin energy—and I'm beginning to recognize Tregart energy in particular, we've run into so many of them."

Chase made a small sound. I glanced over at him. It had

been a Tregart who had almost killed him, who had changed his life forever. He'd been terrified of them since last year, but now the look in his eyes was borderline dangerous. He didn't so much look frightened as pissed.

"So we've got Van and Jaycee—I think we can safely say they're wrapped up in this. They're both sorcerers and Tregarts. We've got a magical club that seems to be connected to everything. Telazhar's most likely involved . . . what else are we missing?"

"The kitchen sink?" Camille snickered, but then pressed her lips together. "Whatever they're up to, you can bet it's no good. Question: why Trixie? Why use her this way?"

"Because she knows about the coyote shifters. Because the Koyanni are out to even the score and they hate their less volatile brethren. Because . . ." A cold sweat washed over me. "Because Marion told us about the Koyanni and they found out, somehow, that she's the one who outed them."

Camille snapped her fingers. "And Trixie might have told them that. Or . . . killing Trixie . . . murder makes good revenge against someone you hate—kill their family members?"

"I think you're right, but it doesn't fully account for them blowing up the Supe Community Center. And why not just kill Trixie alone, why destroy others?" Chase cleared his throat. "I still have a feeling they're trying to drive a wedge between the FBHs and the Supes. Getting Trixie in the mix that was a bonus."

I thought about it for a bit. "You may be right. They could also be trying for a psychological edge. They know we have a small army, so either they must be confident they outnumber us or they're doing their best to psych us out before we meet. Set us on guard. Make us jump."

Camille leaned forward against the backseat again. "So what next?"

"We should check on the other two families and see if there was any link to the Energy Exchange, because that seems to be our primary connection so far." Chase put the car in gear and we headed off to our next victim's house.

* * *

By the time we finished up, we hadn't found any connection between Thomas and Salvatore and the Energy Exchange.

Chase dropped us off in the parking lot. "Sharah and I'll see you tonight at seven." He paused. "So, you don't think it's weird that I'm dating a relative?"

I laughed. "Sharah's so far removed that you really shouldn't worry. And think of it, dude . . . you're related to royalty."

He shook his head, looking a little dazed. "I still can't believe that I'm part elf. A very small part, but . . ."

"Welcome to our world." Camille shook her head. "Guess what, you're part minority now. When Andy Gambit writes his sleaze column, he's writing about you, too. Think about that the next time you lecture me for smacking that pervert's face. I still think I should tell Smoky what he did."

"No! I mean . . . let it be for now. I'll see if I can get through to him that a nice long vacation out of Seattle might be a good idea." Chase headed back into the building as we climbed into my Jeep.

Camille fastened her seat belt. "So what do we do about the Energy Exchange?"

"We do what we always do. Investigate, see what we can dig up on it." I eased the Jeep out of the parking lot and we headed toward home. "And we ask Menolly to convince Roman to tell us about Bryan. In fact, I wouldn't mind a look at that website. Maybe we can find Trixie's postings online."

"You think Roman would tell us even if he has information about this guy?" Camille shrugged. "We still don't know a lot about Roman, or what he eventually wants with Menolly. She's convinced he's okay and I trust her, but let's face facts—he's an ancient vampire, more powerful than even Dredge was, and he's the son of Blood Wyne, the Queen of the Crimson Veil. He's not necessarily going to rat out a fellow vampire."

I'd had my own doubts about Roman but had been reluctant to mention them. And even though Menolly was overtly suspicious of just about everybody, for some reason, she'd let down her guard with him. I had the feeling that reason directly involved the outlet he gave her for the sexuality that she couldn't express with Nerissa. Not without putting her lover at risk. Vampire bloodlust could be a powerful and persuasive force.

"Yeah, we need to check these things out, but tonight is Iris's wedding and there's no way I'm sneaking away from it to go hunt down a club. But tomorrow, we start digging. Menolly can go with us. Derrick can handle the bar." I put the car in gear. "Now, let's surprise Iris by getting home early."

Camille's phone rang. She grumbled as she answered it. "Yeah? What now? . . . Oh, for cripe's sake! Can't you handle—no . . . no . . . okay, we'll be there in ten minutes."

As she hung up and looked at me, I had a sinking feeling in my stomach that just kept dropping and dropping. "Who are we fighting this time?"

"That was Chase. A sizable group of bikers—Shamas says they're Tregarts, but to everybody else they look like a bunch of thugs—are trashing the Davinaka mini-mall. Take Aurora Boulevard and turn left onto Alpine. And let's get there as soon as we can—the owners are caught inside. Chase will get there as soon as he can."

Cursing all the way, I put the Jeep into gear while Camille called home for backup. If the demons put a crimp in Iris's wedding, I'd skewer them and toast them over a bonfire.

The Davinaka was one main shop surrounded by smaller vendors in an enclosed mini-mall, run by Supes, mostly for Supes. The shops contained items that you couldn't find at Target. While the smaller stalls were leased by individuals, the Davinaka itself was owned by Jade Thompson, a shifter of unknown origin. Even she didn't know her background or how she got to be the way she was, but she could shift into several forms and had joined the Supe Community a few months ago.

By the time we got there, Smoky, Morio, and Shade were on their way through the Ionyc Seas. They were bringing our weapons. We swung out of the Jeep just as they appeared in the parking lot, on one of the middle islands near a bare-branched Madroña tree. A bench had been built around the trunk.

We hurried over to them, and Shade handed me Lysanthra, my silver long-bladed dagger with whom I had a symbiotic relationship. Morio handed Camille a dagger.

"What have we got?" Smoky asked. "You said Tregarts?"

"Group of them. There's the prowl car. Shamas and his partner are in there." I nodded to the police cruiser over near the door. The car bore the mark of the FH-CSI on the doors.

As we headed over in their direction, another car pulled in, siren silent but blue and red lights flashing across the top. Chase had arrived. He screeched into a parking lot and leaped out of the driver's seat.

The only ones talking were Morio and Camille. Their heads were together as they whispered. I could feel the dark sparkle of death magic shrouding them. Planning out their spells, no doubt. Ever since Morio had healed up, he'd taken on a decidedly wilder air; he seemed a little more feral than usual. And he'd also taken on a more possessive stance when he was around Camille.

As we approached the door, I looked at Chase. "Do you know how many?"

Chase frowned. "On the radio, Shamas said there were about ten. They're tearing up the joint, and he and Thayus are holding their own but they can't take all of them on. And they can't get to the hostages."

"Thayus is new, isn't he?" Camille shot a quick glance his way.

"Yes. He's Svartan. I don't know if Trillian knows him or not." Chase flashed her a quick grin. "And yes, I know they don't all know each other—no more than all Seattleites know each other."

"Okay, then. So we go in, and we take them out." I swung into the front position. "Let me take the lead. I'm itching for a good fight. It's been too long."

My pulse quickened as the others looked at me and moved aside. I'd been out of commission, healing up, and while I'd helped out as much as I could during Camille's kidnapping, that hadn't been enough. I needed to feel like I was making a difference, that I wasn't letting my family and friends down.

The doors to the Davinaka had been ripped off their hinges and tossed aside, the metal twisted and bent. Tregarts were unnaturally strong demons who mimicked humans. Some of them had *been* human at one point, giving themselves over to the demons for transformation. They looked like a group of Hell's Angels—not a bad thing—but in comparison, the bikers were a troop of Boy Scouts. Most FBHs would sense something unnatural about them but likely put it down to aggression.

We approached from the side and I cautiously peeked around the corner. I could hear a lot of screaming and yelling from the back of the store, on the right side. There didn't seem to be any guards posted—Tregarts were a cocky group.

"Psst. Over here." Shamas was hiding near the end of an aisle, and we quietly joined him. He peeked around the end of the shelving unit, then turned back to us. "It's bad. They caught sight of Thayus and started chasing him—I don't know if he made it or not, but there was nothing I could do to help him. They're on a rampage. The owners and most of the customers managed to reach the back of the store. Jade's a smart cookie. She had a solid steel door made with a lock that resists picking and had it installed on the break room. I don't know what she's been through to make her so paranoid, but whatever it was, that paranoia is saving the life of her and her customers. As far as I can tell, the demons are still trying to break through."

There was blood spattered on the floor near Shamas. Camille reached out and touched his arm. "Is that yours? Are you hurt?"

He shook his head. "No, they managed to catch a few of the customers and . . . let's just say there are casualties. I hid here. They either forgot about me or are more interested in prying that door open."

The image of someone trying to pry the lid off a can of sardines flashed through my head, and I tried to shake it away.

"Anything else we should know before we take them on?" I was thinking more about how they were armed or whether he'd picked out who the leader was, but when he spoke, Shamas managed to knock me off my guard. All of us, really.

He cocked his head to the side and let out a long sigh. "Yeah, there is. I'd hoped to avoid this, but you have to know. I recognize one of them."

"How—where did you see him before?"

Camille let out a little sound that might have been a squeak, and she took a step back. "No . . . oh Shamas, no . . ."

His voice was gruff as he met her eyes. "You know what I'm going to say, don't you? You guessed sometime back but you never confronted me about it."

She nodded, the tension between them crackling. "I've been waiting for you to come clean. Don't make me be the one to say it."

I looked from her to him, then frowned. "What the hell is going on? Shamas? What's Camille talking about?"

After an awkward pause, Shamas straightened his shoulders. "I knew you'd figure it out at some point. Especially since you're married to that one." He nodded toward Morio.

Morio let out a little growl. "As long as you didn't bother the girls, I was willing to let it pass. But they need to know, especially now."

"Will you just fucking tell us what's going on?" Everybody stared at me. I didn't swear as much as Menolly or Camille.

"All right." Shamas caught his breath, then let it out slowly. "One of the Tregarts is from Otherworld. He's one of the sorcerers I trained with. That's how I learned the magic that I used to escape Lethesanar. He was a demon back then and he's even more powerful now." His dark eyes flashed dangerously as he pulled out a silver blade and readied the deadly-looking weapon. "And let me tell you this: He's dangerous, and he hates my guts."

Chapter 7

"What the fuck are you talking about?" I was confused. Smoky and Shade both looked confused, too. Camille seemed to know what was going on, but whatever it was, it was eluding me.

"I'm a sorcerer." Shamas cast his gaze toward the floor, his face pale and pinched. "That's how I escaped Lethesanar. I studied with Feris, a Tregart sorcerer who had managed to gate into the Southern Wastes. He'd worked his way up to Ceredream when I met him. He took me on as an apprentice. No one else in the family knows what I was doing down there. I learned fast. But Feris got pissed when I wouldn't turn myself over to him for the transformation into demon. He might have let that one go, but then . . ."

As he sullenly shuffled his feet, I realized what he was saying. He'd *deliberately* sought out a sorcerer. While not totally absolutely proscribed, sorcerers were routinely ostracized throughout the northern parts of Otherworld for their parts in the great wars. Their magic had laid ruin to a huge region, creating the Southern Wastes, and some of the cities—like Elqaneve—forbade them entrance. Sorcerers tended to be arrogant and chaotic, unlike the witches and mages. They worked primarily with fire elementals and the magic of mind control.

And our cousin had chosen to take that path. Shamas had trained in secret and kept it from the family.

Camille looked like she was going to cry. "I thought it might be true, but I didn't want to believe it. We were such good friends during childhood, Shamas. What happened?"

I could only imagine the betrayal she felt. Sorcerers and witches clashed. The Moon Mother was constantly at odds with Chimaras, Lord of the Sun. Sorcerers often worshiped him, and the ongoing battles between Chimaras and the Moon Mother had been a big factor in the Scorching Wars that had scarred the Southern Wastes.

Shamas shook his head. "We don't have time to talk right now. But I promise, I'll tell you everything," he said, reaching over to brush her cheek with his hand. At Smoky's glower, he pulled away. "After we take care of the Tregarts, I'll tell you whatever you want to know."

It occurred to me that Shamas could have helped us out a lot more in some of our other battles if he had confessed to working sorcery before this. I jabbed him in the ribs.

"Listen, whatever you have that can help, you'd damned well better use it. If you're going to dabble in sorcery, you're going to use those powers to help us rather than hide them under a rock." My voice was gruffer than I intended, and he flinched. But I wasn't about to apologize. Now that he was outed, Shamas had to man up and use what he had to help.

I pushed in front of him and peered around the corner toward where the shouts were echoing from. "Come on, let's go get them."

We kept close to the wall, creeping along. The store was a pastiche of disparate items. Everything from muzzles for rogue werewolves to herbal remedies for Supes who couldn't use standard OTC medications to clothing choices to fit every body from a sprite up to a half giant. Speaking of which—my mind began to meander—we hadn't noticed any half giants lately. There was Peder, of course, the giant who bounced at the Wayfarer during the day. But we still missed Jocko, the bartender who originally ran the Wayfarer. Hell, I missed the *days* before Jocko got offed . . . before the demons made themselves known.

I skirted a jutting shelf that carried specialty harnesses for werewolves who didn't trust themselves under the full moon and wanted a firm restraint. Though they changed into standard wolf form, they were stronger by far than the ordinary wolf—just like a number of the larger predators. In fact, if panther was my primary Were shape and I automatically turned into her instead of my tabby during the full moon, there'd be a good chance we'd have to cage me, considering my Death Maiden abilities.

We slipped past bins filled with the Were equivalent of Milk-Bones—almost all of us with any teeth resembling fangs (and my own were small but not retractable) needed something to keep them from growing too long. We used flavorful hard biscuits to chew on—mostly while in Were form—in order to keep our teeth strong and healthy. I wrinkled my nose at the smell. The scent of beef set my stomach on edge, and now I wished I'd bought the cinnamon bun at Marion's after all.

Shaking my head, I brought my attention back to the matter at hand.

Halfway down the aisle, the wall to my right ended as we came to an intersection. The screams were coming from the right, and they didn't sound human to me. They didn't sound pained, either. I wished the lights were off. We should have thought to douse them, but then, the controls were probably somewhere near the back of the store.

Peeking around the corner, I caught sight of the group of Tregarts. Two were attempting to bust down a metal door but not having much luck. The customers must have taken refuge in there. Three of the Tregarts were gathered around a couple of bodies sprawled nearby in a pool of blood, and they were busily engaged in ripping out and eating the hearts. Cringing, I managed to keep quiet. The rest of the Tregarts were nowhere to be seen.

I quickly pulled back. Fuck. At this range, they could hear if we talked—though the bashing against the metal door wouldn't help them any. But if I tried to tell the others what I saw, somebody would hear us for sure. I glanced at Chase and motioned for him to hand me his notebook and pen. I scribbled down *Group of five. Two trying to batter down door. Three munching on two dead Supes* and passed it back. As soon as everybody had seen it, we were ready.

I sucked in a deep breath, steeling myself. There were always a few seconds before every battle where I wondered if we'd all make it out alive.

People died. *Friends* died. Tregarts were demons, vicious and more than willing to kill anything in their way. We had no guarantees. Hell, with any battle, demons or not, there was always the chance we'd sustain a fatality. Morio had nearly died. Chase had almost died. Camille had been raped and beaten. Zachary had been permanently paralyzed. Trillian had been brutalized. We'd *all* suffered.

As I let out my breath, I felt a tingle as I held Lysanthra in my hand. The familiar hum of her magic raced through me like a comforting old friend. She was sentient, my dagger, and we shared a special bond.

Are you ready? Her voice was lyrical, melodic.

I'm ready. Stand by me. A little spark shot through me, just enough to remind me she had hidden powers and released them only as she saw fit. After a second of indeterminable length, I slammed around the corner, followed by the others, and the fray was on.

We were facing only five of them, but Tregarts were tough. As I swung around the corner, ready to fight, the ones on the floor by the bodies leaped to their feet. The two trying to batter the door down stopped pounding on it and turned their axes toward us. The glint of the fluorescent lights shimmered on the blades.

As I sized up our opponents, I realized they looked bigger and nastier than any other Tregarts we'd encountered so far. Maybe a subspecies? Whatever the case, there wasn't time to speculate now.

I raced toward one who didn't have an ax in hand—better to have longer weapons when attacking someone with a big blade like that. Instead, I aimed for one near the bodies. He was burly and hairy and stank like a dead fish. As I barreled down on him, dagger ready to strike, he let out a loud grunt, pulling out a length of chain.

Oh shit . . . these guys were good with chains. They could wrap the links around a weapon and yank it right out of your hand.

I veered to the right, and the chain went whistling past with barely an inch to spare. As I heard the others engage, I focused on my own battle. That's one thing I'd learned: Don't let your attention waver. *Ever.* It could be deadly.

I ducked the chain and slid in from the side, bringing Lysanthra whistling down. Her tip managed to scar his leather, but I wasn't close enough for the slash to break through. I danced away as he whipped the chain around his head, letting out a yawp. As I darted back, he followed, the chain whirling like a propeller, faster and faster.

And then, before I realized what he was doing, he let go of one end of it instead of just bringing it to bear, and the chain lengthened by half again as it came slashing through the air in my direction.

I dove for the floor, a split second before it would have smashed into my neck and either decapitated me or broken my skull into pieces. Landing hard, I shook my head, trying to pull out of the sudden daze.

As I turned to get up, he was on top of me, raising one fist over my head. My hand did my thinking for me, and I thrust Lysanthra into his balls from my half-seated position. The tip of the blade sliced neatly through the material of his trousers and he screamed. Lysanthra tasted blood and, eager for more, spurred me on. I felt her savage joy surge through my hand and twisted the blade, driving it deeper to feed her thirst.

My opponent dropped his fist; the blade he'd been drawing with his other hand skid across the floor as he furiously clawed at my dagger, trying to pull it out of his scrotum.

Lysanthra screeched in my head, still thirsty, and I ripped her back out of his flesh. As he cupped his balls, trying to stop the flow of blood, I swung her up, underhanded, tip directly under his chin. As the blade slid neatly through the skin, I let out a shuddering breath. Lysanthra sang as the blood satiated her need.

I was on my feet before he hit the ground, looking for the next target. Smoky was finishing off one of the demons, raking long talons across his midsection, and Shade was doing something to another. Camille and Morio were holding hands as a sickly plum-colored haze washed over the fourth Tregart, and—choking—he sank to the ground, scrabbling at his throat.

Shamas faced the fifth. He had a black eye; the Tregart had landed the first blow. Shamas's hands were filled with what looked like blood, but then I realized it was some sort of ectoplasm and, as he thrust his palms forward, the substance splashed over the demon. The Tregart screamed as it slathered him, burning him as a cloud of ash and soot exploded. The demon pawed at his face, not realizing that half of it was gone, and then dove for Shamas.

Our cousin was physically fit, that was for sure. He nimbly dodged the attack, then swung around, his foot connecting with the blistered muscle that lay beneath the flesh of his opponent. The Tregart screamed as Shamas dropped him.

Chase pulled out a pair of nunchakus as the demon fell in front of him. He let go with a whistling blow, and the wooden stick hit the demon so hard we all heard the skull crack. Another blow and what was left of his face vanished into a bloody pool. A third and we heard ribs fracturing.

One look at Chase's expression told me he was making up for lost time. I hurried over to him before he pulverized the body and, one hand on his shoulder, quietly said, "He's dead, Chase. He's dead."

Chase jerked his head up, a look of pure fury on his face.

Then his anger dropped away and he lowered his arm as he stared at the demon's body. He started to say something, but I shook my head. There was no need. We all had demons of our own to exorcise.

"Where are the others?" Camille kept her voice low.

"I'm not sure, but I'm betting they're still around somewhere." I knocked on the door and said, as loud as I could without attracting unwanted attention, "It's safe. We're here to rescue you."

Slowly, a click sounded, and the metal door swung open. A group of Supes peeked out, and I saw that several had changed shape—probably out of fear. There were two dogs, an owl, and three still in human form hiding in the room. We were near an exit—probably where they'd been headed when they'd been ambushed. Shamas peeked outside.

"Do you know how many of the . . . *bikers* . . . there are?" I asked the group.

"Nine, I think," Jade, the owner of the Davinaka, said. "That's all I saw."

Shamas returned. "Safe enough."

"Guide them out—make sure they reach safety." I turned back to the hostages. "We're taking care of the situation. There are still four of the . . . bikers . . . in the mall. So please, follow Officer ob Olanda as fast as you can and do what he says."

The owl flew down to perch on the shoulder of one of the men, and the dogs followed them obediently as Shamas led them to safety. As soon as we saw them near the patrol cars, I closed the door and turned back to the others, leading them into the break room. If the other Tregarts came back, we could shut the door if we needed to—we knew it had already held against them.

The break room was replete with table, chairs, sink, microwave and refrigerator, doors that opened into a small bathroom, and a cleaning closet. A motivational poster hung on one wall—a picture of a werepuma in midchange. The caption read, Be All That You Are.

"Okay, we need to find the others and dispatch them as

soon as possible. If she was right, then we have four left. I just hope they didn't get out into the rest of the mini-mall or we're going to have one hell of a time ferreting them out." I wiped my dagger on a paper towel, wincing as bits of brain matter and blood smeared on the sheet. I tossed it into the garbage can and washed my hands, using the dishwashing soap to scrub away the blood splatters.

"Where would you go if you were a Tregart?" Morio looked around. "How much bigger is this store?"

"Not all that big." I frowned. "I guess we'd better head out into the rest of the mini-mall. Let's wait for Shamas, though. I want to know if any of the five we killed was— what name did he say? Feris—the Tregart he trained under."

Camille let out a small choking sound. "I just can't believe he actually trained with those scum. Not Shamas. He was the only one of our cousins who treated us with any respect—"

I shook my head and held up my hand. "He treated *you* with respect, Camille. Shamas never had a lot to say to either Menolly or me. I think either he had a crush on you or he liked that you work with magic."

She flinched. "No. I refuse to believe it. He wasn't like that . . ." Her voice trailed off as Shamas entered the room. "How are they?"

"Safe. Scared. I found Thayus—he managed to get outside shortly after I led the others out. He said he hid from the others but kept an eye on them. They apparently realized we were beating the crap out of their friends because they vanished. He's not sure how, but they just . . . held hands and vanished."

"Great. *Teleportation.* That's the last skill we need for them to have. By the way, was Feris among the ones we killed?" I stared at him, challenging him. For some reason I was feeling uber-territorial. Camille sounded so bruised that I didn't want him to hurt her. To disappoint her like our father had.

"No. He got away. In fact, I'll bet he's the one who managed to teleport them out." Shamas pulled a chair up and swung one leg over, settling himself on the seat. His hair was pulled back in a tight braid, and his eyes flashed, the same violet as Camille's but without the silver flecks. He was a good-looking man and had not suffered for lack of female company—Shamas picked up dates as easily as I hacked up hairballs.

"Tell us about him. What can he do?" Camille smacked him lightly on the back of the head. "I can't believe you did this, Shamas. I can't believe you studied with the enemies of my order."

He let out a long sigh as Smoky glowered and Morio gave him a cold stare. "I'm sorry. I really am. I didn't mean to hurt you, Camille. I . . . I always envied you. You were studying magic. You were *half human*, but they were still letting you study under the Moon Mother. And I . . . I couldn't get any of the guilds to accept me for study."

"What about Aunt Rythwar and Uncle Foss?"

"*If* my foster mother had backed me, maybe I could have gotten in somewhere, but Rythwar's husband—Uncle Foss—was determined that I join the Court and Crown. I was to be a *nobleman's* son. He wanted me to live on the periphery of Lethesanar's court, never doing anything important, always playing sycophant. And Aunt Rythwar didn't want to rock the boat."

Camille and I nodded. We'd seen it with our father's family. All of them except Aunt Rythwar and Father himself had been intimately connected with the former Queen's court. The Opium Eater—Queen Lethesanar—had been deposed by her sister Tanaquar, who was now involved with our father.

"You didn't want that?" Maybe I'd gauged him wrong.

Shamas rested his chin on his arms, which were crossed across the back of the chair. "No. I wanted to work with magic. I felt called to it—all my life. But I wasn't allowed to follow my heart. You don't know how much I envied the three of you—your father always let you do what you want. Your mother loved you beyond measure. I would have given anything to live with your family." He shot a glance at

Camille with a barely disguised look of longing that confirmed my suspicion. Shamas *had* been fond of her.

Camille hung her head, then leaned down and pressed her lips to his cheek. Smoky stiffened, and she shot him a look that made him take a step back.

"Dear Shamas, you *are* a part of our family. And I'm sorry . . . but sorcery—it's just wrong. You should have just done what you wanted."

He patted her hand and let out a harsh laugh. "Like you did? It was expected of you, that you be difficult and different. You were half-blood. Most of the family wrote you off anyway. I hated the way they treated you, but I didn't dare buck tradition. But I was my mother's prize, and she made sure Uncle Foss knew. It was expected that I make a match with one of the upper nobles—a relative of the Queen. I tried . . . but I just didn't want any of them. I wanted . . ."

"We get it." I broke in, quelling a potentially hazardous admission.

Being a prize cow was common back in Otherworld. Marriages were usually made for economic and political reasons, not so much for love. Father had totally ignored the pressure, but then again, he was a guard in the Des'Estar, not so highly placed. Even so, his choice to marry Mother had left our family ostracized.

"We understand," Camille added. "Please continue."

Shamas caught her gaze, and the two stared at one another for a moment. Then, slowly, he said, "When I had the chance, I ran. I went south, to Ceredream. There I met Feris, and he agreed to teach me for a price. I paid him well, and he took me on as an apprentice."

"What happened?"

"We argued. He was on a vendetta. I refused to participate, and he threatened to kill me. I ran back to Y'Elestrial, where Lethesanar was embroiled in civil war. Feris sent word to the Queen that I was a spy, which wasn't true."

"So Lethesanar caught you and . . ."

"As you say, the rest is history. The triad of Jakaris tried to free my soul before I was tortured. I had learned enough to grab hold of their energy and use it to teleport myself to safety. It's an exhaustive spell, one that weakens the body for months. Sorcerers use teleportation only in dire circumstances or if they're very close to their target destination."

"So that's how you got away." I thought for a moment. "But if Feris used teleportation to sweep the other Tregarts away, he's going to be drained."

"Not necessarily. If they traveled only a short distance it won't be nearly as debilitating as the spell's effect on me. And remember, he's demon. I'm Fae. They have stronger constitutions." Shamas let out another long breath. "I don't know why he's here, but now that he knows I'm around, he'll try to wreak revenge for what he sees as my betrayal."

I played with a napkin, wanting to be up and after the rest of the demons, but that was pretty much a bust. "What vendetta was he on? What could he have wanted to do that made you defy him? Refusing a demon is pretty much tantamount to a death warrant, especially if you've enlisted his help."

I couldn't quite connect the dots. Shamas wasn't stupid. He had to have known refusing Feris would cause a violent reaction. And if he was so desperate to work magic, then wouldn't he have taken on any task?

"I don't want to say." Shamas set his lips. I remembered that pout from childhood. Shamas had gotten his way far more than once by playing a pout.

"Tell us, Shamas. We need to know. It might have something to do with why the Tregarts are here."

"All right. I'm tired of hiding. But you'll hate me." His gaze flickering away, he blushed and hung his head. "Feris was planning to lead a group of sorcerers up to Y'Elestrial, where they were going to attack the grove of the Moon Mother."

Camille gasped, her eyes flaring with anger. "Shamas, how could you?"

"I *couldn't.* Before I ran, I sent word to your order, Camille, and warned them. I made sure Feris knew I'd ratted him out, as you say. I wanted him to *know* the attack would be useless. By the time he and his crew arrived, Derisa would have mobilized an army. So he never bothered staging it. I was headed home to lay low for a while. But Feris got his revenge. He told Lethesanar I was a spy. She believed him, and it almost cost me my life."

I glanced over at Camille, who was staring at him coldly. This would be a hard one for her to forgive. Even if he'd ultimately chosen to do the right thing, the fact that he'd studied with a mortal enemy of her goddess might be enough to mark him forever in her heart.

"Thank you for telling us." I caught sight of the clock. Nearly one thirty. "Crap—we have to get home! Iris is going to go stark raving crazy unless we get there to help." For once, the demons would have to wait. Especially since we had no clue where they'd gone.

Camille slowly moved past Shamas. He reached up for her hand as she passed, but Smoky grabbed his fingers with his own and squeezed. Shamas grimaced, pulling back and shaking his hand. He was lucky it was still attached to his wrist. Morio smacked him on the head—gently, or at least as far as *we* were concerned—as he followed behind them. Shamas stared at the three of them as they left the room.

Chase sidled a look over at me, but I gave him a slight shake of the head that read, *Let matters be*. He picked it up, turning his attention to Shamas.

"Come on, dude . . . we need to get back to headquarters after we make sure nobody else was hurt." He clapped a hand on Shamas's shoulder, leading my cousin out. As they neared the door, he turned back to me. "Thank you, Delilah. Thank Camille and her men for me, too. We needed your help today. We'll see you tonight, at Iris's wedding."

As they left, I sank down next to Shade. He stretched out an arm and I leaned into it, resting my head on his shoulder. He kissed me lightly on the forehead, and I melted into the luxury of knowing that he was there for me. Even in the hardest of times, Shade would be with me.

"I take it your sister's going to be pretty upset for a while?"

I nodded, my face still pressed against his shoulder.

"Um-hmm. As kids, Shamas and Camille were really close. For a while, Menolly and I thought they might grow up and marry, but then we realized that there was no way they could, not with Camille's half-human blood. I think . . . I think that she was a little in love with him. And I know he was, with her. But they grew apart and then he disappeared into Court and Crown life, and she joined the YIA."

"Star-crossed lovers?"

Shrugging, I pushed myself up and let out a long sigh. "No, not really. Maybe. She never talks about him in that way. But I know it hurt her when he cut us off in favor of the nobility. Anyway, let's get going. Camille and I need to stop and pick up Iris's wedding gift and her cake. You go home and help out there."

"What about the demons?"

"Until tonight's over, the demons can fucking eat my dust. Today is Iris's wedding, and nothing is going to put a stop to it. She's waited a long time for this day . . . I won't let anything else interfere."

"Come on, babe. I'll walk you out to the car." Shade draped his arm around my shoulders and as we headed toward the door, all I could think of was that I really, really wanted a vacation.

Chapter 8

❦

Smoky took Morio home through the Ionyc Seas, and Shade traveled on his own. Camille and I stopped in the women's bathroom on the way out to clean up the best we could, then headed toward our first stop: The Scarlet Harlot.

The shop was originally owned by Erin Mathews, an FBH. But when she'd been targeted by Menolly's sire, Menolly managed to turn her before she died and now Erin was essentially Menolly's middle-aged daughter. Tim Winthrop had bought out Erin, and he ran the lingerie store now.

On the way there, I waited to see if she wanted to talk about Shamas, but she just stared out the window. After a few minutes, she cleared her throat.

"I hope Iris loves her gift. And those damned demons better not put in an appearance tonight. Nobody's messing with Iris's wedding."

"No . . . they probably won't. Tregarts can't break through our wards."

"Asheré could—he was a powerful sorcerer." Once again, an edge of fear tinged her voice, but then she paused and took a deep breath. "You're right. They'd be fools to show up when all of the Supes are going to be there. Iris invited at least a hundred people." Camille hung her head, her fingers worrying the material of her skirt. "Why'd he do it, Kitten? Why did he have to do that?"

I pressed my lips together. There was no answer. None that Shamas hadn't already given us. After a moment, I let out a short huff. "He was stupid. Impulsive. He probably didn't think. I don't think he meant to hurt you. I doubt that ever crossed his mind."

She shrugged. "Doesn't matter, I guess. At least it tells us something about one of the Tregarts we're facing."

I didn't want to ask, but I had to. "Do you love Shamas?"

"What?" She jerked around, staring at me like I'd grown another head. "No. I mean . . . not now." Flustered, she stumbled over her words. "Let me start again. Okay, yeah, I did. Many years ago, when we were younger, before I realized that Mother's blood meant I'd never be able to marry him. And while I'm most comfortable with a poly relationship, when it comes to Court and Crown, mistresses take second place. And I *never* settle for second. But now?" She shook her head. "I care about him. I love him—as a cousin. But am I in love with him? No, that ship sailed and sank a long time ago."

She gave me a slow smile. "Chase is worried about a familial connection that's so long-stretched it's barely existent. He would freak about the connections made back home. So, let's talk about something else."

"Good idea. I'm tired of blood and fighting. I want one evening when we can just have fun, let go, and not worry." We reached the Scarlet Harlot—a block or so away from Camille's bookstore—and I veered into an open parking spot. Every time she was in the car, Camille was able to conjure up a parking spot. I always considered her a good-luck charm when it came to shopping.

We hopped out of the Jeep and slammed the doors, heading into the shop. Tim was behind the counter. We hadn't had a chance to really chat with him in ages, and he looked good. Tim had let his hair grow till it was shoulder length. It was curly and gave him a pretty-boy look. He was wearing a black tank, black leather pants, and a silver belt. When he saw us, he put one hand on the counter and swung over the top.

"You've been working out, dude. Look at those abs. I can see them under the shirt." Camille pressed her hand to his chest and gave him a quick kiss on the lips. I crowded in for a kiss, too.

"I've been putting in spare time at the gym as a personal trainer, as well as doing website work on the side. Jason's shop hasn't been doing as much business lately, so we can use the extra money." He tousled my hair. "Still love the hair, girl."

Winking at him, I hopped up on the counter to sit while Camille meandered around the shop. She spent a fortune here, on bustiers and lingerie. I'd bought a few bras and panties from them but felt out of place in lace and satin. But this time a leopard-print bra caught my eye. It was microfiber, which would be comfortable, with just a hint of black lace.

Tim grabbed it out of my hands and unfurled a measuring tape. "You need a bra fitting, my girl. I doubt if you've ever been properly fitted."

I stared at him. "What's to fit? You find one that holds your boobs and bingo . . ."

"No bingo. Now raise your arms, out to the side." He measured me around the bra band and then around the breasts. "What size do you usually buy?"

Frowning, I tried to remember. "I think a thirty-six B."

"You take a thirty-four C." He flipped through the leopard-print bras and brought one out. "Go try this on. Meanwhile, I'll get Iris's present out of the back for you."

I slipped back to the dressing room and tried on the bra. Damned if Tim wasn't right. Suddenly my breasts looked more upright and curvy. And the bra fit a lot better. Heading back into the main room, I saw Camille holding up a gorgeous cornflower blue peignoir. It was perfect for Iris.

"That's gorgeous," I whispered. The lace was hand-stitched, and it was made of sheer silk. "Iris will love it. So will Bruce, for that matter."

Tim nodded. "I'll gift wrap it. Did that bra work out for you?"

"Yeah. In fact, I'll take a few more in this size." While he took the lingerie in back to wrap for the wedding, Camille showed me the garnet and black bustier she'd found for herself. She added it to my pile, along with four pair of black cotton panties. By the time Tim returned, I'd found four more bras and a jungle green chemise. I didn't normally like sleeping in anything but sleep shirts, but it was too pretty to pass up.

"Are you and Jason coming to the wedding?"

Tim laughed as Camille pulled out her wallet to pay for everything. "We wouldn't miss it for the world. We'll be there with bells on. Or something equally appropriate."

"During the reception, let's try to carve out a few minutes to talk about when to hold the Supe Community meeting. I guess we'd better do so as soon as possible."

"I was thinking about the evening of the seventeenth? And Vampires Anonymous has volunteered their meeting hall, with protection included. We can use the phone tree to let people know. What do you say about eight p.m.? I can start the wheels going this afternoon."

Camille gave me a long look. I inclined my head. "The vampires to the rescue. Sounds good. Go ahead. Meanwhile, we have a couple more stops to make, so we'd better get going."

As we left the shop, Tim was already deep into calling the leaders of our phone tree. There would be a lot of buzzing lines this afternoon.

Second stop: a little out-of-the-way boutique that sold the most gorgeous crystal I'd ever seen. We'd ordered a set of cut cobalt crystal dinnerware, for when Bruce and Iris had their own house. Once we were sure it was all intact, we waited while the shopkeeper wrapped the boxes in gorgeous linen paper with an elegant ribbon. After we carried them out to our car, we were off to pick up Iris's wedding cake.

As we pulled into a corner parking spot three shops down

from the Ambrosia Bakery, I had a sixth sense—an uneasy feeling. I paused, getting out of the car, to look around.

A glance up and down the street showed nothing out of the ordinary. Groups of passersby shopping, huddling against the chill of the rain and damp as they hurried by. A cluster of guys in tight jeans and thick jackets loitered on the corner against one of the poles that stretched over the road, holding the streetlights. But the looks they gave us were the same we got anywhere. We had quit masking our glamour most of the time, now that people were used to us, and Camille's outfits and my height always drew notice.

Camille looked at me, questioningly. I shook my head. "Must just be my nerves." I motioned to her and we hustled past the Thai restaurant on the corner, then past a small consignment shop to the bakery next door.

As we pushed through the door, a bell rang and the clerk waved. We'd come in with Iris when she put in the order, after she and Bruce had discussed what they wanted.

They had opted for a three-tiered wonder in white, with elegant roses of blue and silver cascading down the sides. The bottom and top layers were chocolate, with the middle layer vanilla. The frosting was a smooth fondant over vanilla butter cream, and the filling between layers was a chocolate framboise ganache. The smell that filled the bakery set my stomach to rumbling.

"We're parked three spots down; I'm not sure I trust myself with carrying that to the car," I said.

"No problem," Mariah said. "Let me get Jorge to help you—we've got a cart and can make certain you get it to your car intact."

Jorge came out. He was about twenty, muscled and buff, and looked altogether adorable in his Ambrosia Bakery apron. He grinned at us as Mariah loaded the cake onto the wheeled cart.

"Hold on," I said. "Give us six of those cupcakes, please." I glanced at Camille. "Chocolate?"

"Yeah, with the thick frosting." Her gaze was glued to the window of the case. "They should last us till we get home."

As Mariah boxed up the cupcakes—each with a thick topping of icing and multicolored sprinkles—Camille handed her the credit card. Once she signed the receipt, Jorge followed us out the door, back to the car, cautiously pushing the cart with the boxed cake inside.

As we neared my Jeep, I slowed. The guys on the street corner were staring at us, as if they were waiting. They made no move, though, so I tried to shake off the feeling that something was about to go down. But as we neared the side of the car, I stopped, a sick sense of shame sweeping over me. Camille let out a little gasp.

Across the passenger's door, bright red graffiti spelled out *Go Home, Faerie Sluts!* A wash of embarrassment swept over me—the same shame I'd felt when I was a child and we'd been tormented because of our half-human heritage— but then I slammed it down. I wasn't that little girl anymore. And I wasn't taking this lying down.

The smell of the paint was fresh. I glanced at the men on the corner again. One of them gave me a snide grin, and I knew—I knew sure as I knew my own name—that he and his posse were responsible.

Camille followed my gaze. "What should we do? Kick a little ass?" She stood ready to take my lead.

"No, but I am calling Chase. I'm not going to wait here, though. I don't want a confrontation. Not today. Just avoid brushing against the paint. Jorge, can you please transfer the cake into the back of my Jeep?"

"Those motherfuckers do this to your car?" Jorge sputtered, his expression angry as he loaded the cake and cupcakes into the back of the car.

"Leave it alone, Jorge. I don't want you hurt." I didn't want him involved—didn't want the Ambrosia Bakery to be a target—so keeping an eye on the men, I pulled out my cell phone and dialed Chase's number.

"It's not right, miss. Not right at all."

"No, it isn't, but right now, the most important thing to me is getting Iris's cake home safe and sound. So please,

Jorge, go back in the bakery. The cops may come to talk to you, but I don't want you out here. Please?"

"I don't want to leave you two out here alone." He scuffed the ground. "You girls going to be okay?"

"We'll be fine. I'm calling the cops. Now go." As he headed back toward the store, cart in hand, Chase answered the phone.

"Chase, can you get a car down here to the corner of Vine and Wilder? Someone just tagged our car with hate speech—bright red spray paint. I'm going to send you a couple pictures of who I think did it. And of the Jeep."

"Stay there—don't engage them. I have a car on the way." Chase's voice took on a worry that I hadn't heard in a while.

"We won't, but we have to get home for Iris's wedding, anyway. We're running late. And I'm afraid if we stay, we may actually get into a rumble because frankly, if I have to stand here one more minute, I'm going to whale ass on these SOBs."

I punched the End Call button and held up the phone, taking a clear shot of the jokers on the corner. They shuffled when they saw me taking their picture and began to head the other way. Like all bigots, they were cowards inside. That, and our reputation preceded us, apparently.

I then took pictures of the Jeep and sent all of them to Chase's cell phone. Afterward, I motioned to Camille. "Get in. We're leaving."

But before we could pull out, Shamas came screeching into the spot in front of us. He leaped out of the car. By now, a small crowd had formed as several parties came out of the restaurant and stood around to gape.

Shamas took one look at the car, and his usually pale cheeks flared with color. I pointed out the receding figures who were now a block away.

"You take off, we'll deal with them," he said, motioning to the squad car where his partner, Thayus—a man with skin as dark as Trillian's and hair just as silvery-blue—sat. "Go on. And drive safe." He held the door open for Camille, so she wouldn't get tagged by the fresh paint. She gave him a faint smile.

I got behind the wheel, cupcakes all but forgotten, and started the car. "We're not telling anybody at home yet. I'm not casting a pall over Iris's day. I'll just park so they won't see the door of the Jeep and while everybody's busy setting up for the wedding, I'll come out and wash the paint off. If I can."

Camille nodded. "Yeah, I think that's best."

We pulled out of the parking spot and headed for home.

On the way home, Camille unbuckled her seat belt and—just as I was about to yell at her for it—she turned to fumble around in the backseat. After a moment, she plunked herself back in her seat, box of cupcakes in hand, rebuckled the seat belt, and gave me a forlorn smile.

"I don't want to share these at home. I'm sorry, but we've had one hell of a morning, and I want my cupcakes, damn it."

I snickered. "Me, too. Hand me one, would you?"

"Pull off to the side up there, into the parking lot." She pointed toward a small park along the way. Brentmeyer Park. It was one of those little neighborhood greenbelts, where there were a few swing sets, a jungle gym, scattered picnic tables, and a couple of grilling stations. The park wasn't very big, but it had trees and grass and gave the neighborhood kids a place to play.

As I put the car into park and turned off the ignition, Camille opened the door. She swung out, onto the ground, and picked up the box of cupcakes, motioning for me to follow her.

"We need a break." She led the way over to one of the nearest picnic tables and, brushing the raindrops off the bench, sat down. I followed suit, breathing the crisp scent of impending rain. The sky was dark, the ground wet, and I hoped that Iris's tents would hold off the downpour. As we sat down at the table and opened the cupcake box, my gaze flickered over to the side of my Jeep. The red lettering had dried, and now it just looked ugly and garish.

"Stop," she said.

"Stop what?" I wanted to cry. I loved my Jeep and had bonded with it in the same way I had my laptop.

"Feeling sorry for yourself. The cretins who did this are scum. But it's paint. We can clean it off—or we can get your Jeep repainted. What they did was moronic and rude, but it's fixable." She frowned. "Not like the Supe Community Hall—there's nothing that can bring back the victims."

"I know . . . but . . . it's the energy behind it. Seattle was so nice to us when we first came here. Now what's happening?"

"The haters are coming out of the woodwork. They were always there, though. First you hate the blacks and the Jews and Muslims and the gays and the women. When it no longer becomes acceptable to hate them, you find a new target. Anybody different, anybody who makes you realize you aren't the center of the universe. Even Otherworld isn't immune. Look at Father and how he reacted to Trillian. Look at the goblins—they hate just about everybody."

"They're *goblins*. What do you expect?" I shook my head. "We need to counter this somehow. We need something to show people that we aren't the enemy. Maybe . . ."

"Maybe it's time to start focusing on an interactive group? The vamps and the Weres and the Fae all have their own support groups now, and that's a good thing. But maybe it's time to come together? To form a club that's inclusive? That opens up to the people of the city?" She blinked and bit into one of the cupcakes, closing her eyes with delight.

I followed suit, thinking about what she said. As the rich, buttery chocolate melted into my mouth, I sank in the sugary comfort. I polished off one cupcake and picked up another, pulling the paper holder away from the cake.

As I took a long lick of the frosting, it occurred to me that Camille had truly hit on a good point. "What do you think about a community picnic? It's too cold to have it out-doors, but a neighborhood-block-type affair—only have it a

citywide event. Come show your support for *all* the citizens
of Seattle?"

"I think that's a great idea. We could pull people together.
And we should be the ones to spearhead it." She licked her
fingers after finishing her third cupcake. "Tomorrow, after
Iris is safely off on her honeymoon, let's get busy and pull
peeps together on this. The United Worlds Church would be
a good ally to ask for help. In fact . . ." She pulled out her cell
phone and dialed a number.

"Tim? This is Camille. Can you invite representatives
from the United Worlds Church to the Supe Community
Meeting? . . . Yes, that's what I said . . . Okay, thanks!" She
hung up and swung her leg over the table, dusting crumbs off
her skirt.

I followed suit and we headed back to my Jeep. As we
pulled out of the parking lot, I decided that the graffiti color
was as pretty as the words were ugly, and that I'd take it in
and have the entire car painted sparkling cherry.

As we pulled into the yard, I looked for the best way to park
the car so that nobody would see the lettering on the side.

"Why don't you park it next to my Lexus? Let me out first
and then pull up so that there isn't much space between the
two. Then nobody should be able to walk by and notice for
now." She hopped out of the Jeep and I pulled in close to her
car, then joined her. I stared at the cake, wondering if I
should try to carry it, but then Trillian was at our side and
motioned me away.

"I'll carry it." He glanced at Camille, then at me. "You
two okay?"

"Yeah, why wouldn't we be?" I plastered a smile on my
face.

"Because Shamas called and told me what happened.
Delilah, we'll fix your car. And we'll find who did it, and
they will never lift a paint can again."

Before I—or Camille—could say a word, Trillian was
off again, cake in hand, heading toward one of the tents. Oh

man. If the guys knew, then we'd have a situation to defuse. But they also knew better than to take matters in hand today.

"Come on." Camille motioned to me. "Let's see what needs to be done."

It was nearly four by the time we found something to do. Nobody else mentioned my Jeep, and so I hoped Trillian had kept his mouth shut. We hustled into the kitchen, which had been dubbed the staging area, and saw the big basket of flowers that had to be attached to the poles on the front of each tent.

Actually, it was more like five tents pulled together to form one giant one with four wings and the central stage. But each wing had its own entrance through which guests could enter and leave, and tables were set up to host the buffet spread we'd be putting out. Bruce had paid for the caterers, thank heavens, because the final bill for the food and booze had come in at more than two thousand dollars. Supes ate more than most FBHs.

We carried the baskets out to the yard and began wrapping the poles of the tents with mirrors of Iris's bouquet: strings of white tiger lilies, sterling roses in the most heavenly shades of lavender and purple, and long draping tendrils of ivy. Delicate prisms shaped like icicles peeked out from the flower arrangements, catching the silver light reflecting off the clouds.

With the addition of the flowers, the ivory tents suddenly became elegant, dressy, and classic, rather than stark. Balloons in shades of blue, purple, silver, and white with long streamer ribbons hovered near the top of the tents, the helium keeping them aloft. Long tables were covered with starched linen tablecloths and neat stacks of plates and silverware. Within the next few hours, the tables would be filled with chafing dishes and salads and platters of deli meats and cheeses, and—of course—the cake.

Camille and I stood back, eyeing the décor. She burst into a huge smile and clapped. "It's so beautiful. Iris deserves this and so much more. She's been through so much, and for so long."

I let out a long sigh, torn. Iris would still be with us. But she belonged with Bruce now. And she'd be having a baby soon. The little girl in me wanted to reach out, to grab hold of her hands, to say, "Let's run away and play."

But the tents were gorgeous, and in a few hours, Iris would have the wedding she'd always hoped for. And all of her friends would be here. As I stood there, looking at the waiting pavilion, my heart lifted and the little girl who had longed for good friends grew up, right before my eyes. I *had* good friends. I had friends who had become *family*. Tonight, one of my best friends would achieve her heart's desire. And we were privileged to stand by her, to witness and participate in her joy.

"It's been a long past two years since Iris first came to work for me at the Indigo Crescent. And look at where we're at." Camille crossed her hands. "I'm married to three men. Menolly's in a serious relationship, you're in a serious relationship . . . life has moved along."

"That it has," I said with a smile, thinking of Shade. "That it has."

While we hadn't spoken about it yet, Shade and I were exclusive, and would probably remain so—except for my relationship with Hi'ran. In the short time we'd been together, I'd come to rely on my half-dragon lover being there for me. He understood all sides of me—from the tabby within, to the panther, to the half-breed woman. He loved every aspect of me, and I felt it from the top of my head to the tips of my toes.

"Come on." Camille tucked an arm around my waist as we swung out of the tents. "Let's go see what else needs to be done."

And for the first time in a long while, I relaxed and began to enjoy the day.

The candles glistened around the tents, shielded from the wind by cut crystal hurricane lamps. Giving one final look around as the men seated the hundred or so guests who'd shown up, I hurried back inside, into Iris's room. I was wearing an ivory slip dress of silk and satin, flowing down to my ankles, with a pale blue needlepoint shawl, and satin ivory boots that laced up the front. Menolly was there, dressed just like me, her shawl pinned in the front by a blue topaz brooch. My brooch was pearl.

Camille was wearing her priestess robes—flowing and sheer, patterned with peacock feathers. Beneath them, her embroidered bra and panties peeked through. The cloak of the Black Unicorn was tucked around her shoulders, and she was barefoot, as was the tradition of her order, with a silver circlet around her head.

Hanna was helping Iris dress. The wedding dress caught me off guard. It was spectacular. With a strapless corseted bustline, it hugged her curves to her waist, in shades of pale blue and plum, beaded with faceted crystals from Otherworld that shimmered in the light. The skirt of the dress flowed out, a dream of pale blue satin, over which panels of plum and cobalt tulle blossomed, the netting beaded with more sparkling crystals.

A veil of the same tulle draped over her hair, which cascaded to the ground to form a glowing cloak of liquid gold strands. Her veil was held in place by a crystal tiara, delicate and small but brilliant enough to catch the light and send it prisming into rainbows.

Iris held out her hands and Hanna slid on the robin's-egg-blue fingerless elbow-length gloves. We stood there, watching our friend dress for her wedding, and all I could think of was how incredibly beautiful she looked. Her eyes were radiant, outlined with kohl, and her cheeks rosy, and the pale peach lip gloss matched her coloring perfectly. The tattoos on her face glimmered, shining with some internal light.

"You are a vision," I whispered.

"Delilah's right." Menolly's hand fluttered to her heart. "You're so beautiful. I'm so happy for you."

Iris ducked her head, but her smile filled the room with light. "Thank you, for being with me. For standing with me. Bruce . . ."

"Bruce is a lucky man. And he'd better man up and treat you right." I wanted to sound stern, but my threats were hollow. We knew how much he loved her. We saw it every day. Bruce might never be a warrior, but he'd fight for the woman he loved, the woman carrying his child.

I glanced at the clock. It was time. "Are you ready, Iris?"

Camille leaned down and kissed her gently on the cheek. "I'll meet you out there, babe. I have to go prepare for the ceremony." She slipped out the door.

Hanna clapped her hands. "Iris, you look so lovely. You are happy, correct?" Her English might be stilted, but her heart was in the right place.

Iris nodded, blushing again. "I'm happy, and for once my morning sickness is taking a break. I'm probably too nervous to throw up."

"Then, if you're ready, I guess it's time."

After a few last-minute adjustments to her train and veil, I pressed the bouquet of sterling roses, white tiger lilies, and draping ivy into her hands.

"Come on, little mama. Let's go get you married."

We headed out of her room, and I glanced back. She and Bruce would continue to use it after they returned from their honeymoon, until their house was built, but soon it would become Hanna's room. And Maggie would have to get used to Iris not being her primary caregiver. Yes, changes were wonderful, but they weren't without their heartbreak.

With one last smile at the past, I turned to follow Menolly, Hanna, and Iris out the door, into Iris's future.

Chapter 9

꧁❦꧂

The crowds were buzzing with chatter as we approached the main tent. Hanna carried an umbrella in one hand, holding it over Iris's head to ward off any stray raindrops, and with the other, she carried Iris's train, draped over her arm. Hanna had slid into a quiet, supportive role in the family, taking to Maggie with as much love as the rest of us. And Maggie adored her.

Trenyth, the assistant to Queen Asteria, the Elfin Queen, had brought enough soldiers with him that we didn't have to worry about guard duty and could all enjoy the wedding. They were scattered throughout our land, keeping an alert eye out for enemies.

As Iris cautiously held up the hem of her dress, making her way through the wet grass, Menolly and I took our places inside the center tent, on the canvas leading up to the central platform where the handfasting ritual would be performed. There, Camille waited, sitting on a cushioned bench that was draped with a silver cloth. Every chair in the tent was filled.

I glanced around. To the left, I saw the Triple Threat. Titania, Aeval, and Morgaine sat in the front row, along with several others from their court. Trenyth sat with them—as an official representative from Queen Asteria's Court. Next to them sat our extended family, except for my sisters and Smoky.

Behind them were Tim and Jason, along with Chase and Sharah, and several of the other officers from the FH-CSI. And behind *them* were at least fifty members of the Supe Community, along with several FBHs. Iris was well loved.

On the other side were Bruce's peeps—a huge contingent of his friends from both the pub where he'd hung out over the years and the university where he was soon to begin a full-time teaching position. He'd subbed off and on for several years and finally they offered him a full professorship. This summer, he'd start as the head of Irish Studies at the University of Washington.

In the front row, in front of Bruce's friends, sat his family. The O'Shea leprechauns were a handsome family. All twenty of them. Bruce's father looked to be around fifty, which meant he was extremely old in Fae years. His mother still looked young, so she'd probably married for prestige. But the pair held hands and in their shimmering green outfits looked proud as punch. Three girls sat beside them, all fairly young, but obviously related. The rest were an array of cousins and assorted aunts and uncles.

I caught my breath as the music started. Four elves who had come with Trenyth were playing "*The Voice*," by Celtic Woman—two on violins, one on drums, and one—a woman—holding a microphone. They'd spent the past few weeks learning the song. The music reeled and soared as the woman began to sing, her voice echoing through the tents. Smoky stepped forward and turned, waiting. Iris had asked him to give her away, and it only seemed fitting.

As Iris entered the tent and Hanna pulled away the umbrella, the crowd gave a collective gasp as they saw her. She shone in her sparkling princess gown. Cinderella's fairy godmother couldn't have done as exquisite a job on choosing a wedding dress. Every move Iris made brought a glimmer to her body from the beads that shimmered as she walked. Her hair flowed to her ankles, floating on the satin that ballooned out, swaying against the underskirts that gave the dress volume.

As she stepped up to Smoky, one tendril of his hair rose and took her by the arm, wrapping securely around her elbow. She gave me a look, both frightened and wistful, and I realized that for her, this was the fulfillment of a lifetime of waiting.

Hanna, dressed in a pale silver sheath, picked up Maggie in one arm, and with the other she held a basket filled with rose petals. She looked at me, and I nodded. Swinging out onto the canvas, Hanna and Maggie slowly walked down the aisle, with Maggie tossing rose petals every which way. An unlikely flower girl, definitely, but Iris had insisted.

As they neared the halfway mark, Menolly and I took our places in front of Iris and Smoky. Shade took my arm, and Trillian took Menolly's. The music swelled as we began our march down the aisle toward the dais where Camille stood, waiting, looking every inch a priestess.

Behind us, Iris and Smoky waited. As Menolly and I approached the raised platform, we lightly stepped up. Hanna and Maggie had veered off to take their place in the audience. Menolly and I moved to Camille's right as Shade and Trillian took their places beside Bruce, along with another leprechaun—one of Bruce's best buddies. His name was Grayson, if I remembered right.

Everyone turned to look at Iris and Smoky as they stood at the back of the tent. Iris was a vision—her beauty cascading off her like her golden tresses. Smoky stood tall and regal, his hair providing the perfect cushion to support her elbow.

The music dipped, then changed to a slow, sinuous beat as Smoky and Iris began the journey to the altar. The singer began a low chant that wove a hypnotic rhythm through the tent as Camille raised her arms, one hand holding a dagger, one a wand. She stood, legs slightly spread, arms reaching to the sky, waiting for them to approach.

The only sound beyond the music was the rustle of Iris's dress and soft footsteps on the canvas. As Smoky and Iris passed by each row of chairs, the audience stood, a wave rising with their passage. I glanced at Bruce. His eyes were wide, as if he only now realized he was marrying a powerful priestess and not just the love of his life. He caught my gaze and I smiled, which seemed to reassure him.

Smoky and Iris were at the dais now, and rather than trifle with her dress, Smoky gently reached down and lifted her in one swift move onto the platform, then stepped back, moving to sit in the audience beside Shamas, Vanzir, Nerissa, Hanna, and Morio.

Iris stepped forward, her train trailing behind her, and stood beside Bruce. They turned to face Camille. She smiled at them, her expression suddenly wise and knowing. I'd seen her work magic before, but tonight she was wearing the cloak of a priestess, and her aura crackled like lightning.

Menolly discreetly stepped forward and took Iris's bouquet, then returned to her place.

Camille waved the wand in a circle over their heads. "We are here, my friends, to witness the handfasting rites of Iris Kuusi, Priestess of Undutar, and Lord Bruce O'Shea, of the Eire O'Sheas. Marriage among the sprites is a lifelong commitment, spurned only in the case of abuse or of infidelity . . . or of the mutual parting of ways where there is no healing the heart. Oaths are binding, broken only by dishonor or mutual agreement. These rites are the reminders of rituals from long past and are to be respected and honored."

Iris and Bruce both murmured, "We do stand before you."

"Do you recognize me as your priestess, as the one who will hold you to your oath—the sacred vows made, not to be broken?"

Again, their answer came in unison. "We do accept you as our priestess."

"Let all witness, the parties come freely, of their own will, to be joined in the sacred marriage."

Guided by a rehearsal before we started, the audience, still standing, intoned, "We do act as witness," and then sat down.

Camille waited, then, drawing a long breath, said, "Iris Kuusi, Priestess of Undutar, daughter of the ice floes, by mist and snow I bless you. By fire and flame, I bless you. By gale and boreal wind, I call the spirits to take your oath."

She turned to Bruce. "Bruce O'Shea, Lord of Eire, the son of the Rainbow, by sweet grass and meadow, I bless you. By stream and the wild sea, I bless you. By gale and boreal wind, I call the spirits to take your oath."

They knelt before her as she picked up the dagger. "By blood, these oaths will be sealed, by your heart they will be kept. By the gods they will be heard."

Iris held out her left palm, taking Bruce's right hand in hers. They held up their hands, offering them to Camille.

Camille motioned to me and I moved to the altar, where I picked up a thin braided cord of blue, silver, and white. I wrapped it around their entwined hands and wrists, loosely knotting it, then returned to stand beside Menolly.

"Your hands are bound, as is the way, and all oaths you take are bound within this cord. Sacred will be your vows, and to ignore them is to bring dishonor and shame upon your household." She turned to Bruce.

"Bruce, do you accept Iris into your life as your wedded wife, as your spouse and your love, to cherish and honor, to respect and to serve? Will you keep and protect her and any children that come of this union till you depart for the Summerlands? Will you take on the mantle of husband and keep-lord? Will you honor her goddess, even as she honors yours?"

Bruce inclined his head. "I do so vow before the gods, with all my heart."

Camille turned to Iris. "Iris, do you accept Bruce into your life as your wedded husband, as your spouse and your love, to cherish and honor, to respect and to serve? Will you keep the household, and nurture him and any children that come of this union till you depart for the Underworld? Will you take on the mantle of wife and keeper of the keys? Will you honor his goddess, even as he honors yours?

Iris looked almost dizzy. She glanced at Bruce, her eyes shining. For a moment I thought she wasn't going to answer, but then her voice rang clear and firm. "I do so vow before the gods, with all my heart."

"Then seal the pact in blood and with a kiss." Camille reached down and neatly slit a fine gash on Iris's right palm, and Bruce's left. They reached over, clasping hands, joining their wounds so their blood mingled freely, as Bruce met Iris's lips with his own, kissing her long and deep.

As they pulled apart, I unobtrusively wrapped Iris's hand with a bandage to prevent the blood from touching her wedding gown. Bruce's friend did the same for him. Camille lifted her hands toward the sky again.

"In the sight of the gods, in the sight of this gathering, under the watchful eyes of the Moon Mother, I do pronounce you husband and wife. May your lives be long and joyful, and fruitful with a fine family."

And with that, Camille burst into tears, smiling as she leaned over to hug the bride and groom. She unwound the handfasting cord and gave it to them for their family trunk, and then they turned, and everyone stood and clapped, cheering. Iris took her bouquet and—as was the tradition of not separating out the women from the men—tossed it into the audience.

The tightly wrapped flowers took a surprising turn midair—Iris was laughing and waving her hand—and landed right in Nerissa's lap. As Nerissa bundled them to her nose, smiling, Iris blew her a kiss.

And then it was time for the party. As Nerissa and Hanna led Iris off to pose for pictures, I glanced at Camille, thinking that it was over. Iris was married. She would still be here, with us, but she would be having her baby and be raising her own family.

Camille wrapped her arm through my elbow. "We have a date with the photographer, too, so let's get moving. You okay, Kitten?"

As Menolly joined us—unfortunately she would not appear in the photographs—I closed my eyes for a moment. All I could see was Iris's radiant smile and Bruce's deer-in-the-headlights look. "Yeah, I am. I'm fine." And I meant every word I said.

The tents were set up by the time we'd all changed into clothes better suited for dancing and partying. As Shade and I stripped out of our finery and I laid out a nice pair of jeans, a sequined tank top, a sparkling belt, and a pair of stacked-heel boots for my party gear, he was musing.

"Iris certainly looked happy, though I thought she might be having cold feet. She paused there for a moment." He grinned, winking at me as I flashed him my boobs. "Okay, enough talk about Iris. Come here, you wanton pussycat."

I danced my way over to him. "You going to shake booty with me tonight?" Chase hadn't been much for dancing, but I loved it. I loved to feel my body move. All three of us—Menolly, Camille, and I—did. We all had our own styles and music preferences, but we could shake up the dance floor.

"Of course, you know I love to move with you." He wrapped a lazy arm around my waist and slid one knee between my legs, dancing dirty and low and hot. As I settled into his arms, grinding softly against his leg, he whispered, "I love to move inside you, too, babe. You're my sweet pussy, my wildcat."

I caught my breath as the fire of his presence swept through me. Like Hi'ran, Shade ran the same passionate intensity, pulling me deep into his world, dragging me into the shadows where my panther stirred. My skin sparked when he touched me and I could sense how much he wanted me. All I could think of was stripping and fucking his brains out. But they were waiting for us.

A glance at the clock sealed my decision. "We have time for a quickie."

"You sure you don't want long and leisurely?" His lips pressed behind my ear and I gasped, a shiver rippling down my body. My nipples stiffened at the touch of his tongue on my neck.

"We don't have time. Just fuck me. Now." Suddenly so hot I could think of nothing but his sweet, thick cock filling me up, I fumbled for his zipper as he backed me up against the door.

Shade was wearing a pair of cargo pants and a mesh tank top, and the ripple of his muscles through the mesh set me aflame all over again. As I lowered his zipper, I realized he was going commando. I grabbed him by the neck of his tank and yanked him toward me.

"Oh gods, you're hot. So. Damn. Hot. Get over here and get up inside me. *Now*." As I leaned back against the wall, he reached around, cradling me by the butt. I wrapped my arms around his neck and lifted one foot to brace against the desk.

"As you wish, my sweetness." Shade pressed toward me, sliding his cock deep inside as I let out a little groan. And then he was moving, rocking my butt back against the wall with each thrust. As the sensation spread through me like the warm feel of honey, I tugged at his ponytail and his hair came loose, spreading over his shoulders. His eyes flashed, rich and dark, and he buried his face in my neck, nipping lightly on the skin.

Every nerve in my body began to sing, from toes to nipples to head, and the feel of him jostling for position sent me reeling. I slid my hands under his shirt, running my fingers over the rippling muscles, over the scars, over the smooth flesh, then encircled his waist, drawing him deeper inside me.

His hips swiveled against mine, the friction increasing as his gaze took on a determined look. As he increased the pace, his lips traced their way around my neck and, with one hand, he reached down and began to stroke me, stirring a chain of little explosions that drove me toward the edge.

My breath ragged, I let out a cry as my nipples rubbed against the material of his tank in the most irritating sensation. And yet I liked it, in a perverse way. The annoyance set me on edge, heightening the tension.

A flutter began in my stomach as Shade became more aggressive. With one deep thrust, he held me against the wall.

His voice rough, he grabbed my hands and pinned them above my head. "You're *mine*. You're *my woman*. You're my love. You're my passion. Do you hear me?"

I held my breath. Something was happening, and I wasn't sure what it was. And then he grabbed me up and tossed me on the bed, leaping between my legs. And as he plunged back inside me, there was a shift—that's the only way I can describe it—and I found myself soaring, but I wasn't alone.

Can you hear me? Can you feel me? The whisper of thoughts filled my mind. I began to drift on the current . . . my body rocking, every nerve tingling, and then I realized I wasn't just feeling my own response, but Shade's, too. And then, someone else was there with us.

Hi'ran. Hi'ran was there, caught up in the passion, his autumn fires shrouding us with the scent of smoke and soot and the dark, pungent tang of autumn. I turned to see him leaning over us on the bed, and he reached out to trace my cheek with his hand. Shade glanced at him and a feral smile crept across his lips as he kissed Hi'ran's index finger when it came near his face.

"My Lord." Shade acknowledged him, even while he kept fucking me.

Hi'ran leaned down and pressed his lips to mine. And once again, he sucked my breath out of my body and I went spiraling out of my body, finding myself standing between the spirits of both Shade and the Autumn Lord. Shade took me in his arms and began to run his hands over me as a slow drumbeat played in the background. Hi'ran came up behind me and wrapped his arms around my waist, his fingers tripping over my body. We were all naked and entwined together, and I wasn't sure who was touching me where, but it was so delicious, so hot, that I didn't care. And then, someone was in me—or were they both? The heat was so thick that I could barely breathe, but I knew I never wanted it to stop, never wanted this delicious ache to end.

And then the energy of my shadow walker and my liege came tumbling in on me and I could hold back no longer. As Shade cried out, I went spiraling into orgasm, my body one long chord singing in the night as I hovered between heaven and hell.

As I opened my eyes, Shade was sitting by my side, patting my hand. "Delilah, are you all right?"

I blinked, sitting up. "Fuck, what time is it? What happened? Did I pass out?" I grabbed my clothes and began to dress.

He nodded. "Briefly. I think the energy was almost too much for you. Our master is a powerful lord, and he can forget how fragile mortals are. But . . . did you . . . Are you . . ."

I caught his hand up in mine and rubbed it against my cheek, my heart still racing from the orgasm. "I loved it. More than you can know." And then a thought hit me. "Oh no, I'm not—he didn't . . ." The idea that I might be pregnant at this point in the game suddenly scared the crap out of me.

"No, not yet. But it was a test, to see how well you can handle the energy of the Autumn Lord using me as a conduit. I think you passed." He grinned and leaned down to kiss me. I savored his lips.

After a moment, I pushed my way out of bed and began to dress again. "I never thought I'd enjoy two men at once . . . but this was . . . this was different."

"You never know what you might like until you try it." Shade zipped his pants and turned to me. "He won't be with us every time, but we know now that it can work—he can ride me, and touch you in the process. I wasn't allowed to tell you because he feared you might psych yourself out if you knew. If you showed signs of being overpowered, he was ready to vacate instantly. He would never hurt you. Please know that."

I nodded. "I understand. I do. I'm . . . not the little girl I was a year ago. I've grown up. And I like the woman I'm becoming. I feel stronger. I'm ready to shoulder my share of responsibility."

"I love the woman you're becoming. You know, don't you, that he had his eye on you from the moment you were born? This—you belonging to the Autumn Lord—was in the hands of fate all along. You were born to be a Death Maiden." Shade wrapped an arm around me, and I leaned into his embrace.

A shiver of recognition ran through me. "I think I knew. When I saw Arial in the temple of Haseofon, I knew we were both chosen. I still don't know why she's there, but . . ."

"Perhaps you'll find out soon. Now come, they are waiting for us." He stood and held out his hand, pulling me up. "And put on your dancing shoes because I intend to wear you out on the dance floor."

I slapped his butt. "Not a chance. You'll go down before me." And then, abruptly, I stopped. "Tell me something. What is your shadow walker side like? What are the Stradolans like?" I'd never asked before, but now it just seemed a good time.

But Shade looked at me and shook his head. "I will show you, soon. But not tonight. Tonight is for dancing. For celebrating. For family." And, taking my hand, he led me out the door.

The dance floor was rocking. At least two-thirds of the guests were shaking a leg, to a very mixed playlist of rock. Everything from Tempest—a Celtic band—to Lady Gaga to Aerosmith.

Iris and Bruce were in the center, up on the stage where they'd gotten married, dancing the Twist to Suzanne Vega's "Blood Makes Noise." Iris was wearing a pair of pale blue jeans, blue espadrilles, and a sparkling silver tank, and she looked very chic. Her hair was braided in a pattern of intricate loops that kept it off the floor. Bruce was wearing jeans and a muscle shirt, and I was surprised to see how buff he was.

As Shade and I found a space and began to dance, Camille cast a sly smile my way and winked. The music shifted to a new song, and yet another, before Menolly jumped onstage and turned it off.

"May I have your attention, please? It's time to cut the cake and eat! And then, we'll dance the rest of the night away." She motioned to Smoky and Trillian, who carried the cake up on stage. They were careful, and it survived intact. I stared at the tiered wonder, suddenly remembering the graffiti across my Jeep. A wave of anger flashed through me, but I pushed it away. I'd deal with my feelings tomorrow, when Iris was safely on her honeymoon.

Bruce and Iris approached the cake, and she pulled out a silver dagger. As she and Bruce prepared to slice into the cake, there was a sudden noise and Maggie came toddling onto the platform, from the back of the stage.

"Maggie! Maggie!" Hanna's voice echoed from the front of the tent as she elbowed her way through the crowd. "Maggie got away from me! Stop her!"

Iris turned to see the little gargoyle toddling toward her with an unsteady gait. "Maggie, what are you doing, you little imp?"

"I'is? I'is?" Maggie held out her arms and lurched toward Iris. But the next moment she caught sight of the cake, and her eyes grew wide. She grabbed the tablecloth on the folding table and pulled. Apparently, whoever set up the table hadn't done a very good job, because one leg began to buckle as the cloth slid off, taking the cake with it.

"No!" Iris dove for it and so did Bruce, and in the excitement, he tripped over her, pushing them both onto the table, right across the cake.

A collective hush swept over the crowd as we watched Iris, Bruce, and Maggie go down with the cake and table in one big, sugary pile. Luckily, it fell to the side of Maggie, and she just giggled, happily licking her fingers. Iris and Bruce, covered in cake, pushed themselves up to a sitting position. I held my breath, waiting for Iris to throw a fit, but she just picked up a handful of the cake, turned to Bruce, and plastered it on his face.

Bruce stared at her for a moment, then laughed. "Woman, you are going down!" He grabbed her, pushing her down onto the cake. And then, he leaned over her and they were kissing, passionately, oblivious to the fact that everybody was watching them. A few flashes from the guests told me pictures would be forthcoming.

Maggie laughed and ate another handful of cake before Menolly jumped on the stage to retrieve her. She glanced down at the couple and shook her head, then turned to the guests.

"Dinner, along with more desserts, is set up in the tent to your left. Buffet style, so please, form an orderly line. Tables are in the other two tents." And then, taking Maggie with her, she headed for the house to clean up our baby.

As Shade and I headed toward the food, I glanced back at Iris. She and Bruce were sitting up, holding hands. They looked happy. Truly happy.

Hours later, late in the night but still not yet dawn, Bruce and Iris were clean and in their traveling clothes. His family was waiting outside for them. They were traveling together to Ireland for their honeymoon and would be back in two weeks.

I swallowed the lump in my throat as I stood there with Menolly and Camille. Forcing a smile to my face, I leaned forward and kissed the happy couple on the forehead.

"Take care of yourself and come home soon. We'll miss you."

Iris nodded. "I know, I'll miss you, too. But I've waited a long time for this and I want to see the land of Bruce's birth."

Menolly pressed her hand to her lips, her eyes glistening with red tears. "You have to be back by the equinox—that's when Nerissa and I are holding our promise ceremony."

"I will be. Don't you worry—I wouldn't miss it for the world." Iris turned to Camille. "And you . . . will you be okay?"

Camille nodded. "We will be fine . . . *all* of us. Hanna knows what to do, and we are safe here. But please, take care. Bruce, guard her and watch over her. Iris is our sister. Let nothing happen to her."

He straightened his shoulders. "I will, my lady. Trust me—Iris is my joy and my life. And she carries my child. I will guard them both with my life. But now, we must go. My family waits outside."

As they headed toward the door, Camille started to follow, then stopped. We had gone as far as we could. The next two weeks were Iris's to live, without us there, in joy with her new family. Even though I knew she'd be coming back, I began to cry, softly. Life was changing. I only prayed that the future wouldn't tear us apart. Because while I now knew I could weather change . . . I couldn't weather being alone.

Chapter 10

A mist was rising off the street, as I looked around, confused for a moment. Then I realized it was night, and raining, and the raindrops pounded against the city pavement with a staccato drumbeat, hard and fast. The puddles glimmered beneath the streetlights, rippling with each new drop that shattered the surface.

As I looked around, getting my bearings, I realized that this wasn't exactly a dream—I was out on the astral, in spirit, and I knew who had summoned me.

"Greta? Are you here?" I called out the name of my trainer—the leader of the Death Maidens.

After a moment, the petite redhead slipped from out of the shadows and glided over to me, in a robe the color of twilight. Her forehead bore the same tattoo as my own crescent, burning brightly with a flame in the center, and her arms were tattooed like mine, only more intricate and vibrant. Mine would someday be just as vivid.

"Good, you begin to recognize my energy signature. But let us travel. I have a job for you tonight, and it will not be easy." She turned to me, eyeing me up and down. "You need to wear a robe for this. Living or not, when you formally take part in ceremonies, you'll have to wear the uniform."

"I don't have one." I had no clue how to change clothes on the astral, but she held out her hand and a long garment appeared, draped over her forearm. She handed it to me.

"I'll teach you how to change your clothes on the astral. It's a simple matter of focusing your thoughts. You're naked in your bed right now, aren't you?" She smiled. "But here you are dressed in jeans and T-shirt."

I glanced down. She had a good point. Somehow, I had managed to dress myself when pulled out by her call, so I should be able to change clothes. I accepted the robe and held it up. I could just put it on, but I wanted to learn her trick.

"What do I do if I want to mentally shift the clothing?"

"Focus on your body and 'see' it in a different outfit. Close your eyes and feel the image shifting." She smiled. "It helps to think of it not as magic—especially since you don't work magic—but as a mental shift. A perceptual transformation. Think of it like when you shift into animal form."

I closed my eyes and lowered my head, feeling the heavy robe in my hands. Picturing myself standing there, I mentally shifted the robe out of my hands to cover my jeans and tee. Nothing happened. I tried again, this time imagining the robe hovering around me and sliding onto my body. Again—nothing. Finally, irritated, I silently ordered the robe to get the hell on my back. And this time, the material shifted, vanished, and I suddenly felt the weight of it hanging from my shoulders.

Opening my eyes, I looked down. I was wearing the robe. Greta handed me a tasseled belt and I stared at the fringe for a moment, but controlled my urge to play with it. Somehow, I didn't think she'd be as lenient as my sisters were about the G-string.

I wrapped it around my waist and cinched it tight. "Okay, I think I have that down. What's on the agenda tonight?"

For the past few months, I'd been training under the new

moon with Greta, but we'd just passed the new moon a week or so back, and I had the feeling this was a special situation. I'd learned a lot in the training sessions we'd had so far, but something shifted in my stomach and I could sense a big lesson on the horizon.

"Tonight will not be easy for you. Come . . . you are going to be asked to put into action all that you've learned." She looked at me, her face impassive. Greta was petite, far shorter than I, and yet she carried herself with a power and grace that I could only imagine possessing.

As I met her gaze, I realized what she meant. Tonight, I would take my first soul—I would be the conduit to guide someone out of the physical. "You want me to kill someone . . ."

"No . . . you must stop calling it that. Their destiny is set, but you will help with the transition. This is a great responsibility. You have learned to control yourself when you are in panther form. You no longer fear taking down opponents with your Death Maiden powers without permission. Now, you must actually willingly use them."

She took my hand and we began to travel. We sped through the streets, faster than I could ever hope to move when not on the astral, as the steady rain poured around us. At our speed, the drops turned into bullets, sleeting against the ground as they pummeled the pavement. We raced through the night, dark shadows, harbingers of death.

The world fell away and we passed out of the city proper, toward the Sound. It was so dark, I wasn't sure just where we were, but the neighborhood looked familiar, even in the dark. We passed a huge park and my stomach began to flutter. I knew several Weres who lived in this area, and I really didn't want to think about what I might be heading into. Katrina, and Siobhan, they both lived up in this direction.

Please, I whispered to myself as we ran, *please, don't let us be targeting one of them.* I couldn't bear it if I had to take part in transitioning one of my good friends across the veil. I didn't want my face to be the last they saw.

But we turned before we reached the street leading to Katrina's, and we were still well out of distance of Siobhan's house. I sucked in a deep breath—even though out here on the astral I didn't need to breathe—and watched as Greta sped ahead toward a little house on a corner lot. The lot was surrounded by a chain-link fence. A chaise lounge and small side table sat out in front, both soaked through. Greta stopped by the gate and turned to me.

"Do you recognize this place?" She waited for me to take a long look at it. I frowned, taking it in. I didn't remember ever coming here. After a moment I shook my head.

"I don't think so, and yet, there is something familiar about it."

"That's because you know the owner and you can feel his energy even out here. And here, on the astral, this house—this yard, all have his signature embedded into what you see." She motioned for me and I followed her as we slid right through the gate and headed toward the house. The next moment, we were standing inside at a man who was watching a late-night science fiction movie. And then I knew.

"Wylie." I swallowed, hard. Wylie's mother had a sense of humor when she named him. She was a coyote shifter. And so was Wylie. He had become a regular at the Supe Community Meetings. Strong, lean, and a little rough around the edges, he'd still thrown himself into helping out with planning committees and everything else we might need. He was a loner. As far as I knew he didn't have a girlfriend, but he never had a harsh word for anybody, at least that I had seen.

"Is it really his time?" I didn't want to believe it. Wylie was still young, as far as Weres went.

Greta turned to me. "There is much more," she said softly, her eyes dark as the ocean. "You need to take his soul through yours. This one, you cannot just consign to the afterlife. He's not headed for an easy end, Delilah."

I started. "What? You want me to . . ." Pausing, I strove to remember what she had taught me. Some souls we collected for the gods when they couldn't, for one reason or another. Others, we helped transition to the afterlife because they deserved it. And still others, we condemned and sent to oblivion. All of this, we did when the Autumn Lord sent down orders.

"Wylie Smith has upset the balance, bringing too much chaos into a situation. The Hags of Fate have decreed that his soul be sent to the cleansing fires." She stood back, crossing her arms. "You must collect his soul, Delilah. There are things you need to know. Grandmother Coyote spoke with the Autumn Lord, and he has ordered it be done."

Grandmother Coyote *and* Hi'ran? This must be big. I stared at her, nervously tugging at my robe. I didn't want to do this. "How is he going to die?"

"He has a weak heart. As he watches his movie, the rhythm will begin to falter, then seize. He is due for cardiac arrest and will not have time to get to the phone. You will be waiting to collect his soul as he dies. You will examine the images, then consign his soul to the abyss." Her words came out, a neutral flow of information. This was old hat to her.

"You've done this so many times . . . does it get easier?" I glanced over at Wylie, who didn't seem to have a clue that within a few minutes, he'd be dead and his soul cast into oblivion to be cleansed and returned to the primal pool. Part of me wanted to warn him, to give him a chance to right whatever wrongs he'd done, but that wasn't an option.

"No. But each time, I understand my place in the world a little bit more. And so, in time, will you. Do you remember the rites I taught you?" She waited patiently, not pushing me.

I nodded, slowly. I remembered them, but it hadn't fully registered that I'd actually have to use them. Now, there was no avoiding the reality: I was a Death Maiden and while I was still training, my days of standing by as an observer were over. I couldn't very well wear the title without earning it.

"Yeah, I do. You said I have to take his soul through mine?" I'd done this accidentally a couple of times, but never deliberately.

She nodded. "Grandmother Coyote decreed that you need to do this."

When the Hags of Fate made a suggestion, it was an

order. Even if you were a god. Or a Death Maiden. I steadied myself, running through the steps, until I was sure I remembered their order. As I stared at Wylie, I tried to see him as something other than a friendly acquaintance. If he truly did have secrets and had upset the balance, maybe there was something I didn't know that would make it easier. But the only way I'd find out would be to go through with the rite.

I looked over at Greta, who was watching me carefully. "This is a test, isn't it?"

She shook her head. "No. If I were to test you, I'd make it a friend—someone dear to your heart. To see if you could go through with it."

"Have you ever had to . . . collect the soul of a friend?" Our eyes met and I held her fast. Wanted to see her reaction.

She gazed steadily at me, and then slowly blinked. "Yes." Her voice was a whisper on the wind, the rattle of dried corn husks. "My own mother."

I lowered my head. I couldn't imagine doing that. "I'm sorry. I . . . that would be hard to bear."

"It was difficult. I learned too much about her. Things I didn't want to know. But she went on to the afterlife, and I was able to let go after a while. It helped that she was beloved by many, and that her secrets weren't the kind to make me sorry she'd birthed me."

Greta put her hand on my arm. "You will not be sorry you do this. And truly, you have no choice. You are the Master's servant. He has appointed this task to you—and Grandmother Coyote asked for you to do it."

I straightened my shoulders. It was time to man up.

Motioning to Greta, I said, "I'm ready. When . . . ?"

I had to wait until he was on the verge of death before I sucked out his soul. I could do so several ways. With the courageous and those who deserved a hero's death, it would be with a kiss. With Wylie, it would be different.

She closed her eyes briefly. "You have . . . when his clock strikes three twelve, his heart will fail, and you will collect his soul." She motioned to the mantel, where a chiming clock sat. It read three ten.

I prepared myself, standing beside him, waiting. He had no clue I was here, waiting. He had no knowledge, no sense that he was about to die. As I stared down at him, trying to corral my emotions, I felt a spark flare from deep within. There it was—the trigger that Greta had taught me to look for.

It started as a small flicker, but I fanned it to life, nurtured it, coaxed it out and quickly, the flames ignited to a bonfire. When I looked at my target again, Wylie no longer resembled the man I knew, but instead a beacon, ready to explode. The urge to gather him up, to pull him to me was so strong that I had to hold back as I hovered on the edge of time, waiting for the clock to count down his last seconds.

And then, he suddenly clutched at his left arm, and—with a frightened look—stared directly at me.

"Delilah—" His whispered plea was his last, as he began to leave his body. Before he could run, I reached out and touched him, sucked his memories deep into my own. We vanished into a field of mist and shadow, where the moon watched from high over head, a sliver of first light.

And then . . .

Flash. Wylie sat in a room, meeting with other coyote shifters, only I sensed they weren't from the local community. They sat around a table that looked oddly familiar. I'd seen it somewhere before. I racked my brain but couldn't place it, though I'd seen the carved patterns on the edge before.

Then, the door opened and Van and Jaycee entered, with another man—large, bald, and dangerous looking. A Vin Diesel look-alike but with a surly sneer instead of a sexy smile. He was wearing a pendant with a stunning sapphire in the center. *One of the spirit seals.* He fingered it and I could feel the clash of energy waging as he summoned a dark spirit through it . . .

Flash. An ancient man, holding his hands up as an explosion of fire came racing out of his fingers to destroy an entire village. As the smoke roiled off the burning buildings, the screams of women and children echoed through the ash-filled sky. Flames leaped from rooftop to rooftop, catching on the thatch as the village burned to the ground. The sorcerer began to laugh as people ran into the streets, burning like torches. A little girl looked up at him and held out her hands before he engulfed her in another wave of flame.

Flash. Wylie, handing a thick bundle of cash over to Van and Jaycee along with a piece of paper. I leaned closer and saw the schedule for the Supe Community Council printed on it. A sick grin sidled across his face as he said, "Stupid idiots will find out why the Koyanni are nothing to mess with."

Flash. Wylie, meeting with a man who looked as old as time, and as maddened. He looked crafty, and the smell of death and decay hung heavy around his shoulders.

Flash. Wylie, with a woman, beating her senseless as she cowered, trying to fend off his blows. As she crawled toward the door, he gave her a swift kick. "Get out of here, you bitch. And take your fucking rugrat with you." And then I saw the little boy standing in the corner, thumb in his mouth, crying as he watched, eyes wide.

Flash. Wylie, with Van and Jaycee again, talking to someone who was so pale he looked sick. And then the man laughed, and a flash of fangs told me he was a vampire. He pushed a picture of Trixie over to Wylie, who nodded.

Sickened, I slammed the door to his memories. I'd seen enough. Wylie turned to me as I laid hold of his collar and lifted him off his feet.

"What are you doing to me? What's going on?" Fear flashed in his eyes, but I didn't care.

"Fires of the void, come forth to my bidding. Cleanse this soul and pass it through your center." As he struggled, a roar from the skies echoed through the swirling mist, and a wave, riding the night wind, came rushing down to clamor against us. I held him fast against the raging gale.

Wylie screamed, his cries echoing in the night, but a sudden thirst for justice rolled through me and I let out a laugh that reverberated through the night.

"Scream as loud as you want. No one can help you. Wylie

Smith, the Hags of Fate have sealed your destiny. Prepare for oblivion."

The wave of fire rushed over him, a purple flame burning through his essence, clearing the energy and rendering it harmless. As understanding washed through his eyes, he let out one last scream and then, with a final roar, the flames reduced his soul to ashes and swept them up, carrying them away.

"I am the instrument of judgment," I whispered, reaching toward the sky as Wylie Smith vanished forever from the eternal cycle—his consciousness gone forever. His soul was harmless energy floating forever in the great pool from which all life sprang.

As I lowered my hands, I blinked and was standing back next to Greta. I turned to her and she smiled softly.

"Well done, my dear."

There were so many questions I wanted to ask, and yet I couldn't phrase them. I didn't even know if I really understood what they were.

"Why didn't we end up in the training garden—where you took Ronald Wyndham Niece to deliver his soul to Valhalla?" I looked around. We were still standing in Wylie's house, albeit on the astral level. The first time Greta had come for me we'd been in a wild, forested grove with a training circle made of bronze, covered in magical symbols.

"Because that place is reserved for those who deserve a beautiful transition. Who deserve a hero's farewell. There is a darker place where we can take the worst of the worst, but since this was your first official solo, I decided to make it easier on you. The next training session, I will take you through all the places we collect our souls and teach you how to get there."

She stood back. "Do you understand why you were assigned to him?"

I closed my eyes, the kaleidoscope of images from Wylie's mind running through my head. I'd thought him a nice, gentle person, and totally misjudged him. He'd been a traitor, a spy . . . and he'd helped kill Exo and the others. He may not have planted the explosive, but he'd been as responsible for their deaths as if he'd tossed the canya himself.

Don't forget the spirit seal . . . a little voice whispered inside me, and I focused on the image of the man wearing the sapphire. The seventh spirit seal. I tried to zoom in on his face, to remember every nuance so I could tell the others. The spirit seal was out there and in the possession of someone dangerous. *And he knew how to use it.*

"I have to get back." I turned to Greta. "Am I done here?"

She nodded. "Walk softly, Delilah. You are coming to a crossroads. As much as I enjoy your company, I'd rather see you still on the living side of the veil than on my side. Get ready, because the train is rolling down the tracks."

I sucked in a deep breath, feeling a heavy weight descend on my shoulders. "I know. I can feel it headed my way." I paused. "Is Arial around?" Even though I wanted to get back to my body so I could wake up and tell the others about the spirit seal, I missed my twin. It had been a while since I'd seen her, at least in a form in which we could talk.

"Arial is off prowling in her leopard form. She likes to go out and run on the spirit realm, around the grounds of Haseofon." Greta paused, then touched my shoulder lightly. "Your sister is as overjoyed as you are to be able to meet and speak. At some point, she would like to talk to Camille and Menolly. But it would not work for your sister Menolly. To come to Haseofon, either one must come in spirit—and vampires cannot travel out of their bodies in spirit without being yanked out, and then they are only given a time to walk free—or one must journey in the body, and we cannot have a vampire in the halls. It is forbidden."

I frowned. "That doesn't seem . . ."

"Fair? Not all of life is just, or fair, nor understandable. The Master forbids it; therefore we obey. There is no discussion on the issue."

"And Arial cannot take human form out of Haseofon?" I already knew the answer but asked anyway.

Greta shook her head. "I'm sorry, but no. Now, go back to your body, my dear, and attend to your duties."

She vanished and I found myself racing back through the streets, back to where I'd started from. As the city skyline began to lighten, I saw a veiled shadow ahead and instinctively dove for it. As I entered the smoke, I fell into my body and sat up with a start, looking around.

Shade was asleep beside me, but he stirred. As I propped myself up against the pillows and headboard, I thought about what I'd just done. Wylie was dead. Verdict: heart attack. But his soul was gone, forever. I'd sent him to the final death, and there would be no return.

A fierce sense of pride sprang up. I'd done my duty without flinching. And Greta had been proud of me. She'd also given me valuable information. Now I knew for sure Van and Jaycee were behind this. The bald man wasn't Telazhar, that I could tell from watching the sorcerer destroy the village. But he was in possession of a spirit seal, which made him terribly dangerous.

As I climbed out of bed and slipped into a pair of sweatpants and a tank, Shade woke. He blinked, sitting up.

"Is everything okay?"

"No. We need to wake the others. I have information and we need to act on it as soon as possible." I motioned to the door. "I'm heading downstairs. Get dressed and follow. If you could wake Camille and her men, I'll see if Menolly's still up. And someone needs to head out to the studio. This is an all-hands-on-deck meeting."

Shade slid out from beneath the covers and quietly began to dress as I left the room. I scrambled down the stairs, glancing out the window. Dawn would break in a while, but Menolly would still be up for a couple hours. She wasn't in the living room or parlor—which meant Nerissa had gone back to her condo for the night instead of staying over—so I opened the bookcase in the kitchen and raced down the stairs to Menolly's lair.

"Menolly? Are you down here?"

"What's up, Kitten? Is everything okay?" Menolly was sitting on her bed, in a silk bathrobe, reading a book. I glanced at the title. *A History of Vampire Mythology.* She closed it, dog-earing one of the corners as I peeked around the partition that separated her sleeping area from the sitting area.

"Yes. No. Just come upstairs, would you? I've got some important information on the bombing."

She set the book on her nightstand and crossed the room to my side, looping her arm through my elbow. "Did they strike again?"

"No, not yet. But with what I know, my guess is they'll continue on until we catch them. They're out for vengeance."

We headed up the stairs and back into the kitchen. Shade was standing there. We'd given up hiding the entrance to Menolly's lair from family members—everybody had guessed it by now. But we'd insisted on secrecy and had installed a heavy-duty lock on the door, which Smoky had replaced with a reinforced steel one. Now, when Menolly slept, only Camille, I, and Iris could unlock the gate to her world.

Oh, a dragon could bust through it, or maybe a strong demon, but they'd have to find it first, behind the bookcase. But Tregarts and bloatworgles and most other vampires— they couldn't get through to her.

"Camille and the guys are on the way down. I called Rozurial on his cell phone and woke him up. He, Shamas, and Vanzir will be up here in a few minutes. Did you want Hanna?"

"Hanna is already awake." Her voice echoed through the kitchen, and we turned to see her standing there. "What's going on? Is Iris okay?"

"Iris is fine, Hanna. We just have important info to go over. Could you please make a pot of tea, and maybe find something for us to eat?" I turned to the others. "I'm going to wait till everyone is here. And then we have some decisions to make. And a table to find."

"Table?" Camille, blurry eyed, wandered into the room, followed by Smoky, Morio, and Trillian.

"Yeah . . . because we're stuck on the tracks and there's a train barreling down on us. And Van and Jaycee are right up there at the controls."

My nerves were jumping. Somehow, I knew that even Van and Jaycee weren't the ones with the final say on things. The image of the bald-headed man kept flickering through my mind. Bigger, badder forces were at work, and I feared actually finding out just who they were and what they could do.

Chapter 11

~⚜~

Once everyone was gathered around the table, I outlined everything that had happened. I was still high off the catch and felt like I'd had a triple shot of espresso. And I wasn't a caffeine junkie like Camille.

"We have to find that table. If we find the table, we have a starting place. I remember seeing it—I distinctly remember seeing it, but I can't pinpoint *where*." I described it to them in detail, hoping it would spark some memories. After all, most of them had been one place or another with me over the past couple years.

"The bald man—do you have any clue whom it might be? Did he look like a Tregart?" Camille frowned, playing with a cookie. She looked tired and a little worn around the edges. We all did.

"No, but he was summoning something with the spirit seal. A force, a spell, a ghost, an entity—I'm not sure what." I took a long drink of tea and sighed. It was too strong. Hanna hadn't quite mastered the art of brewing the perfect pot yet. "He was wearing the spirit seal, and I get the feeling he was far stronger than Van or Jaycee. And I'm pretty sure the vampire that he and Van and Jaycee were with was Bryan."

"I think we can safely assume you're right about the vampire. Let's see . . . you had several visions. One, with Wylie, Van, Jaycee, and the unknown man. The second . . . Telazhar destroying a village?"

"No—but I think he was the older man in the next flash I had. I think the person destroying the village was the bald man, a long time ago. I'd swear it was in Otherworld, probably during the Scorching Wars, so it had to be a vision of the past."

"Okay, we have a bald-headed sorcerer both in the present and from the past. And Telazhar. Wylie paying off Van and Jaycee and handing them something about the Supe Community Hall. Wylie beating up a woman. Did you recognize her?" Camille was jotting down notes on a steno pad while Morio had commandeered my laptop and began searching the Internet for something.

"No. She didn't seem connected . . . probably just one more memory that stood out in his mind. I wonder if that was his child. But he referred to the boy as 'your' rug rat, so probably not." The memory infuriated me. "If we could find out her name, maybe we could find out more about him."

"Do you think they were in a relationship?" Morio asked. "I could search for Wylie online and see if there's any mention of him on the Net. Maybe they were married?" His fingers poised above the keyboard.

"Yeah, why don't you give that a try." I loved the Internet. It had provided us with an amazing amount of information over the years. "Google *Wylie Smith*, and put the name in quotation marks."

Morio tapped away at the keys. "Okay, we've got a lot of hits. Anything we can narrow it down with?"

"Try . . . *Seattle*. And *coyote shifters*, again in quotation marks." I frowned. I'd become an expert on Internet sleuthing.

Again, Morio quickly typed in the refined search query. He was quick on the keys, far quicker than I was. "How'd you learn to type so well?"

"I had a job in Japan as a data entry operator for about ten years. That was before Grandmother Coyote summoned me to come here." He glanced up. Camille gave him a long look, smiling. She'd obviously known this.

"Really? I thought . . ." I paused. "I don't know what I thought." It occurred to me that we really had very little clue on the backgrounds of some of our loves and allies. "What kind of information did you enter? Was it with a private company or a government?"

He gave me a feral smile. "I worked for a hospital. I was inputting insurance information for patients. It was a boring job but allowed me to live in the city without being suspect. I moved around every ten to fifteen years so people wouldn't suspect something odd when I didn't appear to age."

Camille was sitting next to him. She leaned her head against his arm, and he leaned over and kissed the top of her head. "I'm so glad you're healed up. I was so worried about you."

He pushed the laptop over to me. "Here you go, take a look." And then he draped his arm around Camille's shoulder and began kissing her, long and deep. I glanced over at Menolly, who was eyeing them, an indescribable look on her face. She didn't look angry, but her gaze was hungry, almost predatory. I decided to put a stop to any potential altercations.

"No necking at the table, please. At least not right now." I scrolled through the search results. Wylie had been part of several forums. The Supe Community Forums, for one, but that wouldn't do me much good, considering he'd been hiding so many secrets. But then, two references caught my eye.

The first was FangGirlWannabes.com.

"Well, well, well . . . looks like Marion's sister wasn't the only one trolling this site." I scanned the forums until I found the search function. First, I typed in *Wylie*. I found his profile, but it stated he had no postings on the site—he'd just registered for the forums. He'd registered in October.

After that, I typed in Trixie's name—she'd registered in September and had ten pages of postings. A number were simple fan-girl postings to other fang hags, but then I found a series of posts between Trixie and a vampire who went by the user name of Luv-Bites. They started out flirty and grew progressively more sexual. And then—in one of them—the post to Trixie was signed *Luv U—Bryan*. Another quick search and Luv-Bites' profile showed that he'd registered in October, the same day as Wylie.

"Bingo. We have Trixie and Bryan and Wylie on this site. Wylie didn't make any public postings, but what if he and Bryan were private messaging? They registered on the same day, a month after Trixie joined the site—a couple days after we took out the Koyannis' warehouse."

"Okay. So the Koyanni have been planning revenge since then. That gives them several months to raise havoc that we weren't aware of. Who knows what else they've been up to since then? So, anything else on Wylie?" Camille jotted down a few notes on a steno pad.

"Looking . . . looking . . . here." Another forum site, this one called, Fire Burn Me. But the bulletin board forum system was locked. A strange feeling ran through me as I stared at the logo.

"Camille, look at this. Do you recognize this symbol?" I motioned for her to come look.

She leaned down, staring over my shoulder. "That looks . . . yes, that's Sorcerer's Tongue. Firespeak. Crap, Shamas, get over here. You studied sorcery. You look at it." She shifted to give him room.

Shamas gave her a long look as he headed over, holding her gaze. "Let's get this out in the open. You're pissed at me for what I did. I accept that. But I was stupid and when I realized that Feris had planned an attack on the Moon Mother's grove, I did what I could to stop it. I didn't do this to hurt you, Camille."

Camille turned on him, furious. "You should have known! Everybody knows the Scorching Wars were a battle between the moon and the sun, at the heart. We grew up hearing the stories about the sorcerers and the evil they brought with them. You made the choice—you turned your back on your race, your family . . . on me!"

Shamas lashed out at her. "I screwed up! I fucked up. I almost died for doing so. Nothing can change the past, but I'm not the idiot I was. I'm not the same man. And I can help you with what I've learned." He grabbed her by the shoulders and shook her. "Please, forgive me. I can't stand that you hate me so much."

"I don't hate you—I just hate what you did! Let go of me."

Smoky was at their side instantly, and Shamas found himself dangling from the dragon's grasp. The look on Smoky's face was terrifying and cruel.

"You dare to shake my wife?"

Shamas kicked at him, livid. "She's my cousin and I loved her before you ever knew she existed!"

"You really choose to say that to me?" Smoky turned toward the door, Shamas struggling against his grasp. "I will show you what I do to—"

"Stop." Camille's voice was sharp. "He didn't hurt me. Smoky, you have to let me fight my own battles. I need your help when it comes to the demons and dragons of the world, but not my relatives."

Smoky slowly put Shamas down. "I am trying, my wife. But remember: I am a dragon. This is not easy for me."

"I know." She wrapped her arms around his waist and leaned up to kiss him. "You have nothing to worry about. Shamas and I are cousins. *Nothing more.* What we felt years ago has long changed."

I glanced over at Shamas. I was sure that he didn't feel the same way. He rubbed his neck where his collar had chafed him. After a moment, he cleared his throat and turned to Smoky and Camille.

"I'm sorry. Camille, I've never forgiven myself for not standing up to my family about us. I crumbled. And I ran away because of the pressure." He hung his head. "Forgive me? Please? Smoky, I would never intrude on your relationship. It's obvious Camille's madly in love with the three of you. I just . . . I just want to be friends. Cousins, again. Without her hating me."

The silence in the room was deafening. Shamas looked

heartbroken, his cockiness vanished under a wave of despair and loneliness that was tangible—palpable. Camille closed her eyes, breathing deep. Smoky waited for her move. After a moment, she reached out, took Shamas's hands in hers.

"I believe you. I forgive you. You're with us now. You're helping us. You made a hard choice. We all make mistakes. I should know about that." She glanced over at Smoky, who gave her a nod and took his seat again.

Shamas held out his arms and Camille hugged him, kissing his cheek. "Thank you. I promise, I'll make you proud of me." He gave her a faint smile.

"If you're done with the feel-goods, how about taking a look at this symbol already?" I wasn't sure why the scene bothered me. Maybe it was that Shamas had never had much use for Menolly or me, but it was obvious he chased after Camille. Or maybe it was that I thought Camille was too quick to forgive, and it probably stemmed from her being afraid Smoky would mangle our cousin rather from her truly being okay with what was going on. Or maybe . . . maybe I was just on edge lately and taking it out on everybody around me. We'd all been so stressed, I was surprised we hadn't gotten in more arguments than we had.

Shamas blinked, then shrugged and peered at the symbol. "Sorcerer's Tongue for sure—Firespeak. And that . . . is the symbol for the Subterranean Realms."

"The Sub-Realms." I bit my lip, staring at the website. "What the fuck is information about the Sub-Realms doing on the Internet?"

"There's one way to find out." Shamas pointed to a link. "Register under a fake name and find out."

I shivered. The last thing I wanted to do was hang out in a sorcerers' chat room. "I don't know the lingo. What about you?"

"Me?" Shamas cocked his head. "I could do it. But we need to create a fake e-mail address on one of the webmail servers."

"You learn fast. They could still look up our IP address, but not if I call Tim and ask him if we can use his proxy server. He can route us around so that whoever owns Fire Burn Me will never find us. Or find Tim." That was an absolute *must*. We needed to make sure Tim didn't get caught in the crossfire. I jotted down a note to call him first thing in the morning. "For now, we'll create your e-mail address— how about using webbeemail.com? What do you want?"

Shamas thought for a moment. "Ixsornosum at webbee-mail dot com." He spelled it out for me. "It's a sorcerer's term meaning 'My desire is my Will.' It's a specialized credo that will be recognized by anybody who's seriously studied sorcery. They'll know I'm experienced. No one would use that name without the training to back it up. They'd be setting themselves up for retaliation if they were discovered."

The look on his face scared me. He noticed my reaction and shrugged. "What can I say? There are harsh penalties in the world of sorcery for those who tread on toes. And pretending to be a sorcerer when you aren't brings with it harsh repercussions. So does knowing the secret dialects of Fire-speak if you haven't been given the training. Spies have been killed before for trying to infiltrate the inner societies."

Camille let out a harsh snort. "That figures," she said, but then bit her lip. "I'm sorry. It's a knee-jerk reaction."

"Once you're in the chat room and forums, we can sort through and see if we can find any information to help." I pushed the laptop back after setting up Shamas's new e-mail. "What next? We can't register him until we get the proxy server going with Tim, and I don't think he'd appreciate being woken up at . . . " I glanced at the clock. "Oh man, at four thirty in the morning."

Menolly suddenly jumped out of her chair. "I know where we saw that table! Motherfucking pus bucket." Her eyes turned bloodred and her fangs descended. "If I'm right, and if it's what I think it is, I'm going to feast on Wilbur's blood tonight."

"Wilbur?" I frowned, trying to remember. We'd been inside his house a couple of times, Menolly a couple more than the rest of us, since she was usually the one who showed up on his doorstep when we needed his help.

A blurry memory of standing in his dining room filtered into my head. The cramped chamber had held a large, old china hutch that was filled with books instead of dishes, and there had been several dusty plants, and . . . a dining room table. The table I'd described. "You're right! Wilbur! That's his table."

"I knew it!" Menolly started to slam the wall, but Morio caught her wrist. She glared at him for a moment, then stopped. "Sorry."

"You would have put a hole through it." He held on to her wrist for a beat longer than he needed to, then stopped, looked at her, then Camille, and let go. Menolly pulled her hand back.

"We need to pay Wilbur a little visit," she said. "We can do that now. I don't mind waking *him* up this early."

I sighed. "Might as well. Camille, you coming?"

She nodded. "Sure. But I want Smoky and Shade with us. That should be enough. If we show up en masse and we're wrong, we'll ostracize someone who has been, up till now, a valuable if questionable ally. Morio and Roz, you two wait near his porch. The rest of you stay here and keep an eye on the house."

She stood up. "I guess we'd better get dressed. I sure hope to hell we're wrong. I'd hate to think he's been plotting against us." She yawned. "What I want to know is why these things can't happen when we've had more sleep? An hour just isn't going to cut it for the day."

The thought of being betrayed by Wilbur stung. He wasn't a close friend. In fact, he was a lecher who looked straight out of a ZZ Top music video. A fairly powerful necromancer, he was rude and lewd and had a pet ghoul named Martin who had once been an accountant. But he had helped us more than once, and the possibility that he was working with our enemies would be a harsh blow.

"If he is helping them . . ." I glanced over at Menolly.

"Then we take him out." She shook her head. "If he's on the other side, he's dead. No excuses. I'm going to change. I'll meet you up here in ten minutes." Turning toward the bookcase, she straightened her shoulders and headed down to her lair.

Camille gave me a look that mirrored my own feelings. If we discovered Wilbur had stabbed us in the back, we wouldn't have to worry about him retaliating. Menolly would bleed him dry before we could even touch him.

I gave her a faint smile and shrugged. "I guess . . . we'd better get dressed."

Wilbur's house was known in the neighborhood as "the old London house," though we had no idea why it had been named that. Another Victorian built in a similar design to ours, it was three stories high, but there the resemblance between it and ours ended. Wilbur had no illusions about keeping his property tidy. While it wasn't an issue of junker cars and old refrigerators on the lawn, the driveway up to his house was overgrown with brambles and vine maple.

Wilbur had an old truck, one of those pickups with a rounded top and a running board. He also had a beat-up 1957 Chevy with the tail fins, in a bright cherry red and white. He tore out of his drive on a regular basis, and I wondered if the cops had ever flagged him down for speeding.

We walked down the driveway and across the road to his place, the tension so palpable I could feel it. Menolly was wearing a pair of her stiletto boots—the ones she used to put holes through her enemies. Camille, Smoky, and Shade were all dressed for a fight. And I was wearing jeans, a turtleneck, and pair of Doc Martens. Morio and Roz lagged behind, yawning and quietly whispering together.

I glanced at the sky. Sunrise wouldn't come for over another two hours and it was still dark, but a low, overhanging bank of clouds had moved in, lighting the ground with a faint glow. Though the rain had let up in the evening, it now loomed heavy, moisture saturating the air. The scents of cedar and fir drifted past and I closed my eyes, inhaling deeply. The fragrance of the trees surrounded me with a comforting embrace, and I wished that this could just be a nice stroll down the road.

Camille slipped her hand into mine. "I know. I know."

"You know what?" I gave her a soft look.

"I don't like this, either. I don't like not being able to trust someone we've come to trust. I don't like thinking that he might have duped us. We should be asleep, at home, instead of heading over like a gang of thugs to break into his house and check out his table." She stopped in her tracks. "Great gods, that sounds ridiculous."

"Yeah, I just wish it *were* ridiculous. But it's not." We trudged our way up his driveway, avoiding the potholes. I skirted a patch of stinging nettle that reached out from the side of the road. The feel to the land was odd, but rather than feeling evil, it made me shiver, as if I were being watched.

When we got to the porch, I moved to the front with Menolly. "Let me do the talking," I said. "You're likely to just rip out his throat."

She raised her eyebrows. "You know me too well, Kitten. All right, but don't try to stop me if we discover . . ."

"If he's ratting us out, you can do what you like." We clattered up the stairs, Camille, Smoky, and Shade bringing up the rear. Morio and Roz waited at the bottom of the stairs. I steeled myself, wondering how the hell we were going to approach this, and finally forced myself to reach out and press the doorbell.

No answer.

I pressed again. This time, I heard a shuffling from behind the door and after a moment, it opened to show Martin, in all his undead glory, standing there. In a suit that smelled about five days ripe, he cocked his head—the metal brace around his neck made it difficult for him to turn it too far—and grunted. After a moment he backed up, opening the door.

Wondering what the hell was going on, I cautiously entered, followed by Menolly. The scent of sulfur wafted through the air, mingled with a whiff of mold, a tinge of damp upholstery and . . . something else. Burned flesh? No, not quite.

Martin reached out and for a moment, I was afraid he was going to attack me. Menolly had already broken his neck last year when Wilbur first moved into the neighborhood. But instead, he touched me on the sleeve, then closed his hand around my wrist. The clammy feel of his skin gave me the creeps—it wasn't the same chill of Menolly's flesh—but he just gave Menolly a quick glare and pulled me after him.

I followed him, with Menolly and the others behind me, as he led me through a narrow hallway, the walls covered with dusty tapestries, to the kitchen. A woodstove sat to one side, and a teakettle and cast-iron skillet were sitting on the stove. Right there, I saw what the other scent I'd been smelling was. It looked like someone had been attempting to cook, but the eggs were still raw and smeared across the cooktop, and a raw piece of steak sat on the sideboard, covered with maggots.

Gagging, I turned away and glanced around the rest of the kitchen. There was the table—the design exactly the way I'd seen it in the vision. I slowly moved over to it, rubbing my hand on the wood. The polished surface was smooth. The wood had been well oiled, taken care of in a way that belied Wilbur's rough nature.

Martin grunted again, and I turned to find him pointing at a door next to a built-in shelf unit. I glanced at him. If it weren't for the fact that he was a ghoul, I could swear I was seeing a look of concern in his eye.

"We'd better have a look." I motioned to Camille. "You and Shade keep an eye on Martin, please. Smoky, Menolly, follow me." I gently tapped Martin on the arm. "Go stand over there." After repeating myself several times, he finally shuffled over next to Shade and stared up at him, his eyes glowing. Whether he sensed the Netherworld energy coming off the shadow walker, I'm not sure, but he seemed to find Shade terribly fascinating.

I cautiously put my hand on the doorknob and quietly turned it, opening the door to reveal a stairway heading down. A basement, most likely. With a glance at Menolly, I started down the steps, doing my best to keep from making noise.

Halfway down, I heard a faint groan. It sounded like someone in pain. Concerned, I hastened my pace. By the time I reached the bottom of the stairs, the hairs on the back of my neck were standing up.

The basement was dim, with a single bulb illuminating the room. The room was long and wide, with built in floor-to-ceiling shelving units partitioning off various sections. The shelves were filled with cans and jars and boxes, but overall, the space was organized and far neater than I'd thought Wilbur's basement would be.

"Is anybody down here?"

No answer. I closed my eyes, trying to suss out the energy, but that was Camille's department. I turned to Menolly and gave her a questioning look. She shook her head, and we glanced over at Smoky. He was frowning, sniffing the air.

After a moment, he pushed past me and headed around one of the shelving units, with us following. We found ourselves plunged into darkness—the light couldn't penetrate through the packed shelves. I pulled out a flashlight and flipped it on, shining it into the floor. There, in the gloom, lay Wilbur.

"Wilbur!" Before I thought about what I was doing, I knelt beside him, feeling for a pulse. He was still alive, and he let out a faint wheeze, turning his head to shade his eyes from the flashlight as he looked up at me.

Menolly knelt on his other side. "Wilbur, can you talk? Wilbur? Can you understand me?"

He winced, managing to raise one hand to rub his head. His lips were cracked and chapped, and I wondered how long he'd been down here. He looked gaunt, and Wilbur wasn't a gaunt person. He was a burly guy who never missed a meal. By the looks of things, Martin had tried to bring him food—there were scattered plates around with hot dogs and raw eggs and other delightful concoctions on them.

"Wilbur, can you speak to us?" Menolly frowned. "I don't

want to lift him up because we don't know what happened—if anything's broken. Call Sharah or Mallen. We need a medic here."

"Please ask Camille to call." I motioned to Smoky and he retreated up the stairs. As he left, I took the light and flashed it up and down Wilbur's body, looking for signs of blood or broken bones. He had peed his pants and, by the smell, probably defecated, but if he'd been down here for some time, he wouldn't have been able to help it. As I shone the light down his legs, I noticed that one of them was twisted in a direction that no leg should be twisted.

"Holy crap, look at that." I motioned for Menolly to take a look.

"Broken, possibly crushed." She took the light and examined his head. He murmured something, but we couldn't understand what he was saying. "I think there's dried blood on his head—skull fracture, maybe?" Another look-see at his arms and we found that one sleeve of his denim jacket was covered in dried blood, the material stuck to his skin.

As I stood up, preparing to go get some water so we could moisten his lips, a noise—like the crackling of lightning—sounded from the other side of the basement. Taking the light, I made my way over to the buzzing. As I peeked down the aisle next to the shelves, a shimmer caught my eye from the very end.

I slowly approached, wondering what the hell it was, when a loud flash sent me reeling against the wall. The next thing I knew, I was on my back, and the flashlight had rolled away from me. As I started to sit up, I found myself facing what appeared to be a Tregart. In front of him stood two zombies. And they were heading toward me.

Chapter 12

❦❧❦

"Crap!" As the zombies came at me, two things became abundantly clear. One—these zombies moved faster than normal zombies. Not a good thing. And two—maybe, just maybe, Wilbur wasn't the one betraying us. The jury was still out on the latter, but there was no time to dwell on it. As I rolled to the side and ducked away from a fist that came raging down to hit the floor, I was becoming more willing to give him the benefit of the doubt. That blow could have split my skull. Just like somebody had split Wilbur's.

I came up, swinging with my dagger. As Lysanthra made contact with the zombie's arm, it let out a muted roar and pulled back. A lot of undead didn't like silver. And she sang with the metal.

"Menolly, get over here now!" As I shouted, the zombies surged forward again. I leaped to the side, trying to dodge both of them. Zombies were brainless, no better than automatons. They would fight until destroyed.

The Tregart stood in back of them, arms crossed, watching with a bemused smile on his face. Apparently, he didn't think much of my chances. And that assessment didn't set well with me.

Realizing they were caging me into a corner, I decided it was time to get out of there and into some open space. The basement ceiling was fairly high—an advantage for me—and I'd been working out a lot over the past few weeks. I slid my dagger back into her sheath as I gauged how far I'd have to jump to get out of their way, then coiled and sprang. Using the wall as a springboard, I catapulted myself over the heads of the zombies. Only I miscalculated and ended up directly in front of the demon.

Crap. I pulled out my dagger again as he held up a heavy chain. Just then, Menolly appeared. She took in the situation and immediately attacked the demon, taking him down as she landed on his back. I wasted no time turning my attention back to the zombies and struck the nearest from behind, bringing the dagger up under its left arm.

The only way to kill a zombie was to take it apart and then destroy the pieces. If you cut it into enough pieces, you'd be good to go—they couldn't reassemble, but the hands could run around on their own and grapple things. So: fingers cut from hands, toes from feet . . . hands cut off arms . . . basic slice-and-dice theory.

The zombie turned and, with its too-fast-to-be-normal speed, slammed me with its right arm, knocking me back.

"Damned undead are all too strong for their own good," I muttered, picking myself up off the floor before it could land on me. I shook my head and circled, trying to gauge an opening. If only I fought with a sword, it might do more damage. But I was determined to take one of these suckers down.

I grit my teeth and made a headlong beeline for my opponent. Zombies are too stupid to dart out of the way, so we collided and my weight took him down. I promptly clamped his arms to his sides with my knees and began trying to slice through the neck to cut off his head.

It wasn't pretty. If he'd been a mummy, wrapped in rags,

not so hard. But staring into the face of someone who had once been alive and deliberately sawing his head off with a dagger—rather gruesome.

I steeled my thoughts. *The life is gone from his body. There is no soul here, merely reanimated flesh. Don't be squeamish. You can do this. You have to do this.*

The other zombie was turning my way, but there wasn't much I could do about it now. I wanted at least one of them out of the way. Menolly was thoroughly tangled up with the Tregart and I couldn't tell who was doing what, but I saw blood and it wasn't hers.

As I struggled to keep the zombie down, a noise sounded beside me as the other zombie slammed his fist into my back.

I lurched forward as he fisted my hair and yanked me back. As my scalp screamed, I let out a shout. He lifted me up and the next thing I knew, I was flying across the room like a spinning top. I turned head over heels in the air, barely able to comprehend what was happening before I landed with a thud against one of the shelves. Moaning, I shook my head and looked up in time to see Menolly backing away from the bloody Tregart. He was holding a piece of sharply pointed wood—not a stake, but a sliver he'd broken off a piece of splintered crate.

"Menolly, get away from him!" I jumped up, a little dizzy, and then stopped as the Tregart pulled out what looked like a large cherry. I recognized that—or at least the basic shape. "Firebomb! We have to get Wilbur out of here!" I turned to run, trying to evade the zombies that were now headed my way.

Menolly turned on her heels and headed opposite the demon. At that moment, Smoky appeared. He stared at the scene as I frantically motioned to Wilbur.

"Get him out of here. Now! Firebomb! Firebomb!"

Smoky sprang into action, letting out a roar that brought Shade and Camille halfway down the stairs.

"No! Go back. Run!" I evaded the grasp of the zombies,

dodging to the right and the left as they closed in on my tail. There was a thud and I glanced over my shoulder. Menolly had grabbed one of them and tossed him against the wall in back of her.

Camille saw the demon and what he was holding and squeaked. She turned tail and headed up the stairs. Shade was at my side the next second and he grabbed my wrist and dragged me forward, away from the remaining zombie.

Menolly caught up with us and, seeing that Smoky was headed up the stairs with Wilbur in his arms, we raced across the basement.

At that moment, the Tregart let out a bark of laughter and there was a flash, so bright that it brought a cry of pain from Menolly even though she wasn't facing it. The timbers shook and groaned, creaking, as flames burst against one wall, engulfing the wood.

This was no simple torch or match—magical firebombs were made to catch hold and burn. Water wouldn't always put out the flames. And when they licked against the skin, they stuck, eating away at the flesh.

A cloud of hot smoke billowed around us, so thick it was hard to see. I began to cough as the haze surrounded us. Shade tightened his grip as I stumbled, pulling me back to my feet. I couldn't see anything. Not the turns, not the shelves, not the crates scattered on the floor. I tripped over something and went down again, my knees landing hard on a metal box. It felt like an army trunk. But Shade never let go; he just pulled me to my feet again, and I skirted the trunk.

The flames were licking the basement walls now, crackling as they caught purchase. Somewhere in the mess, a bottle exploded and a rush of fire and heat swelled up, along with the smell of ammonia. Hell! Wilbur probably stored his spell components down here, and no doubt a number of them were flammable.

My eyes were burning and I couldn't stop coughing as Shade rumbled, "Stairs. Watch your feet."

I gently kicked forward and my toes met the first stair.

I felt with my foot and got my bearings. Then, with one hand on the railing and Shade still firmly gripping the other, I struggled up the stairs.

As we stumbled into the kitchen, I saw that the back door was open and headed for it, with smoke spewing out of the basement stairwell behind me. From the kitchen, I could see that Camille was standing outside, along with Martin, whom she'd managed to persuade to come with her. Wilbur was lying on the grass. Morio and Rozurial were running around from out front.

Smoky headed past me, back toward the basement. "I'll be back in a moment. I might be able to quell the flames." He passed Menolly on the stairs as she came racing up them. She was covered with soot, but she held something in her hands.

"What's that?" I headed down the back steps, with her following me.

"I don't know, but it was sitting near Wilbur and at one point, he pointed to it. I thought I'd bring it up, just in case it's important." We stopped beside Camille, who was closing her cell phone.

"Sharah's almost here. And I called the fire department. If Smoky can quell the worst of the flames, the firemen might be able to take care of the rest when they get here." She frowned. "Wilbur is unconscious, but he's still breathing. He's been hurt pretty bad." She knelt beside him in the mud and wet grass and wiped his forehead. "I need a blanket to cover him with."

Shade nodded. "I'll be right back." He headed for the house, and my first instinct was to say, "No, don't go," but then I realized he had the best chance of making it in and out of there without any repercussions.

As we waited, there was another explosion and all the windows on the left side of the house blew as flames billowed out, engulfing the entire length of the walls. Camille gave a little cry and moved forward, but I stopped her.

"They'll be okay. You know they'll be okay." I was scared, too, but we didn't dare go into the tangle of burning timbers and broken glass.

She bit her lip, nodding. "I hope so. I don't trust anything, anymore."

"Not even the Moon Mother?" I tried to cadge a smile out of her as we waited for our men to emerge from the flames.

She gave me a pensive look. "I trust her to do what she can. But I learned the hard way that even she can't control the world, and can't always stop evil when it rises. But she can comfort. The gods are not omnipotent nor omniscient."

We waited—watching, hoping—until a movement at the kitchen door proved the answer to our prayers. Smoky and Shade emerged, both looking a little worse for wear. Camille jumped up and ran over to Smoky's side while I stayed with Wilbur. She wrapped her arms around his waist as they walked back to us. Shade crouched beside me, staring down at the necromancer.

"How is he?"

"Not good, but Sharah should be here any minute. Is the house a goner?"

Smoky let out a sigh. "I don't know, but even when I breathed an ice storm on it, the flames merely flickered. I think Wilbur's house is doomed."

Just then, the medic unit pulled up, siren screaming, and Sharah slammed open the door, heading toward us on the run. She glanced at the house. "You call the fire department?"

"Yeah, but what we need is someone who can counter sorcery. Shamas! He might be able to stop the flames!" Camille turned to Menolly. "Run home, as fast as you can, and get him."

Menolly took off without a word.

Meanwhile, Sharah was examining Wilbur. She motioned to her assistants. "We need a stretcher here. Get his blood typed; he's lost quite a bit and is in shock. His arm and leg are mangled—I suspect his leg is crushed, and his arm is broken in several places. He may have a skull fracture by the looks of things. He's dehydrated and I doubt if he's eaten in several days. I'm surprised he's not dead."

"Martin was trying to feed him, I think. We found plates of food down there. How long do you think he's been hurt?"

She looked over at me as she started an IV drip of some clear liquid into his unhurt arm. "Several days at least. He lost a lot of weight due to dehydration. Okay, once he's stabilized let's get him back to the hospital." She gathered up her stuff. "He must have the stamina of an elephant, to last through the beating he took. What happened to him?"

I shook my head as Menolly returned, Shamas on her heels. He headed toward the building, stopping just below the back porch steps. Camille and Morio followed him.

"I don't know. We came over here, expecting to have it out with him, but Martin dragged us to the basement, where we found Wilbur. While we were down there, a Tregart and two zombies appeared through some sort of portal. The zombies attacked me while the Tregart let loose a firebomb."

Sharah pressed her lips together. She gave me a wan smile and headed toward the ambulance. I crossed my arms in the chill night as a boiling cloud bank drove in around us. Unnatural and growing darker, it seethed with energy and I glanced over to see Shamas, his arms raised to the sky, with Camille and Morio beside him, hands linked, heads tilted back. I wasn't sure how, or in what way, but they were all working together.

A tremendous crash broke through the night and rain pounded down, so hard it hurt against my skin. Hail quickly followed, as thick as snow, and I dodged the pellets, taking cover beneath a nearby tree with Shade and Smoky. Menolly was watching over Martin, and even though he seemed afraid of her, he obeyed when she made him move beneath the overhanging boughs.

So Shamas could work with the weather? Camille could call the lightning, and Iris and Smoky were adept at frost magic, but working with active weather systems was dangerous. Even I knew that.

But sorcerers liked to control as much as they could of the world. They had no compunctions about summoning beings to do their bidding. But right now, I didn't care, because Shamas's rain and hail were drenching the flames. The water must have been charmed for it to quell the magical fires so quickly.

Whatever the case, as we watched, the flames died down, and within five minutes they were extinguished and the house sat, smoldering, a third of it in ruins. But at least it wasn't burned to the ground.

I looked at Martin. "What the hell are we going to do with him? We can't take him home like a puppy dog."

Menolly groaned. "Oh fuck. Maybe we could tell Wilbur he burned up in the fire and put the guy out of our misery?"

Camille cleared her throat. "As much as I'd like to de-animate Martin, we can't do that. It wouldn't be fair. Not unless Wilbur dies. If that happens, then yes, we go ahead and put Martin to rest. But for now, until we know the truth, we owe it to Wilbur to keep his . . . pet . . . alive."

I stared bleakly at the house. "Just what do you suggest we do with him, then? It's not like we can chain him up outside on a leash. Can we?" A hopeful note crept into my voice. After all, I was the optimist of the group.

Smoky let out a snort. "I cannot believe you women are debating what to do with the creature. I think he should be destroyed, but I can tell you aren't going to allow that. Therefore, it stands to reason that we need to lock him up somewhere. I suggest we store him in the safe room down at the Wayfarer." He turned to Menolly. "What say you?"

She groaned and face-palmed. "Oh geez, do we have to? I mean, Erin's living at Vampires Anonymous now, so it's empty, but really, I don't want a ghoul in my bar."

"He won't be able to get out," I said, eager to have him anywhere but at our house. "He doesn't need food or to go to the bathroom."

"He doesn't need food? Of course he does. Ghouls need flesh to feed on. If you think I'm cooking him a steak to keep him from taking a bite out of one of my customers . . ." Menolly stopped, grimacing. She looked from Smoky to me, then to Camille. "I see you have your minds made up. Fine. But I'm not taking him in my Jag. Somebody else has to take him down."

Morio snickered. "We could put Rodney in there with him. Maybe they'd kill each other off." Rodney was a twelve-inch-tall bone golem who could grow to life size. He could have been the love child of Rodney Dangerfield and Howard Stern . . . only worse.

"Oh gods, I can't imagine that. I wish Grandmother Coyote would take him back. I suppose we should make more use of him, but I hate taking him out of the box, the little freak. I wish we could just bury him and leave him there." Camille shuddered. She hated Rodney. So did I. So did Menolly.

"He's supposed to obey me, but sometimes I worry that he's on the verge of being able to break through my control." Morio stood up and motioned to Martin. "Come on, you freakshow. Let's get you somewhere safe until your daddy is out of the hospital."

I stared at him, stifling a laugh. Camille rolled her eyes, and Menolly snorted. Smoky eyed Martin, frowning.

"I suggest Shade take him down to the Wayfarer. Menolly, I can take you."

Shade swiveled around on his heel. "*Me?* Why me? Why not you?"

Smoky shrugged, a half grin on his face. "You are from the Netherworld. Ghouls are undead. It makes sense." He stood back, pushing back his trench and sliding his hands into his pockets. His hair whipped around, almost dancing.

"I see." Shade's lip quivered, and the two dragons locked gazes. Shade was older than Smoky, but he was only half dragon, and that made a difference. After a moment he let out a little huff, then laughed. "Fine, then. I will take the ghoul."

"Whoever takes the ghoul, fine, but if I'm going down there, we have to get moving. I need to get back before sunrise." Menolly walked over to Smoky. He opened his trench and she slid her arm around his waist.

Shade rolled his eyes. He strode over to Martin and, without ceremony, swept Martin under one arm. Martin stiffened, stared at him, sniffed, and then went limp. What the hell? Ghouls couldn't go comatose. They might shut down and sit still for hours until ordered to do something, but there would still be an unearthly light in their eyes. But Martin—he looked like he'd fainted.

With a laugh at our incredulity, Shade said, "I'm part Stradolan. I have many hidden talents." And then, without another word, he vanished. Smoky followed, taking Menolly with him.

Morio grabbed Camille to him and gave her a sound kiss. "Let's get home, wife. This weather is abominable."

On the walk up the road to our driveway, Camille caught up to Shamas, who was walking a few yards ahead of us. She slid her arm through his and laid her head on his shoulder.

"Thank you," I heard her say.

"For what?" Shamas inclined his head, and his arm snaked around her waist. But his hand stayed well off her butt, which was a good thing by the look on Morio's face as he watched.

"For helping us. For putting out the fire on Wilbur's house. Wilbur is a pain in the ass, but he's helped us in the past. I don't believe he betrayed us. At least . . . I hope he didn't." She hung her head.

Shamas reached down and kissed her hair. Then, with a glance over his shoulder at Morio and me, he gently disentangled himself from her, pulling back.

"It's okay. I understand why you were angry at me. I just hope . . . that at some point you can forgive me and accept that I only want to help you. And . . . Delilah and Menolly, too. I've got a lot to learn, still, but I'm trying." He touched her hand, then turned around and walked up to me.

I stared at him, still not particularly impressed. "Yes?"

"I want to apologize. I want to say I'm sorry to you and Menolly for not treating you better when we were kids. For not . . . treating you properly. I'll try to do better." He held out his hand.

I looked into his eyes and, for the first time, saw a genuine warmth sparkling there—for someone other than Camille. I worried my lip—which hurt because one of my nonretractable fangs pierced the flesh.

"Okay. I believe you. You were a real snot-nosed ass, but . . . I really think you have changed. I accept your apology." As I took his hand, I pulled him toward me and he awkwardly gave me a hug. As I wrapped my arms around him, I whispered, low enough so that Camille couldn't hear, "Thanks."

"Thanks for what? I'm just doing what's right. What I should have done years ago." He tilted his head back, grinning up at me. He looked so much like my sister. And our father.

"For caring about Camille. Losing Father's support has hurt her in so many ways. You . . . I think you can help negate some of those feelings. So thank you for caring for her. But, Shamas, I know you still have feelings for her. And trust me, it's not safe. Not with her husbands."

I could see the protest in his eyes and shook my head. "Don't even say it. I know what I see. Trust me, you're better off finding somebody else. Let go any lingering hopes you may have, and you'll be a lot happier. Consider it a friendly warning, unlike the thrashing you'd get from her men. They forgave Vanzir because of the circumstances. You don't have any such excuse."

Before he could say another word, I let go and caught up to Camille and Morio. Motioning for Shamas to join us, we ran the rest of the way back up the driveway to home.

By the time we got home, Sharah had called, and Smoky and Shade were home. Shade was in the shower. I grinned. Somehow, I didn't think cuddling up to Martin had gone over well with him.

Menolly was waiting in the kitchen. "Sharah says they arrived at the hospital without incident. Wilbur's hanging on. He's in serious condition, but she says he should make it, though he still hasn't woken up. He has a skull fracture—and it's nasty but it will heal. His leg may still have to be amputated, they aren't sure. And his arm was broken in three places. He also suffered three cracked ribs, a broken toe, and multiple burns that look like they were caused by electrical shocks. Probably little bolts of lightning."

The look on her face was daunting. Menolly had been through torture—far more than what any of us had undergone—and she hated it when friends and family were hurt. Even though Wilbur got under her skin, I had the feeling she had grown fond of the big galoot.

"You don't think he betrayed us, either, do you?" I challenged her to answer. "Camille doesn't, I know that much."

Menolly frowned, toying with the hem of her shirt. "Honestly? No. I don't. There has to be some other explanation. Today, once you've had some sleep, I suggest you go over to what's left of Wilbur's house and go through it, searching for anything you can find that might be a clue. The Tregart came back to destroy his house—there has to be a reason. I just hope that he doesn't finish the job before we can get to it."

"You want me to go over now?" I didn't want to—I was exhausted and smelled like smoke. But if Menolly thought it was best, I'd drag myself back over there and go through the smoldering ruins.

She frowned, thinking. "No. Wait till morning. Get some sleep. All of you. Go over when it's light, when you can see what might be lurking in the shadows. By then, maybe Wilbur will have woken up and have some information for us."

A glance at the clock signaled the need for her to return to her lair. She yawned, then disappeared behind the bookcase. I stretched and motioned to the others.

"Time for sleep. We have a full day. We have to find out where Van and Jaycee are. We have to figure out who the man with the spirit seal is and what relationship he has to the others. We have to—" I stopped as Shade appeared in the doorway.

"Come on, woman. We have to *sleep*. Let me carry you

off to bed." Shade pulled me up and we waved good night to Camille and her men. They trailed after us up the stairs as the first rays of dawn broke through the living room window, splashing the room with a faint ray of hope.

Chapter 13

The smell of bacon and eggs woke me up. I blinked, stretching my arms wide as I sat up. The clock read eleven ten. Five hours of sleep would have to do for the day. Shade was already up; his side of the bed was empty.

As I pushed back the comforter, it occurred to me that I was now used to sleeping next to someone every night. That when Shade didn't come to bed at the same time I did, I would doze, keeping one ear open for the fall of his foot on the stairs. I loved his smell, the feel of his skin under my fingers, the lazy, smooth tone of his voice, the safe way I felt around him, as if he could protect me from all the world's evil, even though I knew he couldn't.

I love him. I really love him. I twisted the heavy smoky quartz ring around on my right ring finger. It hadn't come off since I'd first put it on, the day I met Shade. Yeah, it seemed at home there. Leaving it, I took a quick shower and then dressed in jeans and a sweater. As I headed down the stairs, my heart felt a little lighter, even though I knew we were facing a long day.

* * *

Camille, Morio, Shade, and I headed over to check out Wilbur's house, while Smoky attended to some business out at his barrow. We always left someone at home to watch over Hanna, Maggie, and the house—and that was especially important now that Iris was gone on her honeymoon. Iris could wield a magical punch that easily rivaled any of our powers, but Hanna was mortal. One of the Northmen, yes, but mortal, regardless.

Vanzir and Roz were on guard duty today. Shamas had gone in to work. And Trillian had volunteered to tackle the grocery shopping on his own, a daunting task for three people, let alone one.

The fire department had made sure all the smoldering embers were out, and now the house steamed lightly but was no longer in danger of burning. Yellow caution tape wound around the structure, but Chase had talked to the fire marshal and he had left the investigation up to us. As we picked through the rubble, looking for any signs of—well, anything important—my phone rang. It was Tim.

"The Supe Council agreed with you that we need an emergency meeting. It's on for tonight at eight p.m., at the Vampires Anonymous hall. Can you be there?" He was shuffling through papers and I heard him take a swig of something. Tim was addicted to diet cola and drank the stuff by the gallon.

"Yeah, we'll be there. Nice of the VA to let us use their hall." Vampires and Weres didn't always get along, and a lot of the Supe Community members were shifters of one sort or another.

"More than just let you use it. Roman apparently sent orders that it be opened, and there will be ambassadors from the Vampire Nation in attendance from the Court of the Crimson Veil." He sounded impressed, and well he should.

I blinked. Menolly must have put in a call to Roman before she went to bed. Roman was one of the sons of the Vampire Queen Blood Wyne. She had recently come out of her reclusive state to stand at the helm of the Vampire Nation again, and within a short period—three weeks—every vampire conclave across the world had knelt to her. Those who chose to ignore her re-ascendance were no longer aboveground. Either they'd been staked by her servants, or they'd gone into hiding. As Roman's official consort, Menolly was privy to a lot of secret information.

"Eight o'clock then. Tim—be careful. And we need to talk—"

"About the proxy server? Shamas called me and explained, the best he could, what you guys were up to. I'm on it. I'll have the info for you tonight on how to route through. Just give me a little time to set it up for you." With that, he kiss-kissed through the phone and hung up.

"Tim is worth ten times what he's getting paid. I wish we could offer him more money, but the Supe Community isn't wealthy." I picked up a charred piece of wood—it looked to be from the dining table—and tossed it to the side. "So much for that table. If Menolly hadn't remembered seeing it, Wilbur probably would have died. In a sense, my seeing Wylie's thoughts inadvertently saved Wilbur's life."

"You're right. The Hags of Fate have a way of weaving their webs, don't they?" Camille headed into the living room, which was smoke damaged but still fairly intact. "I'm going to check through Wilbur's desk."

As she rifled through his desk, Shade and I looked down into the stinking hole that had been the basement. The stairs were gone, and the drop looked precarious. The ceiling of the basement was on thin ice. I didn't trust it not to cave in. And then, an image flashed through my thoughts. *Menolly, holding something, as we knelt beside Wilbur in the torrential rain.*

"Come on!" I headed down the back steps, which had managed to survive the blast, over to where we'd laid out Wilbur the night before.

Shade followed, while Morio stayed inside with Camille. "What did you think of?"

"Last night, Menolly found something that Wilbur had

been pointing to. In all the excitement, she set it aside and we never bothered picking it up. I want to see what it is." I hurried over to where Wilbur had been stretched out on the ground. After a moment of scouting around, I saw it: a small black bag, right near where Menolly had been sitting. "There!"

Shade cautiously picked it up and turned it over in his hands. "Feels awfully heavy for such a small bag."

"Open it."

"I think we'd better have Morio check for traps or magical spells. He has that ability." Shade motioned toward the house, and we headed back. When we got there, Camille was sitting at the desk, absorbed in a handwritten journal.

"What did you find?" Morio said. He was flipping through a sideboard.

"I don't know, but we wanted you to look it over first. You have the ability to decipher magical traps?" Shade held up the bag.

Morio frowned. "Some. Give it to me." He set it on the coffee table and sat down on the lumpy sofa. A waft of dust rose up and I coughed, waving away the slightly stale scents of beer, rotting fruit, and cigar smoke.

Camille glanced up. "Wilbur is one strange puppy. He recorded everything, which can only help us. He seems to have had a pathological need to journal every aspect of his day. And trust me, you do not want to know all of his secrets. There will never be enough brain bleach to cleanse out some of the imagery he's left me with." She shivered.

"Like what?" I was a sucker for bad gossip, but more than that, the more we knew about Wilbur, the better.

"Like, Wilbur was expecting company four nights ago. Apparently he thought some old friends were showing up, from his time in the special ops. But he calls them Mango and Trent and refers to them both as 'he' . . . not Van and Jaycee. Here he said they contacted him via phone call to let him know they were in town and would like to meet up."

"They scammed him. Van and Jaycee . . . you want to make a bet?"

"Not throwing away money on that one. Of course it was

them. But he thought they were old buddies from his military days. They must have done some research on his background." She paused, then added, "He wrote that they were looking for a favor but couldn't talk about it on the phone. He thought they probably needed a place to crash."

"Apparently not. Wonder what they wanted?"

"I can tell you what they were after." Shade looked up from the bag. Morio had examined it, then shook his head and handed it back.

"What?"

"This." He withdrew a small journal and flipped through it. "Background information on you three, on Smoky, Morio, Trillian. On Iris, Nerissa . . ." As Shade flipped through the pages, his frown deepened. "Carter. He knows about Carter and Vanzir—that they're demons. And . . . fuck. A page about the history of the spirit seals. Wilbur knows all of your secrets, including that you've been taking the spirit seals to Queen Asteria."

"How the crap did he get all of that?" I jumped up, panicked. "He knows about Shadow Wing, doesn't he?"

Shade nodded. "Yes, it appears he does."

"Holy fuck. I just found out what the connection between Martin and Wilbur is." Camille looked up, a pained expression on his face. "Wilbur . . . Martin was his brother."

"What?" I cocked my head, frowning. "What do you mean?"

"Martin was Wilbur's little brother. He was an accountant, and he died a few years ago of cancer. Three weeks ago was the anniversary of Martin's death and Wilbur wrote about it. About how he still didn't understand why someone so caring . . . had to die that way." She pushed back the journal, looking vaguely ill. "I guess Wilbur decided to do the only thing he knew how. He brought Martin back, to be with him. Martin's not his slave. Martin's his *family*."

Her words echoed in the room as we stood silent. That Wilbur even *had* a family seemed extraordinary. But then . . . everybody had a family. Even if they were no longer here.

"It's okay." I crossed the room and dropped my arm around her shoulder. "We need to read his journal. We need to know what he's planning. He knows all about us. He knows about the demonic war. That can change the tide of events."

"He hid the information from Van and Jaycee," Camille said. She looked up at me, a pained expression on her face. "He clammed up and hid the information. That's why they beat the crap out of him. They must have returned to see if they could ransack the place and find what they were looking for. But we were already here, so the Tregart did the only thing he could think of and blew up the joint. But he didn't try hard enough."

I sat down beside her, suddenly understanding just what Wilbur had done. He'd put his life on the line to protect us and our secrets. "Somehow, they found out he was keeping tabs on us, and so they pretended to be buddies to gain access to the house. Do you realize that—with the info in this journal—they could mount a raid on Queen Asteria for the spirit seals we've taken her? We can't leave this lying around."

I flipped through the pages, noticing that Wilbur had collected background information that even my sisters and I didn't know about. Like, for example, the fact that Chase's IQ was considered in the genius range. I paused, thinking we could learn a lot by reading the rest of this. But Camille took it out of my hands.

"Either we trust our allies, or we don't. We can't have it both ways." Her voice was soft, but her meaning was clear. "Wilbur didn't betray us. He almost died trying to protect this from the demons."

"You're right." I took the journal and handed it to Shade. "Burn it to ashes. Now."

"No." Morio said. "Seems to me like we want to know exactly what he has on us."

I paused, flip-flopping like a fish out of water. "Morio makes a good point."

She blanched, but shrugged. "Two against one. Shade—what do you think?"

"Lady Camille, I think you worry too much about what your family and friends will think. If no one has anything to hide, they won't mind us reading this. If they do, then best we find out now and not later." Shade took the book and handed it to me. "Delilah, you keep this for now. And when we get home, put it in a safe place where no one can find it. We should make sure there are no magical tracers on it—"

"There aren't." Morio stood, dusting his jeans. "I checked. I guess we should take Wilbur's diary, too. And other than that . . . we're done here?"

Camille's phone rang and she pulled out her cell. "Hello?" She listened for a moment, then said, "We'll be there. Right. Thanks, Sharah," and hung up and turned to us. "Wilbur's awake and coherent. Time to go ask him some questions."

"That should be a ton of laughs." I shoved the dossier into my backpack, and we headed out. Wilbur's life had taken on an oddly familiar feel. And I wasn't sure I wanted to know him as well as I did now.

As we walked into the ICU ward at the FH-CSI, the smell of disinfectant was overwhelming. Machines clicked and beeped, and the sterile white of the bedclothes and walls belied the injuries that came through here. While Wilbur was an FBH, the fact was he was still considered a member of the Supe Community, and Sharah had decided to treat him here rather than take him to the regular hospital.

He was swathed in bandages. His leg was in a splint, his arm in another. He had bandages wrapped around his head, and bruises covered what we could see of his body. Sharah had shaved him, and I was surprised to see that he was actually a decent-looking man under the brush that had been his beard and mustache. He looked woozy, but awake.

"Hey, Wilbur." I walked up to the bed railing and put my hands on them, staring down at his prone body.

"Well, if it isn't the pussycat." His voice was rough, harsh, as if he'd been smoking too long, and he coughed. "I understand I have you and yours to thank for me being alive."

I shrugged. "Yeah, I guess. Actually, Martin led us to the basement."

"You were prowling in my house in the middle of the night." A statement, rather than a question. "You find those sacks of garbage that did this to me? Van and Jaycee? I thought you guys killed them off."

Shaking my head, I glanced over at Camille. She shrugged. He knew far more than we had thought he did, so we might as well be straight about this. But obviously, some of his info was off target.

"They posed as buddies from the service, didn't they?"

His nose took on a pinched look. "You've been reading my journal."

"You've been keeping notes on us. We found them. Fair is fair."

With an exaggerated sigh, which brought on a coughing fit and then a moan as his fractured ribs took the brunt of it, he let out a short bark of laughter.

"I guess, babe. I guess. Yeah, they posed as army buddies. Called me out of the blue. Set up a time to come over and have a beer. I had no reason to suspect them. As far as I knew, Trent and Mango were still alive. I opened the door and they strong-armed their way in. Had a group of them damned demons with them. Demanded to know everything I knew about you. Wanted my notebook—"

A frightened look crossed his eyes—the only time I'd ever seen Wilbur actually look afraid—and he struggled to sit up. Sharah forced him back on the pillow.

"My journal—did they get it?"

"The one you kept all your notes about us in? No. They didn't. We have it. I'd like to know why the hell you are keeping tabs on us, though. But how did they know you had it in the first place?" I was trying to piece together the puzzle, but he was going to have to clue us in on a few things. Wilbur could be an odd duck, but he'd never been stupid.

He closed his eyes. "We talked on the phone several times. I thought it was Trent. He knew about our missions, he knew secrets that only Trent and Mango and I had known.

I told him about you guys, and about that fact that I'd been keeping tabs on you. I didn't mention the demons, though. He . . . pulled a crock of shit over my eyes."

Wincing at the image, I thought about it. "What was Trent? What did he do? Was he a necromancer, too?"

Wilbur shut his eyes. "No, not that I know of. He was into other weird shit, though. I'm not sure what, but it never seemed dangerous, which is why I wanted to see him again. Everything was okay when we last saw each other. We parted on good terms, he to his life, me to mine."

At the tone in his voice, I suddenly understood. Not only was Martin Wilbur's family, but his buddies had been family, too. And like most old friends, Wilbur thought they'd be picking up where they left off. Only it hadn't been Trent. It had been Van on the other end of the line.

"I'm laying bets on the probability that Van had tracked down Trent and got the goods on you some time ago. Maybe even the first time you walked into Van and Jaycee's magic shop."

"The one her dragon butthead managed to thoroughly trash?" Wilbur forced a pained grin at Camille.

She leaned over the railings, making sure her boobs were in full sight. "Dude, they aren't stupid. I'll bet they recognized your abilities and decided to dig up dirt on you in case they ever needed to use you."

"And how do you figure that?" His eyes lit up, but she stayed out of reach of his good hand.

"Because that's something we would have thought of. And if we could have thought of it, you *know* the bad guys are smart enough to."

"Martin!" Wilbur suddenly panicked, struggling again to sit up. "Martin—is he okay? Did they . . ."

"He's fine. We're looking after him until you're back on your feet." I reassured him and, calm again, he rested his head against the pillows.

"I'm sorry," he said after a moment. "I'm sorry I didn't think. I'm sorry I put you guys in danger. I know what you're doing—by now you know that. I know what you're fighting against. I wanted to make sure you weren't out to take over the country but . . . just . . . I'm sorry." He closed his eyes, breathing softly, and I realized he'd fallen asleep.

I patted his hand and motioned to Sharah as we walked outside. "Keep a guard on him. He's in danger until we catch those sorcerers."

She nodded as we walked toward the front of the ward. "He's not out of danger from his injuries either, though I think he'll pull through. But he's probably going to lose that leg. It's so crushed that despite Mallen's needlework, we couldn't connect most of the blood vessels. We'll know in twenty-four hours whether we have to amputate."

"I wish we knew just how much he told Van and Jaycee about us." I held up my hand as Camille started to speak. "I know he didn't mean to—he didn't intentionally betray us, but the fact is that he *did* talk. And now we have no clue if they know about where we took the spirit seals or not."

Camille let out a long breath. "You're right, of course. That's our biggest danger here, isn't it? If they find out Queen Asteria has the spirit seals, Elqaneve will be on the pointy end of the stick. They'll marshal the goblins from Guilyotin and march on the Elfin city. Even if they can't gate enough demons through, they'll use goblins and ogres and whoever else they can pull into their dirty little war. So, where do we go from here?"

"We make sure Martin's okay, and then visit Carter. And then, we head out for the Supe Community meeting." I slid into the passenger seat of the car.

Camille slid into the driver's seat, drawing her feet in and slamming the door before fastening the seat belt. Morio and Shade rode in back; I took shotgun. As soon as we were all situated, she pulled out the parking lot, and we headed over to visit Carter.

Carter, the son of a demon and a Titan, was far more than he appeared to be. He walked with a limp and a brace on one leg, and his shaggy red hair was meticulously kept in a trendy do. Two horns rose, spiraling, from his head, to belie his demonic heritage. Carter kept tabs on the demonic visitations to Seattle, and he had records going back for several hundred years. He also was a member of the Demonica Vacana society, a secret society that observed and—at times—interfered in the goings-on with demons in human society.

He lived in a modest basement apartment in the Broadway district, a haven to junkies and hookers. But he was in no danger, and a magical "go-away" zone surrounded the sidewalk outside the steps leading down to his apartment, discouraging lowlifes and criminals from hanging around.

I knocked at the door and, after a moment, it opened. Carter peered out, eyeing us, then stood back to allow us in. We hadn't been around much the past couple of months and weren't sure just how eager he was to see us.

"What can I do for you?" He was as polite as ever but seemed a little more aloof. Carter had been the foster father to a beautiful mute daughter named Kim, until recently.

"We have something to tell you, and we want your take on the issue." He motioned for us to sit down in the worn but genteel living room. The velvet sofa was spotless; so were the thick rugs that covered up the concrete floor. Everything looked as it always had, but the apartment felt a little more empty.

Then the curtains to his kitchenette opened, and a man walked out, probably in his early thirties, carrying a tea tray with tea and cookies on it. He looked human, but that was no guarantee he was. But Carter smiled up at him, and motioned for the man to sit with us.

"I want to introduce you to my new assistant. This is Tobias. Toby, meet Delilah and Camille D'Artigo, Morio, and Shade." He gave the other man a sly smile, and it was returned in kind. Right then, I knew. Carter had a boyfriend. Nothing about our prior interactions had told us anything about Carter's love life, and we'd never asked.

We murmured hello, and Carter glanced at Toby. "We need some privacy. If you wouldn't mind?"

"What would you like me to do?" Tobias started to stand. Carter reached out and stroked his hand. Toby ducked his head.

"If you could go organize the new photographs we got in, I'd appreciate it." Carter watched as the lithe man excused himself and headed into the back room. After Toby was out of the room, he looked back at us and blushed. Seeing a demigod blush delighted me, for some reason. It meant that, as powerful as Carter was, he still had a spark of humanity to him, even though he'd never been anything remotely resembling human.

"When did Toby start working with you?" I was determined to needle him just a little about it. After all, that was what friends did. And Carter was our friend.

He glanced up at me, and a little smirk crossed his face. "About two months ago. He was working for a client of mine. We . . . the attraction was immediate. So he came to work for me. It won't last. He's one of the djinn, and they don't make good long-term lovers. But it will be fun for the duration. And I needed the company. And the help."

"Can you trust a djinn?" Camille frowned. I knew that look. It said she didn't trust Toby any more than she trusted a skunk in heat.

"No, but that is why he is not allowed access to private information, and why he doesn't have a key to my place. Do not trouble yourself, young witch, I will not compromise the integrity of my operations with a veil of sex haze. But it has been a long time since I've found someone to my liking, and I plan to enjoy myself in the meantime. And before you ask, I don't ask what equipment my lovers have, merely if they want to play."

That was the only time I'd ever seen Carter look lecherous in the least, but the look on his face told me that his mild manner and genteel ways masked a deeply passionate nature, and I found myself catching my breath, a little afraid. Good thing his tastes didn't run to our direction. Demons like Vanzir and Rozurial were easier to identify with than someone who was the son of a Titan.

"Whatever the case. We need to tell you what's been going on and see if you have any suggestions." We laid out everything that had happened. Carter's mood turned from flirtatious to somber.

"Does Wilbur have information on me in that book of his?"

I nodded. I'd flipped through it before hiding it at home when we headed out to interview Wilbur. "Yes. He knows who you are, he knows your background, and he knows about the Society. I have no clue how long it took Wilbur to amass this information, or where he got all of it, but he seems to know too many secrets about too many people."

"Then we will need to take him under our wing. If he resists, we'll have to take further action. In the meanwhile, I will search for information on the man with the spirit seal. If he's connected with the Koyanni, it should not be difficult for me to ferret out his background. I'll call you as soon as I learn anything. In the meantime, walk softly and keep your eyes open."

As we headed for the door, Carter stopped us. "One last thing. You *must* go to the Elfin Queen and tell her of the danger. She has to be prepared, should the unthinkable happen."

And on that note, we headed home for a quick nap and dinner before the Supe Community meeting. There was so much on my mind that I felt a million miles away.

Chapter 14

❧❧❧

Vampires Anonymous was rocking by the time we took a nap, ate dinner, and drove to the hall, in what had once been the home of Sassy Branson, socialite vampire who had been on our side until her predator nature overtook her.

She'd bequeathed her mansion to the group, and now it was used as both halfway house to help vamps new to the life and the headquarters for the Pacific Northwest Regency of the North American Branch of the Vampire Nation. That was the long title for Frederick Corvax's position. But everybody just called him the Regent, according to Menolly.

The mansion was surrounded by an electric fence and patrolled by hired guards during the day, by vampire guards at night. It had taken on the appearance of a fortress, but considering the fear vampires struck among the general populace, that wasn't surprising. They were slowly assimilating into the public's mindset, but while the Weres hadn't had such a hard time being accepted, or the Fae, the vampires were the last bastion of discrimination.

Tonight, the guards were on full alert. I recognized

several vampires from Wade's VA group—including Brett, a comic book fiend who had taken on the superhero alter ego of Vamp-Bat once he was turned. But most looked hardened and experienced. Roman must have moved a new group of soldiers into the area when he officially took over for his mother.

Menolly had gone on ahead, as both Roman's official consort and a founding member of the Supe Community. Even though Roman wouldn't be there, she was expected to put in an appearance.

Smoky had come, along with Trillian, Vanzir, and Rozurial. Shade and Morio stayed home to watch over Hanna and Maggie. I saw a shimmer in the trees and a group of Fae walked through a portal—reps from the Triple Threat, no doubt. This was shaping up to be one of the biggest meetings we'd ever had.

As we pulled through the gates, I steeled myself. Facing the community wasn't going to be easy, considering the pull Exo Reed had exuded. The backlash could tear the Supe Community apart, if our enemies had generated enough fear.

We entered the foyer. In the intervening time since Sassy had died the final death and Wade had taken over, the mansion had gone from genteel home to spacious but official offices. The personal touches were gone, while the elegance remained.

"Hello, the Mistress is waiting in the meeting room." Erin Marshal, Menolly's sired adult child, bounced over, a spring in her step I hadn't seen since before she was turned. Erin had been through a lot, but now she was the official secretary for the VA, and she was doing an excellent job. Wade was helping her make all the adjustments she needed to know for her new life and she was learning far faster than she had with Sassy. She lived here, on site.

"Hi, Erin. Good to see you." Camille raised her hand, shyly smiling. She and Erin had been good friends before Erin was turned. Now, they seldom got a chance to talk. Erin still needed to learn how to react around the living without supervision, and Camille never knew what to say.

Erin gave her a fangy smile and waved, before clutching her clipboard to her chest and taking off again.

We filed into what had been the parlor. Now a meeting room, it—and the smaller office next to it—had been opened up to form one large hall. Devoid of the heavy furniture Sassy had loved, it had plenty of space for a large group to congregate.

Camille and I moved to the front of the room along with Morio, while the others took seats in the first row. Menolly was waiting for us, talking to a European-looking man who wore a very expensive suit. Frederick Corvax. He gave me the chills, almost more so than Roman. Frederick had that same suave European feel that Roman did, but he hadn't had time to assimilate to American culture. Roman had some semblance of familiarity, even though he was a vampire. Frederick was cold and aloof.

As we took our seats up front, I glanced over the sea of faces. They were somber, some tearful. Five deaths in the Supe Community had a far-reaching effect. Everybody had been touched in one way or another. From losing family and friends to the fear of being the next random target, the worry was apparent on every face in the room.

After a few minutes, Menolly and I stood up and approached the microphone. We could probably be heard without it, but considering there were well over one hundred people packed into the room, we decided to go for it.

"Welcome to the February meeting of the Supe Community Council." I took a long breath, then plunged in. We'd do this by the book; that way it would assuage panic. I started with reading the minutes from the past meeting, then moved on to thanking Frederick—and Roman, by default—for the use of the meeting hall.

After a moment, I looked out over the sea of faces. How to dive in? How do you warn a group of people that they may *all* be targets because of the grudge of some madmen?

"We have a problem. By now, I'm sure all of you have heard about the explosion that happened at the Supe Community Hall. Here are the bare bones of the case." I laid out the facts of what had happened, leaving out the demonic overtones. I also made sure to include Andy Gambit's poking around the ruins the next morning. "We don't want you to bother Gambit, but we have to do something to counter him. We have to discuss this as a community. Before we address that, we have a bigger problem. But first, any questions?"

As I looked around, one of the Blue Road Tribe were-bears raised his hand. I pointed to him. "Jonas?"

"Was the explosion a hate crime?" He stood, a big bear of a man, burly and looking like a linebacker in a three-piece suit. With curly black hair and a tidy goatee, he looked like he could rip my head off without blinking.

I shook my head. "Your question brings me to the bigger issue I mentioned. This was not a hate crime in the sense you're thinking. This wasn't the Church of the Earthborn Brethren or the Freedom's Angels who did this. Remember when the werewolves were killed a few months ago? We are facing the same problem again. Koyanni have moved into the area."

Before even the thought of a backlash could occur, I quashed the seeds. "This is not the fault of the upstanding coyote shifters who live here—Marion's family and the others. She lost her sister to them. No, we *know* the Koyanni moved in and they are aiming for her as much as they are for us. They've brought sorcerers with them. The explosion was caused, as far as we can tell, by a fire charm. And before the explosion, they struck at Wilbur Folkes, a friend and neighbor of ours. We found him this morning—still alive, but severely injured. They've also terrorized the Davinaka Mall and killed two people there."

Jonas nodded. "What can we do? Who will they strike next?"

I glanced at Menolly. She nodded for me to answer.

"We don't know," I said, turning back to answer him. "The fact is that we have no idea who they're going to target next. We're following up leads to find them as quickly as we can. But until then, we have to band together. Check with your friends and neighbors. Make certain you don't go out alone—go in a pack."

"How is that going to stop them from blowing up some-place else? It just means more people might get hurt at once." Another man stood. I placed him from the Olympic Wolf Pack but didn't remember his name.

I wanted to reassure him. I wanted to offer some sort of guarantee, but the facts were that we couldn't assure anyone of anything. "It's not. But it may prevent these same sorcer-ers from dragging off lycanthropes again to make Wolf Briar, which they were doing before."

A hush descended over the meeting, and then—after a moment—a lithe young woman stood. She was from the Puget Sound Harbor Seal Pod.

"This is the first time we've heard about the Wolf Briar. Why wasn't this knowledge handed out to the community earlier—like when it happened?"

As I struggled to reassure people that we hadn't deliber-ately tried to deceive them, a movement caught my eye and the next thing I knew, Frederick was standing beside me.

He motioned for me to move away. "People, calm your-selves. The vampires will stand with you. Even though we have a long history of distrust with our Were brethren, the fact remains we are all part of the Supe Community, and the Court of the Crimson Veil pledges its support in this matter."

As the hush in the room died down, a tall, thin woman approached the front. I recognized her as one of Aeval's right-hand women.

"I am Natassia, from the Court of Shadow and Darkness. I am authorized to pledge the support of the Court of the Three Queens. The Fae stand beside the Weres and the Vam-pires." She politely inclined her head and stepped next to Frederick.

Breathing a sigh of relief, I turned back to the room. "We may not have the information we really need right now, but we have allies. The more of us on the lookout, the better."

Menolly set up a couple large photographs—or the next best thing. We'd managed to come up with composites that were nearly as accurate as actual photos.

"These two are . . . sorcerers. They go by the names Van and Jaycee. They'll be hanging out with a rough group— may look like bikers, but don't underestimate them. They're strong and they're deadly. We're going to pass out smaller photos for you to take with you. Show them to friends and family. Keep your eyes open and call us day or night if you see them. Do not take them on yourselves; these suckers *can and will* kill you."

After we'd passed out the flyers, there wasn't much more we could do. I fielded a few questions about sorcery, passing the more technical ones off to Camille. Menolly reiterated the info that sorcerer's fire could seriously harm vampires, too.

As I was trying to think of some way to wind up the meeting on a positive note, the meeting hall door opened and three FBHs walked through. Two women and a man. They paused.

I turned to them. "May we help you?"

"I hope so . . . This is the Supe Community Council meeting, isn't it?" The taller woman stepped forward. She was wearing a leather trench coat over a nice pair of gray trousers and a white turtleneck.

"It is." I paused, waiting. I knew the guards had searched them, so there shouldn't be any danger, but given the events of the past few days, I was leery.

"My name is Amanda Flanders, and this is Neely Reed and Carlos Rodrigues. We're from the United Worlds Church. I'm sorry we're late, but we had another meeting to attend. We have a proposition for your members." She pulled off her gloves and stuffed them in her pocket.

Everyone was leaning forward, listening. FBHs usually weren't invited into our meetings, but I motioned for them to approach the microphone. Menolly cocked her head, giving me a quizzical look, but I just gestured for her to wait.

Amanda stepped up to the microphone and cleared her

throat. "Hello. We are members of the United Worlds Church, and we'd like to bridge the gap between Supes and FBHs by forming an anti-hate organization called All Worlds United in Peace. It will be a secular group focused on working together to promote understanding between the races. Many of us come from families who suffered intolerance and prejudice. It's time to turn Seattle back into what it once was—one of the most friendly cities in the nation."

She passed me one of their pamphlets, and I glanced through it. The premise looked good, and they seemed sincere. I nodded for them to hand out their brochures to the audience.

As people flipped through the pages, I glanced at their mission statement.

The goal of AWUP is to promote harmony between the races sharing this world, whether human, Were, vampire, Fae, or otherwise unknown. We seek to create and implement a vision for the future that is inclusive, rather than exclusive. We seek to lobby for the rights of the entire Supe Community, and to act in unison. When one member of AWUP is harmed, all members come to harm.

As I looked up at the audience, I saw people nodding, and then, slowly, excited whispers began to fill the room. As people moved forward to chat with our guests, I moved back beside Menolly.

"You think they're on the up-and-up?" I was surprised that the thought of duplicity even occurred to me. I was the optimist of the group. But I'd seen too much lately and realized I'd never be naïve again.

Menolly, the one usually quickest to jump to conclusions, paused, watching the interaction out on the main meeting floor. After a moment, she cocked her head.

"You know, I think they are. I have a good feeling about this. We've been needing something to pull everybody together, and the fact that FBHs are extending a peace offering may mean we pull some people off the fence. We aren't out to win over the haters. We need to focus on those who haven't made up their minds—the ones who don't take part in the hate crimes but don't do anything about it."

"Good analysis." I paused as Neely tapped me on the arm. She was a pretty black woman, short and curvy, with short curly hair.

"Excuse me, but the Regent told me I might want to talk to you."

"What can I do for you?"

"May we speak in private?" She looked around, a little nervous.

I motioned for her to follow me into the hall. Once we were out of the hubbub, she sat down on the stairway leading up to the second floor. The steps were polished, the railing newly finished. The vamps had updated Sassy's home and made it shine. It had always been pretty, but now it was exquisite.

"So, Neely, what do you want to talk about?" I sat down beside her, leaning back, resting my elbow on the step behind me.

She blushed, smiling. "I wanted to know . . . I'm studying Inter-World studies at the UW. I want to write my master's thesis on what Otherworld is like. I'd like to arrange for a trip—escorted, of course—to Otherworld for a week so I can get a feel for what it's really like. I hope to eventually write a book on Otherworld from an FBHs point of view."

I blinked. A lot of people had expressed a desire to go to OW, but the OIA had put a kibosh on any unofficial travel. However, we were no longer employed by the OIA. "I can't really help you out right now, but I'll see what I can find out about the possibility of a tour. Meanwhile, it's not the same, but my sisters and I can talk to you . . . answer some of your questions." The United Worlds Church had made an effort to reach out to us; the least we could do was return the favor.

"I'd like that." She held out her hand, and I took it. Her skin was warm and her grip friendly. "You like fish and chips?" she asked.

I nodded, grinning. "Anything that involves French fries or potato chips is good to go by me. Why?"

"Because I work at Abby's Fish House part time to help pay for my tuition. You come by some afternoon and I'll fry you up the best batch of fish and chips you've ever tasted."

As we scheduled a lunch date for next week, my cell phone rang. I held up one finger, mouthed an apology, and flipped open the phone. There was a hushed silence, and then I heard a faint whisper on the other end.

"Delilah, I need your help. This is Marion. I'm at the library. I think someone's following me, and I'm afraid to go out to my car alone. I don't want to ask somebody to walk with me in case it's the Koyanni. They wouldn't think twice about killing some innocent person trying to help."

I'd assumed Marion was at the meeting, but when I thought back to the crowd inside, I realized that I hadn't seen her all evening. "Where are you?"

"I'm at the Seattle Public Library on the Book Spiral. The library's about to close in ten minutes and I'll have to get out of here."

I glanced at the clock. We weren't far away. "Go down to the front desk and stay there. I'll call Chase. If we don't make it in time, he and his men should."

Punching the End Talk button, I immediately speed-dialed Chase and asked him to send a car with two of his burliest Supe officers to the library to meet Marion. "We're on the way."

Waving to Neely and promising to see her in a week, I hurried into the meeting room and dragged Menolly and Camille out. "We have to head to the library. *Now.* Give Trillian your keys and he can follow with the guys if we need them. For now, let's just see what we're facing."

We piled into my Jeep. Menolly followed in her Jaguar. We weren't far from the library, and traffic was sparse. The lights were with me and we sped through the streets without having to stop. Within nine minutes, we were at the library. I saw a squad car parked out front.

As we headed up the sidewalk, we found Shamas and Yugi standing next to Marion by the front doors. The library proper had just closed and we could see librarians working inside, clearing up for the night.

"What's going on, Marion?" I glanced around. The last of the patrons were exiting the building, and no one appeared to be paying much attention to us.

"I was up on the Book Spiral, browsing the stacks. I didn't feel up to seeing a bunch of people tonight, so I didn't go to the meeting. I don't deal well with the whole condolences thing." She bit her lip. "I knew people would be solicitous about Trixie, and I'm just not up to fielding sympathy tonight. You know?"

I nodded. Sometimes grief was hard enough to bear without all of the outpouring of empathy. "So you came to the library to get some peace."

"Right. I was looking for a couple of travel books—I've been thinking about taking a vacation to the East Coast. Maine, maybe the Hamptons, though I'm not that thrilled by being around the upper-crust set. Go beachcombing . . . stay at a bed-and-breakfast, spend the nights reading, the days antiquing in small towns."

She bit her lip and hung her head. "I'm telling Douglas that I want a divorce. We've grown our separate ways. The kids are out of the house; they don't need us anymore. I need some *me* time, to just think about what I want to do the rest of my life."

We had known Marion since we met her while helping out our friend Siobhan, but we didn't know a lot about her home life. I wasn't sure what to say. She seemed resigned, but not terribly unhappy.

"Okay, so what happened?"

"I was in the stacks. I began to feel like I was being watched. I started keeping an eye out—there were a couple of guys a ways behind me. One caught my attention—there was something familiar about him." She looked at me. "You know how you can feel when you're near another Were of your own kind?"

I nodded. There was an unexplainable feeling of recognition when I was around werecats—big or small. A sense of feline connectedness.

"It was like that. I swear he was a coyote shifter, and he felt dirty. I'm not sure about the other one. Anyway, I got nervous, took my books, and moved farther along the Spiral. After a little while, I glanced back and saw them again. This time, they were leaning against the wall, and the shaggy-haired one was still watching me. Right then, I sensed danger—he looked like a coyote watching a rabbit." She shivered. "That's when I called you."

"What happened when you headed down to the first level? Did they follow you?" If they had been among those filing out of the building, we'd lost them.

"I don't know. After I called you, I saw that the elevator was ready to open for an older woman and two other men who were waiting. So, I hurried in with them and pressed the Door Close button. By the time I got to the first floor, I couldn't see them anywhere." She folded her arms, rubbing her shoulders. "Something just didn't feel right about them. I'm scared. I don't scare easy."

Camille leaned against the wall. "Do you know why they might be following you?"

"I don't know . . . except . . . I'm the one who originally told you about the Koyanni. If they found that out, then they might be out for revenge."

"Everything's probably okay, but we'll run you home just to make sure. Come on. Let's go." I motioned for Shamas and Yugi to follow us, giving them Marion's address on the way out. Marion rode with me, while Camille went with Menolly. We left Camille's car for the guys to drive home.

We were within two blocks when we heard the sirens. I sped up while Marion clutched her purse. She leaned forward as far as the seat belt would allow, trying to get a good view out the window, but it was so dark that all we could see were a few sparks flying up into the sky above the roofline.

As we pulled up toward her house, fire trucks came roaring in, sirens blasting, and I swerved to the side, letting them

pass. Marion struggled with her seat belt, unfastening it and
jumping out of the car before I could stop her. She raced
down the street toward her house.

Menolly and Camille were parked behind me; they'd
swung in right behind us. As I unbuckled my seat belt,
Menolly streaked by, on the heels of Marion. Camille came
running by as I hit the pavement and we followed. We passed
two houses and then I skidded to a halt. The next house—
Marion's home—was blazing, flames shooting up into the
air. The fire trucks were there but having a hard time con-
trolling the blaze.

I glanced at Camille. "Are you thinking what I'm thinking?"

"Sorcery? Yes. Shamas just pulled up. He can tell better
than I can." She hailed him as he and Yugi ran down the
block to us. "Shamas—can you tell if those flames are
magical? If so, we'll need you to help calm them so the firefighters can put them out."

"Douglas! Douglas! Are you in there?" Marion was hys-
terical, fighting to run toward the house, but Menolly was
holding her back, her arms tight around Marion's waist.

As Shamas headed toward the fire, I hurried over to help
Menolly with Marion. She was struggling, trying to break free.

"My husband is in there—he took a sleeping pill. He
always takes a sleeping pill!" She tried to break free again,
but Menolly held on tight.

I shook her by the shoulders. "Where's your bedroom?"

"Downstairs—toward the back."

I took a long look at the building. The fire was on one side
so far, flames shooting out of the upper floor. I raced over to
Shamas and grabbed him.

"Come with me. We're going in to see if we can rescue
her husband." Ignoring the firefighters who shouted at us, we
dodged our way in through the front door, which was standing open.

Shamas turned to me. "Let me go first, I can hold back
the flames to a degree and hopefully, if they're magical,
calm them." He moved into the front as I took the back.

Marion's house was lovely—walls a pale shade of gold, trim dark brown. Décor was a mix of northwest and southwest Native American, with terra-cotta urns filled with pampas grass, Northwest art—wood burnings of Raven and Salmon, of the Great Trickster Coyote.

The smell of smoke was thick and beginning to drift down the stairs. Shamas motioned for me to move past him, toward the back of the building. He held up his hands and started up the stairs.

I raced down the hall, listening to the roar of the flames from the floor above. The timbers groaned and creaked, and I glanced at the ceiling. I could see soot marks—black. Only a few minutes and the flames would eat through and it would be too late to attempt a rescue.

I slammed open doors as I went and then stopped. A bedroom, and there was Douglas, asleep on the bed. I'd seen him once, at the diner, with Marion. He was sawing logs. And a cat was curled up on his stomach. I shut the door behind me so the cat couldn't escape and glanced around the room. There was a laundry basket near me, with pillowcases and sheets in it. I grabbed one of the pillowcases and then, as the tabby woke up, I scruffed her and shoved her into the makeshift bag before the princess even knew what hit her. I tied the bag with a loose knot, setting it on the floor, then dragged Douglas out of bed and threw him over one shoulder.

Like most coyote shifters, he was lean. For me, the weight was a burden but not unmanageable. Using my right hand to steady the sleeping man on my shoulder, I opened the door, grabbed the bag in my left hand, and staggered out.

"Shamas! Shamas! Come help me." The cat was struggling, making it hard to hold on to both bag and man.

As I stumbled forward, Shamas came clambering down the stairs. He took one look at me, grabbed Douglas off my shoulder, and carried him to the door. I followed, the sack-o'-cat in my arms. As we exited the house, an explosion reverberated down the stairs; the shockwave sent me sprawling forward.

I landed chin first but managed not to fall on the cat. Scrambling up, I ran like hell. The flames were engulfing the bottom floor now, roaring down the stairwell. Shamas laid Douglas down by Marion's side. The coyote shifter fell to her knees, sobbing into her hands.

"Douglas . . . Douglas . . ." She began to cry as he opened his eyes, blurrily shaking his head. "Wake up, Doug."

As he sat up, coughing, I moved over to her side. "Marion, I rescued your cat." I held out the struggling feline in the bag.

With tears running down her face, she gathered the sack in her arms, crying even harder. She glanced up at the house, then back at her husband.

"Damn you . . . damn it . . . I don't know what I would have done if you died." And before she could say another word, he groggily wrapped her in his arms, cat and all, and kissed her.

In the background, the flames lit up the night as they gobbled up what had been Marion's home and life.

Chapter 15

Marion crouched, her arms wrapped around her husband, as we watched the firefighters try to beat back the flames. Shamas had managed to remove the magical energy from the fire, but he couldn't put it out. The arsonists had also used gasoline. The smell was thick in the air.

I ran over to my Jeep. We always kept a cat carrier in each of our cars, just in case I turned into my Tabby self somewhere and had to be contained until I was ready to change back. I pulled it out and took the pillowcase from Marion, gently easing their cat out of the bag into the carrier and then locking it firmly. I set it down next to her and she smiled, weary and worried, but looking grateful.

"Do you have some place to stay? With one of your children, maybe?"

She shook her head. "No, they're off at college. At least two of them. The third is grown, married, and living in Canada." She hung her head. "We can stay in a hotel—"

"You'll stay at our place. It's crowded, but you'll be safe there for now." I helped her up. Douglas was pretty out of it still, so Shamas guided him over to the prowl car and I led Marion, along with their cat.

After they were tucked inside, Shamas turned to me. "I'll drive them back to the house. You're right—the only place they'll be safe for now is with us. It's beginning to sound like some of this crap is directed at Marion—revenge. Kill her sister, burn down her house, try to kill her husband . . ."

"Yeah, and until we know for sure, I want them safe."

As the house caved in on itself, the flames beginning to die down, I clenched my fists. Marion and Douglas had just lost all of their memories, their safe haven. Shamas handed a book to me. I looked at it. A photo album. I glanced at him, a question in my eyes.

"I saw it on the way out and grabbed it."

A glance through it told me that it was their wedding album and had childhood pictures in it of their kids. A gentle smile springing to my lips, I leaned in and kissed him on the cheek.

"You're a good man, Shamas. And I'm proud to have you for my cousin."

He blushed and turned back to his car, taking the album. "Thanks, cuz. Thanks."

Menolly headed down to the Wayfarer to make sure everything was okay while Camille and I drove home.

"I feel so helpless—our friends are getting hurt and murdered by these freaks and we're just running three steps behind, picking up the pieces." I clenched the steering wheel, my knuckles white with anger. "We need a solid lead and we need it now."

"Well, we have the Energy Exchange, which we could have checked out tonight if we hadn't been putting out fires all day. And . . . Fuck. Fuck me now! I can't believe I forgot about it!" Camille jerked around, her eyes wide as she smacked her head.

"What?"

"The stripper—he got that potion at a shop. Alchemy for

Lovers. I was positive when I talked to him that the place is a sorcery shop and I totally spaced it. That might give us another lead." She slammed back in her seat, fuming. "I'm so stupid. We might have been able to stop this if we'd gone there this morning."

"Stop. Don't beat yourself up." I pulled to the side. "We had a quick nap; we're still good to go despite all the crap we've done today. I don't want to chance the Energy Exchange alone, but what say we take a quick trip down to this shop and check it out? We can at least get a look at what kind of shop it is."

She grinned at me. "Ten to one it's a sex shop, but yeah, let's go. And thanks. I don't think I could sleep anyway. But I'm calling Morio to meet us there. Meanwhile, Hanna and the guys can help settle Marion and Douglas in the parlor for now."

"Misty's going to love the playmate." Camille's ghost kitty that I'd given her for Yule was as friendly as they came, and she'd probably run rings around Marion's cat.

"She'll go nuts. I hope Hanna's cat doesn't mind."

I laughed. "Ha! I wish I were there to see *that* meeting. Make the call while I pull up the directions for the shop on the GPS." We'd all splurged and purchased apps on our phones for GPS service. Camille flipped her phone open and put in a call to Hanna, directing Morio to meet us at the sex shop. Or whatever it turned out to be. She spoke in low tones, then held the phone away from her mouth.

"Morio said he and the others made it home. They were wondering what happened to us."

While she went back to talking to him, I surfed the web for the address on my new smart phone and then plugged it into the GPS app. I'd picked up a leopard-print skin for my phone in honor of my twin, Arial.

When I'd figured out the directions, we headed out. As we drove through the streets, the rain pounded down. In the Pacific Northwest, gray and gloomy were a way of life. We'd grown accustomed to the weather, and actually, I liked it. None of us were much for hot weather. Back in Y'Elestrial, we'd had moderate temperatures during the summer; spring, crisp autumn days; and chilly, snowy winters. Here, there was less variation.

The windshield wipers swished back and forth, sweeping the rain off the glass. Camille stared out the side window as we sped along. The city was pretty seen through the rainy night. The lights twinkled as we turned onto James Street and edged down the steep hill. Seattle wasn't known as the miniature San Francisco for nothing—the entire city, as well as a good share of the East Side, was built on a series of rolling hills caused, in part, by a major underlying earthquake fault system that ran through the entire area.

"What if Van and Jaycee are in the shop when we get there?" I didn't really want to think about the possibility, but if they were there, we'd better be ready.

Camille tugged at her seat belt, readjusting it over her boobs. "You know, maybe I'd better ask Smoky to show up, too."

"Maybe that would be a good idea."

As she pulled out her phone and called home again, I changed lanes in order to make a right turn.

"What do you know." Camille tucked her phone away. "Smoky insisted on going with Morio, so he's already on the way."

I laughed. "You aren't ever going to get out from under his protective wing now. Face it, he's your permanent bodyguard."

She snorted. "Yeah . . . but you have to admit, he's a good bodyguard to have."

The traffic was extremely thin and we were making every light. Another five minutes and we pulled into the parking lot of the strip mall. Alchemy for Lovers was the corner shop. And it was the only one that had lights on in it.

"I'm surprised it's still open. As big as Seattle is, the city closes down fairly early in most parts." Sometimes it felt like we were living in a smaller town, not a big city.

"I'm not. Think about it. Strippers, probably hookers

come here for that potion and other supplies. They primarily work nights. And if this is a haven for sorcerers, well, it's a lot easier to escape notice under the cover of darkness."

I swung around and parked a few spots down from the store. "Might as well keep out of sight until Morio and Smoky get here."

We watched for anybody coming into or going out of the shop, but it seemed to be a slow night. Five minutes later, a car pulled into the parking lot and eased in next to my Jeep. Morio's SUV, with Morio and Smoky. We got out of the car and, joining them, headed for the door.

As I pushed open the door, bells jingled, and I found myself facing an array of brightly colored sex toys. A row of vibrators sat on one table, from neon pink to basic black. I raised my eyebrows. They were shaped so lifelike that I couldn't help but wonder who'd posed for them, especially a couple that looked larger than your average cock. I knew some men came in that size; I'd seen equipment that large before—when Morio shifted into demonic form and was naked. The sight certainly made for fantasy fodder, though I still maintained that Camille was a brave woman.

One wall was covered with various harnesses, leashes, dog collars, cuffs, and other bondage restraints. The smell of leather hung heavy in the air. Another wall was floor-to-ceiling shelves filled with books and DVDs. A large table held a selection of various lotions and creams and a large basket of condoms, but there were no potion bottles in sight.

The clerks, three women, were all muscled, and they looked capable of handling rough customers who might come through. One, wearing a nametag that read Mandy, sat on a high stool behind the counter. The other two—Dona and Marrow—looked like they were just waiting for trouble to erupt. They gave us a thorough once-over. It was obvious we weren't FBHs, but that didn't mean *they* were, either. Tregarts were muscled and tough, both the male and the female demons.

Camille leafed through a rack of racy costumes, then

meandered up to the counter. She leaned her hands on the glass top and smiled at Mandy, behind the counter. "I'm looking for a certain oil for my husband."

The clerk glanced at Camille's boobs, then up at her face. "What kind oil are you talking about? And for your body or his?"

"It's a special oil—one you aren't apt to keep out front. Special blend. A friend told me about it—a stripper. He said he got it here." She winked at the woman. Smoky stiffened but kept his mouth shut.

Mandy darted a glance at the tallest of the women—Dona—out on the main floor, then turned back to Camille. "You sure you can handle something like that? It's pretty powerful."

"Oh trust me, I can handle more than you might believe." Camille batted her eyelashes and turned on the glamour. I watched the woman carefully. Tregarts would be immune to our charms. And this chick wasn't falling for it. But she did give Camille the once-over again and licked her lips, her eyes lighting up with a fierce intensity.

"Marrow—get the lady a bottle of Golden Drops." The cashier looked over at me. "You want anything? Maybe a . . . dog . . . collar?"

I said nothing, but alarm bells began to ring in my head as Marrow turned and swept through a pair of curtains cordoning off the back. I tensed and gave Morio a subtle nod as I moved over to stand beside Camille, landing a feather touch on her arm. She stiffened.

The tension in the air began to rise as we waited. The cashier flipped through a packet of receipts as Dona wandered over to the wall where the harnesses and whips hung.

At that moment, the curtains parted and a group of Tregarts burst through. Dona grabbed one of the whips as Mandy whipped out a baseball bat from beneath the counter.

I hadn't brought my dagger with me, but I had my boot knife, and I snatched it out of the sheath. Morio began to shift into his demonic form—eight feet of terrifying youkai—and

Smoky cracked his knuckles, his fingernails growing into talons. Camille leaped away from the counter as the cashier brought the bat down across the counter at her. The sound of shattering glass echoed through the air and then it was game on—time to bust some heads.

Camille began summoning energy, moving back away from the fray. Smoky turned on one of the bushy-bearded bikers and raked his belly, not deep enough to eviscerate him, but he managed to rip through the guy's leathers.

Morio aimed for Dona as she brought the whip down across his back, the crack shattering the air with its sharp snap. He roared and dove for her, taking her down beneath him. They wrestled—the bitch was strong—and a flash of his fur caught my eye as he brought a fist directly down on her forehead.

Rather than break her neck, as it would for any ordinary human, it just seemed to stun her a little, and she snapped the whip up to coil around his neck. As he pulled against it, she slid out from beneath him and yanked, hard, trying to choke him.

Smoky's talons came whistling down to slice through the whip, and Morio fell back as the leather neatly snapped in two. Smoky turned to Dona and plunged his talons into her midsection. She wasn't wearing leathers and he severed through the flesh, ripping her entrails directly out of her body to splash across the floor. She went down.

Camille turned on Mandy, who was aiming the bat at her. She let loose a bolt of energy that she'd formed between her hands, and, with a brilliant flash, it struck Mandy in the face. The Tregart screamed, clutching at her head, and Camille pulled out a knife from the folds of her skirt and landed a deep blow between the woman's eyes.

I blinked. I knew Camille had been training, but I hadn't expected that maneuver. But I had my own battle to attend to. I turned and sent my knife hurtling into the chest of one of the bikers who was headed directly for me. He yelped, grabbing the hilt and yanking it out of his flesh. Tossing it aside, he barreled down on me. I aimed a round kick for his face and caught him directly in the nose. Grunting, he stumbled back from the force of the blow and I took the opportunity to rush him, knocking him to the ground. I didn't have a blade in hand, so I grabbed his neck and began to squeeze. But his hands were around my waist, so tight I was having trouble breathing.

Everyone else was engaged, so I'd have to get out of this myself. And the one way I could think of was to shift. I forced it to come fast—it would hurt that way, but what the fuck, it would save my life. As I shifted into Panther, the Tregart shrieked, obviously not expecting to find himself hugging a hundred and twenty pounds of muscle, claws, and teeth.

I leaned down and bit him with the killing bite, snapping his neck with one victorious growl. As soon as I smelled his death, I let go and raced over to Marrow, who was backing up, trying to get out of the way. Smoky and Morio were each fighting a couple of the demons, and Camille was readying another spell. I bounded across the room. Marrow saw me coming and—eyes wide—began to stumble back against the wall. I knocked her down, not bothering to toy with her. One good bite across her face and she was done.

I turned back to pounce on one of Morio's attackers. He was pounding the other against the wall head first. I bit the ankle of mine and yanked, dragging him off balance. As he fell, I held him down while Camille landed on him from the other side, dragging a knife across his throat. Morio and Smoky finished off their opponents and we stood down, Morio and I shifting back into our regular forms. While we were transforming, Camille and Smoky turned off the lights and locked the door.

After the shop was secure, Camille called Chase. Morio waited in the front, while Smoky, Camille, and I headed to the back of the shop. The space was bigger than one would think—in fact it looked like they'd rented the shop next to them and opened up into it.

The back offices were as big as—if not bigger than—the main storefront. There were the usual supplies, everything you'd expect to stock a sex shop, but when we began tossing cupboards and drawers, we found evidence that the Tregarts had most definitely been running sorcery through the shop.

Bottles of unknown potions—Camille identified them as magical—filled one drawer. Another drawer held a handful of firebombs. And we found three drawers filled with bags of odd-looking components. Camille stuffed everything into a bag. As she started on the desk, ruffling through the paperwork, my phone rang. I flipped it open and pressed Talk.

"Delilah, it's Chase. We're out in the driveway. Let us in but don't turn on the lights yet."

I leaned out to the front. "Morio, let the cops in. Chase is here."

As Smoky and I headed to the front, Morio opened the door for Chase and Yugi. Chase flashed his light around and grimaced.

"You guys did a number here. What's the story?"

"Tregarts. Demons. They started the fight. This shop is a front for sorcery. Ten to one, Van and Jaycee funded it. What do we do?"

"You're sure they're demons? Nobody will come to the station, missing them?" He frowned, looking around at the mess.

"Nobody. They aren't human. They aren't Fae. And I doubt if Van and Jaycee are going to come knocking on your door to file a missing demons report."

"Then we have the cleaning crew come in here, take care of this. The bodies . . . do you need to take them to Queen Asteria?"

"No . . . but we do need to get rid of them. We also need to make a trip to Otherworld to warn her about the fact that Wilbur may have inadvertently leaked that the spirit seals are with her." I glanced over at Smoky. "Tomorrow, we head to OW."

Camille entered the room, flipping through a date book. "I think I found something. Most of the notes are actually business oriented—one thing I'll say about Van and Jaycee, they're savvy. They were actually already in the black, according to the books. Taking in more than they were expending every week. But that's incidental."

"What did you find?"

She pointed to one of the pages. "On February thirteenth there's a notation for ten p.m. that reads *SCH*. That could stand for *Supe Community Hall*. And here's one for today. *Eight p.m.—Vespa*. Let's see if . . ." She flipped back a week or so. "Yep . . . here it is. *Two p.m.—Folkes*." We've got them on all three incidents."

"But this group . . . they're just the front. You know Van and Jaycee set up the hits. Anything that tells us where we can find them? Phone numbers? If we don't find our way to them, they're going to know something happened here and they'll retaliate even worse." I was now second-guessing our actions. But we had no choice. They'd ID'd us and once they came out swinging, we couldn't back out. Even if we'd left the minute we sensed tension rising, they would have known we were on to this place.

"Phone numbers, check. I picked up their phone book. But it's going to take a little time figuring out who they belong to. Addresses—no. But I suggest you grab the laptop that's on the desk in back. I wasn't sure what cables we needed to go with it." She pocketed the day planner and the address book.

I slipped into the back and retrieved the computer, making a quick search for any CDs or DVDs that might be around. Who knew whether they kept their records on the hard drive or on a disk? When I returned, Chase was talking to a couple of his cohorts. The bodies of the demons were gone. I frowned, looking around.

"Where'd they go? The Tregarts?"

"Smoky, Shade, and Roz took them away."

"Shade? Roz?" I glanced at Camille and she smiled.

"I called them while you were getting the computer. We're closing down the shop and they may figure out we had a hand in it, but they won't be able to tell what went down for certain." She motioned for me to follow her outside.

Morio and Chase followed behind us. Shamas was wait-

ing there, along with a specially trained hazmat team from
the FH-CSI and a number of armed Fae guards. I recognized
them from the Triple Threat's militia. They had arranged a
mutual-aid pact with the FH-CSI several months ago.

As soon as everybody was out and away from the building, the team headed into the building.

"What are they doing?"

"Cleanup. The guards will stick around to protect them.
It won't take them long—apparently they have a number of
magical techniques that standard hazmat teams don't."

I nodded. Sounded like as good a plan as any. There was
a flash from within the building, and mist wafted out. It
smelled vaguely like bleach, but with something underlying.

Camille slapped me on the back. "Come on, let's get out
of here before Van and Jaycee show up. We're not prepared
to fight them tonight."

"Then what *are* we going to do tonight?" I was tired, achy
actually—today had been filled with so much stress, and the
fights of the past two days were wearing on all of us.

"We're going through the computer, day planner, and
phone book to see what we can find out." She slid into the
passenger seat of my Jeep, yawning. "And I'll be damned if
we're setting one foot out of the house until morning.

"Be careful. Don't jinx us." As we waved to the others
and pulled out of the parking lot, Camille's phone rang.

She flipped it open. "Hello?" A second later she mouthed
Vanzir to me and continued to listen. After a moment, she
sucked in a deep breath. "Are you sure? . . . When did he
call? . . . And he's positive? . . . Does he want to see us tonight?
No? Tomorrow? Okay, we're on our way home." She slammed
the phone back into her purse. "Motherfucking hell, to para-
phrase Menolly."

I glanced at her quickly, then pulled my gaze back to the
road. "What's going on? Please tell me we don't have another
explosion or fire to attend?"

"I wish. This is far worse." She slammed her hand against
the dashboard.

"Hey, watch it. Snowdrop doesn't like rough treatment."

"Snowdrop? You named your Jeep *Snowdrop*?" She stared at me with an incredulous look but then shook her head. "Doesn't matter right now. That was Vanzir. Carter called him. We've got a new demon general in town."

Crap. I wanted to hit something, but we were speeding along the freeway at sixty miles an hour and taking my hands off the wheel wasn't the best idea. "Okay, fill me in. I don't want to wait."

"Vanzir will do that at home. All I know is his name is Gulakah and he's known as the Lord of Ghosts. And he's just arrived in Seattle."

I swerved over to the side of the road and parked, flipping on the hazard lights. We weren't supposed to unless we were in a fender bender or had a flat tire, but I didn't give a damn right now. If a cop wanted to ticket me, so be it. I opened my window to let the rain stream in. Usually I hated getting wet, but tonight I just needed a cold shock to the face.

"Can't we catch a break? Can't we deal with just one monster of a problem at a time? I've finally learned that rose-colored glasses aren't any way in which to see the world. I've learned to be tough. I've learned to accept my destiny. But damn it, just once, can't we let somebody else handle the bad guys?"

I wanted to cry, but as I sat there, Camille's hand on my shoulder, I realized that—for now—there *was* nobody else. We had allies. When Shadow Wing broke through, if he did, the dragons would come to help us. And Queen Asteria would send help. And the Triple Threat were marshaling their own army. But for now, for the skirmishes in between, those were just for us. Because we'd landed—either for destiny or chance—on the front lines of this war. And we were here to take care of the vanguard.

Camille stroked my arm, then let out a long sigh. "You know, when Hyto kidnapped me, all I could think about was axing his sorry butt. Delilah, we fought a *dragon* and won. An old, crafty, powerful dragon. And we've killed off three demon generals so far. Now, we face another. So what? We'll kick his ass back to the Sub-Realms. Because that's *what we do*. We fight. And we win. And even when we falter, we still come out to fight again. We're survivors."

Wiping my tears, I rolled up the window. "Yeah . . . I guess you're right."

"Damn straight. Now let's get home so we can go through all this crap, eat ourselves sick on Cheetos, and find out what Vanzir has to say about this new freak."

"Sounds good." And with that, I eased back onto the road, and we headed home.

Chapter 16

❧❦❧

As we burst through the doors, everybody was already in a flurry. Vanzir had the household laptop out and open. Since I used mine a lot, we'd bought a general one for the house so everybody didn't have to keep borrowing mine. He was typing while Morio—still in his coat—was watching over his shoulder.

As we trailed in, Hanna took our coats and bags and pressed mugs of hot soup into our hands. We settled wearily at the kitchen table, where a tray of sandwiches waited. I grabbed one and bit into it, too tired to even notice what it was until an explosion of beef and cheese hit my mouth, along with some spicy spread I couldn't identify. But it woke my taste buds up, for sure.

"Okay, let's hear it. What or who the fuck is Gulakah?" I had no energy to stand on niceties."

Vanzir pushed back the computer. "Carter doesn't have a lot of information on him, but he sounds bad. We're not sure how or when he got over here, but there's no question that he's in Shadow Wing's pocket. This isn't another case like Stacia, where the servant is trying to outwit the master."

"Okay, so he's for real and he's not even going to ask us to play in his sandbox." I tapped my finger on the table. Stacia had tried to bargain with us. She had been out to take over Shadow Wing's position and had tried to win us over to helping her. *The enemy of my enemy* and all that crap. "You mention something about ghosts?"

Vanzir nodded and pointed toward the e-mail that Carter had sent after his call. "Gulakah is known as the Lord of Ghosts. He was originally a god in the Netherworld, where he abused his power over the innocent dead whose souls have not been laid to rest. His brother, Shekah, cast him out to the Subterranean Realms and took his place. He cursed Gulakah to preside over the angry ghosts who exist between the worlds—those who choose not to move on because they're so furious. The curse is to last ten thousand years, and then Gulakah will face a jury of gods to see if he's fit for reinstatement."

"So we've got an angry demon, demoted from godlike status, prowling around Seattle. How long has he been over here?" I was thinking about the spate of ghostly activity that had been going on the past few months. Angry ghosts had almost killed Morio.

"Carter says he doesn't know when Gulakah got here, but it can't have been more than two weeks ago from what he can piece together. I've looked up everything I can find on this demon, but the mentions are sparse. A few websites from paranormal investigators who've turned up the name in séances or through mediums, but nothing concrete." He circled a note on the steno pad. "I've got an idea, but you aren't going to like it."

"Tell us. Right now we have to entertain every possibility." Things were getting worse and worse, and we couldn't afford to lose any more innocent victims.

Vanzir straightened up. His eyes were sparkling. He tipped his head to the side. "We ask Trytian for help. We go to him and tell him we have information he'll want, but in exchange he has to first tell us where to find Van and Jaycee. Then we hand over the info on Gulakah to him."

"Trytian—you want us to deal with pond scum?" Camille slammed her mug on the table so hard the soup spilled. Hanna moved to clean it up, but Camille motioned her away and grabbed a napkin to wipe up the steaming broth.

Trytian was the son of a powerful daemon who was building an army in the Subterranean Realms against Shadow Wing. The daemon had sent his son Earthside—none of us was sure how, and Trytian wasn't spilling secrets—to rally the Demon Underground to help them. Trytian had threatened Camille, tried to blow us all up, and then turned around and offered to build a truce with us. He was about as trustworthy as snake oil.

"I know you don't like him, but look at the facts. He came to us to warn you about Hyto. He reached out first. He's fighting against Shadow Wing, too—"

"That may be so, but he also has no compunction about destroying innocent people who he thinks are in his way!" Camille was pacing the floor. She stopped and whirled to me. "What do you think?"

I looked at the information Carter had sent us. Gulakah sounded like a badass motherfucker, and we were on the end of our tether with regard to Van and Jaycee. The thought of dealing with Trytian was stomach-churning, but the thought of letting the pair of sorcerers go on to cause more havoc was far worse.

"I'm with Vanzir on this one. If Trytian knows about anything at all that will help us catch them, then we need to take advantage of it."

"What about the computer at the shop? The phone book? Can't we go through them first to see if we can find anything that would keep us from having to contact him? If we come up empty, fine then . . . we have Vanzir put in a call and we make a deal with the devil . . . or daemon, rather. But maybe, if we're lucky, we won't need to." Camille clenched her fists.

"Sounds good to me." I looked at the others. "Everybody

willing to pull a late-nighter? If we divide up, we can check out everything that much quicker and get some sleep in the process."

They all nodded, including Hanna. "I'll keep the tea and coffee coming," she said.

"Then, I guess we take a quick shower break to wash off the soot and smoke, and we knuckle down to combing through all of this crap."

After making sure Marion and Douglas were comfortable in the parlor, Shade and I trudged up to the bedroom. I stripped and jumped in the shower first, lathering up and—for the first time in a while—I actually enjoyed the feeling of the soap and water on my skin. Climbing out of the shower, I toweled off and climbed into a clean nightshirt and pair of sweatpants.

Shade was sitting on the bed, waiting for his turn in the shower. He stopped me to gently press his lips against mine. I sank into his arms, enjoying the safety of his embrace, feeling weary and sleepy and wanting only to crawl into bed for a nice long nap. Before I realized what I was doing, I was in my Tabby form, staring at him from the floor.

He sat back down on the bed and held out his arms, whistling for me. I leaped up on the bed, crawling onto his knee. He scritched me behind the ears.

"A little stressed, aren't you, girl?" As he rubbed the fur under my chin, I began to purr and stretched my head for him to reach the sides of my face. It was such a relief to be in my Tabby form. Even though I was still facing the same stressors, when I was in cat form everything seemed muted, like I was wearing earmuffs in the middle of a cacophony.

After a moment, I began to relax. I hopped off Shade's lap and saw my favorite squeaky mouse. Batting it, I felt my blood race at the sound of squeak. I picked it up by the tail and raced out of the room, down the stairs to the second floor where Camille was just coming out of her room. I dropped the mouse at her feet and looked up, twitching my tail.

Camille laughed gently and reached down to scoop me up. "Feeling a little out of sorts, Kitten? Thank you, thank you for the toy. And thank you for making me smile." She buried her face in my fur and kissed me soundly. "But, Delilah, we have a lot of ground to cover tonight. We need you, as a woman. Your reading skills aren't all that developed when you're in Tabby form."

I let out a little mew and then, licking her quickly on the face, I jumped down and moved to the side. She was right. I didn't have time to play with the mouse, or to curl up for a catnip. Resigned and a little sad, I transformed back.

As I shook my head, coming out of the shift, Camille helped me to my feet. I noticed she was wearing a floor-length terry-cloth robe over a loose babydoll. Smoky, Trillian, and Morio were already downstairs.

I took Camille's hand in mine. "Thank you. Sometimes, I still need my big sister . . . though I think I'm finally growing up."

Camille squeezed my fingers. "Kitten, we all need to grow up. But you'll always be Kitten, and you'll always have the playful kitty inside. We need that part of you—it keeps us all hopeful. Just like Maggie keeps us innocent. Menolly can never have that innocence again. I will never be able to trust anybody fully again. But you . . . we need your joy. Please, don't ever lose it."

I misted over. "I'm trying not to. I don't think I'd like myself if I did."

I took the store laptop while Camille started flipping through the day planner and the guys divided up the address book. Settling on the sofa, with a bowl of Cheetos to my right and a big glass of milk to my left, I opened the lid of the laptop. Before we left, I'd made sure that the battery had enough life left to make it home where I could plug it in. I'd been careful not to close the lid so it wouldn't go to sleep. It was still running, so I didn't need the password.

Before I started doing anything, I plugged in an external

hard drive and began to download everything on the laptop. That way, if something happened, we'd have a backup of all the files. I examined the programs. The computer had only a handful of programs on it. I guess Tregarts weren't prone to playing games or writing long documents. I opened the mail and waited for it to download.

Five incoming e-mails. I opened the first and it asked for a return receipt when opened, but I closed the request without answering. No use letting Van and Jaycee know we had the computer. Yet.

It was a simple two-line message asking for the daily report, and giving a heads up that "MV" had not perished yet, with a stern warning that they'd better take care of the matter for once and all.

"You think this group torched Marion's house?" I stuffed a handful of Cheetos in my mouth and swallowed a gulp of milk.

"Doesn't have to be all of them. There were plenty there to play at arson while the others waited at the store." Morio was thumbing through his part of the phone book. He and Vanzir were using the household laptop as well as mine to do a reverse lookup on the phone numbers. We didn't want to call them at this point. Hang-ups would give us away.

"Any luck on finding out who those numbers belong to?"

"Some are listed—dealers, companies, services . . . everything you'd expect for a sex toy business. But there are three I've been unable to trace so far, and two that I came up with names for. One connects to a fortune-teller's shop in the Industrial District. *Future Glimpses.* I looked them up on the Net and they sell spell components, they advertise spells, and they read the cards. But it says they're closed for business until the first of the month."

"Bingo. Sounds like Van and Jaycee's last shop." Camille looked up from across the room, where she was meticulously going through the day planner, jotting down notes. "Who does the other number belong to?"

Morio leaned back. "It leads us right back to the Energy Exchange club."

I stopped. "Right. I knew they were involved and this proves it. Which means they're probably into both the Wolf Briar business as well as magical weaponry."

During our last interaction with the Koyanni, we'd encountered a weapon that we'd been pretty sure was fashioned at the Energy Exchange. It was like a magical stun gun. While Camille and Morio were able to charge it up, to some degree, the exact spell for empowering it with charges still eluded them.

"We have to raid that place. I'll bet you anything Van and Jaycee are holing up there. Come on." I set the laptop aside and jumped up, but a wave of dizziness swept over me and I sank back down to the sofa. "Or maybe not tonight. I'm exhausted."

Camille nodded. "Me, too. We aren't strong enough tonight. I don't care how much caffeine and sugar we pour into ourselves. Vanzir—take one of the laptops and start hunting around for any information you can find on the club. Meanwhile, let's finish going over all this crap. We don't want to miss something that might be hiding right in plain sight."

"I need a nap, though, even just an hour or two." I yawned, stretching.

Camille rubbed her head. "Yeah, we've been burning the midnight oil a lot lately. Okay, you guys keep on with what you're doing. Take over the notes. Morio, are you still good to go for a bit?"

He nodded. "Yeah, and Trillian can take over the planner. You and Delilah get a couple hours of rest. In fact, Smoky, Shade, you go chill, too. We'll keep looking and wake you up in a few hours if we need to. When Menolly gets back from the bar, she can help us."

Exhausted, I dragged myself to my feet and, together with Camille and our two dragons, climbed the stairs. I barely said a word before I climbed into bed and fell into a deep, dreamless sleep.

"Delilah, honey? Wake up." Shade's voice echoed through the room.

I blinked, fuzzy. It wasn't light yet, but Shade was insisting I wake up and I didn't want to. I growled, pushing his hand away. "Go 'way. I'm sleepy."

"Honey? They need you downstairs." Shade pulled the blanket off me, and the chill in the room descended to shock me awake.

I groaned and forced myself out of bed. I glanced at the clock. It was barely three and a half hours after we'd gone to bed. "Gah, I really want a full night's sleep. I haven't had one for a week." As I stumbled into the bathroom, I heard Shade curse. "What's wrong?" I peed, then washed my hands and brushed my teeth.

"I found one of your hairballs. The hard way." He sounded grouchy.

I grimaced as I swished a mouthful of breath rinse and then spit. As I trudged back into the bedroom, he was sitting on the edge of the bed, wiping off one of his feet.

"I'm sorry." I tried to keep a straight face but couldn't help myself. I let out a snicker.

"What are you laughing about? Delilah, honey, can you please clean up after yourself? This is the fourth hairball you've left on the floor after you transformed back. I'll help clean your litter box, but damn it, take some responsibility." He wasn't laughing. In fact, he looked downright out of sorts.

"It's just a bunch of fur and spit." I slipped off my panties and put on a clean pair, then wiggled into my jeans. As I hooked my bra and pulled on a turtleneck, Shade finished wiping his foot.

"That's not the point. The point is that you need to develop better habits. I love you. I can live with the clothes on the floor, and I can handle the empty water bottles everywhere, but you have to start cleaning up your own messes. The hairballs and the dirty litter box and the overflowing garbage can are too much. How hard is it to spend ten minutes a day picking up around here? I thought cats were clean."

I stared at him, both embarrassed and feeling a little

guilty. I'd promised to mend my ways a dozen times—to Iris as well as to my sisters, and now Shade—but I kept forgetting. It just seemed easier to leave it for later.

"I didn't realize my slovenly ways bothered you so much." My face started to feel hot and I pressed my lips together.

"We have to be able to talk about these things—habits that annoy us, things that irritate us. If we don't keep the communication flowing, then we stand the chance of bottling emotions up and that's not a good thing. Especially since I'm part dragon."

He put his hands on my shoulders, but I pulled away. "Well *excuse me*. I'm sorry I'm so disgusting." Hot tears welled up and I dashed them away. I was so weary, and so frustrated, that every thing he said seemed to be colored with disgust.

"*I called you no such thing.* I get that I could have put it better, but Iris herself dumped your litter box on your bed. I live here too, now. Do you want me to go? Is this your way of pushing me away? I will if that's what you want—but I love you. I just want to have a nice, cozy nest where we can curl up in comfort together. Why are you getting so pissed at me?" He looked so confused that I felt a tremor in my stomach.

Chase had lived in his own apartment. He'd stayed over, but we'd never shared a house or apartment. Shade and I'd been in the adjustment phase for the past couple of months, trying to figure out our routine, learning each other's habits. Chase had been a neat freak. I hadn't expected Shade to be one, too, but though I'd tried to ignore the signs, it seems like I'd been paired up once again with a tidy, organized lover.

I sighed, then dropped on the bed, reality crashing in on me. It wasn't just *me* anymore. I wasn't alone. "Fuck. And you know I don't say that often. I'm sorry. I did promise Iris and my sisters I'd try harder. The truth is, I do shirk chores. I hate housework. And yeah, I do make excuses for not doing so." Reaching out, I took his hand and drew him down beside me.

"Change is hard. I know you aren't used to sharing your

space." He wrapped his arm around me and kissed my forehead.

Snuggling into his arm, I looked around the room. When really forcing myself to look at it, what I saw was a giant pigpen. My clothes were scattered everywhere. Two hair-balls had dried on the floor, and the third that Shade had stepped in was still wet. Candy wrappers scattered across the floor beside my side of the bed, along with empty soda cans and a half-finished bag of Cheetos. My closet was a whirlwind.

On the other hand, Shade's closet was ordered, with his clothes neatly lined up on hangers. His nightstand was clear except for what he needed. It wasn't OCD-clean but defi-nitely tidy. As I looked at him, at the warmth in his eyes, I suddenly understood. I was in an adult relationship. I was sharing my life and my room with a man I loved. The house might be in my sisters' names and my name, but it was also Shade's home. And he was here for the long run.

"Okay." I straightened my shoulders. "How about this: We clean together. Every night, we pick up a little. I'll clean up my hairballs and keep the litter box clean. You take out the garbage. We do laundry together. I guess it's only fair. Hanna's going to have her hands full with so many people here, and Iris isn't going to be in any mood or shape to han-dle the work after a couple months."

Shade brightened. "You'd do that, for me?"

"If you do something for me." A thought occurred to me—something I knew that I probably couldn't budge him to do without leverage.

He seemed to sense I was up to something. "And what is that?"

Grinning, I licked my lips. "You know that fantasy I told you about? The Jerry Springer one?"

He closed his eyes and began to shake his head. "No, oh no—I told you I wouldn't be able to keep a straight face."

I pressed my fingers to his lips. "Oh yes. Yes, you will. It's called *compromise*. Couples compromise. I learned that from Camille and her men." Laughing now, I stood and turned to straddle his lap, pushing him back on the bed. "And you, my love, are going to compromise with me."

"Am I really, now? Are you so sure I'm ready to . . . compromise?" He wrapped his hands around my waist as his breathing deepened. I leaned down and pressed my lips to his, feeling the warmth of his breath fill my mouth. I nibbled his neck, tripping my fingers down his chest, sliding my hands under his shirt.

"Oh, you're ready. Trust me." But as I leaned in for another kiss, someone pounded on the door.

"Delilah! Shade! We need you downstairs, *now*." When Menolly spoke in that tone of voice, everybody jumped. "Get off your asses and hurry!"

Whoa. I hadn't heard her that upset in a long time.

We scrambled up and adjusted our clothing, then hurried downstairs. Menolly was already back in the kitchen when we came dashing in. Camille was there, along with Smoky, Trillian, and Vanzir.

"What's up? Please tell me not another explosion." Shade and I accepted mugs of tea from Trillian.

"We got a call from Chase. There's been an ugly incident. We have to get down to the FH-CSI." Camille jumped up and yawned, grabbing her keys.

"What's going on?" A voice from the kitchen door startled me. I whirled around to see Marion standing there, clutching the terry robe tightly around her. She'd borrowed it from Menolly.

"Yet another incident. We have to roll. You and Douglas stay here. Just go back to bed and get more rest." I patted her shoulder. She bit her lip, then nodded. She looked so tired and so lost.

As Marion vanished back to the parlor, Camille let out a long breath. "She's gone through so much. The loss of her sister. The loss of her house."

"Yeah, that's why we're doing this. For people like Marion. To keep the Tregarts—and their boss—from turning this world into a far worse hell than it already is." I swallowed my self-pity. So I'd only had three and a half hours of sleep. At least we still had our house to come home to.

Camille motioned to Trillian and Smoky. "We're leaving Morio at home. He still gets tired easier than usual. I'm making him stay home to sleep."

Vanzir, who was eating a toast and peanut butter sandwich, yawned. "I'll stay here, too. Shamas is still asleep. He has to get up in an hour to go to work and he needs to be on his A-Game while he's on duty. Man, two hours of sleep isn't enough for even me."

"Rozurial's still crashed out." Menolly shrugged. "He looked so peaceful when I went down to the studio to wake up him and Vanzir, I decided to let him sleep. That way Roz and Morio will be fresh later today in case we need down time. We might want to sleep in shifts from now until we catch Van and Jaycee, so we always have fresh blood. And speaking of blood . . ." Menolly glanced at the clock. It was nearly five thirty.

"Maybe you'd better stay home, too. We don't know how long we'll be out and it's almost dawn."

She nodded. "Right. I'll stay here and finish going through the last pages of the day planner and phone book. I don't want to get caught out in daylight and, knowing what's happened lately, if we get caught up in something big, I could fry."

Nodding, I picked up my keys and backpack. Shade and I headed out to my car, while Camille, Smoky, and Trillian headed to hers. As the clouds parted to let the luminous dark through, I breathed in the crisp air. February was a grueling month in the Seattle area. Rainy, cold, sometimes a snowstorm, wind and gloom . . . the city streets never seemed as gritty as they did on a cold February night.

Shade stared out the window as we sped along. After a few minutes, he turned to me. "I love you. You know that, don't you? I've loved you for a long time, far before you met me."

I smiled, keeping my eyes on the road. "I do. And I love you."

"How *much* do you love me?" The tone of his voice suddenly took a solemn turn. I darted a glance his way. He was looking bemused, staring at the windshield wipers as they slashed back and forth.

Unsure what he was up to, I hesitated. "I said I love you. Um . . . you want me to stretch my arms and say *this much*?" When he remained silent, I chewed the inside of my lip, then said, "Where's this going?"

"Where it's going is to the subject of that ring I gave you when we first met. The one you put on your finger to summon me to your side?" He pointed to the chunky smoky quartz that I hadn't taken off since I first slid it onto the ring finger of my right hand.

A funny feeling shifted in my stomach. "Yeah?"

"I told you then, you'd be making a choice. And you made it. Do you regret it? Even a little?"

Suddenly feeling short of breath, I shook my head, praying he wasn't going to break up with me. Sometimes love wasn't enough to conquer differences. Sometimes . . . "No, I've never regretted it. You help me feel complete. If this is about the room—I promise, I'll be less of a slob."

Another pause while I fretted.

Then: "In a way, this is about the room, yes. But not what you think."

"What is it?"

"Just . . . this. I figure, since we're sharing a room and sharing chores, and sharing a bed . . . and since our master has chosen us for each other and it's turned out to be a match made in heaven . . . then why don't we make it official? Promise me that—when you're ready—you'll become my wife?"

Tears blurring my eyes, I pulled over to the side of the road and parked. As I turned to Shade, my heart began to swell. Here was this man who wanted to share my life with me. Who accepted me for all of my faults and flaws. I turned to him. "You and the Autumn Lord are the two loves of my life."

They were both halves of the same whole. One was eternal, one was on my realm. My lips trembling, I reached for him, struggling against the seat belt, and kissed him long and deep. After a moment, I pulled back and took his hands in mine. "I never want to disappoint you. I want you in my life always. Yes, I'll marry you. I'll be your wife."

"When do you want to get married? Any time you want, be it tomorrow, or in ten years. Just name the date."

That, I couldn't answer. I knew that—as much as I was happy to say "yes" to being engaged, I wasn't prepared to actually get married yet. I shook my head. "I don't know. Not yet, I know I'm not ready yet. But I am ready to promise you my future. Is that good enough for now?"

"Oh, Delilah, dirty cat box, hairballs on the pillow, Jerry Springer fantasies . . . it's all part of you. And you, my love, are better than I deserve." He pressed my hand to his lips and kissed it gently. "I leave it to you to name the date. I can wait—I've waited a long time to be with you. I'm a patient dragon."

And, just like that, we were engaged.

Putting the Jeep in gear again, I turned back to the road, and we silently headed to the FH-CSI.

Chapter 17

As we hit the offices, Chase was waiting. He motioned for us to follow him. "Smoky, will you and the guys wait in conference room A? Camille and Delilah? Follow me, please." He led us out the door toward the medical unit.

"Has someone been hurt? Has there been another explosion?" Camille and I were actually hard pressed to keep up with him.

He stopped abruptly and turned, his expression strained. "We've got a situation and it's not one we can—or should—cover up. A woman was gang-raped an hour ago by a group of bikers from the Freedom's Angels. They roughed her up and used a knife to carve the words *Faerie Slut* on her arm. I've got a citywide search going on, but we need to see if she can identify any mug shots."

"This has gone too far." Camille slammed her hand against the wall. "Something has to be done about these freaks."

I put my hand on her shoulder, but she shrugged it off.

"What can we do, Chase? You know the climate of the city better than we do. What's going to help?"

He smiled for the first time, a tight, white smile. "First, you can talk to her, see if she tells you more than she's telling us. Second . . . the way she described a couple of the men, they sound like Tregarts. The more I think about it, the more I think that the demons are infiltrating the Freedom's Angels to divide and conquer. Look at what happened at the Davinaka Mall. Same situation. What if they stir up enough anger between the Supes and the FBHs? It's going to be easier to come in and take over."

"But why—if they're working for Trytian, and were working for Stacia Bonecrusher . . . hold on." A thought occurred to me that I really didn't want to think. "We've been assuming that *all* the Tregarts were working with Stacia, against Shadow Wing, and that all of them are now working for Trytian. But what if Shadow Wing used that assumption to his benefit? What if they've been on his side the whole time? And what about Van and Jaycee? Do we know if they were *really* in Stacia's pocket? What if they were spying on her and reporting back to Shadow Wing?"

Breathless, I dropped to a bench in the hall and leaned my head between my knees, trying to calm the swirl of thoughts running through my head. I wanted to shift, but this wasn't the time. I needed to maintain control.

Camille sat down beside me and took my hand, looking as pale as I felt. After a moment, I let out my breath in a slow stream and sat up.

"You think they might be double agents?"

"It makes perfect sense. Suppose Shadow Wing knew about Stacia Bonecrusher's attempted coup? And suppose he sent her over here, knowing she might betray him, to either prove or disprove her loyalty? And in the meantime, he also sent Van and Jaycee to connect with her and put her to the test. We just accepted that they were totally in sync with Stacia." I shook my head. "We could have been totally off about everything here."

Camille rubbed her forehead, wincing. "If that's so, then there's the chance that Telazhar trained Stacia at Shadow Wing's request. That she turned on him, too? If Telazhar is in the Demon Lord's pocket, then he's over here looking for ways to either rip open a new portal or gate in more demons." Camille gestured helplessly. "If we're right, we've wasted a lot of time assuming Shadow Wing hasn't been active over here for a few months."

Chase exhaled loudly. "This mucks up the works, all right. But I need you to talk to this victim, please. Then we can figure out where to go from here."

We nodded, mutely. If we were right, then the war had taken a darker turn. And, if we were right, then Trytian was playing right into Shadow Wing's hands and the entire Demon Underground was in danger.

I was about to mention this to Camille when we stopped in front of the ER. Chase led us in, after knocking gently. Sharah was standing beside the exam table. The stirrups were still in position, but the victim was sitting up as Sharah stitched up slash marks on her arm. The woman was Fae, with glimmering blond hair and brilliant blue eyes. Her glamour shone through the cloud of shame and anger. She had a black eye, a busted lip, and bruises on both wrists and ankles.

Sharah nodded us over. Chase hung back. We slowly approached the table and I could see the words carved into the victim's arm. *Faerie Slut.* Wincing, I looked at Sharah, waiting for her lead.

She finished stitching up the last of the cuts. "Camille, Delilah, this is Alfina. She's from Otherworld and came over to visit Talamh Lonrach Oll."

Alfina let out a shuddering breath and gave us a short nod.

Camille drew up one of Sharah's swivel stools and sat down, and Sharah pointed me toward the chair at the computer where she input all the wounds and treatments going through the FH-CSI emergency ward. Sitting down was a lot less intimidating than standing up, and regardless of whether she was Fae or human, a rape victim didn't need any more intimidation than she'd already undergone.

"Hi, Alfina . . . my sister and I are from Otherworld, too. From Y'Elestrial."

She glanced up, looking startled. "But you are—"

"Half human? Yes. Our mother was human, our father is Fae. Where are you from, back in OW?"

"Willowyrd Glen." Her voice was a whisper, but a glimmer of hope shone in her eyes. "I live on the shores of the Dahnsberry Lake, and before I moved to Dahnsburg to start work, my mother gave me a gift—a trip Earthside, to learn about the culture. Have you ever been to Dahnsberry Lake? It's so beautiful. Peaceful. We have our problems, but everything is . . . it's just so different than the bigger cities—both over there, and here Earthside."

Camille nodded. "I've seen the lake, briefly. And I've been to Dahnsburg. It's an incredible city, and King Uppala-Dahns is a fair and just leader."

That brought a reaction. "You know the King of the Dahns Unicorns?" For the first time, her voice showed a spark of life.

"Yes," Camille said softly. "I've met the king and I know his son, Feddrah-Dahns. Tell me, what will you be doing in Dahnsburg?" She kept her eyes on Alfina, holding her gaze.

Alfina gave a little shrug. "I'm going to be a clerk in the King's court." She teared up then and held out her arm. "What am I going to say about this? How am I going to go through the rest of my life with *this* on my arm? It's in English, but I'll always know what it says. What they *did*. I wish I'd stayed home, that I'd never come here."

As Alfina burst into tears, Sharah pulled out a salve. "Listen," she said, her voice gentle. "I'm going to put a special salve on this. I've done a really good job on the stitching. There will be minimal scarring. In a year or so, it should fade."

Alfina shook her head, trying to shade her eyes to keep us from seeing her tears. "You don't understand . . . it's a reminder."

I gently took her hands and wouldn't let go. She squeezed, holding tight. "You know that this happens back in Otherworld, too. It's not just here. Rape is a constant . . . it's not confined to one race or world, it's all about power and those who seek to use their bodies as weapons. You did nothing wrong. Your decision to come here didn't cause this to happen."

She let out another sigh and looked at me with those brilliant blue eyes. "What do you need me to do?"

"We need you to look at some pictures and see if you recognize any of the men. And . . . have you ever encountered a Tregart?" I scanned her face, watching for any clue as to what she was thinking.

She held my gaze. Slowly, deliberately, she said, "I'll look at your pictures. And yes, I know what Tregarts are. And at least two of the men were demons. They were bigger, harder, a lot rougher. But the man in the suit was the worst. He wanted to kill me, but the demons said, no, leave me alive as an example. I don't think . . . I don't think the man in the suit realized they weren't human by the way he was acting."

"Man in a suit?" Camille straightened up, looking confused. "What man in a suit?"

"The weasely man who was with the bikers. He was wearing a suit. He was . . . one of the rapists." She turned to Sharah. "Can I get dressed now? I feel too exposed. And I'm scared. I want to go home."

"After you look through the pictures, we'll take you back to your hotel." I motioned to Camille. "We'll wait outside while you dress."

As Sharah handed her a pair of trousers and a long tunic, we exited the room. Chase was in the waiting room. He looked up expectantly.

"She able to tell you anything?"

"Yeah, and I have a really bad feeling about it." We told him what she'd said. "So the demons are infiltrating the Freedom's Angels, stirring up matters. You were right with that supposition. But there's something else. Did she tell you about the man in the suit?"

He pulled out his notebook. "I'm not the one who took her statement. Let me see . . . Thayus took the call. He said . . . yes, there is the mention of a man in a suit. I didn't have a chance to read through it all before I called you. What are you thinking?"

I hooked my thumbs through the belt loops on my jeans. "Show her a picture of Andy Gambit. Ten to one . . . it was him."

"That fucking perv." Chase tapped his notebook. "If it is Gambit, then we've finally got him. But an arrest will make those who follow him go crazy. We have to be prepared. Is there any way you can pull together a counterprotest in case the frootloops come out of the woodwork? Not to confront them, but to balance out the coverage and make Seattle look less like a backwoods KKK enclave. Once this hits the news . . ."

"Yeah . . . I got it." And I knew exactly what to do. "Let me make a call to Tim and to Neely."

"First, let's see if Andy's our man."

Ten minutes later, Alfina was staring at an album open to a page with twelve mug shots on it, Andy Gambit's among them. None of us pointed to him, nobody said a word . . . we just waited.

Alfina stared at the page for a moment, and then without hesitation, she pointed to Gambit's picture. "That's him. That's the man in the suit." She also identified one of the more notorious members of the Freedom's Angels.

Chase nodded, motioning to Yugi. "Get warrants for their arrest and to search their houses. Do nothing until you consult me. If they were OW Supes, we'd extradite them to Otherworld. But they're ours, and their asses are *mine*." He turned to me. "Make your calls and pray we get a big turnout."

Camille and I headed over to the VA with Alfina. She didn't feel safe back in her hotel, so we took her there. Hiding her among Wade's people would be safer than any safe house we could take her to. The men followed in my Jeep.

Wade's assistant—Mari, an ES Fae—escorted us to a private office. From there, I gave Tim a call and asked him to put the phone tree on alert, should we need them. I then called Neely and asked her if we could count on the United Worlds Church to carry through with their promises to stand beside the Supe Community. She gave me her word.

I was just hanging up when Camille's phone rang. She answered and sat up straight. After murmuring a few words, she gave an abrupt "Yes" and flipped the cell shut.

"What was that about?"

"That . . . was Trytian. He wants to meet. He knows about Gulakah and wants to talk to us about him." She kicked the table leg. "I don't want to deal with him, but . . ."

"But considering what we think we know, we'd better meet with him. Like it or not, Trytian's on our side against the Demon Lord, and we need all the help we can get. Especially if Van and Jaycee were playing us all this time."

"Yeah. I told him we'd meet him in thirty minutes at Salsa Ria."

Salsa Ria was a popular twenty-four-hour Tex-Mex all-you-can-eat buffet. I perked up. We'd been going for a while on empty stomachs and too little sleep. Food would be good, even if we weren't looking forward to the most congenial breakfast partner.

Shade, Trillian, and Smoky weren't all that thrilled when we told them we were headed to meet Trytian, but they acquiesced as usual. They knew we weren't going to budge. I called Chase first. He had his men out looking for Andy Gambit, and he promised to call me the minute they found him.

As we walked in the door of Salsa Ria, the smells hit my stomach like a sledgehammer and I began to salivate. We looked around and there he was, sitting at a round table near the back: Trytian.

We hadn't seen him since the night at Stacia Bonecrusher's safe house where she'd escaped and Trytian had nearly blown us all sky-high. He looked a little like Keanu Reeves with an insolent grin, smug and self-satisfied. Only now, his hair was in a spiked shag, a dark mirror to Vanzir's, and he looked stronger than before.

He watched us as we approached, his eyes lighting. I sucked in a deep breath. He'd better watch it, with both Smoky and Shade on hand. They wouldn't put up with any crap from him.

We sat down and a waitress came over. Trytian patiently waited as I ordered beef fajitas and a salad. Camille ordered a chicken wrap, and Trillian asked for a bowl of their corn and red pepper soup.

When she left, Trytian leaned forward and, mostly looking at Camille, said, "Thanks for meeting me. I know you didn't want to, but it's in both of our best interests."

"Get this straight, Trytian." She folded her arms on the table, leaning on her elbows. "I don't like you. *We* don't like you. But there have been a few developments that we all need to be aware of. Including you, because you could fuck things up for us if you don't understand the ramifications of what has happened."

Ignoring the rest of us, Trytian leaned forward across the table, staring at her boobs rather than her face. "Tell me all about it, babe."

Smoky apparently didn't like the direction of Trytian's gaze because he leaned between them and, with one finger, poked the daemon in the chest. "Stop staring at my wife's breasts or I will teach you what it means to enrage a dragon."

Trytian sucked in a quick breath and leaned back in his chair. "A lot like your old man, aren't you? How's it hanging with Hyto, by the way? I hear he met with an untimely end after having himself quite a party." The smirk was back, and his eyes glittered as he challenged Smoky silently.

Trillian grabbed Smoky's arm. "Don't let him get to you. We have bigger fish to fry. Wait till we're done with Shadow Wing." He turned to Trytian. "You can look all you want until Camille decides to spit in your face. But let one finger touch what does not belong to you and you'll lose your dick. Understand matters?"

"Enough!" I was done with the posturing. And with Trytian. "Let's get down to business and leave the testoster-one for later."

Trytian pulled back and shrugged. Trillian winked at me. I waited for a moment and then turned to the daemon. "Talk to me, not my sister."

"Fine by me, kitty-cat."

"Her name is Delilah. You treat her with respect or you'll have two dragons on your tail." Shade drawled out his words in a lazy tone, but the threat was implicit.

Trytian snorted and was suddenly all business. The game had apparently worn thin. "Whatever. Let's get on with this. You know about Gulakah, then?"

"We do, at least to the degree that he's here, he's in Shadow Wing's pocket, and he rules over angry ghosts. We now believe that Telazhar, Van, and Jaycee are also in Shadow Wing's pocket. We think Shadow Wing knew Sta-cia was out to take his spot, and he was setting her up. Test-ing her loyalty before he let her get mowed down by us."

Trytian shifted in his seat, the smirk fading from his face. "Is this speculation or fact?"

"We're not positive, but we have circumstantial evidence. We think that Shadow Wing sent in Tregarts, who are now infiltrating the Freedom's Angels. We know for a fact they've been trying to cause a schism between the FBHs and the Supes. In fact, want to make a bet that whoever started the Church of the Earthborn Brethren is a plant for Shadow Wing? And those same Tregarts, why not use them to spy on the son of the daemon who's leading the opposition down in the Sub-Realms? You thought Van and Jaycee were on your side because they hung out with Stacia? Think again."

He pressed his lips together. I could see the wheels turn-ing in his head. After a few minutes, he blinked, slowly, and said, "All right. You've given me the heads-up, but since you won't work with me on my terms, I'll take care of my own backyard. Trust me, the Tregarts in my employ will be gone by morning. And they won't be on a flight home. Now, since you've done me a favor, I'll give you something in return. You've heard of the Energy Exchange?"

Camille cleared her throat. "The magical bar. We're thinking Jaycee and Van are behind it. We've run across a lot of references to the club in our investigations the past couple of days. We also know that a magical stun gun most likely came from there during our last dealings with the Koyanni."

"You're right. Only you won't find the pair on the owner's certificate. One of the Tregarts I've been talking to spilled that little news while drunk. He didn't count on my booze being of a much stronger nature than the Earthside alcohol." He laughed, his voice coarse. "Most people—demon or otherwise—underestimate my abilities."

Again, his glance shifted to Camille. *You're really walking on thin ice, dude,* I thought. I snapped my fingers, and he shook his head and shrugged. "Yeah . . . well, that aside, what were you saying about the bar?"

"The Tregart told me that his bosses had opened the bar to attract recruits. He said that anybody who walked in there and stayed would be the kind of people *they* were looking for." Trytian picked up a sugar packet and began playing with it, tapping it on the table. He ripped the top off and poured it into his coffee and stirred.

"They who?"

"I asked him that. He was sufficiently drunk to let names slide, for which—no doubt—he could have been killed. He said two Tregart sorcerers named Van and Jaycee. They apparently owned a magic shop that got torn apart by some explosion a few months back. He told me they smelled dragon in the air." With a long look at Smoky, Trytian let out a slow laugh. "Ten to one, I know who."

Smoky just growled.

"Yeah, I made you, right. They hurt your woman, right?" He glanced at Camille, who gave the smallest of flinches, but apparently Trytian was good at picking up on nuances. "What did they do? Beat you up? Set you on fire?"

She let out a long sigh. "Rolled me in broken glass during a fight. I survived, though I felt like a pincushion."

"That sounds about right. They're sadists. I knew that already. But I'll admit it: I really thought they worked for Stacia. I was wrong. They didn't work for her. Or, it turns out, for me. I had no clue they had this vendetta going on that involved your Koyanni shifters. I don't dabble in the affairs of most Supes. I'm only interested in building a force against Shadow Wing."

At the last, his eyes flashed and I saw a glint in them that made my stomach shift. Daemons were often more powerful than demons, and we still didn't know what abilities Trytian possessed. I wasn't entirely sure we wanted to find out, either.

"We were both played."

"Apparently so. Hold on one minute." Trytian stood, walked to the side, and pulled out a phone. The clamor in the restaurant was so loud it was hard to think. While we were waiting, the waitress deposited our meals on the table. Camille, Trillian, and I dug into our food.

After a moment, Trytian returned. He sat back down, leaned forward and cocked his head to the side. He interlaced his fingers, cracking his knuckles.

"Listen, puss—" He stopped as Shade shifted in his chair. "*Delilah.* Nobody plays me and survives. That phone call I just made? Every Tregart in my house will be dead within the next five minutes. Before you're done with your meal, every Tregart in my training camp will be dead. They won't know it's coming until it's over."

I blinked. "How many?"

"Forty-five . . . fifty. My Second knows for sure. But not Van and Jaycee—I only deal with them on a business arrangement. They aren't in my camp and they don't know the inner workings of my plans." He was cool as a penguin on ice. He didn't even blink.

"And you're comfortable killing them all, knowing that maybe some of them are truly loyal to you?" Once again, the difference between Trytian's methods and our own seemed so clear.

"Oh, don't try that with me, pussycat." He held his hand up as Shade stood. "Get over it, Stradolan. Yes, I know what you are," he added, giving my startled lover a quick, cold smile. "The fact is, you kill off every Tregart you come across, don't you?"

I stammered. "Well . . . yes . . . but . . ."

"You don't know if they're sent over here from Shadow Wing, if they're my soldiers, or if they're—possibly, just possibly—trying to escape their past and live a relatively normal life. *The only good Tregart is a dead Tregart.* Isn't that the way you work?" He slapped the table—one, quick, hard slap.

"He's right." Camille sat up, wiping the corner of her lips with her napkin.

I swiveled my head and started to say something, but she shook her head.

"We *do* operate that way. The Tregarts are our enemy. We fight them, we kill them. Trytian's correct." She ignored his snort. "He did us a favor, because no doubt at least a good share of them were working for Shadow Wing. Forty-five? Fifty? That many fewer demons we have to worry about."

I swallowed my protest. "Yeah, I guess so."

"So, what's our next move?" Trytian asked.

I didn't like the implication of that little statement "*Our* next move? What makes you think we're working together?"

"I don't think we have any choice on this. We were both deceived." He gave a little shrug.

Trytian had repeatedly offered to work with us. On *his* terms. But I still didn't trust him. We could definitely add to his army—we'd knocked off three demon generals already. But he knew we'd never kowtow to his orders, so what was he expecting? He had threatened Camille last time—it was obvious he wanted her. But no, Trytian would fuck her if he had the chance, but he wouldn't go to these lengths just for sex. He was an opportunist, not obsessed. So it had to be something else.

And then, I knew. There was one thing he could be hoping to gain—and obviously, he knew about it even though we had conveniently left out mentioning it when we told him what we knew.

"Tell us who the bald-headed man is who's hanging out with Van and Jaycee. He's not one of the Tregarts, but he is a Koyanni, and you know about him, don't you? You know what he carries. And *that* is why you want to work with us." He wanted the spirit seal, and he knew we could lead him to it.

Trytian licked his lips, but then he leaned back, locking gazes with me. "Let us proceed on the supposition that you're correct. We each hold pieces of the puzzle. Without the other, we flail in the dark . . . at least for longer than we would if we lay our cards on the table. Separate, we're strong. Together, we're stronger."

Trillian snorted. "What's to prevent you from turning on us when we find . . . what we're looking for?" He was playing with his knife and now pointed it directly at Trytian.

"Put your blade away, Svartan. You deserted the Sub-Realms like the rest of us. You're no better than me." He let out a huff. "I'm growing bored. Okay, I tell you who the bald-headed Koyanni is, and you let me in on the fight when you find out where he is. Better hurry. My offer expires in the next five minutes. I'll give you some privacy to discuss it while I make a trip to the john."

As he left the table, I let out a long sigh. "He wants the spirit seal. He knows who this guy is, and he knows he has one of the spirit seals."

"Do you buy the bit about him killing the Tregarts?" Shade looked skeptical, but both Camille and I nodded.

"Oh hell, yes. Trytian would sacrifice his own mother if he thought it would gain him another rung up the ladder. He's on a mission for his father, and nothing's going to stop him from his goal. And that goal is to raise an army to fight Shadow Wing. A spirit seal would go a long way in helping his cause." I slapped the table. "Damn it, I hate dealing with him, but we need to know who this creep is."

Camille's phone rang and she answered. A minute later, she hung up. "We deal with him."

"Why? Who was that?"

"Chase. There's a massive rally going on there between the hate freaks and the United Worlds Church. This is getting out of hand. We have to get over to headquarters and get the counter-rally started."

Trillian stood up and silently stalked into the men's room. Within seconds, he was back, Trytian behind him. The daemon looked at me, expectantly.

"Fine. We deal. Now tell us what you know about the bald-headed Koyanni." I pulled out my notebook.

Trytian laughed and reached into his coat pocket, withdrawing a sheaf of papers. He tossed them on the table. "Here's all the information I've gathered on Gulakah, on the Koyanni, on your bald-headed man. And here's the deal: You have my cell phone number. When you're ready to take him down, you call me. Whoever gets to him first gets the prize, and no fighting over it afterward. You have my word. Now keep yours."

"The word of a daemon." Smoky simmered, glaring at him. "How do we know you're good to your honor?"

With another laugh, the daemon shrugged. "You don't. But you don't have much choice, now do you?" And with that, he turned and exited the restaurant.

Chapter 18
❧❧❧

"I'm beginning to feel like we live here," I said as I eased into the parking lot. As we neared the building, I began to see a crowd. The signs they carried were ugly, and there were scattered members of the Freedom's Angels throughout the throng, along with a fair number of FBHs. The majority carried signs in support of Andy Gambit. *Andy Gambit the rapist and hatemonger.*

"I didn't think they'd actually gather here." I glanced at Shade as I maneuvered into a parking spot away from the crowd. The last thing I wanted was a rock through my windshield.

"Makes sense. This is where they're holding Gambit." Shade shook his head. "Crowd looks pretty mild right now, but those Tregarts in the mix aren't going to help anything. They'll do their damnedest to make trouble and stir up people who normally probably wouldn't do more than stand around shouting clichéd slogans."

I shrugged into my jacket as Camille pulled in next to us. "I don't understand how they can back him. How can they defend someone who raped—and helped slice up—a woman. She could have been one of them."

"But she wasn't. They see her as the enemy because Gambit and that sleazy rag he writes for paint her as the enemy. Gambit's no better than a two-bit Hitler. Give him enough power and he'd declare open season on the Supe Community." Shade leaned against the car, folding his arms.

"He's already done that." I punched in Tim's number, and when he answered, I said, "Get the phone trees in action. We need people down here at the FH-CSI to counterprotest Gambit's supporters. Pick them carefully, though. We need people who aren't going to fly off the handle and cause a stink. Levelheaded . . . that's the key."

"Will do. And, Delilah—you guys be careful. Please." He paused, not hanging up. "Listen, would you like some support from the GLBT community?"

It took me a moment to decipher the acronym, but when I did, my heart gave a little leap. "Of course we'd welcome your friends' support. Why would you think we wouldn't?"

He laughed. "No reason. No reason at all. I'll call our local support group and alert them to get busy, too."

I said good-bye and then called Neely. She sounded sleepy—apparently I'd woken her up. I glanced at the clock. Seven ten. The sun would be up in a few minutes. Menolly was already deep in her lair, falling into that dark slumber that summoned her each morning.

After I explained what was going down, she promised she'd get the United Worlds Church into action. Hanging up, I headed inside. Shade and the others followed.

As we walked past the crowd, they began to chant epithets, *Faerie whores* and *Fleabags* being among the unimaginative fare. Smoky turned to them and let out a low rumble that echoed through the parking lot and they stopped, staring at him. Camille tugged on his arm and we hurried into the building. As soon as Chase saw us, he motioned for us to follow him to one of the conference rooms, where we gathered around the table, all looking just as tired as we had earlier.

"It didn't take them long, did it? What did Gambit say when you hauled his ass in? I wish I could have been a fly on the wall for that one. Or better yet, there to watch his face and laugh at him when you put the cuffs on him." My hatred for Gambit had skyrocketed ever since we met Alfina.

"You are not going to believe what's happened. The news about Gambit got out on the early news, plus his photo. We've had five women come in already, claiming he raped them, too. Three FBHs, another Fae, one elf."

"That motherfucking piece of trash—"

"Yeah, I agree. Of course, Gambit's protesting his innocence and went into martyr mode. He used his phone call to contact the editor of his yellow rag, who first staged the protests and then called a lawyer for Gambit. And the guy he hired is apparently on the payroll with the same attitude that Gambit has. This is going to be sticky, because two of Gambit's victims are from Otherworld. Technically, I could extradite him, but the crowd out there would go insane."

"If we could get him to confess, it would make it so much easier." I didn't like the thought of Gambit on trial. There were too many things that could go wrong in a rape trial. Even with a serial rapist. Alfina was a gorgeous woman; the mindset that a woman deserved what she got was still far too ingrained in society—both Earthside and parts of Otherworld.

"That's not likely to happen. Unless . . ." Chase jumped up. "Wait here."

As he left the room, I opened the packet of information Trytian had given me. The top page was a photo of the bald-headed man—or at least *a* bald-headed man, but he was gaunt and lean, and tough looking, so he was probably our Koyanni. Around his neck was a pendant. One of the spirit seals.

"That's our man." Trillian picked up the dossier on him and began to read. "Name is Newkirk. No address, but it says here that he's been spotted at the Energy Exchange. In fact . . . it says here he's one of the regulars."

Camille leaned over his shoulder. "Looks like we're going clubbing tonight. What else is in that packet of info?"

I flipped through the pages; there was information on Gulakah—mostly what we already knew. He sure looked like a buttload of laughs. On the last page was a schematic of the bar. As I examined the layout, it became apparent there were several hidden areas, including . . . a tunnel.

"Want to make a bet there's an entrance from Underground Seattle?"

"What better place to use to hide things you don't want the cops to find out? Or to hide when enemies come looking?" Shade drummed his fingers on the table.

"I think the real question is, do they know what that pendant is? Do they understand the significance? The Koyanni looking for Amber's spirit seal didn't. All they knew was that it was of great religious significance to them, and it gave their leader powers." Camille shook her head. "I'm not betting the Koyanni know the true nature of the gem, but want to make a bet that Van and Jaycee do and they're biding their time to try to retrieve it for Shadow Wing?"

I skimmed through the pages until I found what I was looking for.

"It's no coincidence that Gulakah showed up here at this point." I pointed to one of the paragraphs. "Here—it says that Newkirk showed up on the scene a couple weeks ago. Van and Jaycee took an immediate interest in him."

"They recognized the spirit seal?" Trillian rapped his fingers on the table.

"Yeah. My bet is that they've figured out that Newkirk really does have one of the spirit seals and that they called home to Shadow Wing for help. Chances are, they don't know how powerful Newkirk is—yet. If they try to steal the seal by themselves and fail, that's going to look really bad to Big Daddy back home in the Sub-Realms."

"So, call for help and that way, it removes the responsibility from Van and Jaycee should something go wrong," Smoky said. "Which means the demon general knows exactly who has the spirit seal."

"Which means we're not the only ones after Newkirk. A three-way race against someone determined to keep what they've got. Us, Trytian, and the demons." The potential results of that race didn't make me altogether comfortable. In fact, two out of the three possible end scenarios weren't in our favor.

Chase opened the door and slipped back in. We looked at him, waiting. He cocked his head to the side, a faint smile flickering across his lips. "I just went to check on something and we may have lucked out. Turns out one of our FBH rape victims reported the attack when it happened a year and a half ago. They got DNA off her, but no hits were ever made, and though she described her attacker to the sketch artist, there were never any leads. We already ordered a DNA swab from Andy Gambit in Alfina's case. We'll know in a couple of days. I put a rush on it."

"It's going to be positive. You know it is, and then we make that pervert fry. Now, we've got some info for you about one of the spirit seals. We have a new demon general in town." My cell rang and I stopped to answer it. The Caller ID read *Trytian*. Crap, what now?

I flipped it open, listened to what Trytian had to say, and then turned to the others. "Don't they ever give it a rest? Van and Jaycee have been spotted over in one of the graveyards. They're with Telazhar, raising the dead—who knows for what purpose? Looks like they're intent on wreaking as much havoc as possible." I turned to Chase. "Can we borrow weapons? Not guns, of course, but my dagger's at home and so is Trillian's sword, and Camille's knife."

Chase nodded. As he called for Shamas to get a couple of long daggers from the armory, we grabbed our jackets. "I wish I could go with you, but I need my men here, in case things get ugly. Gambit's incarcerated here, and I don't want a situation where there's a run on the station."

"No problem. We can take care of this," I said, with more confidence than I felt. At that moment, Shamas hurried in and handed Trillian, Camille, and me each a good-sized dagger. They weren't silver but they were sharp, with cool steel hilts. As we headed toward the door, I gave them directions.

"We're headed to Freeburg Cemetery, a secluded graveyard in the West Seattle area." West Seattle wasn't all that far from the Industrial District, where the Energy Exchange bar was.

As we burst out the doors, we saw that the protest had swelled dramatically. There were three times as many protesters as there had been when we entered the building, but the majority of the new ones carried counterprotest signs. The media was having a field day, news crews all over, taking photographs and filming the relatively peaceful mob. I spotted Tim, standing with a bullhorn. He stood next to Neely, who had another bullhorn. Waving to them, I scrambled into my Jeep and put the car into gear as Shade joined me.

"I wish I'd brought Lysanthra," I muttered. "She's silver and works really well against the undead."

"Yes, but at least we have blades." Shade nodded. "We'll just have to get along with what we have. We don't have time to go home."

"Yeah, I know. But from now on, we go armed everywhere. I've been caught twice in the past few days relying on what I had on hand. Not again."

As we peeled out of the parking lot, following Camille's Lexus, life felt all too chaotic. I longed for the days when we were a small band, fighting what seemed like a relatively tame enemy.

Freeburg Cemetery was the home of the unclaimed dead, the final resting place for those with no money for fancy funerals or family to acknowledge them. A group of churches—including the United Worlds Church—contributed to the upkeep, as well as the burial of the indigent, the homeless, and the nameless.

The size of a small city block, the graveyard was surrounded by an iron picket fence that was falling over in some places. The budget for maintenance apparently didn't extend far enough to cover nonessentials. But the grass was neatly mowed, and a few rose bushes were scattered here and there among the maples and cedars and firs. Three statues of angels rose from the center of the park to watch over the dead.

I scanned the lot. The thickets of trees shaded lurkers, but even though it was midmorning, there weren't many mourners in sight. In fact, I doubted that the Freeburg Cemetery ever saw anybody come through to leave flowers or say a prayer for the dead, at least after the initial burial.

"There—over there behind that stand of cedars." Camille pointed to the right. I squinted and followed her direction. Figures were milling around what appeared to be a cluster of graves.

"Has to be them. Unless some family has suddenly discovered that one of their missing members was planted here. Come on, let's go. Stick to the trees." We slipped between the trees, crouching down. With luck, they hadn't spotted us.

"I'll be damned," Camille whispered. She was kneeling behind a large fern that filled the space between two large Douglas firs. The fern must have been growing there for years because it was at least four feet high and stretched between the trunks with ease. Camille parted the fronds and peered through them.

"What do you see?"

"It's Jaycee. Van and Jaycee are *here*. And there's somebody with them." She turned back to me, her face pale. "I think it might be Telazhar."

"Telazhar? How do we handle *him*?" I thought for a moment. "Do you see any sign of Newkirk?" The last thing we were prepared for at the moment was a Koyanni with a spirit seal. Especially one who knew how to use it.

She shook her head. "No, and I only see two other Tregarts standing lookout. But there are other figures out there, lurching around."

"Lurching? That doesn't sound promising." Lurching meant a lack in the motor skills department. And that much of a lack of coordination implied undead. Either that, or Van and Jaycee were hanging out with a bunch of drunken frat boys, and that didn't seem likely.

"Wait—Telazhar just . . . vanished." She shook her head. "He's able to teleport."

"Either that or he used a gate spell. Remember, we think he's the one who gated Stacia over here. At least with him out of the picture, we can probably take on Van and Jaycee. Are you ready to rumble?" I unsheathed the dagger Shamas had given me. While it wasn't silver, it had a wicked serrated blade. "Well, now, this will do some damage."

Camille smiled, then inhaled slowly, the crackle of magic rising around her. Holding out her hands, she began to summon energy—by now I could spot it a mile away when she was gearing up for a spell. "Yeah. I owe Van a nasty fucking roll in some glass."

I looked at the men. "You guys ready to go in?"

They nodded.

"Then . . . let's go. And this time, let's try to avoid letting them escape." I moved to the front, motioning for Shade and Smoky to follow me. Camille and Trillian moved to the side. Without another word, we went racing from behind the trees.

Van and Jaycee looked just about like we remembered them: dangerous, lying, scum. They were wearing jeans and polo shirts—and combat boots with nasty looking steel toes on them. They whirled as we came running out and barked an order.

Two more Tregarts—they looked like lackeys—stepped in front of the pair. But standing between the four demons and us were a half dozen ghouls. Or zombies. I wasn't sure which. Zombies were easier to kill than ghouls, so we'd find out the hard way.

Camille moved to one side and immediately let loose a bolt of energy directly at Van. She had a score to settle with him, and it looked like she wasn't wasting any time. I moved in to help her, but one of the zombies moved toward me, cutting off my view of what Van was up to. I tried to dart around the fiend, but even though it was slow, it was quick enough to cut off my access. There was no evading it. I'd have to fight.

Zombies would fight till they were torn apart. They were merely reanimated bodies. They had no souls, they felt no pain. Ghouls had some semblance of intelligence, warped as it was, but zombies were mere cannon fodder. Ghouls fed on flesh and energy, while zombies merely ate flesh and destroyed anything alive that they came across.

As the creature shuffled toward me, I sized up my options. Shamas had given us good, solid blades, and it wouldn't take much to carve up the creature if I planned my attack. I was faster and quicker than the zombie. They were dangerous in the sense that they were strong and hard to stop, but they normally weren't speedy.

A spin kick knocked the creature back. As it reeled away, I took the opportunity to slice through the zombie's gut and watched as the embalmed organs dropped out. Damn, Shamas had given me a sharp blade!

The corpse grunted but ignored the rain of organs pouring out of its stomach. It swiped at me, but I managed to keep it at arm's length with the dagger. As I glanced over to my left, I saw Smoky ripping one of the zombies to shreds. Shade had taken care of one of them, too. That left four.

A shout echoed from behind the zombies and a flash lit up the air. The next moment, my opponent began to move faster, a gleam in its eye. Hell! What spell had Van cast now?

I didn't have time to think about what was going on because the shambling lump of rotting flesh had become a freight train, bearing down on me. The zombie managed to evade my knife as a fist slammed into my side. I stumbled back from the blow—I felt like a concrete ball had hit me. As I struggled to catch my breath another flash lit up the sky as a woman shrieked.

"Camille!" I tried to dart past the zombie, but it blocked my way.

"Wasn't me! Keep fighting."

She sounded fine, so I turned my attention back to the corpse—it was coming in fast with another blow, but this time I managed to sidestep the attack and stabbed again, this time hitting its shoulder. Instead of pulling the blade out, I dragged it over the top, pressing to break the joint and slice the arm off. The zombie grunted again.

Before he could turn, I managed to slip around behind the creature and bring my dagger across the base of its neck, cutting through the vertebrae. As its head flopped forward, severed except for a thin line of flesh, gravity took over and the skin ripped, the head falling to the ground. Still grunting, the mouth snapped open and shut, unable to do anything. The body lurched blindly, and it was an easy matter to begin parceling out the rest.

A slice here, a slice there, and the other arm fell off. I severed the fingers and thumbs from both arms, and they flopped uselessly like fat grubs, unable to pull themselves along the grass. Within minutes, the zombie was an assortment of body parts. So much dead meat. The flesh quivered and jiggled, attempting to move, but the spell would wear off and this time, the corpse would stay dead in the ground once we reburied it.

Another shriek—this time it *was* Camille. I raced to help her, but one of the Tregart thugs jumped in my path.

"Ah, crap." I went into fighting stance as the demon laughed, approaching. He had the usual chain that Tregarts seemed to love to wield, whirling it as he eyed me with a glint in his eye.

"Come on, Blondie. You like it rough?" He lunged forward, his chain whistling toward me. I dove to the side, coming up with knife at the ready, turning my body so I was protected as well as I could be. As long as he had that chain, he could keep me at arm's length unless I could dart in too close for him to use it.

Looking for an opening, I stepped to the right. He turned to follow me, and I quickly darted back to the left before he realized what I was doing and drove my knife straight into his side, moving in close enough for the chain to be a liability. He dropped it as he screamed, grabbing for his belt knife. I shoved against him, using the hilt for leverage.

He let go of the knife, flailing to keep his balance, and we both went tumbling to the ground. I yanked my dagger back as he reached for my throat. Blood fountained out of his side and—as he grappled for my neck—I brought the hilt of the blade down on his forehead. A crack on his skull and he let go of the knife. Another good crack and his head fell to the side.

I jumped up, looking for his partner, but the other Tregart goon was already dead, and by the looks of the rake marks across his midsection, Smoky'd had a go at him. As I frantically tried to assess the situation, Camille screamed again. I whirled around to see her holding her side, doubled over. Smoke was wafting off her and the ground around her.

As I frantically looked for Jaycee, a body on the ground caught my attention. Jaycee! Camille had managed to drop her—or . . . Shade stepped out of a shadow cast by the tree and I realized he'd been the one who took Jaycee out. He and Smoky were bearing down on Van, whose sneer quickly vanished.

"Dragons!" He let out one shout and turned to run. As Smoky and Shade gave chase, there was a flash, and Van disappeared. Camille was crawling over to Jaycee, still holding her side. Trillian was trying to keep her still. In three quick strides, I was by Jaycee's side. She was still alive but stunned. Something had managed to knock her out, but she was coming around and the minute she was conscious, she'd be a danger.

I ripped her shirt off her and tossed it to Trillian. "Tear it into strips! Now!" He caught it, using his dagger to start the tears.

"Wha—who are . . . Where . . . ?" Jaycee shook her head.

Trillian handed me the strips of cloth and I stuffed one of them in Jaycee's mouth, tying it around her head to form a tight gag. As she began to push against me, Trillian caught her hands together. I wrapped a strip of cloth around them and tied them tight as she struggled. He used another strip to bind her ankles, and I rolled off her. There wasn't much she could do while bound and gagged.

Van had effectively left the building. The Tregarts and zombies were dead. Telazhar was still out there. But . . . we had an ace in the hole now. I looked around. It was easy to see where they'd gotten the bodies for the zombies from . . . I could count the six open graves from here, and there were broken shards of caskets scattered around.

"Ouch." Camille struggled to stand up. Smoky was examining her side.

"You're hurt. Can you stand?" He held her elbow as she forced herself to stand straight. "We need to get you to medical help."

"No. Hanna can handle it. The bolt only grazed me. Let's get Jaycee someplace where we can question her. The safe room at the Wayfarer. That way she can't throw any magic around." She winced but forced herself to start walking back to the cars.

"I'll take you—" Smoky reached to pick her up but she waved him away.

"Will you and Trillian rebury the bodies? They don't have any headstones, not really; they didn't have any family, and then Van and Jaycee came along and dug them up and we have no clue why. We can at least say a prayer for the dead over their graves."

I turned to Shade. "Can you carry Jaycee to the Jeep and wait for us?"

While he hoisted Jaycee—she was struggling like a fish on a line all the way—and carried her to the car, Smoky and Trillian began gathering the remains of the zombies and Tregarts and replacing them in the graves.

I took Camille's arm and helped her back across the lawn. "Tell me what happened."

"What's to tell? Van's damned good with the lightning bolts. He shot one at me at the same time I was aiming for him." She winced again.

"He hit you with a lighting bolt? How did you survive

that? He's freaking powerful!" I stared at her. Had Van somehow tripped up? If so, then maybe we had a chance.

She glared at me. "Don't get cocky. He misaimed and it went awry. He didn't touch me."

Confused, I cocked my head. "Then how did you get hurt?"

"Oh fuck, you're going to make me say it, aren't you?" She blushed. "My spell backfired and blew up before it left my hands. Somehow I managed to keep my fingers from getting blistered, but the force of the bolt hit my side and scorched me. I kind of . . . hurt myself."

I stopped, turning to her. "You toasted yourself?"

She grinned, then. "Yeah. Got butter?"

"No, but we can stop for some on the way." I laughed and, carefully wrapping my arm around her waist, hurried her to the parking lot.

We headed directly to the Wayfarer, with Trillian driving Camille's car, while Shade kept an eye on Jaycee in the back of the Jeep. I pulled down the alley and hopped out, opening up the back of the bar. All three of us had copies of the keys to everything we owned.

As I slipped into the back entrance, Shade followed, carrying Jaycee. It just wasn't a good idea to show up on the main city street during daylight carrying a bound and gagged woman. Chase would understand, but he wouldn't necessarily be the one getting the call.

We got her down to the basement. Kendra jumped up as we came in. An elf, she was one of the guards watching over the portal. She was on on-call duty and today was covering for the usual guard.

"You need any help?"

"Can you get Martin out of the safe room? We'll have to find another place to put him—a safe place—for now. Jaycee needs to be kept under lock and key. She's a sorceress and she's dangerous." I unlocked the door to the safe room and opened the door. "Oh, gross. It stinks in here."

Martin was sitting in a chair, staring at the wall. Ghouls didn't exactly need a lot of entertainment. I glanced around the room. He'd been fed recently, that much was apparent, and he'd gone to the bathroom, not in the toilet, but on the floor.

"Oh, Martin, aren't you housebroken?" Cringing, I motioned for Shade to wait outside. "Kendra, can you get me some rubber gloves, a bucket of soapy water, a garbage bag, and some paper towels?"

She nodded, running upstairs. I shut the door, keeping Martin inside till we were ready to move him. As Shade and I sat near the portal, waiting for Kendra, there was a long, low hum, and a crystal on the table lit up. I jumped up. The portal had been activated—I knew because this was the same portal my sisters and I had come through a couple years ago.

Shade made sure Jaycee was comfortable on the sofa and stood beside me. As we waited, I sucked in a deep breath. It was probably nothing. Probably just a visitor from OW.

As a form shimmered into view, I squinted, waiting to see who it was. And then, a leg stepped through, and then another, and we found ourselves facing someone I didn't think I'd ever see again.

A tawny-haired older man with a ponytail and feral eyes stood there. His eyes lit up when he saw me. It was Venus the Moon Child, the shaman of the Rainier Puma Pride, until he'd been carted off to Otherworld to join the Keraastar Knights under Queen Asteria.

"Venus! What are you doing here? You didn't bring the spirit seal with you, did you?"

"No, don't worry about that. I wouldn't carry it over here." He smiled sadly. "I've come for Zachary. He's going home with me. For good. He can run free in Otherworld a lot more safely than he can here. And I can watch over him. He contacted me and asked me to come get him."

I stared at him, reading between the lines. "Is he making the final transformation?" Zach was a Were, and the only time he could run, or walk, was when he was in puma form.

Venus the Moon Child put his hand on my arm. "Yes, my dear. He's decided that's what he wants to do. I'm going to help him."

There were rituals that could permanently shift a Were to his or her natural animal form. My breath quickened and I bit my lip as tears rose to the surface. This was real. Zach was leaving for good. He was going to go back to Otherworld with Venus, and once the ritual was done, he'd be a puma. *Forever.*

I'd wanted to love Zach because he'd fallen so hard for me, but I couldn't. I'd been attracted to him and the sex had been great, but it had become apparent to me that while I could love him as a friend, I couldn't *fall* in love with him.

During a battle with Karvanak, one of the demon generals we'd fought, Zachary been paralyzed saving Chase's life. He'd lost everything. His Pride had rejected him because he saved an FBH. He'd lost his job and was living on the grudging charity of the rest of the puma clan.

Venus saw the look on my face, and he pulled me into his arms. "There is no blame. Zach asked me to find you and give you a letter."

I caught my breath. Zach had rebuffed my friendship. He'd turned me away after he'd been moved to the rehabilitation center. "He wouldn't talk to me the last three times I tried to see him. He wouldn't see me."

"Zachary had to come to terms with the changes in his life." Venus handed me a letter.

I took it, opening the folded paper. The handwriting was Zach's.

Dear Delilah:

I asked Venus to talk to you, to give you this letter before he came to take me to my new home. Please, don't blame yourself for this. I don't. You thought I was angry at you, and I can understand why. But I needed time alone, without distractions or influences, to decide what was best for me.

And the best thing I can do for me is to live free in Otherworld. It's not the disability that is holding me hostage, but my own memories, my own fear, and the fact that my family has turned away from me.

The Pride resents me for helping out Chase, for putting myself in danger for someone outside the clan. I do not regret what I did, but their rejection is more than I can handle. I could never live in the city, and I can't live in a center like this where I'll never feel truly at home. I've always been more comfortable in my puma form. My Were nature longs to be free. To run wild and not feel caged. So, I've decided to go with Venus.

I never expected my life to go like this, but destiny has a way of taking us on unexpected journeys. I like to think that even if I hadn't been hurt, I might have made this same choice. In fact, I think I always knew that I was meant to prowl the mountain ranges, to run high among the rocky crags. I'll just do it in Otherworld, not in the Cascades.

Please, don't feel sorry for me. I don't. Not anymore. I'm looking forward to the next phase of my life. And I wish you—and all your loved ones—the best lives you can have. I pray you are able to win your battle against the demons. And I hope that you, especially, find the love you so dearly deserve. I loved you, Delilah, but now I have to love myself. So I'm letting your memory go, and moving on.

Chapter 19

I stared at the letter in my hand, then looked over at Venus the Moon Child. "Oh, Venus . . . he's sure about this?" I didn't want to think of Zach desperate. Or feeling trapped.

Venus wrapped me in his arms, pulling me close. He patted my back. "Yes, little panther. He is. We've talked long and hard. Queen Asteria gave me leave to come back home whenever Zach needed me. I no longer belong to the Pride, either. They're looking for a new shaman."

He cupped my chin and gazed into my eyes. "You know, deep in your heart, that he's not making a rash decision. Zach will have a better life over there with me than he would staying with the Pride."

I exhaled, slowly. I trusted Venus. He would tell me the truth. He wasn't one to lie. "Do you need an escort?" I asked, jotting his name down in the book and the purpose of his visit.

He shook his head. "No, I remember my way around. And Zach's waiting for me. We'll go back through the portal at Grandmother Coyote's. I just wanted to deliver his letter first. I was going to leave it here in the bar for you—I didn't expect you to actually be here."

I wanted to pour out my troubles to him, to tell him about what we were facing now. Venus the Moon Child seemed to invite confidences, but that wasn't his job anymore.

"Thank you. I'm glad we had a chance to talk." I couldn't just leave things this way. I sought for something else to say, wanting to hold on to Venus. He reminded me of life before it had been totally shot to hell. "Tell Queen Asteria we're on the track of another spirit seal, would you?"

He nodded. "I shall. I'll see you . . . well . . . sometime in the future, I imagine." And he headed up the stairs, passing Kendra on the way down.

She gave me a quizzical look, but I shook my head. "I know him. He's safe." I accepted the cleaning supplies and—while she babysat Martin and Shade watched Jaycee—I cleaned up the disgusting mess Martin had made of the safe room. That was what we got for keeping a ghoul around. Wilbur's house had been cluttered and dusty, but it hadn't smelled bad. I wondered just how he kept it clean around Martin. It seemed like a good question to badger him with once he was out of intensive care.

As I was finishing up, Camille, Trillian, and Smoky showed up. She was walking better. "Where did you guys go?"

"We stopped at Tenzos for some ointment for my burn."

Tenzos was a new chain store that had sprung up—it was geared toward Supes, containing a variety of common herbal remedies for Weres and Fae alike. Branches had been opening throughout the United States in most of the larger cities.

"Good. You don't want that getting infected. Let's get this show on the road. We have to interrogate Jaycee." I had my doubts about how much the sorceress would talk, but we could always let Menolly loose on her if we needed. Menolly had no compunctions about putting the strong arm on someone when we needed information.

Shade carried Jaycee into the safe room, where we cuffed her to the bedpost. Even if she got loose, she might be able to trash the room but she'd never be able to escape. As I removed the gag from her mouth, she let out what sounded like the words to a magical curse, her eyes gleaming. When nothing happened, she looked confused.

"Not gonna happen, Jaycee. Your magic won't work in here. Face it, we've got you, you're ours, and you might as well answer some questions." I straddled a chair, leaning my elbows on the back. "Now, tell us where you guys are holed up this time."

She let out a choked laugh. "You really think I'm going to talk? What are you, a moron in addition to being one of those stinking Weres?" She wrinkled her nose at me. "I smell cat shit."

I cocked my head. "You know our sister Menolly's a vampire. Tonight, she'd be more than happy to come question you, and she's not always a very nice person." Intimidation, I could do. Or at least a good semblance.

"You really think I'm going to turn in my partner? You're stupider than I thought. I'm a Tregart. We know the meaning of loyalty."

Camille joined me. "Loyalty? You're so loyal you'd spy on Stacia Bonecrusher for Shadow Wing, wouldn't you? You were so loyal that you set her up because your boss—Mr. Big and Mighty—thought she was a danger to him."

At the mention of Shadow Wing, Jaycee blinked. Aha—we were right.

"We know you're working with Shadow Wing; you might as well tell us the truth." I stood up and motioned for Camille to stand back.

"If I'm working with Shadow Wing, what makes you think I have any intention of talking to you? I'm not getting out of here alive. I'd be an imbecile to think so. You can do what you like, but I'm not talking."

Her bluster was real. I could see it in her eyes. She was waiting for us to kill her. Which we'd have to do. We'd never turn her to our side. Even if we did manage to secure her cooperation, we wouldn't be able to trust that she was telling the truth.

I shoved her back on the bed. "Shade, hold her down while I search her pockets."

Jaycee struggled, but Shade was too strong for her and I went through all her pockets, searching for anything that might help. I found her wallet and phone, and stepped back.

"No, those are mine—give them back!"

"I don't think so." I sat at the table with Camille and we started going through the wallet. "Our demon here has a driver's license, and her address is printed on it. And it's not the safe house they used last time." I jotted down the address.

"Found her smart phone. Let's see what we have in here . . ." Camille frowned. "It won't work."

"Remember? Most electronics won't work in this room. Step outside and check it out." I was still going through the various receipts and cards in Jaycee's wallet. Camille exited the room.

"Jaycee, I see you spend a lot of time at the Energy Exchange. Care to tell me more about the club?"

"Eat me out, pussycat." She just glared.

"I'm more into men, thank you. But I'll pass the invitation on to my sister, the vampire." My gaze flickered up to meet Jaycee's, and I saw the barest of flinches. So she *was* afraid of vampires.

After a couple of minutes of useless insults flying back and forth, Smoky frowned and slipped outside. I wondered where he was going, but the next minute he slammed the door back open.

"Get out here now—we need your help!"

Stuffing Jaycee's wallet and information in my pocket, I gave her a dark glare and then followed him out of the room, along with Trillian and Shade.

There was a major fight going on near the portal. Three Tregarts were tearing up the place, while Kendra and Camille were doing their best to hold them off. Camille had her dagger out that Shamas had given her, and I saw slashes on one of the demons' arms. Kendra was trained in martial arts and

she was involved in a brawl with the shortest one—she'd just
knocked him against one wall with an uppercut to the chin,
but it merely stunned him for a second and he was charging
at her again.

I unsheathed my dagger and charged in, helping Camille
with her opponent. Smoky and Shade divided up on the
other two, Smoky aiming for the one Kendra was fighting,
while Shade and Trillian took on the third.

I managed to land a blow on the Tregart's bald head,
gashing a long wound on his skull. He groaned, staggering
back. Camille rushed in, her dagger aimed at his heart. Her
blade bit deep and he stumbled, grunting. But then he shook
off the pain and gave a hard shove, throwing her back across
the room.

A flash caught my attention, but I didn't have time to
look. I attacked the Tregart, slamming him against the wall,
and drew my dagger across his throat as he struggled. A
fountain of blood sprayed my face and shirt as the demon
slid to the floor.

"No!" Camille's scream echoed and she took off on the
run toward the safe room. I whirled around to see Trillian
and Shade following her. Unsure of what was going on, but
trusting that it was something we weren't going to like, I followed them as Smoky finished off his demon, his talons gut-
ting him like a fish.

As I skidded into the safe room, I saw Shade and Camille
grappling with another Tregart. Jaycee was lying dead on
the bed, her throat cut from ear to ear. Shade caught the
demon in a chokehold and, with one quick movement,
snapped his neck. Camille knelt by Jaycee, then looked up
and shook her head.

"She's dead. He got to her before we could stop him."

"Van sent an assassin to kill his own wife? Or partner? Or
whatever the hell they are?"

"To keep her from talking, you bet he did."

"Question is, how the hell did they know about the safe
room? That we'd be keeping her here?"

"Oh great gods, I know how they knew!" She paled.

"Remember when Trytian sent the daemon to warn me that Hyto was around? We brought him down here. And we let him go afterward. He must have talked about it in front of the Tregarts. And since the Tregarts are working both sides of the fence, they told Van and Jaycee about it. That makes the Wayfarer an effective target. They may not be able to destroy the safe room, but they can destroy this building and put us out of commission. And now the demons know there's a portal down here, too."

Holy crap, she was right. I sank down on the nearest chair. "But why haven't they shown their hand till now, though? I'm surprised they haven't charged in to destroy the place and take over the portal. They can get to Otherworld through it."

Smoky frowned, then shook his head. "They may know about it, but they can't use it to get to the Subterranean Realms. And that is where their focus lies. They want to start ripping portals open to bring a number of demons over Earthside. They don't want to take a holiday jaunt to Otherworld. Not just yet."

Shade nodded his agreement. "You're probably right. Once they have a free-flowing portal between Earthside and the Sub-Realms, then they'll be looking for a way over to Otherworld. And then, this portal—along with Grandmother Coyote's portal, and all the others—will be targeted."

I started to haul Jaycee's body out of the room. "I'm not leaving her in there for Martin to feast on, regardless of how much we despise her."

With a queasy look on her face, Camille nodded. "I'm going to go check on Kendra and make sure she's okay. I suppose . . . we head back to the FH-CSI to see what's going on with the protest. Then, we make plans for tonight. All roads are leading to the Energy Exchange."

"Right . . . but we're going in the back way. Through the entrance in Underground Seattle. And if we're *really lucky*, maybe we'll run into some more ghosts down there." I grimaced.

Camille reached out and knocked on one of the walls. "Don't jinx us, babe. Don't jinx us."

Kendra was fine. I told her to call in extra help, just in case the Tregarts returned. As we headed out toward the door, I asked her to call Peder, the day bouncer—who was a giant— and have him take Jaycee's body and the dead Tregarts through the portal and dump them in OW, away from the city.

Once again, we were on the road. Traffic had picked up, and pedestrians were out in full force despite the wind and the chill. Men and women in three-piece suits hurried toward their jobs in the skyscrapers, shoppers in Prada and Armani scoured the boutiques, students waited for the bus, on their way toward the universities, their backpacks and Starbucks firmly in hand. Cars and Metro accordion buses crowded the streets as we edged our way through the morning bustle. The sky was overcast, but the rain had let up for a little while.

Finally, we were out of downtown Seattle and nearing the FH-CSI headquarters. As we pulled into the parking lot, I could see that the crowd had swelled even further. Andy Gambit's supporters were backed into one small area of the lot by now, and the crowd protesting against the hate groups was a good four times their size. Someone was handing out papers, and I grabbed one as we headed in the building.

The headline read, *Seattleites Refuse to Accept Hate Crimes or Rapists.* That was promising. I scanned the story as we pushed through the doors.

Apparently, the city had been looking for a good cause, because the quotes supporting the Supe Community were coming from housewives, students, cops, and businessmen alike. The statistics showed what I'd thought: the Church of the Earthborn Brethren's membership wasn't nearly as big as they'd let on, and most of the people polled wanted to see them run out of town on a rail. They were just a terribly vocal minority.

"Hate can only exist where people refuse to speak out

against it." Chase had been quoted, and the picture of him standing next to Sharah spoke volumes.

While Camille, Smoky, and Trillian stayed outside to talk to Tim and Neely and get the lowdown on what was happening, Shade and I pushed through the doors. Yugi waved us over. He had turned on the television that was mounted on the wall. The news was on.

The reporter was new; I'd never seen her before, but she looked bright and perky. I wondered if there was a finishing school for TV news reporters and talk show hosts where they were trained in the fine art of looking like they were on a perpetual high.

She cleared her throat and said, "And in other news, today, at the Faerie-Human Crime Scene Investigations headquarters, a protest involving around fifty people was staged in support of Andy Gambit, reporter for the *Seattle Tattler*, who was arrested on rape charges this morning. Accused of raping several women, including a woman from Otherworld, Gambit remains in custody without bail.

"His supporters—primarily members of the Church of the Earthborn Brethren—were passing out anti-Supe literature. A counterprotest ensued, sponsored by a combined effort from the United Worlds Church, the Rainbow Community Action Center, the Reclaim the Night Women's Coalition, and the Supe Community Council, and quickly swelled to encompass more than four hundred people."

The scene cut to a reporter interviewing people at the scene. They showed a montage of comments, cutting from one person to another.

"Seattle has no place for hate crimes. If he did it, Gambit should be locked up for good—"

"Rapists deserve to be castrated—"

"The Church of the Earthborn Brethren have been stirring up trouble for a while . . . we want people to know that most of Seattle doesn't feel this way—"

"If the Supes don't want to be targets, they should get out of town—"

"Hate groups have no place in this area. It's time Seattle woke up and took care of them before they become a serious problem. There's no room for supremacists here—"

And then Neely came on screen. She smiled and held up a new pamphlet that looked fresh off the presses. "We invite anyone who doesn't want Seattle to seen as a mire of hate and bigotry to join our new organization. Sponsored by the United Worlds Church, the Supe Community Council, Vampires Anonymous, and the Sovereign Nation of Talamh Lonrach Oll, we have formed an inclusive organization—All Worlds United in Peace. AWUP. Please, feel free to take some of our literature if you are interested."

And the comments went on. After a moment, Yugi turned down the sound. "As hard as it is to say, considering Alfina's injuries, the attack may be a blessing in disguise. This seems to have woken the city up. People don't want their home to be known for hate crimes."

I stared at him. Yugi was usually as sensitive as they come. "You're saying you *glad* Gambit raped her? Don't let Camille hear that garbage when she comes in here."

"*No!* I'm not saying that. But let's face it—as we've seen, this doesn't seem to be his first attack. We still need to get the DNA back, but there's no doubt in my mind that he attacked all those other women first. And there may be more. He may be a murderer. After all, from what Alfina says, he was all for killing her afterward, but the Tregarts wanted to leave her alive. They wanted to make the city believe that the FBHs were hurting the Supes and maybe start a fire."

He sat down at his desk. "I'll bet Gambit was quaking in his boots when he realized she'd be able to tell us about him. The Tregarts sold him down the river along with the Earthborn Brethren. We'd better pull our unsolved cases and see if we can match any of them up with him."

As he flipped through some papers on his desk, looking for something, Chase came striding out of his office.

"Good work on the protests. Thank Tim for me, will you? That news coverage did us a world of good. I've already gotten five requests to talk to neighborhood watch associations who don't want this kind of crap in their part of town. Did you catch the report right before it about the rise in hate crimes lately? They segued nicely into the piece about the protests."

We headed back to his office. "Chase, are you going to be available tonight? We're planning a raid on the Energy Exchange, and it would be helpful to have a member of the FH-CSI there to shut it down officially if we can capture Van. We know he ordered the bombings—"

The phone on Chase's desk rang and he held up one hand. "Yes? . . . Where? Oh crap, all right, we'll get a unit right over there. How many injured? . . . Right." As he hung up, he pushed himself out of his chair. "Come on. The Supe-Urban Café just went up in flames. Five injured so far, no known deaths at this point."

"Motherfucking son of a bitch. Van's going to wreak havoc on the city because we caught Jaycee and he had to kill her to make sure she didn't talk." I followed him out, Shade on my heels.

"What? You caught one of them?"

"Yeah, but Van sent in Tregarts to kill her. I'll explain how they found us later. Right now, we'll see you at the café."

On the way out, we caught Camille and the others coming in from talking to the protesters. I waylaid her. "To Marion's café, now. It's on fire."

Camille groaned. "Let me guess—Van's on a rampage?"

"Looks that way. He's out to scare the hell out of this city, and what are we going to tell the press about all this? *Demons terrorizing the city!?* I'm worried about Tim's business and all the other Supe businesses and homes. And what about Vampires Anonymous? We have to stop him or he's going to burn down the city." I pulled out my keys. "How's your side?"

"I'll live. Meet you there." She ran to her Lexus, Smoky and Trillian right behind her.

I stared at the Jeep. I was so tired of running around town, trying to put out fires—in this case, literally—that I could scream. But there was no choice. But before I got in, I pulled out my phone and put in the call that I really didn't want to make.

"Hanna? Put Marion on, please." As I waited to tell my friend that she'd lost not only her house, but her business, I looked up in the sky. The clouds were massing again. A crack of thunder split the sky and lightning flashed as rain began to pour, beating against the pavement. At least it would help the firefighters put out the blaze at Marion's—the drops were as fat as orb weaver spiders, breaking apart as they hit the ground.

Marion came on the phone. "Delilah? Hanna said you wanted to talk to me?"

"Your café's on fire. There are injured. We're headed there now."

"Oh, Great Coyote Master . . . we'll get down there right away—"

"No!" I was overexcited and yelled at her. "No, Marion. You stay there. We can't chance you being out in sight. We caught Jaycee, and the Tregarts killed her before we could get anything out of her. Put on Roz, please."

Marion protested, but I convinced her that she needed to leave the job to us. Roz came on.

"Listen, you and Vanzir tell the guards around the house to beef up security until we catch Van. Things are reaching an explosive level. Once they have more guards come in, get all our weapons ready for tonight. And if we're not home when Menolly wakes up, tell her we're going hunting tonight."

"That bad, huh?"

"Yeah, I think it will be. We're going to have ourselves a party at the Energy Exchange and it's likely to get bloody. Ask Morio to prepare whatever spell concoctions he and

Camille are likely to need. And make sure you don't forget to grab my dagger. I don't know if we'll have a chance to make it home first."

"Gotcha. Okay, we'll get everything together and I'll restock my armory." By his armory, Roz meant the coat full of weapons he routinely wore. He challenged Neo in the Matrix for most dangerous duster of the year. "So, you're expecting this to be big?"

"Yeah, we are. Van, Telazhar, Newkirk—"

"Who's Newkirk?"

"Our bald-headed man. He's a Koyanni with a spirit seal. Van and Jaycee have been posing as Trytian's lackeys while they've been double-timing first Stacia and then him. They work for Shadow Wing. Things have just gotten incredibly chaotic, and we have to take them down before they go on a spree. Right now they're targeting specific organizations and people, but that could snap at any time."

Spree killers didn't care what or who they hurt, and while—in the long run—that was essentially the nature of the demons, right now our singular focus was preventing a wider massacre.

"We'll get everything together and meet you . . . where do you want us to meet you?" I could hear Roz scribbling notes on a pad.

"Meet us at the Energy Exchange. I'll call you with a time." Flipping my phone shut, I slid into the car. Camille and the guys had already taken off.

Shade gave me a long look and I leaned my head back against the seat. "This sucks. Just a couple days ago we were having fun, preparing for Iris's wedding. Now we're running around like maniacs trying to stop a group of trigger-happy Tregarts. At least Iris and Bruce are having a better time than we are."

"Yeah, but look at it this way: We're not bored." And with that, he pulled me in for a kiss, then snapped his seat belt shut. I started the ignition, pulled out of the parking lot, and headed for the Supe-Urban Café.

Chapter 20

~~~~~

Marion's café was smoking. The front windows were busted out, but the building was still in one piece. Flames licked the timbers, but the fire department had managed to catch it before it engulfed the whole place, and the fire appeared to be normal, not magical. Maybe they'd run out of canya. We could only hope.

Two fire trucks were there, with firemen pouring water on the structure. Three ambulances were parked by the curb, treating customers who'd been overcome by smoke and light burns.

Chase and Shamas were there, running operations. Camille was searching through Jaycee's phone while Smoky, Shade, and Trillian talked to the customers milling around on the sidewalk.

I folded my arms against the rain. The pouring skies were helping put out the flames. As the scent of ash and smoldering wood filled the gloomy afternoon, I felt rage rise up. Marion didn't deserve to lose her house and her business.

Alfina hadn't deserved to be raped. The Supes didn't deserve to lose five members and their meeting hall. The demons were running rings around us.

Camille edged over to me. "I found several text messages on Jaycee's phone. And she has a calendar. Tonight she was supposed to meet 'N' at the Energy Exchange and the notation reads: *Bring payment.*"

"Payment? For what?" I ran through everything that we knew about the Koyanni. "Remember what Van and Jaycee were making for the Koyanni?"

Understanding lit up her face. "*Wolf Briar.* If they're to bring payment . . . then maybe the Koyanni are back to snatching werewolves. Or maybe they were about to be paid for the drug. Have there been any more reports of missing male beta lycanthropes?"

"I don't know. I didn't keep track after we shut them down the first time. Damn it!"

Wolf Briar was a dangerous drug, made from various glands of beta werewolf males who'd been caged and hyped up on steroids. The werewolves were terrified, angered, and at the height of their rage, they were flayed alive and dissected. When mixed with various herbs, this created a drug that would subdue most werewolves when inhaled. It also played havoc with some witches. Camille had been knocked unconscious when she triggered off a trap. Another exposure could possibly kill her.

"They're back at it. I know it. They're back at making that fucking drug!" I slammed my hand against a telephone pole.

"That's got to be it. That's why Newkirk and the Koyanni have targeted Marion. She gave us information about them. The Koyanni found out, and they consider her a traitor. She's friends with the Weres—werewolves and all. So they're systematically destroying her life. They killed her sister. They burned down her house and tried to kill her husband." Camille pressed her hand to her stomach. "What if they've already gone after her kids? She has three."

"I hesitate to have her call them—if there's trouble, there's no way in hell we'll be able to stop her from going to help them, and that could get her killed. We can't go along to protect her." We were stretched too thin as it was.

Camille pressed her lips together. "We don't have a choice. These are her kids. She *has* to know they're in danger, and she'd better call to make certain everyone's okay. And she has to warn them to be cautious."

As much as I didn't want to, I called Marion again and told her to check on her kids, make sure they were safe, tell them to be careful, and then call me back. As the smoke poured out of the now-smoldering but no longer flaming restaurant, I paced, wondering how much it would take to refurbish the café.

"We're not doing any good here. What next?" Camille leaned against her Lexus, watching the crowd that had gathered. She stiffened, nodding to a group that were just arriving. "Oh, hell—look at the slime that creeped out from under a rock."

I glanced at them. Protesters, carrying signs that read *Good Riddance* and *Burn, Supes, Burn* and other hate slogans. I jammed my hands into the pockets of my jacket and was about to head over to warn them off when another throng—about twice as big as the first—arrived on hand. They were carrying picket signs, too, only they were in support of Marion and the Supe Community. The minute the hate crowd began chanting, the others slid between them and the yellow caution tape cordoning off the café and overpowered their outbursts with a louder one.

"Looks like Neely and Tim have managed to coordinate things. They're right on top of it." Camille gave me a brief smile. "That's one of the first pieces of good news we've had."

"Think we're needed here?"

"I think they can handle it. Hopefully nothing will get out of hand." She signed and called to the guys, who began walking back to us.

"We can't hit the Energy Exchange yet—I want to go in at night, when we have a better chance of catching the Koyanni and Van. And when we have Menolly—and maybe

Roman—on our side." I mulled over what we could do in the meantime. I wanted a nap—curling up in one of my cat beds seemed like the ideal thing to do for a few hours—but we didn't have that luxury.

Then it hit me. "We were going to go talk to Queen Asteria. We've got a good five or six hours until we can even think about going to the club. What say we take a quick trip to Otherworld and visit the Queen? Or at least talk to Trenyth?"

That brought the first real smile from Camille I'd seen since Iris's wedding. "What say? I say *hell, yes.* You know, Chase has always wanted to see Otherworld. Why don't we take him? He can leave Yugi in charge for an afternoon. He can use a break."

And so, within half an hour, we were standing at the edge of Grandmother Coyote's wood, ready to portal-jump to the Elfin City.

Since we weren't planning on staying long, we decided to skip dressing for travel. The portal in Grandmother Coyote's wood would take us directly to Elqaneve and the city wasn't rough, or hard going, so we didn't need to worry about hiking gear. Chase looked nervous. Even though he'd been dragged into a different realm not long ago by one of the Elder Fae, he'd never been to Otherworld. And he'd never been through one of the regular portals.

We stopped at home first, to gather weapons and make sure everything was okay, and decided to leave Trillian and Shade behind. We didn't need them to update the Queen on the situation, and they could spend the afternoon finding out everything they could about the Energy Exchange and preparing for the evening.

Chase stared at the portal that shimmered between two large trees in the middle of the forest. Grandmother Coyote wasn't anywhere in sight, but we had license to use the portal anytime we needed to. The shimmering blue energy crackled and snapped.

"Is it like the one that I got dragged through by that freak show spider-Fae woman?" He eyed it suspiciously.

"Don't sweat it. The principle is similar, but it won't feel as weird. Well, *I* don't think it feels as weird." I patted him on the back, and he forced a smile. "I thought you wanted to see Elqaneve?"

"I do . . . I'm just . . ." He paused, then shrugged. "What the hell, I'm going to have a long life unless I get murdered or do something stupid. I might as well learn how to be adventurous." Sucking in a deep breath, he followed the three of us to the portal. Camille went first, then Smoky, then Chase, and then I stepped through.

Traveling through a portal is like stepping between giant magnets—with your body rippling apart into atoms, breaking down to the primal energy that makes up both spirit and form. Then every atom, every cell, goes singing through time and space. Within seconds, the body slams together again, in a dizzying whirl, and you find yourself standing a world away from where you began.

We were near the Barrow Mounds. Centuries ago, they'd been the home to the Elfin Oracle, Sarasena. She'd been killed by bandits, and after that, no plants ever grew again on the barrows. The ghosts of elves, long dead, walked between the mounds, whispering to themselves, thinking whatever distant thoughts they thought. They lingered, the victims of old battles, memories that would not rest.

There was a haunted feel to the Mounds, and every time we came through them, it gave me chills. Camille could see the spirits, and so could Shade and Morio. I was beginning to feel them more, the longer I trained with Greta. Eventually, she told me I'd be able to see ghosts and spirits with ease.

I looked around. By now, Morio should have used the Whispering Mirror to contact Trenyth, the advisor to the Queen. And . . . there he was, right on clockwork.

Trenyth, like all elves, looked younger than his years by far. He was loyal to the heart, and though he didn't seem to realize it, he was in love with Queen Asteria. I secretly hoped that one day she'd realize his feelings, but the age difference was probably too great for her to allow a tryst to take place. Not to mention the difference in caste.

Trenyth broke out in a wide smile. "Camille—Delilah! Welcome. Morio contacted me and said you'd be coming over. Are you staying for a while?" He noticed Chase and inclined his head. They'd met before. "Chase—what an unexpected surprise."

Chase held out his hand and Trenyth, used to the greeting by now, took it. "I hope you don't mind that I tagged along with the girls."

"Not at all." Trenyth motioned toward an enclosed carriage pulled by two horses. Noblas stedas—a variant of Earthside Clydesdales, they were gorgeous, broad shouldered, and regal.

"We can't stay long—a few hours at most—but we must talk to you and the Queen. It's imperative. We have some unwelcome news." I followed Trenyth, trailed by Camille, Smoky, and Chase. Chase, his eyes wide, darted glances every way as we headed to the carriage.

"This is incredible." Chase caught up to me. "The air is so clear here. I can't believe how easy it is on my lungs. I feel like I did when I quit smoking. Almost dizzy." Chase had stopped smoking when we were going out, and he had managed to stay off the cigarettes after we broke up. He cocked his head. "There's something else . . . I feel . . . tingly . . ."

"Magic." Camille accepted the driver's hand as he helped boost her into the carriage. "You're feeling the magic that permeates the air and the land. Otherworld is magical down to the core of each atom. With the changing nature of your abilities, you're becoming more sensitive to these things."

With a nod, he climbed into the carriage after her. The rest of us joined him, along with Trenyth. Smoky's head brushed the roof. As we headed through the cobbled streets, the horses' hooves clipped smartly against the cobblestones. Chase was looking out the window, an expression on his face that I'd never before seen.

"You know, even though I've seen things that, five years ago, I didn't even believe existed . . . I feel like I've stepped into Wonderland. I feel like Alice, down the rabbit hole." He looked so excited and his face was so lit up, that I couldn't help myself. I reached out and kissed him on the cheek. He pressed his hand to his face, grinning at me, then stared back out the window.

"The houses! They're so different."

Trenyth smiled softly, then turned to Camille. "Not to bring up a sore subject, but has your father been in contact with you at all?"

She hung her head, shaking it mutely.

"Why? Did Tanaquar decide she needed a new paramour?" I snorted. "Trenyth, unless you know something that we should, our father is a sore subject. Especially for Camille."

"I know, but . . ." He rubbed his chin and let out an exasperated sigh. "There are rumors . . . I don't know how true they are, but there are rumors going around that the Ambassador has had a falling out with Queen Tanaquar and she has tired of his attentions. She hasn't officially labeled him pariah, but reliable sources have told me that your father no longer holds the ear of the Queen."

So Daddy was on the outs with his lover, and his job might be on the line. I wanted to be empathetic, but after what he'd put Camille—and Menolly and me—through, it was hard. I couldn't help but have a little niggle of schadenfreude.

Camille, however, said nothing. But a sad smile escaped and she folded her hands in her lap as Smoky rested his arm around her.

As we traveled through the streets, the quietude of the city began to settle through me and I leaned back and closed my eyes, a feeling of longing resonating through me like ripples on a pond. I missed Otherworld. I missed my home . . . but where was home, really?

"We really are windwalkers, aren't we? No true home."

Camille cocked her head. "Oh honey, no. Windwalkers have no place to call home. But we—we don't have just one home. We have *two*. We're so much luckier than some people." She leaned across the space between the seats and took my hand. "It's all in the perspective."

Silent, meditating on what she'd said, I stared out the window as we clattered up the main road leading to the palace. Gleaming with alabaster, the palace was elegant in its simplicity. Surrounded by gardens, the royal courts were as clean and clear as the air. The road leading to the palace was spacious, paved with brown bricks. It ended in a cul-de-sac, with an island of grass at the end, where an oak tree grew so tall it was hard to see the top. A circle of early blooming jaspa flowers—they were a lot like Earthside crocus—surrounded the island, their fragrant white blossoms stark against the verdant green of the grass.

The carriage rolled into the cul-de-sac, stopping in front of the entrance. The driver opened the door and helped Camille and me out into the chill air. It was still early spring in Otherworld, too. The men followed. The driver bowed to Trenyth as a guard came up to lead us into the palace.

We followed Trenyth through the expansive halls, into the throne room. Chase turned this way and that, craning his neck to take in all the sights. He paused by a wood carving that ran the length of one wall. The bas-relief was etched out of oak and showed a procession of elves in the middle of the woodland, north of Lake Arvanal, where the elves held their sacred rituals. The raised edges were kissed with liquid silver, and the metal sparkled in the low light coming through the stained-glass windows of the hall.

Chase reached out, stopping a finger's length before touching the carving. "This . . . there is so much magic in here. So much history."

Camille joined him. "Yes, there is . . . but don't touch it. That would be considered bad manners." Then, she paused. "That's right—I almost forgot with all the frenzy over the Tregarts. You have a distant ancestor who was an elf. Enough, perhaps, for your blood to recognize this place."

He nodded, pressing his lips together, then returned to us. Trenyth motioned for us to hurry. We followed him into the

throne room. There, on a throne of oak and holly, sat the
Elfin Queen, as old as the world, as young as the spring.
She wore a gown made of silver and blue, and her hair was
bound up in braids like Iris often wore.

Even though Queen Asteria was as old as the hills, her
hair was still pale and flaxen, though her face was lined with
wrinkles. Elves aged so slowly that I couldn't imagine when
the Queen had been young—it had to be thousands upon
thousands of years ago. She was wisdom incarnate, although
we questioned a few of her decisions, and when she stood,
all elves in the room knelt at her feet. Camille knelt in a deep
curtsey while the men and I bowed low.

She motioned for us to stand. "Rise, my friends, and rest
yourselves in my chamber. Eat, drink, please."

As we sat down on the velvet benches at the sides of her
throne, serving women offered us goblets of the clearest nectar ever gathered, and delicate cakes that melted in our
mouths.

Queen Asteria slowly made the rounds, stopping before
each of us. She motioned for us to stay seated. She smiled
softly at Smoky. "Young beast, we meet again. You have
been through difficult times recently. Word travels even
here. But you have proven brave and loyal, and the Dragon
Reaches are lucky to have you as one of their lords. Say hello
to your mother next time you see her."

Smoky took the offered hand and pressed his lips, then
his forehead, to the top of her palm. "Your Highness, I will
convey your message. Thank you."

The Queen moved on to Camille. She leaned down and
cupped Camille's face. "My dear . . . there is nothing I can
say except . . . I am proud of you."

Camille's eyes flickered, and she looked like she might
cry, but then she merely nodded and smiled softly.

My turn was next. These rituals went back thousands of
years. Though we had pressing business to discuss, protocol
was to be followed. Tradition was the foundation of the
elves, even more so than the Fae. Countless years went into
forming the rites, and each generation learned from the last.

The elves were the backbone of Otherworld—they provided continuity.

"And we have Delilah. She who was born craving the sunlight and now must walk among the stars. The Immortals are not always kind, but I think . . . if you have to serve one of them, you are lucky with he who chose you. And you are lucky with the man you've chosen." She lifted my hand and looked at the smoky quartz ring. "He is constant. He is loving. And he will never betray you."

I pressed my lips to her fingers. "Thank you. I knew that, but I'm glad you said so." Suddenly realizing that Chase was sitting next to me, I glanced at him, but he was smiling at me and he mouthed *I'm happy for you* as the Queen moved on to him.

Queen Asteria stopped in front of Chase. She gazed at him, then reached out and touched him on the head. She closed her eyes and stood there, and Chase let out a little moan. After a moment, she let him go and he gazed up at her, his eyes sparkling.

"Even though the beginning of your line was so long ago that it is shrouded in the centuries gone by, like recognizes like, and blood recognizes blood. Chase Garden Johnson, you have been our ally over Earthside. Now, I offer you something you never knew you wanted." She motioned to Trenyth and he slipped to her side. She whispered in his ear and he nodded, then exited the room through a curtain off to the left.

"Chase, you know nothing about your elfin heritage. But I can give you history. I can give you names."

"I—I—you can?" He sucked in a deep breath and looked at me, a hopeful gleam in his eye that I'd never seen.

"Yes, I offer you a glimpse of your past. Distant as it may be."

Trenyth returned with a small chest, carved from a chunk of cedar with only a few runes engraved on the lid. He set it down next to the Queen, and she gestured for him to open it. He lifted off the lid and pulled out a journal that looked like it was ready to fall apart, then handed it to Queen Asteria, who opened it to a page somewhere in the center of the volume.

Without thinking, I blurted out, "You knew! You knew about Chase all this time and you never said anything."

Queen Asteria smiled, laughing lightly. Her voice rang with the sound of wind chimes. "I have known since this young man first came into the employ of the Otherworld Intelligence Agency, but it was not time to tell him. We had to wait and see how his destiny played out. And now, we have some glimpse of his future."

Chase coughed. "You know my destiny?" He sounded terrified.

"No, Chase. No one can ever predict destiny except for the Hags of Fate. But we have seen possibilities . . . and we want you to be prepared, so when you come to a crossroads, you can make an informed decision."

She held up her hand. "Back along the lines of your maternal blood line, a thousand years ago, one of our people met a woman named Rosalia. She was an herbal woman, living on her own in what is now Italy, near the coast along the Ionian Sea. She never married, but an elf named Tristan fell in love with her. She became pregnant but was too afraid to come over to Otherworld."

Chase was listening raptly. It was as if the rest of the room had disappeared and her voice was the only sound in the world.

"Rosalia bore twins—Io and Cris, and both thrived. They were half elf, and Tristan interacted with them. Io chose to return to Otherworld with his father when he was a young man, while Cris stayed Earthside. Cris hid his heritage, but he married and had children, and they grew strong. He told his children about their lineage, but he fell off a ledge when he was still young—by both human and elfin standards— and died. But his children remembered his story, and passed it along as they grew and had children. Elves and those with elfin blood are long-lived, but accidents were common in those days, and many of them died young."

"I never heard any of those stories. None of long-lived

relatives or romantic trysts with Otherworld beings." Chase exhaled slowly, shifting in his seat. He absently reached for another cake.

"I am not surprised. As the generations evolved, the bloodline thinned, especially with no new infusion of elfin blood, and the stories of Rosalia and Tristan disappeared into legend, and finally, into history. But Tristan always kept watch over his children and grandchildren and their grandchildren from a distance." She paused. "Would you like to meet him? Tristan, the father of your line?"

Camille jerked her head up. Smoky stared at Queen Asteria as if she'd just grown a second head. And I . . . I did a spit-take, cake crumbs spewing out of my mouth.

Chase grabbed my hand and squeezed it so hard I almost flinched. "Can . . . is it possible?"

Queen Asteria glanced at Trenyth. "While I talk to Delilah and her sister, please escort Chase to meet the elf who fathered his bloodline?" And before we could say a word, Trenyth had swept Chase away, through one of the doors, to meet his past.

While Chase was off learning about his distant past, we filled Queen Asteria in on what had been happening in the recent present, with Van, Jaycee, and the Tregarts. I reluctantly revealed the fact that Wilbur had been spying on us, keeping a journal, and that—although he wasn't a traitor— our info, including the fact that Queen Asteria had the spirit seals, may have found its way to Shadow Wing.

The Queen sighed. "This is sorry news. If Shadow Wing breaks through to Otherworld, we'll be the first stop on his journey. And even if he does not, surely he'll enlist the goblins or the ogres or perhaps the sorcerers down in the Southern Wastes to do his dirty work for him."

"That was our fear. Jaycee is dead. We're going after Van and Newkirk tonight. If we win, we'll have another spirit seal to bring to you. If not . . . then who knows what the hell will happen to it?" I kicked the floor. "What about the

Keraastar Knights? You said they were going to be able to help us repair the portals?"

"Not until we have all seven knights. Nine—with nine seals—would be best. But for now, we have only five. I found a match for one of the spirit seals not possessed by Ben, Venus, and Amber. In fact, Amber's brother Luke possesses the spark . . . so he has become one of our knights along with his sister. But the fifth seal, it is waiting for the right person—for the right knight to come along. By the way— Amber had her baby and she has a healthy, happy little girl. As to whether the spirit seal's powers may have altered her in the womb, we aren't sure. We won't know what to expect until she grows up and has her first moon-time transformation to werewolf."

The Keraastar Knights were a society that Queen Asteria had formed, composed of some of those who had possessed the spirit seals. She'd summoned them to Elqaneve and taken them in to train with her mages. For what purpose, we weren't clear, and she wasn't taking questions. My sisters and I didn't think it was such a good idea, but till now, we hadn't questioned her plan.

"Do you really think this is wise?" Even though it was a serious breach of protocol to express doubt, I couldn't help it. "Queen Asteria, we're worried. The spirit seals corrupt— they aren't evil, but they corrupt and twist the mortals who try to wield them."

Camille gave me a frantic look but then came to my defense before the Queen could speak. "Please, don't be angry. But Delilah's right. We are worried. You, yourself, told us that the spirit seals aren't trifles or baubles, and they should be hidden away. We've seen what they can do—"

"Stop." Asteria held up her hand. "No more doubt. Trust me, my girls. Trust me and have faith. And . . . for what it's worth, rest easy. The true nature of my plan . . . that is hidden from *everyone*, regardless of what you think you know. There is no one to betray me because no one except the Hags of Fate knows the truth of the matter."

That meant that King Uppala-Dahns and Queen Tanaquar didn't know as much as they thought they knew.

Camille gently shook her head at me. We'd expressed our concerns. And that was all we could do.

"We have to leave soon. We just needed to warn you. Keep watch to the Goblin lands, and to the other Cryptos. Who knows what the Tregarts have been up to?" I stood, looking for Chase.

"Your detective will be out shortly. Fear not. We will keep the watchtowers lit and active. And the grapevine runs in my favor. Now go home and do your best to corral this new threat. I will send more guards to watch over your house."

As Chase reappeared, a bemused and easy look on his face, we stood. After we made polite leave, Trenyth escorted us out and back to the portals. But I couldn't help but feel that giving the spirit seals to the knights instead of locking them away was a huge mistake, and I knew Camille thought it so.

As we hugged Trenyth good-bye and stepped through the portal, I hoped to hell that the Queen wasn't making a mistake that could bring down both of our worlds.

Chapter 21

Chase wasn't talking about his experience yet. I was curious, but Camille and I'd agreed we wouldn't push him. There was so much for him to accept. First with the Nectar of Life, and now this. He'd never met his birth father, but now he'd met the father of his family line, the line through which his mother was born. And that had to be huge.

By the time we got home—Chase accompanying us—it was nearing sundown. We had time to eat and rest for an hour or so before heading out.

Hanna was cooking dinner and Marion was helping her. Marion confirmed that all her kids were fine, which was a relief, and that she and Douglas had talked it over and decided to rebuild after all the mess was cleaned up. She glanced at me, and I saw in her eyes that all thought of divorce was gone. Somehow, the threat to their lives had rekindled whatever it was they thought was lost.

"We're not letting the Koyanni push us out." She gave me a cold smile, and her teeth suddenly looked sharp and vicious. "I'm not a pushover. They killed Trixie, they took my house, they burned my café. It ends here."

I patted her arm. "I understand. Hopefully, it will end tonight. Meanwhile you are welcome to stay here as long as you need to."

"I've got all your gear ready. Go take showers and get dressed." Roz had laid out all our weapons in the living room.

After we showered, Hanna put dinner on the table. Her cooking wasn't as good as Iris's, but she made a mean pea soup—thick and hearty—with smoked sausage that had been fried up with onions and garlic.

We gathered around the table. Morio started to set up the computer, but Hanna shook her head. "Food first. You have time after you sup to go over your plans. Now—sit. Eat."

I snickered. Hanna was getting more comfortable in her place with the family, and now that Iris was on her honeymoon, she seemed to be blossoming out. When Iris was around, Hanna was careful never to step on toes—she respected Iris's place in the hierarchy. But now, she seemed to be growing into her place in our home.

Trillian laughed. "The cook makes the rules." He winked at Hanna and she blushed. Her hair was the color of spun wheat, pulled back in a braid that reached her shoulders. Though she showed her age—and maybe a little more—from the years serving Hyto, she was still an attractive woman. She would have been close to forty if she'd been human, and her eyes were a warm hazel.

Hanna reached for the breadbasket, but Roz jumped up and took it from her. "Let me help you." He touched her arm, lightly, as he took the breadbasket from her and set it down on the table. She gave him a shy smile, and he returned it. It was almost as if . . . no . . . they couldn't be sleeping together. Could they?

Roz was an incubus; he wasn't capable of sticking to one woman. But then again, Hanna didn't seem interested in settling down, either. In fact, she was learning new traditions, trying to adapt to a world unlike any she'd ever seen before.

I gave Camille a long look and flickered my gaze to Hanna and then to Roz. She furrowed her brow, took a quick peek at both of them, then lightly shook her head at me. But she was smiling.

As we finished dinner, Menolly entered the kitchen. We filled her in on everything that had happened during the day while we helped Hanna clear the table. Afterward, while Hanna and Marion started on the dishes, Morio pulled out the computer and called up the blueprints.

While he was fiddling with them, Menolly floated up to the ceiling—she liked life at the top of the world. "Asteria won't even think of discussing the spirit seals?"

I shook my head. "We expected Queen Asteria to shoot down our concerns. She's going to do whatever she wants. Even if it fucks up the portals further, there's not much we can do about it. And really, what can we do? Steal the spirit seals back and hide them . . . where? They're probably safest where they are right now."

Camille paced back and forth, gesturing toward Menolly. "The problem is, they aren't being protected—not the way she promised. When we took her the first one, Queen Asteria promised to hide them away, to keep them under lock and key. If they're out and about, they could be targets."

"And again—what can we do about it?" I paused, not wanting to bring up a sore subject, but we had to address it. "What about Father?"

Menolly cleared her throat. "So you say our dear *pater* is on the outs with Tanaquar? She must have found another lackey who's more useful. But I'm surprised she didn't just add a paramour. It's not like we're naturally monogamous."

Camille ignored her, turning to me as she shrugged. "What about him?"

"Do you . . . did you want to talk to him?"

"Just because he's no longer dipping his wick in Tanaquar's pussy? You think that because she dumped him, I'm going to be all touchy-feely? That I'm going to excuse what he did? Until he comes begging me to forgive him, until the day he admits he fucked up and that he's sorry, you can bet our father isn't getting a free pass from me." She dug in the cupboard and pulled out a box of cookies, biting into one before tossing the package to me. Obviously this was the wrong avenue of discussion to focus on.

"Right." I caught the Oreos and pulled out a handful, passing them around. "Let's focus on tonight. Morio's got the computer ready. Let's plan out our raid."

We gathered around the computer.

"Okay, somebody has to stay home. We need Morio and Camille together, for their death magic. And Smoky and Shade. I'm going, and Menolly." I looked around. "That leaves Chase, Trillian, Vanzir, and Rozurial."

Menolly shrugged. "With the extra guards, I'd say we can get away with just Trillian and Chase here. Chase, would you mind hanging out for the evening?"

Chase let out a sigh. "Always the babysitter. Ah well, I haven't seen Maggie for a while. And if a call comes in—if somebody blows something else up—I'm going to need to head out anyway, so sure. Trillian, you up for a game of chess?"

Trillian rolled his eyes. "I can beat you with one hand tied behind my back, Johnson."

"Bring it on." Chase lifted Maggie out of the playpen and cuddled her as Trillian started to set up the chessboard on one corner of the table. Maggie pinched Chase's nose and licked his face. He laughed and tickled her tummy and then sat down with her in the stove-side rocking chair and began to sing a lullaby to her.

The rest of us went over the plans. The Energy Exchange had several hidden rooms in the back, as well as the connections to Underground Seattle. It was hard to tell from the schematics whether they had cordoned off a part of the underground tunnels for their private use, but it seemed likely.

Morio pointed out the route to get there, which ran through parts of Underground Seattle. Back in the late 1880s, a glue pot caught on fire and the resulting blaze destroyed twenty-five city blocks. When they went to rebuild, they decided to

(a) build out of stone and brick rather than wood and (b) regrade the streets one to two stories higher than they'd been. The resulting tangle created a maze of buildings; some that had escaped the blaze were now two stories belowground, reachable only by ladders. So as the new roads were built, the businesses relocated to the new street level and what had been the storefronts and streets now existed hidden, below the main city. Part of the labyrinth was still reachable via an underground tour, but a great deal of Underground Seattle had been forgotten, left to the Supes who made it their home.

"So, do we go in the front or come in from below?" Morio asked.

"If we go in the front door, they'll have time to escape." I stared at the plans. "The only thing is . . . the ghosts. We may have to face ghosts down there again. Ivana Krask couldn't have gotten all of them. Could she?" I turned to Menolly.

"No. She got the ones around the area where we were chasing the serial killer, but that was it. I doubt if she's been back down there on her own." She glanced at Morio. "You okay with going back there?"

Morio shivered. "I admit it, I'm not that thrilled about the idea, but I'm not about to shy away. I'm not going to panic."

Vanzir was leaning against the doorjamb. "We should take Shamas. He's a sorcerer."

"Good thinking. He should be home soon, but I'll call him." Camille crossed to the corner where she could phone him without our chatter interfering.

"So, we go in from below. We sneak through the tunnels, come up the back way. Which means we'll get a chance to see their dirty secrets first. But we have to be prepared for guards." I held up Lysanthra. My blade shimmered and sang to me. She was sentient, alive, and tingled in my hand. The longer I'd been a Death Maiden, the stronger my connection with the blade had become.

Menolly glanced at the clock. "We should head out. Any word on Shamas?"

"He'll be here by the time we're out to the cars. He was

just turning into the driveway when I called." Camille pulled
her hair back in a ponytail. She was wearing an Emma Peel
catsuit, with a leather bustier over the top and a short skirt
that wouldn't impede her movement. Her ankle boots were
grannies, laced up, with kitten heels.

I'd changed into a pair of well-worn jeans that bent easily
with my movements, and a V-necked tee, over which I pulled
a denim jacket. My boots of choice were a pair of steel-toed
hiking boots. Menolly wore her usual black jeans and long-
sleeved turtleneck, and Doc Martens.

The guys were decked out in their usual fare; Roz flashed
us with his freshly stocked duster, and it looked like he had a
bunch of new toys in there.

"I swear, you're a walking time bomb. Someday, someone's going to piss you off and you're going postal on them."
I picked up the printouts of the Energy Exchange. "I guess
we're ready. Let's go."

Camille, Menolly, and I stopped to kiss Maggie good-
bye. "Take care of her, Johnson," I whispered as I tousled the
fur on her head.

"Come back, Delilah . . . all of you." Chase gave me a solemn nod.

As we headed out the door, I stared into the darkened sky.
The rain had let up, but it was threatening to return. A sliver
opened in the clouds and a single star shone through. I held
on to the glimpse like a lifeline. A promise that this time,
we'd all make it through unscathed. Superstition? Maybe.
But sometimes wishing on a star was all we had to hope for.

The drive down to the Energy Exchange was quiet. We took
Morio's SUV and Camille's Lexus. Morio drove Shade,
Vanzir, Menolly, and me. Camille took Smoky, Roz, and
Shamas. We had decided to go in from a block away. There
was an entrance to Underground Seattle near there. It looked
like an old sewer grate, but it actually led down to the
tunnels.

We'd come prepared this time with gloves. The rungs

were iron and would hurt Camille and me. Iron burned
Menolly, too, but she'd heal from it a lot faster than we
would. But with thick fleece gloves, we were able to climb
down the ladder into the tunnels without a problem.

Underground Seattle was a spooky place, filled with cob-
webs and memories of times long gone. The tunnels were
cool and damp, and they smelled like an old tomb—musty
with a tang of mildew. The floor and walls, unlike the sew-
ers, were brick and wood, with nooks that had once been the
basements of shops. We'd gone down two stories in this area,
a good fifteen to twenty feet.

I flipped on the light that was clipped to my belt. We'd
discovered a delightful mountaineering store with all sorts
of wonderful gadgets, including belt lights, rope as strong as
the rope made out of spidersilk, and other goodies. Roz had
taken a buttload of money down there and gone wild a couple of months back, and now we had gear out the wazoo.

The passages were narrow in this area. I took the lead
with Shamas and Menolly; behind us came Camille and
Morio, then Smoky and Roz. Shade and Vanzir brought up
the rear. We started down the passage, cautious not to touch
the sides of the walls. There were viro-mortis slimes down
here, and while the green variety was a nuisance, the purple
could kill. Trouble was, neither was easy to see and clung to
the walls just waiting for victims to put their hands, or any
other body part, against the bricks.

I nervously glanced to the right and left, keeping an eye
out for any ghosts. The shadows that hung out in Underground Seattle were dangerous and usually pissed off. Glancing over my shoulder, I said, "Camille, can you or Morio
sense any supernatural activity here?"

We paused while she, Morio, and Shade lowered themselves into trance. After a moment, Shade's eyes flew open.

"Incoming behind us! Something, though I'm not sure
what. It's from the Netherworld, all right."

We turned just in time to see a woman come running
toward us. She was translucent, a look of horror splashed
across her face. She looked like she was screaming, but no

sound came out of her mouth and she raced through us—a cold breeze rattling by as she ran on ahead. Suddenly, she stopped, turned, and flailed. It looked like something had grabbed her around the waist and tossed her over its shoulder, though we couldn't see what was carrying her. The girl reached out, a knife in her hand, and slit her own throat. As the blood began to pour, she faded from view.

"What the fuck was that?" I was still cold from her passing through us.

"I don't know," Shamas said. "But let's go look where she disappeared."

We stopped where she'd faded, and I knelt down, aiming my light toward the ground. There, on the bricks, was the stain of dried blood. It didn't look terribly old, either. I glanced around. Off to one side, something caught my eye. A knife—it looked like the one that the girl had been holding.

"Well, we know she was real. And that her spirit hasn't rested." There was an alcove near me, and something was sticking out of it. I peeked in, cautiously, just in case it was a bloatworgle or something equally noxious. But it was a body, probably dead for around three weeks. And it was our girl.

I leaned down to examine her. "I wish we had a corpse talker with us. She hasn't moved on, she's still here."

Shade looked over my shoulder. "She was a Were. I can see her astral form still around the body. A werewolf."

"Crap. But they don't capture female werewolves for Wolf Briar." I shook my head. "I have no idea what they were doing with her, but I'll bet you anything that she was kidnapped by Van and Jaycee for some reason. Maybe prostitution, maybe just to have a little . . . fun . . ."

"We can't do anything for her. See if she had any ID— that way we can let her family know—and let's get moving." Morio turned to Camille. "Let's prep a protection spell for the group."

While they prepared their spell, I gingerly hunted through her pockets and found a wallet—it was a small clutch, with a checkbook in it. I eased it out of her skirt pocket, wincing as

I tried to avoid the decomposing flesh. Opening the purse, I glanced at the name on the checking account. Clarah Rollings. I flipped through the contents of the wallet.

Thirty-two dollars in small bills. Fifty-seven cents. A picture of Clarah—I thought it had to be Clarah by the spirit we'd seen—hugging another girl who looked a lot like her. Maybe a younger sister. They looked so happy it made my gut hurt. And—a driver's license. Clarah Rollings, all right. I tucked the license, the money, and the picture in my pocket. The gods willing, we'd at least have these things to give back to her family. And we could come back to pick up her body when we were done with the bar.

"That's all we can do here. Let's move."

Re-forming ranks, we headed down the passage. As we neared the area leading into the tunnels directly below the club, we came to a wall stretching across the passage.

"Looks like somebody decided they wanted some private space." Shamas moved forward, looking at the wall, but not touching it. He motioned to Morio, who joined him. "Can you find any traps, or maybe, the entrance?"

Morio examined the bricks. "The trigger to open the secret entrance is down here, but I think there's something . . . stand back." He moved to the side and held out his hands. With a soft whisper, he flexed his fingers as pale blue light began to emanate from them. It clung to the wall, creeping across the bricks like a misty cloud. As it reached the central point in the wall, a crackle of sparks raced through the fog, and the scent of sulfur filled the air.

After the light cleared, Morio examined the wall again. "It's clear now." He reached down and a soft *click* sounded. An entrance appeared as a secret door swung open.

"We're in," he said, moving back to his place beside Camille.

Shamas and I took the sides of the doors. We peeked around the corner, and—surprisingly—saw a string of dim lights running along the artificially lowered ceiling. The passage was empty, and so we cautiously entered. I motioned for Vanzir to close the door behind him.

"They could have built a level between the basement of the club and where we are." I kept my voice low, just in case the place was bugged, or in case somebody came down from above.

"Want to make a bet it's not a pleasure palace?" Camille muttered. "Okay, we head up the ladder. While we're climbing, Morio and I won't be able to cast a spell, but we have a protection charm prepped and we can cast it now. It should give us protection unless someone interferes. If we're attacked, it will break since we can't concentrate on it while we're on the ladder, but there will be a few seconds lead time." She shrugged, smiling grimly. "Some protection is better than nothing."

We all nodded.

"What do you need us to do?"

Camille motioned for us to stand at an arm's length apart. "It's simple, just close your eyes until we tell you to open them."

As Morio moved in back of us, Camille took the front. They moved as a pair, arms out, down the line, energy racing around us, from Morio's hands to Camille's, and back again, creating a circle. I closed my eyes, but the crackle of magic was unnerving. I could feel it tingle as it slid over my body, into my lungs.

They began to singsong back and forth in a counterpoint, low chanting on the currents of air, but powerful enough to make my skin crawl.

"Spirits of water, spirits of earth . . ." Camille's voice was rich, like sloe gin, throaty and warm.

"To our spell come forth, give birth . . ." Morio echoed back at her, soft-spoken and smooth.

"Spirits of fire, spirits of air . . ."

"To all unwelcome, beware, beware . . ."

"Spirits of the Netherworld take heed . . ."

"Hear us in our hour of need . . ."

"Circle 'round, protect, defend . . ."

"Until this spell breaks and ends . . ."

The passage seemed to take a deep breath, and then

Camille asked us to open our eyes. We couldn't see any difference, but the feel of magic was there, saturating the air. Shamas's eyes were bright, sparkling, and he stared at them, his expression flickering between envy and admiration.

"We're ready. Let's go." Camille stepped back into place, as I motioned for Menolly to take over the lead, followed by me, then Shamas, and then the others in order. Menolly would be the least vulnerable if somebody was waiting up top.

The rungs led into a narrow vertical passage. As we climbed, I saw that there was, indeed, a second level before reaching the street. As I stepped onto the landing that led to a metal door next to the rungs continuing up, Menolly had her ear pressed against the steel, trying to catch any sound coming from within.

"All I can hear is a shuffling behind the door."

Once we were all crowded on the landing, I checked the lock while Shamas held a light on it. Easy to pick—obviously they didn't think anybody would be coming through their barricade below. I pulled out the set of lock picks I carried around everywhere I went, and within seconds I had shimmied the pins. With a soft *click*, the door opened. Holding my breath, I pushed it open and Shamas and I slammed through.

The room was long and wide, lined on both sides with cages. Three held prisoners—men, manacled to the walls. They were in pain, and two were frothing at the mouth. There was no doubt in my mind they were werewolves. When they saw us, they rattled their chains and tried to lunge forward, but the manacles only gave them a lead of a few inches from the wall.

"Crap. We have to shut them up so nobody hears them." As I scanned the rest of the room, I was relieved to see nobody else around. Shade made sure the door was shut behind us and leaned against it, just in case someone tried to come in.

"Leave it to me." Roz pulled out three quarter-sized black balls with a wick on each end, and a lighter. He lit the wick on the first and sent it skidding toward the first werewolf.

A small puff of smoke rose up from the smoldering bomb and then a *pop* as a shower of sparks set off the spell. The man let out a sharp cry, then slumped, unconscious. Roz moved to the next cell, and then the third. "That's all I have of those—they're pricey, but we can look around in peace now."

As we ransacked the room, Camille let out a little cry. She was at the very back, and she motioned us over. "I found their dissection table." A queasy expression crossed her face, and though I didn't want to see it, I looked.

We'd seen this before, when we were dealing with Van and Jaycee the first time. The table was more like a long sink—seven feet long—set into a stainless steel counter. It was a good ten inches deep, and drains on either end led down to pipes below the fount. A faucet with a sprayer attachment was fixed to the center of the drain board. The sink was porcelain, and heavy reddish-brown stains spotted the length of it.

"*Wolf Briar.* This is their setup. But how do they dispose of the bodies?" I looked around. There was a cloaked-off section to the right. I hoped to hell we wouldn't find a special surprise like a Tregart or two hiding behind the curtains. But as I pulled them back, what we did see was even more disturbing. There was a portal there. It was between two obsidian obelisks that were about four feet high, and it crackled with orange light.

"Where the hell does that lead? I don't think I want to stick my head through to find out." As I drew closer to the vortex, it sizzled and popped.

Shamas approached, motioning me back as he knelt near it. "I think I know." He held out his hands, closed his eyes, and whispered something I couldn't catch. After a moment he pulled away and turned around. "I was right. This portal leads to the elemental plane of fire. Ten to one, they shove the bodies through and take care of them that way. They just burn away in the heat."

"Their version of a crematorium." I stared at the portal. "Is there any way to close that down? It seems way too dangerous to leave open."

Shamas nodded. "You're right. It is dangerous. We do not need fire elementals running rogue over here, and believe me, they can come through. I can close it, but whoever opened it is going to know sooner or later. If they're not focused on something else, they'll feel the spell break, because this isn't a naturally occurring vortex."

"Do it. The minute you're done, we'll head topside and take out the club. And . . . crap . . . what about the were-wolves? We can't just leave them. Somebody might decide to come down and slit their throats to keep them from talking, or out of spite."

Smoky shrugged. "Rozurial and I can take them through the Ionyc Seas. We'll take them to the FH-CSI—the medic unit can take care of them."

"Good thinking. Shamas, while you close that, we'll get the guys out of here."

I started to pick the locks on the cells, but Menolly motioned me aside and just broke the lock by yanking open the door. She bent the chain link, tearing the manacles from the wall. Smoky gathered up two of the men. Roz took hold of the third, and they vanished from sight.

"One of these days, I expect one of them to overshoot and end up in the middle of Puget Sound," Camille said, attempt-ing a smile. "How's Shamas doing with the vortex? I've a good mind to go check on him."

"I wouldn't." Morio grabbed her arm. "If he's still work-ing on closing the thing, and you disturb him, it might get ugly. That's pure flame—the core essence of fire. And the last thing we need is a rush of energy to come flowing through to light everything ablaze."

She acquiesced. "You have a point—oh, here he comes."

Shamas hurried over. "Closed, but whoever built it was one fucking powerful sorcerer. Telazhar?"

"Telazhar is a necromancer, not a sorcerer." I scratched my head. "Jaycee . . . I don't think so. But Van . . . I'll bet you Van opened it up. I had the feeling he was the more pow-erful of the pair."

"Well, whoever it was did a damned good job of warding

it, and you can guarantee he knows it's been shut down. So we'd better get up to that club now." Shamas grabbed my hand and started leading me back to the door. Just then Smoky and Roz reappeared.

"They get settled in?"

"Yeah." Roz frowned. "They were in pretty sorry shape."

"Well, we'll have to worry about them later. Come on, we have to rumble." I swung onto the ladder, followed by Shamas. "Let's go take them out, guys." And so we crept up the rungs, on our way to what I felt in my bones was going to be one of the toughest battles we'd faced yet.

Chapter 22

❧⚬❧

As we approached the landing leading into the back of the club, I began to get nervous. But Menolly was going first, so I couldn't see if she was about to run into anybody. As she shimmied off the ladder, there was a shout and sounds of a scuffle. Crap—someone was up there.

I swung myself over the edge, pulling Lysanthra out as I did so, and saw Menolly wrestling with a Tregart. He appeared to be the only one, and as I hustled over to help her, she fastened on his neck and he stopped struggling. As she drained him of blood, he went limp in her arms.

As he fell to the floor, she turned and I saw a stake sticking out of her turtleneck. I started to scream but she motioned for me to keep quiet and pulled it out. Blood oozed slowly out of her side.

"Another four inches and he would have dusted me. But he missed my heart. This will heal." She looked shaken—just in the slightest—and she tossed the stake over the edge of the landing. "Fucker was hiding in the shadows. By the looks of his weapons stash, he's a clone of Roz—prepared for anything."

I examined his body. "Hey, he has another one of those magical stun guns, and it looks fully charged. I handed it to Vanzir. "Here, you can use this."

He took it, nodding. "Let's get in there. Who knows if he had time to raise an alarm. What else he have?"

"Various daggers—be careful, they look like they might have poison on them. Smells goblin in origin. The usual chains these fuckers like to use, a second stake, and . . . hmmm . . . a ring of keys!" I held them up, then pocketed them. "Want to make a bet one of them opens those cells down below?"

Menolly examined the door he'd been guarding. "This door isn't locked." She yanked it open, almost pulling it off the hinges. As it went swinging back, she stormed in. Shamas and I followed, and then the rest.

We spilled into a back room. Music pounded from somewhere inside the club. Whoever was out in front wasn't going to hear us until we started tossing furniture around. The room was obviously an employee lounge, with long tables, a counter with a microwave and coffee maker on it, a refrigerator, and a series of lockers. Camille stopped, pulling out her cell phone.

I stared at her. "Who the hell are you calling?"

"We promised Trytian a piece of the action. If we don't stick to the bargain, we make another nasty enemy." She paused, holding up one finger. "Trytian, get your ass down to the Energy Exchange. We're infiltrating from the back. If you hurt any of us, I'll take your butt down so hard you won't be sitting for weeks. Got it? . . . You *what*? . . . Right . . . think again, hotshot. Okay, see you in the fray. We're not waiting for you."

She hung up and began yanking open the lockers, dumping the contents. I was about to ask what he'd said to her but, with one glance at Smoky, decided on discretion. Trytian was crude, and his manners over the phone weren't any better than they were in person.

Camille tossed through the lockers. "Not much here, a few skimpy outfits, mostly lingerie. I'll bet we find a few brothel rooms. This one's locked. Smoky?"

Smoky broke the lock on it and Camille opened it.

"Hello . . . I think I found Van's locker." She motioned to Shamas. "You know what any of this crap is?"

He peeked inside. "Spell components. A couple firebombs. A bottle of . . . Wolf Briar. It's labeled. Another bottle that's got pixie dust in it. I'll bet the pixies hate him." Taking both bottles, he shoved them into his backpack. "We won't leave these here for anybody else to find."

Roz took the firebombs, and Camille grabbed a bottle of dishwashing soap off the counter by the sink and poured it liberally over the rest of the things in the locker.

"Spell components need to be untainted. This will ruin them for anybody's use. Even if he rinses them, the chemicals in the detergent will have altered their energy and they'll be useless." She threw the bottle on top of the components, grinning. "Anything to screw him over."

"Okay, are we ready? We head through that door, and this is it. We're going to be walking into a den of vipers." I glanced at them. "Remember, there's a spirit seal out there—and we have no idea what Newkirk can do with it."

I went first, with Menolly and Shamas right behind me. As I opened the door a crack, I could see a hall to the right and the left. Directly ahead was a beaded curtain leading to what I assumed was the main club. There was laughter coming from down the hall, and moans, blending into the throbbing music from out front. Van probably wasn't with the whores, but there was no telling whether they were here voluntarily. For all we knew, Clarah Rollings was destined for this joint. If the prostitutes were prisoners, then their customers might not think twice about cutting the girls' throats if they thought they were being raided.

I motioned for Vanzir and Shade to check out the rooms, and then, with a wave to the others, I burst through the main curtains.

The Energy Exchange was packed. The dim green light

gave an eerie neon glow to the room. A deep heavy beat
throbbed beneath the wailing music; the reverberation had
to be some form of magic. The bar was lined with patrons,
drinking everything from beer to tall glasses foaming with
steam that spiraled up, sending a pungent smell into the air.

Dancers writhed on the floor, and the booths were filled.
Camille and I scanned the room for Van. Camille pointed to
a table near the bar. Van was sitting there with the bald-
headed man—Newkirk. They looked like they were waiting
for someone.

As we waded through the dancers, I wondered how the
hell we were going to get away without hurting anybody not
involved in this mess. Van wouldn't hesitate to put innocent
people at risk—and the minute he saw us, he was going to
come up swinging.

"Over to the bar. Now. Everyone." Camille whispered
loud enough for all of us to hear, then—as we moved to
obey—she and Morio pulled back, and they linked arms.
They were staring out over the crowd. Fuck, they were up to
something and it felt big.

As they murmured softly, drowned out by the music and
crowd, a shadow began to emanate from their hands, and it
grew larger, then billowed up, a cloud of smoke that rolled
over the dance floor. People began to scream as the cloud
took the form of a large winged creature. Whatever it was
scared the hell out of me, but I managed to stand steady.

Several dancers looked confused but not frightened, and
they held their ground, but a stampede toward the door
started as the shadow dove into the crowed, screeching over
the music. I glanced over at Van to see him jump up, looking
around wildly. Newkirk sat still beside him, unmoving, staring straight at Camille and Morio. Crap. We'd been made.

As the crowd pushed through the door, leaving ten dancers behind—all looking suspiciously like Tregarts—an
older man huddled in a booth in the corner. He had grizzled
hair and a scruffy five o'clock shadow. Shade and Vanzir
popped through the curtains right about then and gave me
a nod.

"Van, I just punked your stash in the back." Camille stepped forward.

"Bitch. I'm going to gut you." He motioned toward Newkirk. "The three girls are mine. The rest—you deal with."

I glanced at the older man in the booth, but he just sat, watching, a smile playing over his face. And then, I *knew* who it was. Telazhar. Fuck, he was going to play cat and mouse with us—and probably with Van. I fell back to where Smoky and Shade were standing. "That's Telazhar—"

But I'd barely gotten the words out when he slowly stood and flexed his fingers, then pointed at me and I screamed as a burning blast caught me on the arm. Slammed back against the floor, I rolled over to staunch the flames that were blazing brightly.

Van whirled, staring at Telazhar. "What the fuck are you doing?"

"Shut up." The necromancer held up his other hand and a ghostly host appeared in back of him. Five etheric figures, all terrifying and mist-shrouded, headed our way.

"I think we have company!" I pulled out my dagger.

At that point, Morio yanked out a miniature coffin, opened it, and tossed Rodney onto the floor. "Grow, fight them, and keep your mouth shut." Rodney grew to full size, a terrifying sight considering he was a skeleton with an attitude, and he headed directly toward Telazhar.

I felt something brush by my side. Arial was here—I could sense her. She raced past me, headed for Telazhar.

The Tregarts on the dance floor were converging, along with the ghosts. This wasn't going to end well. Shade vanished into the shadows. I didn't bother looking to find him—I didn't have time to waste seeing what he was going to do.

Smoky took on the Tregarts. He rushed in, talons sharp, a blur of white against their somber black. A whir of chains flashed through the air at him, ending in garbled cries as he took down two of the demons, bashing their heads together with a tremendous crack. Blood poured from fractured skulls as he tossed them to the side, grinning wide.

Menolly and Roz joined Smoky on the dance floor, while Vanzir raced by, catching up to Rodney, and they were a blur of demon and bones on their way to face the necromancer. Fuck—Vanzir didn't have his demonic powers anymore! He could get himself killed. I didn't give a damn if Rodney got toasted, though he was helpful when he kept his mouth shut, but I kind of liked Vanzir and wanted to see him come out of this alive.

Just then, I turned to see Newkirk focusing on Camille and Morio while Van was homing in on me. The hairs on the back of my neck stood up as he let loose with a blast. Before I could move, the energy bolt hit me and knocked me off my feet, slamming me a good ten feet back. I landed on my butt, skidding even farther back till I hit the wall.

Shaking my head to clear the ringing in my ears, I jumped up and—not wanting to wait for his next attack—raced forward, Lysanthra poised to stab through whatever flesh I could find. For such a pale, bland man, Van was incredibly powerful. Looks could lie, and lie big.

He was ready for me, laughing as he held up his other hand and a wave of flame emerged. I managed to duck to the left, away from the blast, and as I did so, I spun around and lunged toward him. Lysanthra sang as she clipped Van in the side, ripping his jacket and slicing the skin below.

Van narrowed his eyes, his nose pinched and turning white.

"Cunt." He let loose with another spell, and this time it hit me square in the chest, knocking me back again. And this time, it was fire and I was suddenly aflame again. I screamed as a shower of ice pellets and mist hit me, putting out the flames. Smoky was there. He yanked me to my feet, gave me a quick once-over, and, seeing that I was still in one piece, whirled around to face Van, his talons long and glistening sharp.

I pushed myself off the floor. My shirt was charred and I was mildly burned, but the flames hadn't had time to do any real damage. Thank the gods I'd kept my hair short.

A shout to the left, over near the table where Van and

Newkirk had been sitting, caught my attention. The bald-headed man was playing with the spirit seal and Morio was on the ground, thrashing. Camille was screaming, holding her head as she slowly sank to her knees. I started in their direction, but the next moment, Shade appeared and backhanded the man with such force that it knocked him over the table. As he scrambled to his feet, Shade was on him, pummeling his face. Whatever spell he was playing with broke, but Camille and Morio stayed down. Smoky glanced at Camille and panic set in his eyes, but he forced his focus back to Van and grabbed the sorcerer around the throat with both hands.

At that moment, there was a commotion from the front of the dance floor and a rough laugh burst out in the room. Try-tian entered, followed by two lesser daemons—horns on the head and all. They engaged the Tregarts alongside Roz and Menolly.

There was a loud shout and a flash lit up the room over by the booths along the wall where Telazhar had been sitting. He was on his feet, and he was trying to do something to Vanzir and Rodney, but whatever it was didn't seem to be working. In fact, Vanzir was standing there, head thrown back, soaking in the energy. Good gods, had he regained his ability to feed off life force?

Before I could figure out what was happening, Telazhar broke off his attack and stood back, gesturing with his hands. Magic flowed between them, and then another flash and there was a spinning vortex in the room, and something was coming out of it. Oh fuck, what the hell was going down now?

Everyone stopped to turn and stare, including Newkirk and Shade. Smoky kept his hands tightly clenched around Van's neck, and I heard a snap as something in the demon's throat broke. His head lolled to the side and he slumped. Smoky tossed his body aside.

I hurried over to Camille and Morio, who were slowly struggling to their feet. I grabbed Camille's arm and helped her up, then turned to see what the hell we were facing now.

The portal was spinning, and runes lit up the sides, hanging in midair like eye catchers.

Camille gasped and moved forward, staring at Telazhar. "No—you can't! You're fucking insane!" As she started to run forward, Newkirk lunged and grabbed her around the waist. He slammed her over the table, against the wall, and then Smoky was on him, ripping his face with one long sweep of his talons. Morio managed to shake out of the stupor as I ran toward Camille. Menolly took the opportunity to break the neck of a nearby Tregart, and now she and Trytian were attacking yet another.

Vanzir and Rodney began to back up as a noise came through the portal—it was the sound of trumpets thundering, of crackling fire and the screams of the damned.

"A Demon Gate. Telazhar created a Demon Gate!" Morio looked petrified. "What the fuck—"

Camille was nursing her wrist as she staggered to her feet. A nasty lump on her forehead was going to hurt a hell of a lot worse later on. She heard Morio and, before I could stop her, was racing headlong toward Telazhar.

Morio staggered after her, and I gave chase after him.

Vanzir glanced at them, then moved in again on the other side of the necromancer while Rodney tackled the last Tregart. The bone golem grabbed the demon's balls and twisted, hard enough to rip them off. A sharp scream echoed through the room and the demon fell to the ground, blood saturating his pants.

I caught up with Morio and pushed him aside, then reached out and yanked Camille back. As she fought me, I pushed her together with Morio. "If you have any magic left, now's the time to bring it on!"

A clap of thunder and the room filled with mist, pouring out from the Demon Gate. Trytian was suddenly beside me. He grabbed my arm and yanked.

"Get the fuck away—you do not want to be in the way when the guest of honor comes through." He dragged me out of the way as a hooved foot stepped out from the gate. I caught my breath. *Not Shadow Wing—please, don't let it be Shadow Wing!*

Newkirk lunged forward, blood pouring down his head. One eye was hanging by the optic nerve, dangling on the side of his face. He was clutching at his chest—holding the spirit seal. A flicker of light shone from it as it began to reverberate, and Newkirk dropped his head back and let out a crazy laugh.

The figure emerging from the Demon's Gate was a reptilian creature; he was nine feet tall and looked a little like one of the Sleestaks from *Land of the Lost*, but his head was sporting a lovely do of weaving tentacles that draped down his back like crazy dreadlocks. His eyes were flat and black, if it was a he. It was rather hard to tell. I thought I saw a penis, but I wasn't looking all that hard. My attention was focused on the razor-sharp teeth and the claws that passed for fingernails. He was a dirty olive green, and his gaze darted this way and that.

Four shadows followed him out of the gate, and I groaned as pictures began to fly off the walls and spin through the air. Morio yelped and ducked as a chair went over his head all by itself.

Next to me, Trytian let out a sharp gasp. "Gulakah! Motherfucking son of a bitch, that's Gulakah, the Lord of Ghosts! Get the fuck out of here or *we are dead*." He motioned toward his bloatworgle lackeys. "Get the seal! Now!"

Oh hell! Trytian was making a play for the spirit seal. I barreled headlong toward Newkirk, dodging the creatures. I was faster than they were, and as I pulled up in front of the Koyanni, a light shot out of the spirit seal, hitting me like a fist in my stomach. I lurched, falling across the nearest table. The daemons were hot on my heels, but they, too, ended up sprawling on the floor. Smoky and Shade were coming in from two different angles, but then Gulakah was suddenly in front of the Koyanni, moving in a blur. As the ghosts following him entangled the dragons, Gulakah gutted Newkirk with one hand while with the other he ripped the spirit seal from his neck.

"No!" Menolly raced forward, but Trytian tripped her as she went by, turning to the Lord of Angry Ghosts in her place. He tried to snatch the spirit seal out of Gulakah's hands, but one of the ghosts rushed through him and the daemon went sailing back across the club, landing in a heap against the wall.

Camille let loose a ball of energy and it landed square on the demon general but bounced off and managed to take out one of the ghosts. Gulakah snaked his neck around to stare at her and, with a whimper, she scrambled back, turning to race for cover. In the next moment a black slither of energy came sailing out of one of the moving tentacles that he called hair, and it hit her in the back, sending her sprawling. She screamed, so loud I thought she was dying, and Smoky and Morio flew to her side.

Menolly and Roz were side by side, and they both threw ice bombs at the demon general at the same time, but they just exploded and shattered another one of his ghosts.

Telazhar was heading toward the Demon Gate, and Gulakah, spirit seal in hand, followed him.

"No—you can't take that!" I leaped forward, but the next moment, the two vanished through the gate, and the gate disappeared. They were gone, and so was the spirit seal.

"*Fuck*. We were right. Telazhar *was* working with Shadow Wing all along, and now he's helping Gulakah. They took the spirit seal. Shadow Wing has two now . . . no . . ." I could only whisper as the shambles around us began to come into focus.

"Camille needs help! Delilah, get over here." Smoky sounded frantic.

I crawled over to her side. Something black and leechlike was affixed to her back. It had eaten through the cloth. "Motherfucking . . . what is that?"

Trytian stomped over. "Good going. Now neither of us has the seal."

"Fuck you and the horse you rode in on. Do you know what the hell is attached to Camille?" I shoved him in front of me. "Because if you do, fix it."

He gave me a long, cold look but turned back to her. "Devil leech. You need to freeze it off her. And I'd do so soon, or it will burrow through the flesh and take hold of her heart, and then she'll belong to the enemy." And with that, he motioned to his henchmen and they strode out of the club.

We sat there, in the midst of absolute carnage, as Smoky sent a blast of freezing cold over Camille's back. The leech let go and fell off, and Camille groaned. She rolled over and slowly sat up, looking as bruised as I felt. We'd all been slammed around, including Menolly.

"Well . . ." The sudden silence was deafening and I felt like somebody had to say something. "What do we do now?"

"I'm not sure," Shade said, "but whatever it is, I don't want to make the decision from here in this club. At least Newkirk is dead, and Van and Jaycee."

"Yeah," I whispered. "But at what cost?"

Camille rose, unsteady on her feet. "If that . . . *thing* . . . that was on my back is any indication of Gulakah's powers, then he scares the crap out of me. Because I could feel it worming its way into my heart . . . like it was planting seeds of evil within me. When it died, they died, but if you'd been much longer, I would have been fighting for Shadow Wing."

"That's worse than the Karsetii demon. Instead of draining your powers, it turns you. And it came out of one of those tentacle-snakelike things on his head." I turned to Shade. "Do you think he's gone back to the Sub-Realms?"

"Probably to deliver the spirit seal, but he'll be back. I guarantee it. We lost this round. Shadow Wing isn't going to let that go unnoticed."

Smoky shook his head. "No, he won't. And Shade is right. You can be sure that Gulakah will return. And Telazhar with him. They are working in concert, that much has become obvious." He glanced around. "Where'd that punk Trytian go?"

"Back to the Demon Underground, probably to let his father know what happened. I think . . . as much as I hate to say it . . . we're going to have to contact him and work out some sort of long-term alliance. His army's been decimated since he killed off most of the Tregarts who were following him, but we can't count Trytian out." Camille stretched, wincing. "What about the women in back?"

"We told them to stay put . . . bunch of Weres who'd been kidnapped. I think it's time we tore this place apart. We need to find their armory and confiscate everything we can. Then we need to level the wall down below and close this place down for good."

"Blow it up? The building's empty except for the bar. There have been a number of explosions here tonight. We can pin it all on Van, and Chase can announce that the mad bomber was caught and killed." I looked around, wondering just what had gone down in this club over the past few months.

"Sounds good to me." Menolly glanced at Smoky. "You and Shade willing to rattle the rafters?"

"Oh, let me," Vanzir said, with a sly grin.

"You? You have dynamite or something?" I stared at his eyes. They whirled as usual, a pool of unnamable colors, but there was something behind them—something new.

He shook his head. "Don't need it. Trust me."

We got the women out, calling Sharah to come pick them up and check them out. She also took the body from the tunnels and I gave her the girl's wallet and belongings. Sharah promised to notify Clarah's family.

After busting out several walls, we found a stash of weapons, including a number of magical stun guns. We cleared the bar, including some of the better-quality booze, and stepped outside. Vanzir stood in the archway to the entrance. He held his hands up to the sky and let his head drop back, staring at the ceiling. There was a creak, then a groan, and then a shift. After a moment, the concrete walls began to buckle. The ceiling wavered, and with a shriek, the metal struts gave way and bent, breaking through the cement.

Vanzir was sweating, his face set in a horrible pain-racked visage. He took one last deep breath and then, as he exhaled, the club began to crumble, imploding in on itself, screaming girders and all. As the thunderous sound of falling concrete filled the air, Vanzir stumbled back and Smoky caught him before he fell. We watched as the club slowly disintegrated before our eyes, and then . . . it was gone in a cloud of roiling dust.

Chapter 23

❦

We phoned Chase, asking him to meet us at the FH-CSI. Everybody needed to be looked over. As we straggled in, bedraggled and bruised—except for Smoky, who was clean as fresh snow, of course—Chase stood, his mouth agape.

"What the hell happened to you?"

"Don't ask. But the explosions should stop, at least all of the ones as of late. Menolly was almost staked, Camille's got more bruises than a prizefighter, and I think I might have sprained my ribs again. I also think I bruised my tailbone when I was slammed against the wall." I looked at the others. We still hadn't asked Vanzir about what the hell he'd been able to do. Obviously, he had some new sort of power but how, and from who?

Morio rubbed his neck. "Look me over, too—check out my injury. I think I'm okay, but I got banged up pretty bad."

Sharah nodded. "What about the rest of you? I doubt if I have to ask Smoky and Shade. What about you, Roz? Vanzir? Shamas?"

They shook their heads, mostly just dirty and bloody.

"We'll wait in the waiting room," Shade said. Sharah took Camille, Morio, and me back to the exam rooms. None of us were in need of hospitalization, but Sharah spread salves and lotions where we needed them, and she made sure there weren't any lingering tendrils from the devil leech. After twenty minutes, we were pronounced fit to go home.

Chase was waiting with the guys. Roz was gone. He'd left for home to make sure there were enough people guarding the house. We gathered in the conference room and examined everything that had gone down.

"Jaycee and Van are out of the picture. Dead and gone. Most of the Tregarts are gone, too. Newkirk, dead. The Koyanni will be on the run, now that their new fair leader's dead. They aren't very effective without a good leader, and I have the feeling, having lost their Wolf Briar contacts, they won't be showing their heads much around the area. Of course, that's what I said the last time." I ticked off notes on a steno pad.

"The Energy Exchange is gone, and Vanzir trashed the place." Camille turned to him. "And just how the hell did you do that? You were stripped of your powers."

He ducked his head. "The Triple Threat . . . when Camille was in the Northlands with Iris, they began taking me through a series of rituals. I didn't know why, but Grandmother Coyote told me that I needed to cooperate. When one of the Hags of Fate gives you a direct order . . ." He stopped. Nobody questioned *that* little piece of news. We all jumped when Grandmother Coyote said jump.

"What did they do during the rituals?" I started to asked, but Camille stopped me.

"He can't tell you." She gave Vanzir a long look. "Rituals are private affairs, just like my initiation was. I knew you were studying with the Triple Threat, but I wasn't sure why. We won't ask how or why—not right now . . . but if you have other powers, you better tell us if you can. If you know."

They locked gazes, and then, with a glance at Smoky, Vanzir gave a half shrug. "I feel like some of my prior powers are coming back, but they feel . . . different. I don't feel pushed to feed on anybody now, but I feel like I could reach out and . . . I don't know just yet. Like tonight, I knew that I could bring the club down. I still don't understand how I did it, but I felt like I could reach out, take hold of the atoms making up the walls, and shake them into falling apart."

"Very well," Smoky said. "But you keep us informed." He and Vanzir were on speaking terms again, but I had the feeling Smoky still didn't trust him.

Vanzir nodded. "Save your huff and puff. I promise. I'll tell you when I sense something new." He slid back in his chair, examining his fingernails.

"And now, for the elephant in the room." I tossed the pencil onto the table. "We have a new demon general to deal with. He managed to steal one of the spirit seals. We all know he isn't going to stay back in the Sub-Realms. He struck a blow for Shadow Wing here, and he's going to be shipped right back here to wreak more havoc. And Gulakah . . . there's no way we can take him down easy, especially when he combines his powers with Telazhar."

Menolly floated down from the ceiling. "He's the Lord of Ghosts. We're going to have a long haul getting rid of him. Not to mention the freak-show cavalcade of spirits he'll bring with him. Those motherfucking ghosts he trotted out tonight were probably the mere bullies of the party. I can't wait to see him call up the big boys."

I rubbed my temples. I had a raging headache. "There's nothing we can do about that right now. We have to be satisfied with the fact that we took down Van and his cronies."

Yugi knocked at the door, then peeked in.

Chase motioned him in. "What is it, Yugi?"

"Gambit is dead." Yugi glanced over at us, looking grim.

"What the fuck happened?" Chase jumped up. "We had him in custody—he was going to stand trial and we were going to put him away."

Yugi placed a series of photos on the table. "Here—these are printouts caught by the security camera. This man just . . . showed up in the cell block. We have wards down there to prevent magic, but somehow he got in. The next shots show him in Gambit's cell—with it still locked—and then, a blur, and then—Gambit's dead and the man's gone."

We glanced at the pictures. *Trytian.*

"Fuck—how did he get past your wards?" I slammed my hand on the table. "I'm not sorry that Gambit's dead, but what's this going to do to the hate groups? They'll martyr him."

"No, I don't think they will," Chase said. He handed me the evening edition of the *Seattle News*. The front-page headline read, Three More Women Report Gambit Raped Them.

"So, he really was a serial rapist?" I flipped open the paper. Sure enough, apparently three more women had come to the headquarters during the evening to swear out complaints, stating that Gambit had raped them, too. The *Seattle Tattler* had withdrawn its support of him, basically throwing him to the wolves.

And Trytian . . . had shown up and killed him.

"There's no way to bring him in," I told Chase. "We can't arrest a daemon—he'd be out of here so fast that . . ."

"Yeah, I know. I'll swear out an arrest warrant on John Doe, but this is one case that will remain unsolved. Once the DNA comes back—providing it proves it was him—the public isn't going to mourn Gambit's death. Good riddance, even though I can't say so in public. At least not until I have the DNA proof in my hands." He paused. "So, where does that leave us?"

I just wanted to go home and go to sleep. The past few days had been brutal, and we'd lost a hell of a lot. But we'd also gained allies, and support. And we'd taken out some of the bad guys. And maybe, just maybe, we'd started a movement to squelch the hate crimes that had been building in the city.

Camille laughed. "It leaves us . . . well . . . we prepare for the return of Gulakah and Telazhar. With Gulakah being the Lord of Ghosts, and Telazhar being an ancient necromancer, they're well suited to work together. So . . . what next?"

I shook off the bone-weariness that had settled in my

body. "I supposed . . . we tell Queen Asteria we lost another spirit seal. We see about getting Wilbur out of the hospital so we can give Martin back to him. We build an alliance with Trytian. We tear down that wall below what remains of the Energy Exchange. We help Marion rebuild her café and help her and Douglas find a new house. Just a simple morning's work."

Snorting, I stood. "At least we got Van and Jaycee off the streets, out of the picture. No more Wolf Briar, at least for now. And Zach . . ." I told them about Zachary, as hard as it was. "He's gone out of our lives for good, I think. But it's his path. It's what he needs to do. He's running through the hills of Otherworld by now, free and healed."

After a pause, where we all stared at the table, Shade grabbed my hand. "Before we take off for the night, there's one more thing we have to address."

I looked at him, unable to think straight. "If there's anything else, I've lost track of it."

"Delilah has conveniently forgotten that I asked her to marry me. And she said yes. Well, she said yes to *someday* becoming my wife." He grinned, and as Camille and Menolly clapped, I blushed. While everyone was talking at once, I moved over to the window, staring out on the squad room. Chase joined me.

"Delilah," he said softly. "I want you to know . . . I'm happy for you. Truly." He offered me his hand and I took it, squeezing his fingers.

"Thank you. I'm content. It's right. Shade and I . . . we fit together. We're a match, in a fashion I never knew I could have."

"I know you are. I can see it. I have some news of my own."

"About your family tree?"

He shook his head. "I'm still not ready to talk about that yet. It's all so new. No, this is something bigger than that. I asked Sharah if I could tell you." He scuffed the floor. "Please, don't tell the others yet. We didn't plan for this to happen. But sometimes, things just . . ."

I looked at him, waiting.

He shrugged. "Sharah's pregnant. I'm the father. She's keeping the baby. Beyond that, I have no clue what the future has in store for us. But we'll tell your sisters in a day or so."

And then, before I could say a word, Camille and Menolly were hugging me and discussing wedding plans. I suddenly found myself crying. The stress of the past few days had taken its toll. But they were tears of joy as well as sorrow. So much had changed in so little time. And so much was still changing.

Linking arms with my sisters, we sailed out of the room, toward the parking lot, with the men following. Chase raised his hand as we left, and our eyes met. He was smiling at me, and I beamed at him. He was headed toward fatherhood. And, while he would always be our detective, I had the feeling that his path was leading him into so much more than that.

And me? I . . . I was headed . . . who knew where? But Shade would be at my side wherever I was going. And one day, when I was ready, I would become his wife. I didn't believe in happily-ever-after anymore. There was always an "after." My rose-colored glasses had been shattered—collateral damage in this war we were fighting. But I *could* believe in happy *for now*. And overall, considering what we were facing, that was enough. I was ready to face my future. And our lives were pretty damned good.

CAST OF MAJOR CHARACTERS

The D'Artigo Family
Sephreh ob Tanu: The D'Artigo Sisters' father. Full Fae.
Maria D'Artigo: The D'Artigo Sisters' mother. Human.
Camille Sepharial te Maria, aka Camille D'Artigo: The
    oldest sister; a Moon Witch. Half-Fae, half-human.
Delilah Maria te Maria, aka Delilah D'Artigo: The middle
    sister; a werecat.
Arial Lianan te Maria: Delilah's twin who died at birth.
    Half-Fae, half-human.
Menolly Rosabelle te Maria, aka Menolly D'Artigo: The
    youngest sister; a vampire and *jian-tu*: extraordinary
    acrobat. Half-Fae, half-human.
Shamas ob Olanda: The D'Artigo girls' cousin. Full Fae.

The D'Artigo Sisters' Lovers & Close Friends
Bruce O'Shea: Iris's husband. Leprechaun.
Carter: Leader of the Demonica Vacana Society, a group that
    watches and records the interactions of Demonkin and
    human through the ages. Carter is half demon and half
    Titan—his father was Hyperion, one of the Greek Titans.
Chase Garden Johnson: Detective, director of the Faerie-
    Human Crime Scene Investigation (FH-CSI) team.
    Human with a smidgen of elf in his distant past, who has
    taken the Nectar of Life, which extends his life span
    beyond any ordinary mortal and has opened up his
    psychic abilities.
Chrysandra: Waitress at the Wayfarer Bar & Grill. Human.
Derrick Means: Bartender at the Wayfarer Bar & Grill.
    Werebadger.
Erin Mathews: Former president of the Faerie Watchers
    Club and former owner of the Scarlet Harlot Boutique.
    Turned into a vampire by Menolly, her sire, moments
    before her death. Human.

Greta: Leader of the Death Maidens; Delilah's tutor.

Iris (Kuusi) O'Shea: Friend and companion of the girls. Priestess of Undutar. Talon-haltija (Finnish house sprite).

Lindsey Katharine Cartridge: Director of the Green Goddess Women's Shelter. Pagan and witch. Human.

Luke: Former bartender at the Wayfarer Bar & Grill. Werewolf. One of the Keraastar Knights.

Marion Vespa: Coyote shifter; owner of the Supe-Urban Café.

Morio Kuroyama: One of Camille's lovers and husbands. Essentially the grandson of Grandmother Coyote. Youkai-kitsune (roughly translated: Japanese fox demon).

Neely Reed: Founding Member of AWUP—All Worlds United in Peace. FBH.

Nerissa Shale: Menolly's lover. Worked for DSHS. Now working for Chase Johnson as a victims-rights counselor for the FH-CSI. Werepuma and member of the Rainier Puma Pride.

Roman: Ancient vampire; son of Blood Wyne, Queen of the Crimson Veil. Menolly's official consort in the Vampire Nation.

Rozurial, aka Roz: Mercenary. Menolly's secondary lover. Incubus who used to be Fae before Zeus and Hera destroyed his marriage.

Shade: Delilah's fiancé. Part Stradolan, part black (shadow) dragon.

Sharah: Elfin medic; Chase's girlfriend.

Siobhan Morgan: One of the girls' friends. Selkie (wereseal); member of the Puget Sound Harbor Seal Pod.

Smoky: One of Camille's lovers and husbands. Half-white, half-silver dragon.

Tavah: Guardian of the portal at the Wayfarer Bar & Grill. Vampire (Full Fae).

Tim Winthrop, aka Cleo Blanco: Computer student/genius, female impersonator. FBH. Now owns the Scarlet Harlot.

Trillian: Mercenary. Camille's alpha lover and one of her three husbands. Svartan (one of the Charming Fae).

Trytian: Son of a powerful daemon sent over Earthside to form an underground group of discontent demons, devils, and daemons against Shadow Wing. Out for his own agenda, not trustworthy, but ultimately fighting against the same foe as the D'Artigo Sisters.

Vanzir: Was indentured slave to the Sisters, by his own choice. Dream-chaser demon who lost his powers and now is regaining new ones.

Venus the Moon Child: Former shaman of the Rainier Puma Pride. Werepuma. One of the Keraastar Knights.

Wade Stevens: President of Vampires Anonymous. Vampire (human).

Zachary Lyonnesse: Former member of the Rainier Puma Pride Council of Elders. Werepuma living in Otherworld.

GLOSSARY

Black Unicorn/Black Beast: Father of the Dahns unicorns, a magical unicorn that is reborn like the phoenix and lives in Darkynwyrd and Thistlewyd Deep. Raven Mother is his consort, and he is more a force of nature than a unicorn.

Calouk: The rough, common dialect used by a number of Otherworld inhabitants.

Court and Crown: "Crown" refers to the Queen of Y'Elestrial. "Court" refers to the nobility and military personnel that surround the Queen. "Court and Crown" together refer to the entire government of Y'Elestrial.

Court of the Three Queens: The newly risen Court of the three Earthside Fae Queens: Titania, the Fae Queen of Light and Morning; Morgaine, the half-Fae Queen of Dusk and Twilight; and Aeval, the Fae Queen of Shadow and Night.

Crypto: One of the Cryptozoid races. Cryptos include creatures out of legend that are not technically of the Fae races: gargoyles, unicorns, gryphons, chimeras, and so on. Most primarily inhabit Otherworld, but some have Earthside cousins.

Demon Gate: A gate through which demons may be summoned by a powerful sorcerer or necromancer.

Dreyerie: A dragon lair.

Earthside: Everything that exists on the Earth side of the portals.

Elemental Lords: The elemental beings—both male and female—who, along with the Hags of Fate and the Harvestmen, are the only true Immortals. They are avatars of various elements and energies, and they inhabit all realms. They do as they will and seldom concern themselves with humankind or Fae unless summoned. If asked for help, they often exact steep prices in return. The Elemental Lords are not concerned with balance like the Hags of Fate.

Elqaneve: The Elfin lands in Otherworld.

FBH: Full-Blooded Human (usually refers to Earthside humans).

FH-CSI: The Faerie-Human Crime Scene Investigation team. The brainchild of Detective Chase Johnson, it was first formed as a collaboration between the OIA and the Seattle police department. Other FH-CSI units have been created around the country, based on the Seattle prototype. The FH-CSI takes care of both medical and criminal emergencies involving visitors from Otherworld.

Great Divide: A time of immense turmoil when the Elemental Lords and some of the High Court of Fae decided to rip apart the worlds. Until then, the Fae existed primarily on Earth, their lives and worlds mingling with those of humans. The Great Divide tore everything asunder, splitting off another dimension, which became Otherworld. At that time, the Twin Courts of Fae were disbanded and their queens stripped of power. This was the time during which the Spirit Seal was formed and broken in order to seal off the realms from each other. Some Fae chose to stay Earthside, others moved to the realm of Otherworld, and the demons were— for the most part—sealed in the Subterranean Realms.

Guard Des'Estar: The military of Y'Elestrial.

Hags of Fates: The women of destiny who keep the balance righted. Neither good nor evil, they observe the flow of destiny. When events get too far out of balance, they step in and take action, usually using humans, Fae, Supes, and other creatures as pawns to bring the path of destiny back into line.

Harvestmen: The lords of death—a few cross over and are also Elemental Lords. The Harvestmen, along with their followers (the Valkyries and the Death Maidens, for example) reap the souls of the dead.

Haseofon: The abode of the Death Maidens—where they stay and where they train.

Ionyc Lands: The astral, etheric, and spirit realms, along with several other lesser-known noncorporeal dimensions, form the Ionyc Lands. These realms are separated by the Ionyc Seas, a current of energy that prevents the Ionyc Lands from colliding, thereby sparking off an explosion of universal proportions.

Ionyc Seas: The currents of energy that separate the Ionyc Lands. Certain creatures, especially those connected with the elemental energies of ice, snow, and wind, can travel through the Ionyc Seas without protection.

Koyanni: The coyote shifters who took an evil path away from the Great Coyote; followers of Nukpana.

Melosealfôr: A rare Crypto dialect learned by powerful Cryptos and all Moon Witches.

The Nectar of Life: An elixir that can extend the life span of humans to nearly the length of a Fae's years. Highly prized and cautiously used. Can drive someone insane if he or she doesn't have the emotional capacity to handle the changes incurred.

OIA: The Otherworld Intelligence Agency; the "brains" behind the Guard Des'Estar.

Otherworld/OW: The human term for the "United Nations" of Faerie Land. A dimension apart from ours that contains creatures from legend and lore, pathways to the gods, and various other places, such as Olympus. Otherworld's actual name varies among the differing dialects of the many races of Cryptos and Fae.

Portal, Portals: The interdimensional gates that connect the different realms. Some were created during the Great Divide; others open up randomly.

Seelie Court: The Earthside Fae Court of Light and Summer, disbanded during the Great Divide. Titania was the Seelie Queen.

Soul Statues: In Otherworld, small figurines created for the Fae of certain races and magically linked with the baby. These figurines reside in family shrines and when one of the Fae dies, their soul statue shatters. In Menolly's case, when she was reborn as a vampire, her soul statue re-formed, although twisted. If a family member disappears, his or her family can always tell if their loved one is alive or dead if they have access to the soul statue.

Spirit Seals: A magical crystal artifact, the Spirit Seal was created during the Great Divide. When the portals were sealed, the Spirit Seal was broken into nine gems and each piece was given to an Elemental Lord or Lady. These gems each have varying powers. Even possessing one of the spirit seals can allow the wielder to weaken the portals that divide Otherworld, Earthside, and the Subterranean Realms. If the all of the seals are joined together again, then all of the portals will open.

Stradolan: A being who can walk between worlds, who can walk through the shadows, using them as a method of transportation.

Supe/Supes: Short for Supernaturals. Refers to Earthside supernatural beings who are not of Fae nature. Refers to Weres, especially.

Talamh Lonrach Oll: The name for the Earthside Sovereign Fae Nation.

Triple Threat: Camille's nickname for the newly risen three Earthside Queens of Fae.

Unseelie Court: The Earthside Fae Court of Shadow and Winter, disbanded during the Great Divide. Aeval was the Unseelie Queen.

VA/Vampires Anonymous: The Earthside group started by Wade Stevens, a vampire who was a psychiatrist during life.

The group is focused on helping newly born vampires adjust to their new state of existence, and to encourage vampires to avoid harming the innocent as much as possible. The VA is vying for control. Their goal is to rule the vampires of the United States and to set up an internal policing agency.

Whispering Mirror: A magical communications device that links Otherworld and Earth. Think magical video phone.

Y'Eírialiastar: The Sidhe/Fae name for Otherworld.

Y'Elestrial: The city-state in Otherworld where the D'Artigo girls were born and raised. A Fae city, recently embroiled in a civil war between the drug-crazed tyrannical Queen Lethesanar and her more level-headed sister Tanaquar, who managed to claim the throne for herself. The civil war has ended and Tanaquar is restoring order to the land.

Youkai: Loosely (very loosely) translated as Japanese demon/nature spirit. For the purposes of this series, the youkai have three shapes: the animal, the human form, and the true demon form. Unlike the demons of the Subterranean Realms, youkai are not necessarily evil by nature.

PLAYLIST FOR *SHADED VISION*

I listen to a lot of music when I write, and when I talk about it online, my readers always want to know what I'm listening to for each book. So, in addition to adding the playlists to my website, I thought I'd add them in the back of each book so you can create your own if you want to hear my "soundtrack" for the books.

3 Doors Down: "Kryptonite"

Adam Lambert: "Mad World"

Aerosmith: "Come Together"

Air: "Napalm Love," "Clouds Up," "Playground Love"

Amanda Blank: "Something Bigger, Something Better," "Might Like You Better," "Big Heavy"

Android Lust: "Dragonfly," "Stained"

The Asteroids Galaxy Tour: "Around the Bend," "The Sun Ain't Shining No More," "Sunshine Coolin' "

Bangles: "Walk Like an Egyptian"

Black Rebel Motorcycle Club: "Shuffle Your Feet"

The Bravery: "Believe"

Buffalo Springfield: "For What It's Worth"

Cat Power: "I Don't Blame You"

Celtic Woman: "The Voice"

Chris Isaak: "Wicked Game"

Cream: "Sunshine of Your Love"

Creedence Clearwater Revival: "Run through the Jungle"

Crosby, Stills, and Nash: "Woodstock"

David Bowie: "Cat People," "I'm Afraid of Americans"

Depeche Mode: "Dream On"

Fatboy Slim: "Weapon of Choice"

Faun: "Konigin," "Punagra"

Gary Numan: "My Breathing," "Haunted," "Down in the Park"

Gorillaz: "Stylo"

Haysi Fantayzee: "Shiny Shiny"

Hugo: "99 Problems"

In Strict Confidence: "Forbidden Fruit," "Silver Bullets"

Julian Cope: "Charlotte Anne"

King Black Acid: "Haunted"

Korpiklaani: "Shaman Drum"

Lady Gaga: "Born This Way"

Ladytron: "They Gave You a Heart," "They Gave You a Name," "Paco," "I'm Not Scared"

Low: "Half Light"

Men at Work: "Down Under"

A Pale Horse Named Death: "As Black as My Heart," "To Die in Your Arms"

PJ Harvey: "The Colour of the Earth," "Let England Shake," "The Glorious Land," "The Words That Maketh Murder," "All and Everyone," "In the Dark Places," "Hanging in the Wire"

Ricky Martin: "She Bangs"

Ringo Starr: "It Don't Come Easy"

Roisin Murphy: "Ramalama (Bang Bang)"

The Rolling Stones: "Gimme Shelter"

Sister Sledge: "We Are Family"

Stealers Wheel: "Stuck in the Middle With You"

Suzanne Vega: "Blood Makes Noise," "If You Were in My Movie"

Tangerine Dream: "Grind," "Dr. Destructo"

Three Dog Night: "Mama Told Me (Not to Come)"

Tina Turner: "One of the Living," "We Don't Need Another Hero"

Tingstand & Rumbel: "Chaco"

Traffic: "Hidden Treasure"

Warchild: "Ash"

Zero 7: "In the Waiting Line"

Dear Reader:

I hope that you enjoyed Shaded Vision, *the eleventh book in the Otherworld series, as much as I enjoyed writing it. So much happened in this book that it opens up a lot of paths for the coming books in the series. I'm looking forward to exploring the world and seeing it expand as the adventures continue. Next up in this series: Menolly's next book,* Shadow Rising, *which will be book twelve, coming November 2012.*

But before then, I hope you're looking forward to reading Night Seeker, *book three of the Indigo Court series, which will be available July 2012. I'm including the first chapter from* Night Seeker *here to give you a sneak peek.*

For those of you new to my books, I wanted to take this opportunity to welcome you into my worlds. For those of you who've been reading my books for a while, I wanted to thank you for revisiting the D'Artigo Sisters' world once again.

Bright Blessings,
The Painted Panther
Yasmine Galenorn

The night was still. Snow drifted slowly to the ground, where it compacted into a glazed sheet covering the roads. Favonis—my Pontiac GTO—silently glided through the empty streets as I navigated the icy pavement. We had to be cautious. The Shadow Hunters were out in the suburbs tonight, searching for those who braved the cold. They were running amok, and New Forest, Washington, had become their hunting grounds.

Equally dangerous, Geoffrey and the vampires were also out in full force, patrolling the streets. Clusters of dark figures in long black dusters wandered the shopping areas, their collars turned up, hands in pockets, searching the crowds for Myst's hunters.

At least we could bargain with the vamps and have a chance of winning through reason. But it all boiled down to the fact that two bloodthirsty predatory groups now divided the town. And they were aching to shake it up, looking for any excuse to throw down.

As for us? We were on a reconnaissance mission.

Kaylin was riding shotgun. My father—Wrath, King of the Court of Rivers and Rushes—and Lannan Altos—the vampire I loved to hate who had become an unexpected ally—sprawled in the backseat.

We were on our way to see what was left of the Veil House, if anything. We'd been holed up for two days, planning out our next moves. Finally, tired of being cooped up, I suggested an expedition. If we could sneak back into Vyne Street, we might be able to scavenge something useful from the ashes.

I dreaded seeing the pile of rubble. I expected to find a burned-out shell filled with soot and charcoal, soggy from the snow. But when Rhiannon had suggested coming, I stopped her. Better that I go. My cousin Rhiannon had grown up at the Veil House. She'd lost her mother there. Asking her to go on a raiding expedition would have only been cruel. Besides, the four of us were the ones least likely to be killed.

A glance over my shoulder told me that my father was doing his best to avoid touching the metal framework of the car. The iron in the car hurt him, but he swallowed the pain, saying nothing. I admired his strength and reserve, and thought that finally, I had a role model—someone I could be proud of in my family.

"You don't think I'll develop a weakness to iron, do you? Favonis has never bothered me." I'd only recently discovered that I was half Cambyra Fae and that Wrath was my father.

"You are worried about this?" Wrath leaned forward, still looking ill at ease.

"I'm just wondering . . . The more my Fae lineage comes to the surface, will it make me more vulnerable to the things you are?"

"Eyes back on the road, please. I don't fancy dying in this contraption." He gave me a slight shake of the head. "If you were to develop our intolerance to iron, it would have happened by now. The only reason you didn't discover your owl-shifter capabilities earlier was because I laid a spell on the pendant I hid for you—and on you—when you were a child, that you not come into them until you were where I could teach you."

"Good, because I love my car." I longed to flip on the radio, to listen to some sound other than the quiet hush of our breathing, but it wasn't a good idea. We were trying to avoid drawing attention to ourselves. I'd wanted to do this during the day, but Lannan couldn't travel then. And during the day, we'd be far more visible to Myst and Geoffrey's spies.

"What are we looking for?" Lannan asked. "I don't understand why you want to go back to that burned-out shell. I have money. If you need something, I can buy it for you."

I shook my head, glancing at the rearview mirror, even though I knew I wouldn't see his reflection. "Not everything we need can be purchased. At least not now. I want to see if we can find any of our magical supplies. I'd just made a lot of charms for Wind Charms, and if any still survive, they might help us. And . . . I just need to see . . ." I paused.

"You need to see the Veil House and what happened to it," Kaylin said.

I kept my eyes on the road, even as my voice was shaking. "Yes."

"You need the reality to settle in," Kaylin added.

"Exactly." I nodded. "But don't even say the word 'closure' to me. There can never be closure, not until Myst is dead and routed out of the wood."

I pressed my lips together, still bitter over the way things had worked out. Two of our most powerful allies had turned their backs on us because I refused to go along with a plan that would have changed my nature forever, that would have put me in danger of becoming a monster.

As if sensing my thoughts, Wrath leaned forward and put his hand on my shoulder. The weight and strength in his fingers reassured me. "You chose the correct path. It may be more difficult than the one Geoffrey offered you, but you must trust in your instincts, Cicely."

I nodded, trying to calm the feelings of betrayal that ran

through my heart. What was past was past, and we'd have to
do without either Lannan's people or the Summer Queen's
help. As I turned onto a side street, I turned off the headlights. We'd wing it in the dark from here. Favonis fishtailed
and I eased the wheels into the skid, slowly pulling out
before we bounced off the curb. The silent fall of snow continued, as the long winter held us hostage in her embrace.

Fifteen slow minutes later, we approached the turn for Vyne
Street. A cul-de-sac, this street—and the Veil House—had
been the only home I'd ever truly known. For years I'd
longed to get off the streets, to run away from my mother
and return to New Forest, Washington. Now that I had my
wish, all hell had broken loose.

As we approached the end of the road, where the Veil
House had stood until two nights ago, I realized I was holding my breath. What would we find? And would we have to
fight off a host of Myst's Shadow Hunters to get through to
the ruins?

I pulled into the drive, finally daring to look over at the
house. A blackened silhouette stood there—and my heart
began to race. I reached for the car door handle.

"It's not all rubble! There's something left!"

I started to jump out of the car, but Lannan snaked over
the backseat and his arm looped around my neck, yanking
me back. "Be careful, my beautiful Cicely. The night is filled
with predators. Don't go running over there without us in
tow." His voice was seductive but oddly protective.

I glanced back at him. Lannan Altos, the golden boy, with
jet black vampire eyes that gleamed in the dark, set off by
the golden hair that fell past his shoulders. He was gorgeous,
and a freak, and his fingers lingered on my skin. I tried to
ignore the lurch in my stomach at his touch.

"Good idea." I'd been so eager I'd almost lost my head.
And that could lead to losing my life. I was learning, but
over the years I'd had plenty of occasions where I'd had to
leap without looking, and I'd gotten used to running hard

and fast. But here we had to bide our time, because the hunters who dogged our heels were far more deadly than any perv or junkie or cop on the street.

I leaned back in my seat, staring at the house. Beyond the three-story Victorian stood the Golden Wood, which spread out, buttressed against the foothills of the Cascades on its far edge. But the golden glow of the Summer Queen was only a memory, and now the forest belonged to Myst, with her spiders and her snow. The aura of the trees glowed with a sickly greenish-blue light, and I began to tremble. Evil lurked within the woodland, and a ruthless darkness.

I closed my eyes, calling for Ulean. We were bonded, she and I—she was the essence of the wind, an Elemental linked to my soul, and we worked as a team.

Do you sense anything out there?

Her words came in a rush through my mind. *Yes, there are two of the Vampiric Fae hunting around back of the house. If you creep up on them, I'll keep your scent from traveling ahead of you.*

Anything else I should know?

She is out there, far in the forest, weaving her magic. And she is hungry, and angry. You stole Grieve back from her— she wants your blood and your soul. Myst is growing stronger even as the winter strengthens.

I nodded, then turned to the others. "Two of the Shadow Hunters are on the far side of the house. Ulean will run interference for our scent, but be prepared to take them down. No prisoners, no survivors."

No prisoners. That had become our creed. I was still getting used to the feeling of being a killer. It wasn't a label that weighed easily on my mind, but it was what it was, and Myst was who she was, and it was either us or them.

We quietly climbed out of the car and I craned my neck, listening. My father was doing the same. Lannan and Kaylin stood, poised for trouble.

A gust of wind howled past and I projected myself onto the slipstream. A whisper rushed by. *What did you find? Does anything live?*

And then, *Only trinkets. She will not want them. No flesh. No life. Nothing of importance.*

They were searching for the cats, most likely. But we'd managed to save them all from the flames and falling timbers. I turned to the others. "We go in. Take them down. Wrath, can you go in your owl form? They won't be expecting that."

My father nodded, stepping away from us. He shimmered, and then, in a blur, lifted his arms. They became feathered wings, an almost six-foot span. His body transformed, shrinking into owl form, and then, there he stood, nearly three feet tall and just as regal—a great horned owl.

I sucked in a deep breath, my blood recognizing his. Beside me, Kaylin let out a little sound, and Lannan stiffened, watching with almost too much interest. His obsidian eyes glittered, taking in every nuance of the metamorphosis.

When Wrath was ready, he launched himself off the ground and took to the air, circling us until I jerked my head at the others and crouched, moving forward slowly and cautiously. Wrath disappeared around the house, his wings silently propelling him through the night.

Are you ready? We're about to move forward.

Ulean's hushed reply echoed through me. *Yes, I will fly ahead and disrupt your scent. They will not know you are coming.*

And so we moved. I took the lead, with Kaylin behind me and Lannan moving silent as the night behind him. For some reason, Lannan's stealth surprised me, though I don't know why—vampires made no sound when they chose not to. Perhaps it was because he was so flamboyant. Perhaps because he always had to have the last word. Whatever the case, we moved in unison, stooping through the shadows, keeping to the sides of the ruined Veil House.

My fan was looped around my wrist. With it I could summon up gale-force winds against our enemies, even a tornado, but Lainule had warned me to use it with caution. Magical objects had a way of taking over their owners if you weren't careful. In my other hand I held a dagger my father had given me. Kaylin was armed with shurikens, and Lannan carried no weapons. He *was* a weapon.

We circled the house, the scent of sodden ash and charcoal filling my nose. I caught my breath, once again struck by the loss we'd endured. But worse yet was the loss of my aunt Heather. She had been the heart and soul of the Veil House. Thinking about her, living under Myst's rule, made me cringe. I forced my attention back to what we were doing. There would be time enough to assess the Veil House after we were done. As for Heather . . . she was long lost to us. There was nothing we could do but attempt to release her spirit.

As we rounded the corner, there they were. *The Shadow Hunters. Vampiric Fae.* They lurched up off their haunches as we rushed in, and one of them let out a low hiss. The cerulean cast to their skin glowed in the light of the falling snow, and their eyes were dark like the vampires, with sparkling white stars glittering through them.

I rushed forward, trying to reach them before they transformed. As I moved in toward one, Wrath came winging down with a shriek and grappled the other by the shoulder.

The Shadow Hunter screamed and twisted as my father raked his skin and then flew just out of reach as Kaylin sent a flurry of shurikens into the man. I launched myself at my opponent, with Lannan right on my heels.

"Bitch!" The Shadow Hunter saw me coming and pulled out an obsidian blade. Crap. Their blades were usually poisoned, so sharp that they could rip through skin like a hot knife through butter. And I had a particularly hard time with obsidian. I'd learned how easily its nature could unleash my predatory nature.

I darted to the side as he brought the blade to bear and lunged past his outstretched arm to drive my own dagger into his side. He let out a scream and began to transform as Lannan came in from the other side.

The Shadow Hunter shifted, his mouth unhinging as his jaw lengthened and he went down on all fours, turning into a monstrous doglike beast with razor-sharp teeth. He rushed toward me, even as Lannan landed on his back and brought his fangs down onto the back of the creature's neck, distracting it.

I grabbed the chance, plunging my blade between its eyes. As the Shadow Hunter screeched, Lannan reared back and plunged his fangs deep in the flesh as he ripped open the veins. A fountain of blood bubbled up, spurting into the air, foaming over the side of the beast. With a throaty laugh, Lannan began to drink from the wound.

I stumbled back, yanking my dagger out of the creature's skull, unable to look away. There was something primal, something feral and wild and passionate about watching the vampire feed, and I wanted to reach out, to run my hand through his hair, to brush his lips with my own . . .

Ulean howled around me. *No, Cicely, keep hold of yourself. Watch your yourself—you are stepping too close to the flame.*

Shaking my head, I forced myself to turn away and brushed my hands across my eyes. *Damn it.* Ever since I'd drank Lannan's blood there'd been a bond between us that I did not want. But I couldn't shake it, no matter how hard I tried to deny it existed. I'd noticed, over the past few days, that I felt him when he was near, like a shadow creeping behind me, waiting for me. As much as I tried to hide my feelings from Grieve, I was afraid he'd noticed.

Shaky, my knees weak, I turned to see my father—back in his Fae form—and Kaylin finishing off their opponent. Wrath was carrying a curved dagger and he slit the man's throat quickly and quietly, stepping away as the Shadow Hunter clutched at his neck and went tumbling to the ground.

After a moment they were both silent bodies in the snow, and a pale stain of blood spread around them, dyeing the brilliant white with dark crimson. Lannan pulled away from the creature, who had reverted to his Fae form. He wiped his mouth on his hand, his eyes glittering. His shirt was stained with blood, and he fastened his gaze on me.

Stepping forward, he reached for my hand and, unable to look away, I let him take it. With a slow, sinuous smile, he lifted my fingers to his mouth, kissing them with his bloody lips.

A shiver raced through me, a live wire that set me aflame. There was something about the blood splattered on him, about the savage way he'd tore into the Shadow Hunter, that had set me off. As if he could sense my thoughts, Lannan's smile turned into a smirk, and he squeezed my hand so tightly I almost screamed. And then he slowly let go, one finger at a time.

My wolf growled and I pressed my hand to the tattoo on my stomach. Grieve could sense my feelings, and he wasn't happy. I quieted him, even as Lannan leaned close to my ear.

"I can smell your arousal," Lannan whispered. "I'll fuck you right here if you want me to." But before my father could hear him, he backed away.

I turned to find Kaylin staring coldly at me, suspicion in his eyes, but he said nothing. Instead, he motioned to the house. "We should get in there and see what we can find before any of their kinfolk arrive."

Not trusting my voice, I nodded and looked at the house. This side had been the most damaged, and I wasn't sure how much I trusted the roof over the kitchen. Most of it had burned away, but there were still patches held up by support beams that had survived the inferno, albeit heavily damaged. The front of the house had looked much more stable.

"We go in through the front," I finally said. The others followed me. Kaylin stopped to pocket the obsidian knives from our enemies. We hurried back around the house and up the front steps.

The house is clear?

Ulean shivered against me. *Yes, the house is empty, but do not tarry. The woods are alert tonight. The hunters are awake and active. They are searching for you and Grieve. And all who helped him escape.*

"We have to hurry. Myst's people are out in full force and we don't have a lot of time." I jogged up the stairs and pushed open the door. We hadn't had time to lock it when we were rushing to escape.

As I entered the living room, it hit me just how much had happened in the past few weeks—and how much we'd all lost.

My name is Cicely Waters and I'm one of the magic-born, a witch who can control the wind. I'm also part Cambyra Fae—the Shifting Fae—and can shift into an owl. On that front, I only recently learned about my heritage and have in no way honed my abilities. But in a few short weeks I've learned to love being in my owl form, and I've found a freedom I've never before experienced.

When I was very young, Grieve—the Fae prince of the Court of Rivers and Rushes—and his friend Chatter came to my cousin Rhiannon and me and taught us how to use our innate abilities. It was Grieve who bound me to Ulean, my wind Elemental, telling me I would need her help. In a sense, he was foreshadowing my life to come.

When I turned six, my mother dragged me down the stairs of the Veil House, and we headed out on the road. Both Heather and the only stability I'd ever known vanished in the blink of one afternoon.

I learned early on how to survive on the streets. I'd longed to return to the Veil House, but Krystal—a meth head who used booze and drugs to dim her own gifts—wasn't capable of surviving on her own, and so I stayed with her until she died in the gutter, a bloodwhore who'd serviced one bad trick too many. Until that day, I'd kept us going, using my ability to hear messages on the wind to stay one step ahead of the cops and the drug runners.

And now my mother was dead, and I'd finally returned to New Forest, Washington. But too little, too late. My aunt had been captured by Myst, and my cousin Rhiannon was terrified for her life. Now, Myst holds the town in her icy grip, and she's out to spread her people throughout the land, to conquer the vampires and use the magic-born and yummanii—the humans—as cattle.

In a life long, long ago, I was Myst's daughter. And Grieve

had been my lover. We'd defied our families to be together, rampaging through the bounty hunters and soldiers who sought for us. We'd hidden behind rocks and trees, snared them in traps, and I'd torn them to shreds, reveling in the blood.

Grieve and I fought for our love, killed for our love, and, at the end, when we were cornered and couldn't escape, we chose to die, binding ourselves together forever with a potion designed to bring us back together again in another life.

And now we're back, and we've found one another. And once again, we're caught between the Cambyra Fae, the vampires and the Vampiric Fae, with Grieve bound to the Indigo Court when Myst turned him into one of her own. And me? I'm tied to Lannan's shirttail by a contract that he insists on enforcing.

Some of our allies have chosen to betray us, so once again, we're in hiding, on the run, fighting against overwhelming odds. Only this time, it will be different. Neither Myst nor the vampires will win. Grieve and I will weather the storm. We have no other option.

Once we were inside, I flipped on a pale flashlight. The living room had weathered the fire, with soot and smoke damage, but the weather was creeping in through the caved-in roof in the kitchen, and I shivered as I saw the ravaged state of the room. Myst's people had been through here, that was apparent. The upholstered sofas were shredded as if by wild dogs. Holes marred the walls; the beautiful old antiques had been scratched and broken.

I slowly walked over to my aunt Heather's desk. She'd never need this again—not now—but the sight of the injured wood made me glad that I'd come instead of Rhiannon. It was bad enough to lose her mother to the enemy, but to lose her house and the memories of her childhood?

As I ran my hand over the wood, my heart ached.

"I'm sorry." Kaylin's voice echoed softly behind me. "Can I do anything to help?"

I turned, gazing into his smooth, unlined face. He was gorgeous, Chinese by descent, with a long ponytail. Lithe and wiry-strong, Kaylin Chen was more than one hundred years old. He had been wedded to a night-veil demon in his soul in the womb, and had never been fully human.

I sought for something to say, but there were no words. I was in a dark spot, and I didn't know the way out. Finally, I looked hopelessly around the room, shrugging. A picture on the wall of Heather and Rhiannon spurred my tongue.

"Let's see what we can find. If you see any pictures . . . for Rhiannon . . . like that one . . ."

He nodded, taking the picture off the wall, and then began to hunt through the sideboard on the opposite side of the room. After a while he moved out into the next room.

I turned back to the desk and yanked open one of the drawers that had somehow remained untouched. And there was the first sign of hope I'd seen. Aunt Heather's journal, with her magical notes in it. It was intact, with the map that showed the Veil House as a major power juncture on several crisscrossing ley lines.

I pulled out the journal. It was cold in my hand, slightly damp, but unharmed. I shoved it in my bag, then shuffled through the rest of the drawer. The bank book, an envelope of cash—of course, they would have left these things. Myst's people had no use for money, but we could use it.

After a quick look-see, I just swept everything into the bag and then glanced at the piles on the floor surrounding the other upended drawers. Not much had been left intact, but there—a ring of keys. Not sure what they opened, I added them to the bag. One of them looked like it was for a safety-deposit box.

Lannan had vanished, but after a moment he reappeared, carrying a large bag stuffed full of plastic bags and jars. "I found your herb stash. Thought these might be useful."

I nodded, fishing through them. Some of these I could use. Some had been herbs that Leo had used to make healing salves. *Leo.* "Crap."

"What's wrong?" Lannan was on instant alert, darting a

look over his shoulder at the door. "Do you sense something?"

"No. I was just thinking about Leo and how he fucked us over." I pressed my lips together and finally looked into Lannan's eyes. A mistake—you should never stare at a vampire directly—but I didn't care.

Lannan's eyes were the center of the abyss, cold and unfeeling. "Leo made his choice. I told you that Geoffrey was not to be trusted." He hefted the bag over one shoulder. "Don't blame the boy. He is choosing immortality over frailty."

"Don't *blame* him? Leo trashed Rhiannon's world. They were *engaged* and he turned his back on her. He fucking hit me across the face. And Geoffrey . . ." I shuddered. "Geoffrey wanted to turn me—the same way he'd turned Myst. He wanted to use me as a weapon to bait her."

Eons ago, Geoffrey, the Regent of the Northwest Vampire Nation and one of the Elder Vein Lords, had attempted to turn the Unseelie Fae. It was then that Myst had been born, turned from his lover into a creature neither vampire nor Fae. A terrifying half-breed, she was more powerful than both Unseelie and vampire. And she was able to bear children. She had become the mother of her race and Queen of the Indigo Court.

Lannan brushed away my fear. "Forget about Geoffrey." His voice coiled seductively around me as he leaned against my back, one hand around my waist.

"*I* want to turn you, but not in order to use you against Myst. I want you for a playmate. But you, Cicely Waters, you would be no fun if I made it too easy. I like a little fight in my playthings."

I caught my breath, steeling myself as his lips tickled my ear, his fangs dangerously close to my neck. "I hate you." I pushed his hand away from my waist. He let go, only to grab my wrist, his fingers holding me in an iron grip as he delicately rubbed against my skin, setting off yet another unwelcome spark in my stomach.

"Remember your manners, Cicely. Or I'll have to give

you another lesson in etiquette." His words were soft but threatening.

The glimmer of the flashlight on his hair made him sparkle as if a golden nimbus surrounded him. A memory flared, with me caught in the blood fever, crying out, *"My angel of darkness, make it light for me . . ."* My words echoed through my thoughts and I let out a little moan. I was walking on thin ice—I'd felt the sting of Lannan's perverted lessons too many times now.

Lannan watched me closely, a look of delight spreading across his face. "You're thinking about me. Inside you. If only we hadn't been interrupted, I could have finished and you would have been mine. Can you *really* think that I don't revel in your reluctance? But you have to admit, I've become a valuable ally."

I let out a long, slow breath and nodded. "Perhaps, but I don't trust you."

"Good. You shouldn't trust *anyone*. I don't understand why you trusted Leo to begin with. His nose is pushed so far up Geoffrey's ass that I'm amazed you didn't suspect him earlier. He's just doing what his nature begs."

"Stop, please. And don't defend Leo."

Lannan snorted. "Girl, if Geoffrey gives him what he wants, your cousin had better lock her doors at night, because he'll be coming for her. I know his type."

"If he hurts her, I'll never forgive him." If Leo came after Rhiannon, I'd stake him myself.

Tipping my chin up with his index finger, Lannan shook his head. "My sweet Cicely . . . Leo won't bother asking for forgiveness. Vampires have neither need nor desire for atonement. I am what I am. I'm a predator. I'm your master. And I have no remorse for any of the things I've done in my life. Save, perhaps, for leaving my beautiful sister in that house with Geoffrey."

I pulled away and kicked at the rubble. There was nothing else of value here. "You had to. You didn't have a choice."

"Perhaps, perhaps not. But we should go, if you are done.

Here comes your father and Kaylin." And once again, he was all business.

We carried what bags and boxes we'd found out to the car and, before Myst found out we were here and sent a scouting party, we eased out of the driveway and headed back to the warehouse that had become our temporary home. All the way there, Lannan leaned over the backseat, resting a hand on my shoulder.

I knew Wrath and Kaylin were watching, but there was nothing I could do to stop him. Lannan was an ally we needed, and if I protested, he'd only find another way to screw with my head. And another mind-fuck was the last thing I needed right now.

"Yasmine Galenorn is a powerhouse author;
a master of the craft."

—*New York Times* bestselling author Maggie Shayne

From *New York Times* Bestselling Author
YASMINE GALENORN

Courting
Darkness

Camille D'Artigo is Priestess of the Moon Mother
and wife of a dragon. But her dragon father-in-law
doesn't want her in the family. Captured and
swept off to the Dragon Reaches, she must find a
way to escape before her husband's father breaks
her spirit . . .

penguin.com
galenorn.com
facebook.com/ProjectParanormalBooks